DANGEROUS EMBRACE

"What is it, Faith?" Hunter rested a hand on my shoulder, turning me back so that I had to meet his gaze. "Is there something about this part of the island that troubles you?"

A quivering began deep inside me, banishing all words from my befuddled mind. I stared deep into his eyes, trying to frame the questions I must ask, trying to read his answers; but I saw only my reflection, the longing naked in my eyes.

His fingers stole, warm and caressing, along my jaw. He was going to kiss me. I knew it and did nothing to stop him . . .

THE LOST LILACS OF LATIMER HOUSE

SHARON WAGNER

ZEBRA BOOKS
KENSINGTON PUBLISHING CORP.

ZEBRA BOOKS

are published by

Kensington Publishing Corp.
475 Park Avenue South
New York, NY 10016

Second printing: April, 1992

Printed in the United States of America

Chapter 1

Nassau, Bahamas, 1861

"Faith, come quickly, there is a steamer heading in." My cousin Caroline's voice carried easily through the halls of the Potter house, summoning me from the flowers I had been arranging. I left the bright red blossoms scattered on the table as I ran up the stairs to the second floor.

"Is it David's ship?" I called even before I reached the door of Caroline's room. It was a foolish question, for one blockade-running steamer looked very much like another, but I could not control my impatience. It seemed months not weeks since my younger brother had set sail on a ship carrying a load of arms to be delivered to our friends and relatives who were fighting for the Southern cause.

Caroline turned from the open window with a sigh. "They all look alike at this distance, Faith." She was three years my junior, being just seventeen, but she looked at me as though I were a fool; her calm decorum a reprimand for my unladylike behavior.

"I am just anxious for David's return." I knelt beside her on the window seat and leaned out, squinting in the sunlight that danced on the water of Nassau Harbor. The low-lying gray-painted steamer was indeed heading for the docks to unload its cargo of cotton.

"Do you wish to go to the dock to meet it?" Disapproval underscored Caroline's tone.

"Of course." Since my mother's death in the spring, I had been feeling more and more a burden to the Potters; but with David now gone most of the time on his daring mission to help supply the Confederacy, I had little choice about remaining here. My mother's sister, Minerva Potter, made that clear whenever I spoke of perhaps going back to Charleston on one of David's voyages.

"Do you wish me to accompany you?" Caroline leaned languidly against a cushion on the window seat.

"Not unless you desire to do some shopping." I preferred going alone, even though I knew Aunt Minerva would disapprove. A year ago when my father first insisted that mother, David, and I leave Charleston for a lengthy visit to mother's English family in Nassau, I had hoped that Caroline would be the little sister I had always wanted. For the first few months we had been close and it had been easy to put thoughts of secession and war aside while I enjoyed the island society, but now everything seemed different.

"I think I shall just remain here, Faith. Mother may wish me to read to her later and it is so warm for September." Caroline cooled herself with a fan of woven straw.

"Thank you for telling me about the ship." I hurried out before she could change her mind. Whether or not the steamer approaching was the *Sea Sprite*, I wanted some time to talk to her captain and find out what he had learned while he was in Southern waters. Having Caroline with me would make conversation difficult because she would only want to flirt with the young officers.

Sighing, I touched the heavy gold signet ring that I wore on a chain around my neck. Maybe I would have had more patience with her flirting had I not been betrothed before I left Charleston. As it was, most of my questions to the steamer captains dealt with the plight of the brave soldiers who had gone to Virginia to defend our fledgling country. And, of course, I always hoped that one of them would bring me a letter from my handsome intended, Tommy Anderson, from whom I had heard nothing in nearly six long months.

The docks were seething with activity. There were a number of English tramp steamers unloading their cargos—the arms and other supplies that would be transferred to the smaller vessels which would carry them through the Northern blockade to the Southern ports where they were so desperately needed. Still, my heart pounding with hope, I had no trouble finding my way through the mass of people to where the ship I sought was already being secured.

My excitement drained away as I read the name—the *Sea Pearl*. Was that one of the Latimer boats? David had listed them for me once, but I could never remember all the names. Sighing, I watched the people on the crowded deck. Even if this steamer had no ties to the *Sea Sprite*, they might have some word . . .

"Were you looking for someone, miss?" A hand touched my elbow, startling me.

I turned quickly, nearly stumbling as my heel caught in the folds of my skirt. "Yes, I . . ." The words I had been going to say died in my throat as I looked up into the bluest eyes I had ever encountered. "Captain Latimer," I gasped, overjoyed to recognize the handsome man with whom David had sailed.

He tightened his hold on my elbow, steadying me, even as his gaze made my heart beat faster and brought a warmth to my cheeks that had nothing to do with the tropical sun. "Have we met?" His black brows drew together in a puzzled frown. "Surely I would not have forgotten so charming a young lady."

That sobered me, for we had indeed been introduced. I managed a cool smile. "My brother David Richards sailed

7

with you aboard the *Sea Sprite*. He introduced us several months ago."

As I spoke, the import of my own words suddenly shuddered through my mind. Being insulted because he had not remembered me paled in importance when I thought of all that could have happened to the *Sea Sprite*. If Captain Latimer had a new ship, where was David?

"Ah, so that is it." His smile came easily, his teeth very white against his tanned skin. "You must have met my brother Harlan. I am Hunter Latimer and I assure you, I would never have forgotten our meeting, Miss Richards." He released my elbow and took my hand instead, holding it lightly between both of his.

Relief flooded through me even as I asked, "Is the *Sea Sprite* safe then?"

"I have heard nothing to the contrary. But, please, I can see that our meeting has disturbed you. Though we have not been formally introduced, might I escort you to one of the nearby inns where we can get a cool drink and talk about our brothers?"

His eyes gleamed with a light of mischief as they met mine, making me think he was younger than the thirty I had assumed him to be. Aunt Minerva would be furious with me if she found out that I had gone off with a stranger; but then, how would she know, unless I told her? I was very tired of her strict rules of conduct and my "poor relation" status in the Potter household. After all, sending us to Nassau had been my father's idea, not mine. I had wanted to stay in Charleston to be near Tommy.

Thinking of Tommy sobered me a little, but Captain Latimer had already taken my arm and started across the dock area to the streets of town. I could hardly refuse his invitation without being rude, I told myself. Besides, there was always news to be learned from any new arrival in port. I slanted a glance in his direction. He certainly looked like the Captain Latimer I had met with David.

He seemed to read my thoughts. "My brother and I are

8

twins, Miss Richards. People are always mistaking us for each other. But tell me more about your brother. I have little chance to get to know the crew of the *Sea Sprite* since we are seldom in port at the same time."

Since talking about David was one of my favorite pastimes, I needed no more encouragement. No one in the Potter household seemed interested in hearing about David, so it was pleasant to extol his virtues to this handsome stranger. In fact, I was so busy describing his bravery and devotion to the cause, that I gave no notice to where we were going until it was too late. I nearly groaned aloud when Captain Latimer guided me into the King George Inn. As I feared, several familiar faces turned our direction. So much for keeping a secret in Nassau.

Captain Latimer was oblivious to my discomfort as he handed me into a chair and ordered cool drinks and a plate of cakes. I sought desperately for a new topic, but my thoughts were distracted by the curious stares I felt coming from several directions. "What . . . what news do you bring, Captain?" I asked desperately. "Have there been more battles? Is this dreadful war going to end soon?"

A sigh seemed to drain some of the animation from his lean features and even his eyes lost their gleaming. His lips formed a thin line as he scowled into the distance for a few minutes. I felt a chill in spite of the heat. After a few moments, he seemed to notice my anxiety, for his scowl eased away and his lips once more were relaxed into a smile.

"I'm afraid the men I trade with have little news of specific battles, Miss Richards; but I suspect that this war is going to continue for some time. The blockade is becoming more difficult to slip through each passing week. I wonder how much longer I will be able to continue to make my supply runs." He sighed again. "But tell me more about yourself. How is it that you live in Nassau if your home is in Charleston?"

9

As we sipped the cool drinks and ate the cakes, I explained that my father had decided to send us away as soon as the election of Abraham Lincoln had set the South firmly on the path of secession. "My mother was not well and he feared that she would be unable to withstand the rigors of war should it come. Her sister Minerva Potter and family live here, so he sent the three of us to visit." I could not keep back a sigh. "It has been a very long visit."

"There are many in the South who would happily trade places with you, Miss Richards. Your father was wise to protect his family while he could. Will he be joining you here?"

I shook my head, then lifted a hand to smooth back the honey-colored tendrils of hair that always seemed to escape from my pins to curl around my face. "He was not much in favor of secession, but he would never desert the South now. I only wish that I could be with him. Since my mother's death, I really have no place here."

"But I thought you made your home with your relatives?" His gaze was full of sympathy. "Are you so unhappy?"

His question embarrassed me as it made me sound ungrateful. I hastened to explain. "It is only that I should like to be doing something more than just waiting for David's ship to come to port. For the last several years before I left Charleston, I helped my father with the ledgers for his various businesses and that fall I expected to become an instructor at the girls academy where I was educated."

My words seemed to interest the captain, but they shocked me. Until I spoke the complaints aloud, I had not realized just what is was that sat so heavily on my spirits. I was bored with the life that Caroline seemed to find so pleasant. I was sick to death of drifting sleepily through the days, then going about to dull parties in the evenings. In Charleston my life had been full; here I had devoted myself to caring for Mama until her death. Now it seemed

10

there was nothing to distract me from the endless waiting.

"Would you be interested in employment, Miss Richards?"

"What?" My question was rudely uttered, but his words had shocked me out of my reverie. I quicky made an effort to recapture my sense of decorum. "Excuse me, but I am not sure what you are asking, Captain."

"I hope that I am not speaking out of turn, Miss Richards, but your comments have reminded me of a mission my sister-in-law asked me to undertake for her." The intensity of his gaze warmed my cheeks. "If I may explain?"

"Please do." I had a strong suspicion that I was going to like whatever he had to say. What worried me was why that should be so since he was a stranger to me.

"As I am sure your brother has told you, Latimer Trading Company has been located on English Wells Island for over forty years now. That island has been our family home as well, but recently my brother has begun building on a small nearby island and Harlan and Sarah are planning to move there. Their home is nearly finished, but before they move to the island, Sarah wishes to have a proper governess to care for the children. So far none of the ladies she has spoken with have fulfilled her requirements."

He stopped speaking, but I could not think of a single word to utter. He was offering me a position, I realized. Me, who had never worked for anyone but my father. I suspected that Aunt Minerva would be appalled at the prospect, then I wondered. Perhaps she would be glad to be free of the responsibility of my care. She certainly found fault with everything I did these days.

"Have I offended you, Miss Richards?" Captain Latimer drew my attention back to him. "That was not my intention. It just seemed that you might be the sort of person who could offer Sarah friendship as well as helping her with the children." His gentle smile spoke of

11

his fondness for his sister-in-law. "Dark Thunder has few residents and I suspect that Sarah's urgent need for a governess comes from a fear of loneliness since both Harlan and I are so frequently at sea."

"It is just that I had not thought of seeking employment," I murmured, feeling foolish. I forced back my shyness and met his gaze. "It was only as we spoke that I realized what was missing from my life now that David is away so much of the time."

"You would be able to spend more time with him if you were on Dark Thunder, for he could accompany Harlan to the island each time the *Sprite* is in port." His grin was contagious, I felt myself smiling back at him, forgetting all the reasons why his suggestion was impossible. "But then, I must not press you, Miss Richards, even though I would like very much to have you consider my proposal."

"I find the prospect interesting," I admitted, "but I fear that my aunt and uncle would not look kindly on the idea of my leaving since my mother entrusted me to their care." Just saying the words made me feel like a mere child instead of a mature young lady who would have been a wife and mother by now, if not for the war.

"Perhaps I could call upon them to discuss the position, if you are interested. As it happens my brother and I have had frequent dealings with Edward Potter, so he might be more disposed to give you permission if he knew the details."

"You know my uncle?"

He chuckled. "Surely you did not believe that your brother would have been allowed to sail with a captain of whom your uncle disapproved?"

I could not keep from laughing with him. "To tell the truth, I have seen my brother only once since he left the Potter household and when David refused to visit the family while he was in port, I feared he might have left without permission. I knew how determined he was to join in the battle for our cause."

12

Captain Latimer sobered. "I only hope that our efforts will be sufficient help to our friends." He sighed. "I grew up just outside Savannah. Harlan and I were thirteen when our father was killed in a riding accident and we moved to English Wells to live with our grandfather. He is the one who founded Latimer Trading. Our father was in charge of company operations in Savannah and I hope to return someday to reopen the offices there; but now with all the unrest . . ." He let it trail off.

"Perhaps after the war is over," I began, then stopped, suddenly aware of how often I said or thought those words each day. The war seemed the one constant; everything else was just an illusion. For months I had done nothing but make plans and dream about a time to come, while making no effort to fill the days until then. In that moment, I realized that I could live that way no longer.

I took a deep breath and straightened in my chair, making a decision I suspected might change the course of my life. "If you would speak with my uncle, Captain Latimer, I should like to be considered for the post of governess to your sister-in-law's children."

"Bravo, Miss Richards." His hearty laughter brought stares from all sides. "I can see that you share your brother's courage. Sarah will adore you. You will make a fine addition to the Latimer household."

I could feel the heat in my cheeks, but it came from pleasure this time. I had looked into his eyes and seen the admiration there and I liked it. Being sweet, demure, and obedient might suit Caroline, but I was mightily tired of simply accepting life as it came. If David could take action, why should I be forced to wait for life to happen to me?

"I shall be . . ." I stopped as I noted the change in Captain Latimer's expression. He had sobered abruptly.

"Faith, is that you?" My uncle's voice was like a cold north wind as he came to stand beside me. "I could not believe it when I was told that you had been seen here

13

with Captain Latimer." Disapproval blazed from his eyes.

Captain Latimer rose, smiling, to offer his hand. "Ah, Mr. Potter, how pleasant to see you again. I had just explained to Miss Richards that we are business acquaintances. I planned to call at your office as soon as I saw this young lady safely home."

I sifted through my spinning thoughts for some excuse that I could make to explain my presence, but none came to mind. I had left the house unescorted and without even telling Aunt Minerva where I was going, mostly because I knew she would never allow me to go alone. My dream of independence seemed to be ending before it had even begun.

"My clerk can see Faith home, if you have business to discuss." Uncle Edward's frown eased as he accepted Captan Latimer's invitation to join him. He signaled to the doleful Mr. Hodges, who had been waiting like a faithful dog, and ordered him to see me to the house. To my shame, I was dismissed like a recalcitrant servant.

Fury and embarrassment at my uncle's treatment burned in my cheeks and brought the prickling of tears, but I blinked them back as I rose and politely thanked Captain Latimer for his kindness. What would the captain think of me? He had applauded my courage and now I was forced to slink away like a . . . I stole a glance at his face and was shocked when he winked at me. His lips formed the words "later," then he turned back to my uncle.

"If you are ready, Miss Richards?" Mr. Hodges offered his arm politely and I felt a pang of pity for him. I knew he was only a year older than I, yet he seemed without spirit or hope. Swallowing a sigh, I allowed him to lead me out of the inn and along the streets to the Potter house.

The next few hours were the longest I had ever spent. I stayed in my room watching the street below, hoping to see the captain's dashing form approaching or even to see Uncle Edward returning home from his appointments. Though time dragged past, I refused to even consider the possibility that Captain Latimer might fail to speak to me.

Impatience and anger stirred within me as I changed into a more suitable gown for the evening, then returned to my window. Was I destined to spend the rest of my life waiting and watching? By the time Caroline came to walk down with me for the evening meal, I was ready to scream.

To my surprise, Aunt Minerva met us at the foot of the wide staircase. "We are to have a guest tonight," she announced. "Edward sent his clerk with a note informing me that Captain Hunter Latimer will be joining us at table." She cast a questioning glance my direction. "Is he not the captain with whom your brother sailed?"

"He is the twin brother of that Captain Latimer," I replied, hoping that she would not ask me how I knew. "They each have their own ship."

"Was his the steamer that came in this afternoon?" Caroline asked, then gulped guiltily. "I saw it from the window, Mama. We thought it might be David's ship."

Aunt Minerva started to speak, but before she could say anything, the front door opened and Uncle Edward came in with Captain Latimer. Both Caroline and Aunt Minerva turned to welcome him, but Captain Latimer looked first to me. When our eyes met, my heart began to pound with excitement. Though he said nothing beyond greeting me, I sensed that he had kept his promise to talk to my uncle and my spirits soared.

In spite of my high hopes, dinner proved to be an interminable meal. The governess position was not even mentioned; instead conversation concentrated mostly on business and, naturally, the latest rumors about the tides of war. Through it all, Caroline flirted so shamelessly with the captain that I wanted to strangle her.

By the time we ladies retired to the parlor, leaving the gentlemen to their port, I was beginning to fear that I had been wrong. I braced myself for questions from Aunt Minerva since Uncle Edward had mentioned my presence at the inn with Captain Latimer. Luckily, I was spared

15

that when one of the maids came almost immediately to summon Aunt Minerva back to the dining room.

"Whatever do you suppose they want to ask Mama?" Caroline whispered even before the door closed behind her mother. "She knows nothing of business."

"I wish I knew." Actually, I wished that I could be sure it was something other than my future they were discussing. If Aunt Minerva was as angry about my behavior this afternoon as she appeared to be, I doubted that I would be allowed to leave the house, let alone Nassau.

"Perhaps it has something to do with your visit to the dock this afternoon," Caroline speculated. "Is it true that you went to an inn alone with the handsome captain?"

I nodded. "When I first saw him, I thought he was the man I met when David was in port last time. They are twins so . . ."

"I doubt that your having been properly introduced would have made any difference to Mama. A young lady simply does not go to such places with a gentleman she scarcely knows, Faith. Surely your mama would not have approved either."

"I suppose not, but I was so hoping he would have word of David. There are such fearsome stories of what happens to the blockade runners who are caught by Northerners and David should have been back several days ago." I could not hide my anguish. The open market was rife with new rumors every day and because of David, I listened to them all.

"Of course I understand, Faith, but I do hope you can mollify Mama's anger. She does feel she must watch after you since your dear papa is so far away and you have not heard from your betrothed in so long."

The mention of Tommy brought a blush of shame to my cheeks, as he was rarely in my thoughts these days. Recently it seemed I could barely recall the details of his features—did his nose really turn up at the end and were

16

there freckles sprinkled over it? I remembered his eyes were green and his hair golden, but his kisses and the promises we had made to each other seemed to have happened in another lifetime.

"I should not have mentioned your Tommy," Caroline murmured with a sigh. "I know it always makes you sad, Faith. But perhaps the next steamer will bring you word. Who knows, David may have spoken with someone who has seen him. He did promise to make inquiries, did he not?" Caroline's light blue eyes held a plea for forgiveness that I could not ignore. She truly seemed to want my friendship and approval most of the time and I felt guilty about my resentment. It was no more her fault that I was here than it was mine.

"I am sure he is doing his best to find out about everyone we left behind," I murmured, seeking for another topic that might be easier for both of us. "Do you think . . ." The door opened and Aunt Minerva came in, her face flushed, her eyes stormy.

"Have you truly been so unhappy with us, Faith?" she demanded, standing before me, instead of sitting down. "What have we done to make you feel you must leave us?"

"Leave?" Caroline gasped before I could answer. "Faith, what have you done?"

"She has sought employment!" Aunt Minerva's tone made the word sound ugly.

"That is not the way it happened, Aunt Minerva," I began, sensing hurt behind her anger. "I did not seek a position. Captain Latimer and I were making conversation and I happened to mention how much I missed working with my father and my dreams of teaching at the academy where I received my education. That was when the captain told me of his sister-in-law's desire to have someone who could be a governess for her children and a companion for herself."

"You said nothing of this longing for employment to me." Aunt Minerva calmed enough to sink down on the

17

settee beside me.

"Truly, I had not realized it myself. When my mother was so ill, my time was filled with caring for her and watching out for David. It is only since he has been gone that the hours have grown long. I had no desire to trouble you, Aunt Minerva. This only seemed a special opportunity because it would give me a chance to spend more time with David. I would never have considered it otherwise." That last was not exactly the truth, but I could never admit that having Captain Latimer suggest I was right for the post made it more attractive to me.

Aunt Minerva sighed. "Then you do wish to go? I could not believe it when the captain said so. You would be little better than a servant in their household, Faith. Here you are like another daughter to me. Surely your father would not approve."

I had a strong suspicion that she was right, but I refused to admit it, choosing instead to state my case in the best light possible. "Papa was willing to allow me to teach and he did encourage my interest in his ledgers and my understanding of his business dealings. He said that a woman should be able to care for herself and be strong."

"By accepting a post as governess?" Clearly Aunt Minerva was not convinced.

Knowing that I would have to tell her more, I continued, "I think he felt thus because his sister Emily suffered terribly before Papa learned that her husband had proved unworthy." The scandal of the man's long-ago desertion of my aunt and her children had rocked our household, but I was sure Mama had told the Potters little about it. I mentioned it now only so that Aunt Minerva would not misjudge my father.

She shook her head. "I do not approve, Faith, but Edward and the captain have come to an agreement, so I will not stand in your way. If you wish to accept this post after you meet Mrs. Latimer and her children, you may."

"I may?" For a moment I was too stunned to feel

anything, then excitement surged through me. It took all my self-control to keep from leaping to my feet and dancing around the room like a happy child.

"You are to sail day after tomorrow with Captain Latimer. He will take you to English Wells to meet with his sister-in-law. If you do not wish to stay, he has promised to bring you back when he returns for his next cargo." She sighed. "Fortunately, the wife of one of his crew has made the journey with him, so you will be properly chaperoned on the trip." She met my gaze squarely, her expression stern. "Do promise me that you will think carefully before you accept the position, Faith. Your mother entrusted your future to my care and I would not want to fail her."

Remorse swept over me as I saw that she truly meant the words and that in her fashion, she did care for me. Impulsively, I leaned close to hug her. "Thank you, Aunt Minerva, I promise you I will do as you say. I do appreciate your advice."

For a moment, she held herself stiff, than slowly her arms came around me and she held me as my mother had so often. It was a feeling I had greatly missed. "I know that you are a grown woman, Faith," she murmured, "but until you are safely wed, you need protection. English Wells is not far from Nassau, but with the blockade causing troubles . . . Just take care and remember that you will always have a home here with us."

"I shall remember and I thank you for being so good to me." There was more that I would have said, but before I could order my thoughts, the gentlemen came to join us and I was quickly swept into making plans with Captain Latimer. I felt much as I had as a girl when the small boat I was riding in was caught by a storm tide and nearly swept out to sea.

It seemed that my quiet life had begun slipping free of constraint the moment Captain Latimer took my arm and

19

invited me to have a cool drink with him. But this time, unlike that long-ago day, I found the rushing tide exhilarating and had no desire to turn back. Whatever happened in English Wells would come about because of my decision, not because someone else was planning my life. I could hardly wait!

Chapter 2

"Oh, how I wish I were going with you, Faith." Caroline followed me about my room as I selected several changes of clothing for the maid to pack for me. "Do you realize I have never left New Providence Island?"

"Perhaps you will be able to come for a visit one day." I put back the two shirtwaists and one skirt I had selected and brought out another dark gown. What did a governess wear? Party gowns seemed unlikely, but would I be expected to go about in dowdy dark colors or could I wear some of the bright island print gowns I had made during the long hours I spent at Mama's bedside? Now that the time of my leaving was approaching, I was beginning to have a few flutters of doubt.

"To think you will be sailing off with Captain Latimer." Caroline's sigh seemed to come from her toes. "He is so handsome and exciting, why I would swoon, if I were going."

"If you did, he would probably leave you at home." I put the dark dress back in the wardrobe and selected a green and blue island print for packing. I could wear what looked best on me at least until I accepted the post and I certainly did not want Captain Latimer to think of me as dowdy.

"If you were not already betrothed, I would envy you more," Caroline continued. "Though I suppose he has a

21

lady waiting for him on English Wells. A man like that must be much sought after."

I gritted my teeth, not wanting to think about some lovely young lady waiting for Captain Latimer. "I am more concerned with making a proper impression on Mrs. Harlan Latimer," I stated firmly, wishing that it were true. My dreams last night had definitely not been about matrons with young children in need of my care. But why did I have so much trouble avoiding thoughts of Captain Hunter Latimer? As an honorable young woman, I must remember that my heart belonged to Tommy Anderson and I should not even think of the captain as an eligible man.

I returned to the wardrobe for my ivy-colored shirtwaist, the one that brought out the green highlights in my hazel eyes. It would look well with my brown traveling suit, I decided. Not that I wanted to attract the captain's eye; it was only my need to look attractive for my first meeting with Sarah Latimer.

"What time do you sail?" Caroline held one of the bright-hued gowns I had rejected against her rather flat chest and circled the room, dancing and swaying as though in a man's arms.

"Before dawn tomorrow." A small chill slipped down my spine as I said the words. I had not seen Captain Latimer since last night's dinner, but his note had been very specific. He would send a wagon for me about five in the morning and he expected me to be ready as he would not be able to wait.

"It is just like a story in a book," Caroline wailed. "You will be sailing off into the unknown and I shall be left here alone again. You are so brave and independent, Faith. I would be frightened to death of going to a strange house to live among people I had never met."

I smiled at her sadly, remembering how frightened I had been when Papa put us on the ship in Charleston harbor. This would be my second voyage to live with strangers, but this time I had made the choice to go.

Strangely enough, that fact did not make it any less intimidating.

The house was dark and still when the maid came to advise me that the wagon had arrived. The streets were empty of life so early in the morning, at least until we reached the mooring area. Here men moved purposely from the dock to the deck of the *Sea Pearl*, some loading supplies, while others came and went on missions less obvious. The sailor handed me down from the wagon, then shouldered my traveling case and carried it aboard without a word.

I looked around, hoping to spot Captain Latimer, but he was nowhere to be seen. Determined to show no fear, I lifted my head and followed the sailor up the gangplank. I had accepted the challenge of this voyage because I wanted to take charge of my own life, I certainly had no need for Captain Latimer's welcome.

"Miss Richards, you are on time; how nice."

My heart skipped a beat as I turned to see him emerging from the shadows cast by some cargo stowed on deck. His smile seemed to beam out of the predawn darkness and when he took my cold fingers in his warm hands I became aware of a quivering deep inside me. "I would not want to delay your sailing, Captain," I murmured when I managed to catch my breath.

"I have been anxiously awaiting you as I have had good news since our last meeting." His fingers were strong and slightly rough, not the hands of a city-bound gentleman, and their touch made the quivering worse, yet I had no desire to free my hand.

"News of David?" I gasped, hope banishing the odd emotions he had evoked.

"Of the *Sea Sprite*. It was spotted safely on its way to English Harbor. A fisherman caught sight of it on the open sea and came to tell me late last night."

"Bound for English Harbor and not Nassau?" My first

23

joy fled quickly as I recalled what David had told me about his blockade-running. "But I thought the cotton was always brought here for transfer."

Captain Latimer's smile faded. "How much did your brother tell you about our activities, Miss Richards?"

"Just that he would be coming to Nassau often as the cargo transfers to and from the English tramp steamers would be made here." I sensed there was something that he was not telling me and that frightened me. "Is that not true, Captain?"

His sigh did nothing to relieve my fears. He released my hand and raked his fingers through his thick black hair as he stared away from me toward the bulk of the island that protected Nassau Harbor from the sea. "It is true, Miss Richards, and I have no idea why the *Sea Sprite* is making for English Wells instead of Nassau. I fear we shall have to wait until we reach the island to find out."

"But what . . . ?" I could not easily accept his words, not when I suspected that David might be in some danger.

"The ship appeared undamaged, according to the fisherman, so it may be that they found no cotton waiting or perhaps they were unable to make their rendezvous at all. The blockade tightens with every passing day, so sometimes those awaiting the supplies are forced to trade something other than cotton for them."

"So it becomes very dangerous." A chill formed around the bread and cheese that I had swallowed before I left. In the weeks since David had joined the blockade runners, I had done my best to ignore the dangers, but now they were all too real.

"War is always dangerous, Miss Richards, but no more so for those of us on the sea than the brave men fighting for the cause. Try not to worry. I know my brother will take good care of David and the rest of the crew." He smiled at me and my spirits lifted in spite of my worries. If Harlan Latimer was half as brave and strong as his twin, I had no doubt that David's safety was in good hands.

"I know you are right. It has just been too long since I have seen David." I allowed myself to be soothed, remembering that Captain Latimer was speaking of his brother, too.

"Then you should be especially pleased that we are ready to cast off. With luck, we shall be seeing them this afternoon when we reach English Wells."

His words buoyed my spirits even further and I settled myself at the rail to watch the ritual of casting off and to enjoy every moment of our voyage. The steamer moved quickly through the crowd of anchored ships, leaving the harbor and taking on the rolling waves of the midnight-colored sea as the sun rose to greet us. My heartbeat quickened as the breeze tugged at my protective bonnet and spray kissed my cheeks. I was truly on my way!

Though I had entertained vivid fantasies about spending much of the voyage in Captain Latimer's company, in fact, I had very little chance to talk with him except while he, Mrs. Green, and I shared the midday meal in his cabin. Since Mrs. Green, who was large with child, spent much of the journey lying down, I had far too many hours to spend wondering about what I might find in English Wells.

What if Aunt Minerva proved correct about my being little more than a servant in the Latimer household? What if I discovered that Sarah Latimer was unfriendly or her children rude and difficult? What if . . . ? My imagination produced so many horrible images that I was driven to pacing the deck in spite of the afternoon heat. In fact, I was so lost in my dark thoughts that I did not even hear Captain Latimer approach and when he spoke, I had to choke back a scream.

"My dear Miss Richards, when I invited you to journey with me to English Wells, I had no idea you meant to walk there." His tone was light and teasing. "Or are you perhaps anxious because I have been forced to neglect you?"

Embarrassment darkened my already heated cheeks and it took all my self-possession to face him with a weak smile. "I know you have many duties, Captain, so I had no expectation of your company on this journey. It is simply that I long to see my brother to assure myself that he is safe." Not exactly the full truth, but enough of it that I could speak the words with a clear conscience.

"And, no doubt, you wonder what kind of welcome you will receive, since you have not met Sarah." His gaze warmed me and at the same time seemed reassuring. With most people, I felt the need to keep a proper demeanor and hide my feelings, but Captain Latimer breached my defenses with his understanding.

"I did make my decision in haste," I admitted, my anxiety ebbing even as I acknowledged the cause.

"I doubt that you will repent it. Sarah is not much older than you and no one could resist Penny and little Harlan." His grin deepened. "I admit to being a doting uncle."

"You have no children of your own?" Though Caroline had learned from Aunt Minerva that the captain was unmarried, I asked in hope of finding out if there was a specific lady with plans to be a part of his future. Not that it should matter to me, of course.

"My brother married the most beautiful girl on English Wells, so I have been wed to the sea." His tone was light and teasing, but I caught a gleam of curiosity in his eyes as he asked, "And what of you, Miss Richards? Surely the young men in Nassau have not all become blind since your arrival."

"Before I left Charleston I was betrothed to a young cavalry officer." I spoke the words quickly, hardly aware of what I was saying, since I had answered that question so often in the first weeks after my arrival in Nassau. Guilt swept through me as images from those long-ago days filled my mind. For the first time I realized that I had tried so hard not to think worrisome thoughts about Tommy, that I had very nearly banished all the good

26

memories we had shared.

"I had no idea you were betrothed, Miss Richards. Your uncle did not mention it." The note of censure in his voice surprised me. Did he perhaps think that I had asked uncle to withhold that fact?

"My uncle may well have forgotten. It has been a very long time since I have had word from my intended. Still, I hope when David returns that he will bring me some word of Tommy's welfare." I paused, then added, "Would my betrothal be a problem if I should accept the post of governess?"

"Of course not. It is only that I was surprised." His grin had faded and there was a touch of sadness in his eyes as he looked past me toward the distant horizon. "And you may soon know if your brother has any news for you. See that green smudge rising out of the sea? That is the island of English Wells."

I followed the direction he was pointing and swallowed hard. Ready or not, I would soon be there. Hope and anxiety knotted my stomach as I hurried below to wash the dried salt spray from my face and tidy my hair, then returned to the rail as we neared the green expanse of English Wells.

"Blast!" Captain Latimer came to join me. "Where can they have gone?"

"What do you mean?" I turned to him, startled by the anger that radiated from those piercing dark blue eyes.

"The *Sea Sprite* is not here." He waved a hand at the beautiful expanse of aqua, green, and pale blue water that formed the harbor. There were a dozen boats either anchored in the deep water or tied up at the long, white-painted dock that extended out from the beach; but none resembled the *Sea Sprite*.

"Could they not be anchored elsewhere around the island?" I had already noted that David's ship was not in the harbor, but assumed that an island the size of English Wells might offer a private anchorage, perhaps near the family home.

"There is no other safe anchorage. Much of the rest of the island is plagued with rocks or shoals." The captain sighed. "Mayhap they have gone to Dark Thunder for the day. Harlan is most anxious that the house be finished and ready for the family, so perhaps . . ." He sounded much like a man trying to convince himself.

"And if they have not?" I forced the question past the lump that formed in my throat.

"Then we shall find out where they are." His smile was confident, but it did not quite wipe out the worry in his eyes. "Do not trouble yourself, Miss Richards. The sea can be a fickle lady and there are many things that can delay a ship's passage. It might be that Harlan took on cargo to be delivered to one of the other islands. I simply assumed that he was headed home; the fisherman only told me that the *Sprite* was not bound for Nassau."

I nodded. "And if Mrs. Latimer is not on English Wells?"

"You will be perfectly safe at the house. Mrs. Higgins will see to that, I promise you. She and her husband Karl have taken care of the Latimer house and grounds for years. But I suspect that we will find Sarah here as she is in no hurry to leave this island."

A note of sadness in his voice made me turn to look at him, but I could read nothing in his rugged features. His fondness for his sister-in-law had been obvious from the first, but from his tone and words, I sensed that he was more concerned about this move than he had told me. How I wished I could be rude and ask all the questions that came to my mind.

Memories of how much I had misunderstood my aunt's feelings toward me should make me more cautious about forming assumptions about others. It seemed I had a great deal to learn about getting to know people. To my shame, I too often accepted their outward appearances without trying to understand what might be behind them.

As we neared the expanse of water that formed the

opening between the twin arms of land that embraced the harbor, Captain Latimer left me so he could take charge of the steamer's approach to the dock. This gave me plenty of time to study the collection of shops and houses that followed the curving shoreline in both directions from the main dock. Pastel and stark-white buildings vied with the glowing colors of the tropical plants that grew in great profusion. The few dusty streets meandered casually between the buildings, appearing nearly empty of life this late in the afternoon.

It was only after we entered the harbor proper that I glimpsed the people gathered in the shade of a huge fig tree or seated on benches in the shadows that edged what appeared to be a big warehouse. Had everyone on the island come to greet us?

I peered at the multicolored houses, wondering if one of them could be the Latimer home. It seemed unlikely as most were small and none seemed suitable for someone like Hunter Latimer. Still, I realized that I knew almost nothing about him or his family. Not for the first time, I regretted my inattention to all the facts about his new life that David had tried to give me. Back then I had only wanted to hear what David had learned about life in Charleston and what was happening to Papa and the friends we had left behind.

As we eased up to the dock, the people came hurrying out, calling eager greetings to Captain Latimer and his crew members. It was then that I realized why they had all been so anxiously awaiting our arrival—they were the friends, brothers and sisters, wives and children, even the parents of the crew. I felt an instant kinship with them because I had done my share of waiting since David joined the crew of the *Sea Sprite*.

The moment the gangplank connected the steamer to the dock a tall, slender blond woman broke free of the group and came running toward the deck. Even as I looked around to see whom she might be greeting, Captain Latimer dashed by me and caught her in his

29

arms. A sharp pang stabbed at my heart and I had to bite back a groan. Wed to the sea, indeed! Not with a woman like this waiting on the shore for him. I started to turn away.

"Oh, Hunter, have you any word of Harlan? Is he safe in Nassau? What has happened to delay him so?" Her voice was soft, but so full of anguish I knew at once that she must be the woman I had come to meet. Shame at my foolish jealousy made me want to slink below deck so that I would not have to face Sarah Latimer.

"Now, Sarah, you must not allow your imagination to run wild," Captain Latimer began, his tone light and teasing. "The *Sea Sprite* made it safely back from the rendezvous point; it was spotted by a fisherman yesterday."

"Then where is he? Why was he not in Nassau with you or on his way there? You did not meet him?" Her eyes, which were a dark gray, never left the captain's face. He had let her go, but she still stood very close to him.

"The fisherman said that he was sailing this direction, not toward Nassau, so I thought he might already be here." He took her hand. "Perhaps he stopped at Dark Thunder on his way home. You know how anxious he is to have everything ready for you."

"I just want him here." Her shoulders slumped and I became aware of the dark circles beneath her eyes and the sadness of her expression. "I wish he would forget his plans for that accursed place."

"Ah, Sarah, you know that Harlan just wants the best for you. Meanwhile, I would like to see a smile. I have a surprise for you." Captain Latimer beckoned to me with his free hand. "I think I may have found a governess for the children and, with luck, a friend for you, too."

I swallowed hard as I stepped forward, intimidated by the beautiful, but unsmiling face and the scrutiny of those dark gray eyes. I suddenly felt hot and mussed and dowdy in my wrinkled brown suit. David had neglected to tell me that his captain's wife was very much a lady.

Captain Latimer made the necessary introductions and I waited for Mrs. Latimer to speak, but the silence between us drew on and on as she frowned at me. Finally, I could bear it no longer. "I am sorry if my presence is awkward, Mrs. Latimer," I began. "I will return to Nassau as soon as possible, but I would like your permission to remain until the *Sea Sprite* docks since my brother David is aboard."

"David is your brother?" A smile lit her face. "I could not fathom why I felt that I had seen you before, but it must be simply that you and David look so much alike. Welcome to English Wells, Miss Richards."

"You know David?" Relief swept through me like a warm tide.

"He has spent many evenings with us. Most of my husband's crew have family on the island, but since David was alone . . ." She reached out and took my hand. "Come along, Miss Richards, I have the pony cart. I shall take you to the house so we may begin getting acquainted while Hunter tends to all the details of the ship."

I cast a quick glance in Captain Latimer's direction and blushed when he winked at me again. He had the look of a fat cat licking cream from his whiskers, yet there was a warmth in his gaze that touched me and set my heart to pounding in a way I knew it should not. My heart, like the rest of me, was promised to Tommy Anderson; I could ill afford this attraction to Captain Hunter Latimer.

The people crowding the dock smiled our way as we strolled the length of it and stepped into the shade of the fig tree. Being on solid ground felt wonderful to me, even though I was a good sailor rarely troubled by rough water. Mrs. Latimer paused, giving me a moment to look around, then moved slowly between two of the buildings.

"I hope you will forgive my earlier lack of welcome, Miss Richards," she began as she untied the sleepy pony that was hitched to a bright red cart. "I fear I let my worry overcome my sense of decorum too often these

31

days, especially when Harlan's ship is several days overdue."

"You have no need to explain, Mrs. Latimer," I assured her as I climbed into the cart beside her. "I have discovered the troublsomeness of waiting. In fact, that is precisely why I decided to find something to occupy my days. Living with my aunt and uncle I had nothing to think about except my brother and the danger he might be in."

"Then you have not been employed as a governess?" She clucked to the pony, which started along the dusty street without any direction from the reins she held.

"Before my father sent my mother, my brother and me to Nassau from Charleston, I assisted him in keeping his business ledgers and sometimes acted as his clerk. At that time, however, I planned to become a teacher at the academy where I received my education. I hoped to teach until my marriage. I am betrothed to a cavalry officer." I decided to make my status clear from the beginning so that Mrs. Latimer would have no reason to question my honesty.

"And your family agreed to your considering this post?" Her frown was back drawing her pale brows together.

I explained quickly about my mother's death and my father's refusal to allow me to return to Charleston now that the war had begun in earnest, then summed it up, saying, "So you see, David is really the only close family I have in the area and Captain Latimer assured me that I would be able to spend far more time with him here than I could in Nassau. And should you wish my services as governess for your children, I would also have real duties to occupy my time while David is away."

"You appear to be a very resourceful and independent young lady, Miss Richards. I am not sure I would have the courage to leave a familiar place to face the unknown. Truly, I am finding it difficult to leave English Wells even to go to the wonderful new home my husband is

32

building for me on Dark Thunder Island." Her uncertain smile made her look as young as Caroline, though I knew from Captain Latimer's conversation that she was three years my senior.

"I had little choice in leaving Charleston and, though my aunt and uncle were very kind, Nassau has never been my home." I chose my words with care, not sure that her assessment of my character was meant as a compliment. Besides, I was tired of talking about myself when there was so much I longed to know about her, her family, and the governess position.

Not sure how to change the subject without being rude, I looked around and gasped with pleasure. We had left the populated part of the island while we talked and were now passing through a cultivated valley that reminded me of the area outside Charleston where Tommy's family lived. "It is lovely here," I murmured. "Have you always lived on English Wells?"

Her eyes glowed as she followed my gaze. "I was born here just six months after my father brought my mother to the island from England. Nassau is the farthest I have ever been from home. We used to live just over there." She pointed toward a high ridge. "All this land belonged to my family and the people who till it were our tenants."

"No wonder you want to stay." I peered at the ridge, seeing nothing but the lush tropical foliage that seemed to grow wild wherever the land had not felt the plow. "Is your home on the other side of the ridge?"

"My home is gone, as is my family. They were all swept away by a mud slide during a terrible storm when I was just a girl of fifteen." Her sigh spoke of great sadness, then she banished it with a smile. "But let us talk more of the future. Precisely what did Hunter tell you about the position?"

"Only that you were seeking a governess for your children." I decided not to mention his comments about her need for a friend and companion because of the move to Dark Thunder Island.

33

"Actually, the position might not offer much challenge to someone with your training. Little Harlan is only two and still has a full-time nurse to see to his needs. Penny is just four, but very bright and so full of curiosity that I feel she will need someone once we leave here. You see, there are no children her age on Dark Thunder and I fear that she may be lonely, so I thought she could benefit from learning to read and write, if you think she is old enough."

"If she is interested in books and drawing, I suspect she could be taught, Mrs. Latimer. My mother instructed me when I was very young and I loved my lessons. David resisted until he was nearly six, but I suspect that was because he preferred exploring with his friends to sitting in the garden with Mother and me." I had watched her face as she spoke, reading in her eyes the love and concern she felt for her children. I could not help but respond to it.

"I am so happy to hear you say that, Miss Richards. Or may I call you Faith? We are not much for formality here on the island and I would be happy if you would call me Sarah. When anyone speaks of Mrs. Latimer, I still think of Harlan's grandmother, even though she has been dead for several years. She was a grand lady, but she terrified all of us when we were children."

Understanding her words, I chuckled and recounted my own story about Miss Adams, the bane of all the pupils in Miss Hammond's Academy for Young Ladies. "Never have I been more surprised than I was the day I went to the academy to say good-bye to everyone. Miss Adams was actually crying because I would not be coming to work with her."

"You have lived such an exciting life, Faith," Sarah murmured as the pony turned off the road we were following onto a slightly narrower pathway. "I cannot imagine living in a city and attending a real school. Are you sure you would not be lonely and unhappy living on an island like Dark Thunder? There are scarce thirty

34

souls altogether."

"If David will be stopping there often, I should be content as long as I am busy." I spoke without thinking, then swallowed hard, realizing that my words would give the impression that I had accepted the position, if Sarah was, indeed, offering it. To find out, I decided to be blunt. "Are you saying that you would like me to become governess to your daughter, Mrs. . . . Sarah?"

"I think I would like you to become a part of my household, Faith, though I suspect you would be as much my companion as Penny's governess. We could buoy up each other's courage when the *Sea Sprite* is gone too long." Her eyes met mine levelly. "How would you feel about that?"

For just a heartbeat, a shiver of uncertainty traced a path down my spine, then I forced it away. I liked Sarah Latimer and I had trusted Captain Hunter Latimer enough to undertake this visit to English Wells, so why should I have any doubts about accepting the position? For a year I had met no one in Nassau that had become a special friend. Now, however, I sensed that Sarah and I shared a bond that might well become true friendship. "I shall look forward to it," I told her, deciding to trust my instincts this time.

We shook hands as solemnly as men of business, then giggled like schoolgirls as the cart passed between high, flowering hedges and stopped abruptly in front of a weathered old building that was nearly hidden by the thick tropical foliage that trailed over its very walls. "Welcome to the Latimer House," Sarah said as a young boy came around the corner of the building to hold the pony's head while we stepped down from the cart.

I waited while she gave the boy orders to take a wagon to the dock for my luggage and the captain's, then heart pounding, I followed her up the spotlessly clean steps to the dimness of the wide veranda that hid behind the curtain of greenery. The door opened even before we reached the top step.

35

"Miss Sarah, was it Mr. Harlan's steamer that was sighted?" The woman was in her forties, and from her plain dark gown and manner, I guessed that she must be Mrs. Higgins, the housekeeper that Captain Latimer had mentioned.

"It was Hunter this time, Mrs. Higgins, but he said that Harlan's ship was sighted by a fisherman yesterday, so perhaps he will be here this evening, too. Meantime, I will need you to have a guest room readied for Miss Richards. Hunter has brought her here to be Penny's governess."

My smile of greeting froze on my face as the housekeeper turned my way. She spoke politely enough, acknowledging the introduction Sarah was making, but the look in her eyes was less than welcoming. Hunter and Sarah might want me here, but for some reason Mrs. Higgins had reservations about my presence.

Chapter 3

"If you will come this way, Miss Richards, I will have . . ." Mrs. Higgins let the words trail off as we all heard the sound of hurrying footsteps approaching.

"Miss Sarah, thank the Lord you are back. 'Tis Miss Penny, she be doing it again." A buxom woman of about thirty skidded to a stop in front of us. "I went to fetch her from her nap and she were gone and . . ."

"Calm down, Dorry," Sarah commanded brusquely. "Where is Penny now? Have you seen her?"

"She be in the attic a walkin' around all spooky like." The woman ran a nervous hand over her disheveled red hair. "I was gonna stop her, but I heard the cart comin' and . . ."

"Is something wrong, Sarah?" I asked as both the servants simply stood staring at their mistress.

"Penny has recently taken to leaving her bed while still asleep." Sarah's eyes met mine and I read the fear in their depths. "I have no idea why she does it and it . . . it unnerves all of us, I fear. Do you . . ."

Relief swept through me; sleepwalking was something I knew how to handle. "If you will show me where she is, perhaps I can help. My brother used to do it. Sleepwalking looks scary, but if your daughter is like David, she will soon outgrow it."

"You will not be disturbed by it?" Sarah's relief

glowed in her face as she led me along the hall and up a stairway to the second floor, then through a door and up another narrower staircase to the dim heat of a crowded and dusty attic. There we all paused, Mrs. Higgins and Dorry behind us as we looked around.

I felt Sarah stiffen as I caught a glimpse of a tiny form moving like a shadow near the windows along the side of the room. Sarah pulled in a deep breath, but before she could make a sound, I lifted a finger to my lips to silence her. "Let me," I whispered. "If you call to her, you may frighten her badly."

"But . . ." Sarah began, but I took no time to argue. Instead, I hurried to the outer edge of the room and ran lightly toward the windows. Though I could no longer see the child, I knew she had to be there somewhere and if the windows were not securely fastened, she could be in real danger.

She stepped out from behind a massive highboy just as I reached it and I nearly crashed into her. She looked like a lost angel, her golden hair curling around a face pale and perfect as porcelain, and she was heading straight for a window. Controlling my urge to snatch her up before she stumbled into danger, I reached out and very gently took her relaxed little hand in mind.

She stopped immediately; but I did nothing else, just waited to see what would happen, as I knew from experience that any interruption of her sleep would frighten her. As I watched, her long brown eyelashes stirred against her cheeks and I knelt down to take her in my arms before her eyes opened. "Hello, Penny," I whispered as she looked up at me with eyes as blue as the captain's. "Did you have a nice nap?"

For a moment her gaze held only blankness, then a flicker of fear, but my smile seemed to reassure her. "Who are you?" she asked, relaxing against me.

"Penny? Are you all right, darling?" Sarah had come up behind me. "You are not frightened?"

Penny looked up at her mother and then beyond her to

the room and her face seemed to crumple as big tears filled her eyes. "I did it again, Mommy. I'm sorry. I try not to." She pulled away from me to bury her face against her mother. "Please don't be angry."

"Now why would anyone be angry with you, pretty Penny?" I asked before Sarah could respond. "You can no more stop walking in your sleep than you can stop a bad dream or a good one. My brother used to do it all the time. We never knew when it would happen, then one day he just stopped and never did it again."

"Will I do that?" Penny's gaze nearly broke my heart, she looked so hopeful and so frightened.

"I am sure you will." I could not resist wiping away one of her tears. "Meantime, you have no need to cry."

"Would you be wantin' me to take Miss Penny down and dress her proper like, Miss Sarah?" Dorry finally joined us, looking both distracted and ashamed.

"Please, then bring her and her brother to the parlor for some milk and cakes. Faith and I will be waiting there." Sarah hugged her daughter once more, then let her go with the older woman. Only after Penny, Dorry, and Mrs. Higgins had left, did she turn to me, frowning slightly.

Realizing that she might resent the way I had just taken charge, I swallowed hard and sought for a proper apology. "I am sorry if my behavior offended you, Sarah," I began. "I feared that one of the windows might be unbolted. Sleepwalkers can injure themselves in falls."

"I am grateful you knew what to do. But how did you know? I asked everyone on the island and they all told me I must wake her immediately every time she did it. I had her screaming with terror so often, I feared she would never sleep again. It was dreadful."

I nodded. "My mother was told the same thing when David began sleepwalking, but she refused to listen to them. Instead, she just took him by the hand and led him back to bed. He would never know that he had been up."

"Is that what you were trying to do?"

"It would have been less frightening for her, but she was too close to waking, so I held her. That always helped with David. They feel safe in your arms, so it is easier for them to accept the fact that they have no memory of leaving their beds."

I stepped away from the towering highboy. Now that the excitement was over, I was feeling a little strange myself. The attic was both hot and airless and the piles of furniture seemed to be closing in on me, making it hard to breathe. My discomfort must have shown in my face, because Sarah took my hand.

"Are you all right, Faith?" She urged me along the narrow cleared area toward the door where we had entered.

"I am afraid the heat and my long journey have taken their toll," I murmured, drawing in several deep breaths as I followed her down the narrow stairs to the second floor.

Sarah led me along the hall to a door near the head of the main stairway. "Please come in here. You can wash your face and relax for a moment while I make sure that Mrs. Higgins has one of the maids preparing your room." She opened the door to a magnificent suite of rooms that I knew at once belonged to her and her husband. "Rose will have left fresh water on the washstand in the bedroom and if you wish to lie down, I will certainly understand. Please make yourself at home; I shall be right back."

I crossed the sitting room slowly, admiring the handsome furnishings, the elegantly carved desk, the book-laden shelves along one wall, and the rich fabric of the twin loveseats that were drawn up to the well-swept hearth. The bedchamber beyond was equally sumptuous and I could easily understand Sarah's sorrow at leaving such a beautiful home. Still, if her husband had ordered a house built just for her it would likely be even more elegant than this place.

40

For a moment images of Hunter Latimer filled my mind and I pictured myself clinging to his arm as we strolled along a white stone pathway to a mansion that was designed to please my every whim, a home where our children could . . . What was I thinking? Heat rose in my cheeks as I realized exactly what my fantasy meant.

Swallowing hard, I hurried across the room to the marble-topped washstand and used one of the cloths to pat cool water on my face. A glance in the mirror told me that my fancies were truly foolish, because I could never match the cool blond beauty of Sarah Latimer and from Captain Hunter's own words, I knew her to be his ideal. Not that it mattered, I reminded myself firmly; I was, after all, promised to Tommy Anderson.

The cool water soothed both my skin and my heated thoughts and by the time Sarah returned, I had tucked all the dark gold strands back into place and adjusted my pins. Her happy smile lifted my spirits.

"I stopped by Penny's room and she seems no different than she was before this sleepwalking started, Faith. And she is most eager to see you so she can thank you properly. If you are feeling well enough?"

"I am fine, Sarah. It was only the heat and a feeling of being enclosed. I mislike being shut in and sometimes even windows are not enough to make the feeling go away. I would love to get to know Penny better, especially since we will be spending a lot of time together." I watched her face as I spoke, hoping she had not changed her mind about my being Penny's governess.

"You have no doubts about accepting the position after what happened? I would understand if you did, since you were not told about it." Sarah met my gaze and her relief was evident. "Dorry has threatened to leave because she feels she cannot keep watch over little Harlan and Penny, too."

"I am simply happy to know that I can help her, Sarah. She is a charming child and this will pass

41

quickly, I suspect."

"I hope so. Harlan was very disturbed about it. He seemed to feel that Penny was somehow . . . flawed and he feared that little Harlan might begin doing it, too." Her smile faded. "I will be so happy when he returns, Faith, then we can give him the good news."

"I am sure David has already relieved his worry. He surely remembers the times he woke up in strange places."

"I doubt that David knows of Penny's problem. Harlan refused to tell anyone, even Hunter." Sarah sighed. "But enough of this chatter. Shall we go have some refreshments? I am sure you must be ravenous after your long journey and Cook has prepared a sumptuous tea for us. Hunter is her favorite, so she always makes extra treats when she knows he is in port."

I glanced once more at my image in the tall mirror that stood beside the washstand and wished that I had been allowed to change before seeing Hunter Latimer again. Sarah looked so cool and beautiful in her bright-colored gown, I felt like a brown wren fading out of sight as a tropical bird came into view. Not that I should care whether or not Hunter Latimer found me attractive, I reminded myself firmly. But, of course, I did care.

The next hour proved an intriguing one as I began to get better acquainted with the Latimers. As soon as Sarah and I were settled in the parlor, a maid arrived with tea, cakes, sandwiches, and several varieties of biscuits. As we began to eat, Dorry brought Penny and little Harlan, a dark-haired toddler with an infectious grin, to join us.

Though both children were shy at first, I found it easy to win their trust. What surprised me was the joy I felt when Penny climbed into my lap and whispered her "thank yous" to me. Like most girls, I had grown up dreaming of the day I would marry and have a family; but until this moment, the children had been only vague images. Now I could clearly picture myself with a daughter like Penny and even a little boy as winning as

Harlan, Jr. When Hunter joined us and the children both raced to greet him, my dream circle seemed complete.

"Have you any word of the *Sea Sprite*?" Sarah asked after Hunter had hugged, tickled, and given trinkets to both children.

"As a matter of fact, I have," Hunter replied as he accepted a plate and began selecting food from the laden tray. "Hixon came in from fishing just as I was leaving and he claims to have seen the *Sprite* heading for Dark Thunder this morning."

"Was she all right?"

"If the ship was in any difficulty, Harlan would never have gone to the island, Sarah. We still lack the facilities to make major repairs there. Most likely, he had some cargo to unload at our new warehouse. He will probably come steaming into the harbor either tonight or tomorrow." Hunter grinned at me. "I thought you were going to help me keep this lady from worrying so much."

The glint in his eyes told me that he was teasing, but his gaze seemed to scramble my thoughts and I could come up with no suitable reply. Instead, I felt the familiar heat rising in my cheeks and wished that I had more practice at making social conversation with gentlemen.

"Now you must not be teasing Faith, Hunter." Sarah leaped to my defense. "She is not used to your troublesome ways. Besides, she has been a wonderful help to me already."

"I knew I had found the perfect person for you the moment I saw Faith." Hunter seemed unworried by Sarah's reprimand. "She is exactly what this family needs."

"You are right about that." Sarah smiled first at Hunter, then at me. "I am so glad you brought her here."

I looked from one to the other feeling embarrassed by the praise, but foolishly happy, too. It had been a long time since I had felt like a part of a family, and I very much wanted to believe that I could fit in here. Still, I was grateful when the children claimed Hunter's at-

43

tention once again. I seemed to have a great deal of difficulty thinking clearly when he looked my way.

Rose, the middle-aged maid, came in just as Hunter and the children were devouring the last crumbs of food on the tray. "Your room is ready, Miss Richards," she informed me. "Would you like me to help you unpack?"

"That would be most kind," I began, rising from the chair. I was in no hurry to get my dresses hung, but I felt the need of some time away from Hunter's intriguing presence.

Hunter rose immediately. "Before you go upstairs, Faith, I must tell you, there is a fishing boat leaving for Nassau in the morning. If you would like to compose a note to your aunt and uncle, I could ask Hixon to deliver it to them. I am sure they would welcome the news of your safe arrival."

I looked up into his dark blue eyes and again felt the odd quivering inside me. His gaze was bold, but so admiring that I could not resent it, not when it made me feel both pretty and exciting. "Thank you, I should like to send them word," I murmured, suddenly aware of the time that I had spent just looking into his eyes.

"If you wish, I am sure that Hixon would bring your belongings back with him when he returns. It would save you waiting for the inter-island ferry, which only calls here every other week." He reached out and took my hand. "You are going to stay with us, are you not?"

"Of course, she is." Sarah rose, too, a quizzical frown furrowing her pale forehead. "We are going to have a wonderful time together, especially when Harlan and David return."

The mention of David broke the mesmerizing power of Hunter's touch and I managed to pull my hand away. "I shall go up now and write that note. Thank you for suggesting it, Hunter. You have been most considerate."

"It was my pleasure, Faith." His grin was both teasing and flattering, a combination that made me happy to escape with Rose. Hunter Latimer had brought me here to help his sister-in-law, I reminded myself. To read anything else into his manner would be to invite trouble. Somehow my firm resolve did nothing to still that persistent quiver inside me.

Rose proved both an efficient maid and an excellent source of information as she shook out and hung my dresses, skirts, and shirtwaists in the wardrobe. From her I learned that she had come to Latimer House with Sarah at the time of her marriage and that the other maid was Olivia Watts, younger sister of Hannah Watts, the cook. Rose, herself, was a distant cousin of Karl Higgins, the housekeeper's husband and the household man of all work.

"It sounds as though you are all one big family," I observed as I tucked my folded underclothes into a drawer of the handsome old bureau.

"'Tis that way when you live on an island, miss," she agreed. "The Latimers and the Donovans have employed most of the families what live here. Without them, there'd be little work and less hope."

"Donovans?" I frowned, trying to remember if I had heard the name before.

"Miss Sarah's family. Her grandpa and old Mr. Latimer settled the island between them. Mr. Latimer built the dock and warehouse and set his dreams upon the sea, while Mr. Donovan was after growin' crops and taking his fortune from the land." Rose smiled. "My pa served the both of them and they were a pair. Always aquarreling and acting as rivals, but when trouble came to English Wells, they acted together to defend the island. 'Twas a sad day when the hurricane took them both."

"Both. How dreadful. Sarah told me her family was killed in the storm, but I had no idea that Hunter's grandfather . . ."

"That storm took half the buildings on the island and near every member of Miss Sarah's family when her home was caught in a mud slide and dragged into the sea. She and I were spared only because the storm caught us here at Latimer House when she was visiting the twins' grandmother."

"What a terrible tragedy. Sarah must have been devastated." Having recently lost my mother, I understood only too well.

"'Twas a dark time for all. Luckily, Mr. Harlan and Mr. Hunter took charge or dear knows what would have become of us. They were but lads of twenty then, yet they convinced us all to start rebuilding."

"They took charge?" I was intrigued as I tried to remember what Hunter had told me of the man who had raised them after their father's death. "What happened to their grandfather?"

"He was at sea when the storm struck and there were many who blamed him for bringing it down on us by ignoring the curse." She sighed. "As it 'twere the old gentleman went down with his ship. All hands lost. 'Twas an evil storm what took someone from near every family on the island."

"How terrible," I began, then I realized what she had said. "Did you say something about a curse, Rose?"

Her ruddy complexion darkened. "I should never have mentioned it. Miss Sarah says 'tis all plain foolishness, but I still think . . ." She turned away.

"What is all foolishness?" I knew it was rude to press the woman for answers, but I could not help myself. If I was going to be a part of this household, I felt I had a right to know what was going on.

"It has to do with that accursed island, miss. The story is that long ago it was home to pirates and that when they left it, they placed a curse on any who would claim it."

"What island?" Though the room was warm, I had a chill feeling that I was not going to like her answer.

"Dark Thunder."

"But I thought people already lived there," I protested, remembering that Sarah had mentioned only that there were no children Penny's age among the residents.

"Descendants of those who served their pirate masters and guarded the secrets of the island. Leastwise, 'tis what I have been told. There'd been no new families on the island in near seventy-five years afore old Mr. Latimer won title to it in a wager with some strangers on one of the out islands."

"He won the island?" I studied the maid, suddenly sure that she was playing some sort of game with me; but her gaze was steady and her expression held no humor. In fact, she looked frightened at the very idea.

"I know nothing of such things, miss, but Miss Sarah agreed 'twas all legal when Mr. Harlan showed her the papers before he set about building a house there." She sighed. "Like his grandfather, he refuses to believe in the curse and he is that set on taking us all to live there."

"Do you not want to live there?" I asked, a shiver tracing down my spine as I remembered Sarah's lack of enthusiasm for the move. Could this be the reason?

"'Tis not for me to say." Rose closed my traveling bag with a snap, obviously sorry for having said so much. "Is that everything, miss?"

"For now. My remaining belongings will be arriving from Nassau in a few days. Thank you very much for your help." I had a lot more questions, but the determined set of Rose's jaw told me that I would get no more answers.

Once I was alone, I tried to concentrate on the note I had promised to compose, but I found the words elusive. I could write glowingly of Penny and Sarah and the beauties of English Wells and the Latimer House, but my thoughts were on Dark Thunder and Rose's story of the curse. Though I realized it was no more than foolish superstition, I longed to tell Caroline the story, just to see her shiver. For my part, I could hardly wait to see what a pirate's isle looked like.

When I finally finished a passable letter, I changed from my wrinkled traveling suit into my favorite blue and green gown, then took the letter downstairs. Though

Hunter had not told me when he would be returning to the dock area, I hoped to find him still in the parlor. The room, however, was empty; all signs of our pleasant tea long since cleared away.

I hesitated in the doorway, realizing that I should have simply rung for Rose and asked her to see that Hunter got the letter. Only I wanted another meeting with him. That realization bothered me. Being somewhat shy, I had never been one to seek a gentleman's attention, so why did I feel so drawn to Hunter Latimer?

"May I be of service, Miss Faith?" Mrs. Higgins stepped out of the room across the hall from the parlor, closing the door behind her.

"I . . . a . . . was looking for Hunter." Why did her polite gaze make me feel like a naughty child? "He suggested that I write a note to my family to let them know that I had arrived safely. I thought I should bring it down as soon as I finished it, so he could give it to the fisherman who is going to Nassau in the morning."

"Mr. Hunter is busy at the moment, but if you like, I can give it to him before he goes to the dock." Her smile seemed much more genuine, but I still sensed that she had reservations about my presence, though I had no idea why.

"Oh, thank you, I . . ."

"Faith, I thought I heard your voice." Hunter opened the door Mrs. Higgins had just closed. "Have you finished your letter already? Why don't you come into the study for a few minutes? You could rescue me from my ledgers."

His charming grin drew me like a magnet and I followed him into the book-lined room without even glancing toward Mrs. Higgins. He waved me into a chair, then sank down behind the desk, frowning at the account books that were stacked on it. "Did you truly help your father with his ledgers?"

"From the time I was fifteen." I laughed at him. "He was no fonder of keeping records than you seem to be."

"And you?"

"I was always fascinated by the way everything could be put down. When I was younger, I kept count of the numbers of bales and barrels that passed through his warehouses, but in my mind I saw the people who produced the goods that were shipped to us and the other people who would put them to use. It made the accounts far more interesting."

"I had never thought of it that way." His smile told me that he found my words entertaining and not foolish as I worried he might. David told me frequently that I was too fanciful. "When I keep ledgers, I fear I am more inclined to think of what price the cargo will bring and how the money can be put to good use."

"That should be interesting, too. Especially when you are building your own company." My heartbeat quickened further as I met his gaze and read admiration in his face. At least he did not resent my interest in business matters as my uncle had.

"But enough talk of ledgers and accounts, Faith. Tell me, are your accommodations to your liking? I know your stay here will be brief as I am sure that Harlan stopped at Dark Thunder to make certain that everything is ready for the move, but I want you to be comfortable."

"Everything is fine. The house is lovely and everyone has been most kind." I was sorry at the change of subject because it made me feel as though I were just an ordinary employee. Which was exactly what I was, I reminded myself as I turned away from his gaze, shocked to realize that I had been attempting to flirt with Hunter.

Had he noticed? I wondered, feeling ill at the thought. What must he think of me, coming here to be a governess, then acting as though I were an invited guest to be entertained? If Caroline had behaved this way, I would have laughed at her. It was humiliating.

"Faith, what is it? Has something troubled you?"

Blast my transparent features! Would I never learn to keep my thoughts from showing in my face? I got to my feet, doing my best to gather my tattered dignity around me. "I am sorry, Hunter, I just realized that I am keeping you from your work. If I might give you my note, then I will leave you to your ledgers."

"I much prefer your company, but Harlan will be after me if he returns and finds that I have neglected to bring everything up to date for the *Pearl*." Hunter took the folded note from me, his fingers brushing mine and sending a shiver through me as he escorted me to the door. "Till later, Faith." His gaze made the words more promise than polite conversation.

I stood outside the closed door until I caught my breath. This was ridiculous. I was no schoolgirl to be mooning about a handsome ship's captain; I was betrothed to Tommy Anderson and here only to care for Penny and spend time with David. Sure I was. I kept repeating the words over and over in my mind as I went up the stairs, but repetition could not make me believe them.

"Ah, Faith, there you are." Sarah came to the top. "I was just looking for you to give you the good news."

"What news?"

"One of the lads from the village just came to tell me that the *Sea Sprite* has been sighted outside the harbor. I sent him back with a message for Harlan asking him to make sure that David dines with us tonight." She giggled. "I neglected to tell him why, though, since I thought you might like to surprise your brother."

"They will be here tonight?" I could hardly believe my ears.

"I knew your arrival was an omen of good luck," Sarah said. "This proves it. We shall all be together tonight. I must tell Cook and Hunter . . ." She raced down the stairs like a young girl, her happy laughter trailing behind her.

I watched her for a moment, hating myself for the envy that I could not deny. If not for the war, I might have been like Sarah, a wife eagerly awaiting my husband's return. A chill touched me as I realized that the man in my daydream looked far more like Hunter Latimer than Tommy Anderson.

Thank heavens, David would be here tonight, I thought as I continued toward my room. Surely once my brother was back in my life, I would stop thinking so much about Hunter. Meantime, I could hardly wait for David to discover what I had done so as to be closer to him.

Sarah stopped by my room on her way back from talking to the cook and at her insistence, I agreed to stay in my room until she sent Rose to bring me down to surprise David. It seemed forever, but finally, Rose tapped on the door. As we went down, I could hear voices coming from the parlor, but Rose led me to the door of the study. "He be in there, miss," she whispered. "Miss Sarah thought 'twas best that you have a few moments alone afore you join the family.

"Thank you." My fingers shook as I opened the door and stepped inside to face the tall, handsome stranger my brother had become.

"Is there something I . . ." David stopped and I could scarce contain my giggles as his mouth dropped open. "Faith? Whatever are you doing here?"

"Why I came to spend some time with you, of course. Sarah has offered me a position as governess to Penny and I have accepted, so I can stay. Is that not wonderful?"

"You what?" David's expression showed none of the joy I had been expecting. In fact, he looked almost angry.

"I shall be living on Dark Thunder with Sarah and the children. Hunter says we will have much more time together." I tried to sound enthusiastic, but it was hard when I could find no answering joy in David's face. Feeling betrayed, I glared at him. "I thought you would be pleased to see me."

For a moment he continued to frown, then at last his familiar grin split his face and he held out his arms to me.

51

"I am happy to see you, Sis."

I ran into his embrace. "Don't you want me here, David?" I asked after I caught my breath.

His grin faded. "If you were going to be here, it would be perfect; but since you are not, I would prefer that you go back to Nassau rather than to Dark Thunder, Faith."

I wanted to laugh, to believe that he was only teasing, but his green eyes were solemn as they met mine and I could read something very like fear in his face. It frightened me as well. "Surely you do not believe in some pirate's curse," I gasped, remembering Rose's story.

"I believe there is evil in the world, Faith, and so should you. I have just come from Dark Thunder and there is something strange there. I felt it from the moment we tied up at the dock. You will be safer in Nassau."

"I will die of boredom and loneliness in Nassau." I met his gaze squarely. "I have given my word to Sarah and I mean to honor it, David." I reached up and rumpled his thick brown hair as I had when he was a little boy. "Trust me, David, everything will be perfect; no old curse is going to bother me."

He ducked away from my fingers and gave me a mocking glare then joined in my laughter. But even as he agreed that I could handle any ghost he had ever seen, I sensed the doubt behind his words. Something had happened to make my usually down-to-earth brother superstitious and that frightened me more than any ghost story I had ever heard.

Chapter 4

"So what news do you bring, David?" I asked, eager to change the topic of our conversation to one I hoped would prove less disturbing to both of us. "Did you perhaps see Papa this trip?"

He shook his head, but his smile was reassuring. "We missed our regular contact this trip, but I did ask the man we met with and he said that he knew Papa to be well and working hard for our cause." His smile faded then and he turned away, seeming to look at something outside the window. He did not fool me for a moment.

"What else did he tell you? Did he know something about Tommy? Or someone else we left behind?" My happy spirits fled as thoughts of the war intruded.

David turned back to face me. "I asked him about Tommy and he said only that there has been no news of him at all, not for nearly six months. His parents are terribly worried. That was all, Sis, truly. And it could mean that he was captured or something."

It was the 'or something' that chilled my heart, but I forced my dark fears away. I wanted this night to be a shared celebration since I was finally with David again. I met his solemn gaze, then managed a smile. "So are you happy sailing with the Latimers?" I asked, changing the subject once again.

"I love it. Once the war is over, I hope to have my own

ship and work with Papa to restore trade between the Confederacy and the rest of the world. Meantime, I can really help our friends in Charleston by getting their cotton crops to market and delivering the supplies they need."

"But what about the blockade? Do you really think . . ." A knock on the door interrupted me.

The door opened and Hunter stepped inside. "I hate to interrupt your reunion, David, but Sarah asked me to tell you that the evening meal is ready to be served." He turned to me. "And Harlan is most eager to see you again, Faith, so he can thank you for easing Sarah's mind about Penny."

"We will be right out," David promised before I could speak. Once Hunter retreated, however, he turned to me. "What is this about Penny?"

"She has begun sleepwalking and everyone was beside themselves with worry over it. I simply told them that my wayward brother used to do it all the time." I could never resist teasing David. To my surprise, he immediately relaxed into a grin.

"So that is what was troubling Captain Harlan this trip. I feared I had angered him somehow, he was so out of sorts. I wish he had asked me, I could have shown him how well I turned out."

"I thought you wished to relieve his worries? Thinking that poor Penny might turn out to be such a . . ." I dodged away as he tried to pull one of my escaping curls and danced out of the library, feeling lighter of heart than I had since we set sail from Charleston. It was being with David again, I told myself, but my heart skipped a beat when Hunter came to take my arm to escort me in to dinner.

Since we were but five at table, I had ample time to study Hunter and his brother Harlan. While they were remarkably alike in feature, I quickly saw little physical differences—a small scar nearly concealed in Hunter's left eyebrow, Harlan's oddly bent little finger. More

54

importantly, as the meal went on, I noted the deeper differences between the brothers. The open glow in Hunter's eyes, the habitual narrowing of Harlan's lips when he was not speaking, Hunter's ready grin, the detached appraisal in Harlan's gaze. I knew at once that I would never have trouble telling one from the other as Harlan's smile did nothing to make my heart beat faster, while Hunter's . . .

Foolish fancy. I almost shook my head in despair at the way Hunter Latimer haunted my thoughts. I had counted on David's nearness to stop my wayward imagination, but it seemed the long months of loneliness had left me more vulnerable than I realized. To fight the attraction, I decided to concentrate on learning more about my position with the family.

Directing my gaze to Harlan, who sat at the head of the table, I offered a smile and observed, "Sarah has told me that we are soon to move to another island, Captain Latimer."

"Harlan, please, Faith." His lips relaxed into a smile nearly as charming as Hunter's. "And that is true. In fact, we will begin moving furnishings within the week as the house is finally ready for us. That was what delayed our return to English Wells. Our last cargo contained a number of items I thought would suit our new home, so we stopped at Dark Thunder to unload them."

"You never told me that, Harlan," Sarah spoke up, her eyes bright with curiosity. "What sort of things did you leave there?"

"If I told you, you would not be surprised." His gaze was filled with love and I felt an instant longing to share a feeling like that with someone special.

"Oh, you are maddening." Sarah's breathless tone held no anger and she giggled like a girl. "Always surprises."

"I thought you liked surprises." He looked even more like Hunter when he gazed into his wife's eyes.

The teasing had a heat that both intrigued and

embarrassed me as I had never been around a couple who seemed so oblivious to the rest of us. My parents had shown their love with rare shy kisses and the Potters were so unfailingly stiff and correct in company that I suspected they were only slightly less so when they were alone.

My own thoughts embarrassed me and I was glad when Harlan spoke again, addressing his remarks to me. "I am most anxious for you to see the house I have had built for my family, Faith. Since you have been in the finer homes in both Charleston and Nassau, I will look forward to hearing your opinion of the design and decoration."

"Harlan has created a home even more beautiful than Latimer House." The warmth of Sarah's fond smile did not reach her eyes and I sensed again how little she wanted to make this move.

"It must be truly magnificent if it outshines this house," I said, looking around at the elegant dining room. "This is a lovely home."

"It has served the Latimer family well," Harlan agreed, "but the harbor facilities here on English Wells belong in part to other people and the ones we are building on Dark Thunder will be ours alone. If we are to expand our company, we must have total control of . . ." He let it trail off, chuckling. "But I must not bore you with business matters, Faith. Instead, perhaps you could tell me what you will be teaching my little Penny."

I had to swallow a protest, since I most definitely was interested in learning all about the Latimer Trading Company. Still, I was here as a governess, I reminded myself grimly, and I had best learn quickly to act like one or I might find myself on a ship back to Nassau. My answers to Harlan's questions and a lengthy discussion of sleepwalking kept my concentration on the realities of my life and safely away from any daydreaming I might be tempted to do.

Though I had expected to retire from the dining room with Sarah when the meal ended, Hunter got to his feet before Sarah could suggest the usual exit of the ladies. "David, I expect Harlan would appreciate your taking charge of the *Sprite* tonight, so if Faith is willing, we will drive you down to the dock."

David looked as stunned as I felt, but he got to his feet obediently. "I would be happy to oversee things if you wish me to, Captain," he murmured, his expression solemn, but a twinkle coming to life in his eyes.

"I think that is a fine idea." Harlan rose and held out his hand to Sarah. "We have much to discuss . . . many decisions to make about the move to Dark Thunder."

Bright color warmed Sarah's normally pale cheeks, but her eyes glowed as she moved to her husband's side, calling polite words over her shoulder as they left the dining room. I tried to banish the embarrassment that had my cheeks flaming, but I longed to escape to my room where the atmosphere would be less charged with passion.

"Forgive my high-handedness, Faith," Hunter said, turning to me with a gentle smile that relieved some of my discomfort, "but I thought you might enjoy a pleasant carriage ride to the dock and Harlan has been long at sea. Shall I ask Rose to fetch a wrap for you? The night air is always cool near the water."

"Thank you, that would be nice." I slanted a glance at David, then immediately regretted it. He was clearly enjoying my embarrassment. Being in the company of seafaring men had obviously changed my shy brother more than I realized. I was glad when Hunter stepped out of the room to summon Rose and to order the carriage brought around, but I braced myself expecting more teasing from David.

His words proved me wrong. "If you wish to remain here, I can take one of the horses and ride to the dock, Faith. You need not accept Hunter's invitation if you are weary from your long journey."

"But I would enjoy the ride." The words were out before I could stop them. I might be a bit embarrassed by

57

the open display of affection between Harlan and Sarah, but I rather liked it, too. It seemed much more honest than the studied politeness that I had noted between most married couples. If Tommy and I had wed, I would have liked to feel that way about him and to know that he still cared deeply for me.

David frowned at me for a moment, then shrugged. "I guess if I had been locked away in the Potter house as long as you have, I would enjoy going anywhere."

"It is very good to be with people who still remember how to laugh," I agreed, ignoring the fact that my eagerness to go had more to do with getting to know Hunter better than a need for activity.

"Just be on your guard, Faith. Remember you are betrothed to Tommy and you should be safe enough."

"What do you . . ." I began, but before I could question the implication of his warning, Rose arrived with my wool shawl and it was time to go out on the veranda with Hunter to await the carriage.

The night was stunningly beautiful, the velvet sky set with more stars than I ever remembered seeing from the Potter house in Nassau. Flower scents drifted gently on the night breeze that whispered through the palm fronds and a few sleepy birds discussed our presence until the stable boy arrived with the small carriage.

Though I had feared that conversation might be stilted on the short drive, I found myself fascinated as Hunter and David discussed their separate voyages through the blockade waters. Hunter's trip sounded almost routine, but David's tale was more exciting.

"We tried twice to make the proper rendezvous point and both times we were nearly intercepted. There was just no way to reach the cargo of cotton hidden there. That was when Captain Harlan suggested that we try this secret dock farther along the coast. Said he had heard about it from another captain in Nassau."

"I am surprised he would risk the *Sprite* by meeting with an unknown contact." Hunter sounded almost

58

angry. "He always accuses me of taking risks."

"Well, it was not completely unknown." David's voice held a note of pride. "I remembered that the dock belongs to a man my father has done business with."

"You guided him in?" Though I knew my interest would be considered unseemly, I could not keep silent. "Oh, David, you are becoming a real man of the sea."

"We had a cargo to trade and I suspected that Daniel Jones would be a man able to give us a fair value for what we carried. Luckily, I was right. He had no cotton, but he did have other goods to offer in trade."

"Perhaps you should give me some directions to this landing area, David. Just in case I encounter the same difficulties when I take a cargo in next week." Hunter sounded impressed.

"I would be pleased to draw you a map of the area," David agreed, "but I doubt he will have cotton for you either. He showed no interest in making arrangements with us for another meeting."

"Perhaps you should wait to take your cargo until you have more definite word about your rendezvous," I suggested, hating the thought of Hunter steaming into a trap or pursued by some vicious Yankee captain who might . . . I refused to even think of what could happen to him.

"My cargo is promised, Faith, I have to try to deliver it. I have had little difficulty in the past, so Harlan's problems were probably the result of a temporary interest by the blockaders. Most likely by the time I get there they will be looking elsewhere for ships."

"Hunter is right, Faith," David spoke up quickly. "The coast is long and the Yankees are having their troubles, too. We cannot let them stop free trade. Our people need what is in the *Pearl*'s hold and they need the money their cotton will bring. If we fail to help them . . ."

"I just mislike the thought that any of you are in danger," I murmured, embarrassed by my own outburst, yet unwilling to sit quiet while they discussed the risks they were taking.

"Perhaps our usual contact will have news of Papa or Tommy," David said. "Jones knew very little about what was happening in Charleston, even though he had some contact with the Andersons."

"I will be sure and ask for you, Faith," Hunter promised, but I sensed an odd edge in his tone.

I had overstepped my bounds again, I realized, swallowing a sigh. Paid companions and governesses no doubt were expected to hold their tongues and offer no opinions or suggestions. It was going to take me some time to get use to that. Still, if I wanted to stay with the Latimers, I would have to learn. I was trying to find words of apology when Hunter stopped the horse and I suddenly realized we had reached the dock.

"We shall see you in the morning, David," Hunter said as my brother hugged me before climbing out of the carriage. "Come early and we shall arrange a picnic or some such diversion for you and Faith. I know you want to spend as much time as possible with her since she has come to be near you."

"We do have a great deal to discuss," David agreed, then gave me a quick wave before turning toward the dock where the second steamer was tied up near its twin. "See you tomorrow, Faith, Hunter."

Silence dropped over the carriage as his footsteps faded and the breeze traced cooling fingers along my cheeks. I peered out at the now deserted dock area and suddenly felt very much alone in the dark with Hunter Latimer. Was this what David had meant to warn me about? I waited for apprehension and felt only anticipation—no way was I afraid of Hunter.

"Your brother is proving himself a real asset for Latimer Trading," Hunter said, shifting slightly in the seat, but not slapping the reins to start the horse on the homeward trip. "It may be that when the war is finally over Latimer Trading can work out a contract with your father that will allow both companies to expand trading."

"I only hope it is over soon." I could not keep the longing from my tone.

Hunter sighed, then started the horse to moving. "Do you miss your home so much?"

"Charleston?" The question surprised me, but I gave it some thought, sensing that it was not idly asked. "I miss my papa and some of my friends, but I know living there will never be the same now that Mother is gone. Mostly, I just wish that I could see what the future will be. It seems as though all my plans and dreams have been halted until the war is over."

"And what would have happened had there been no war?"

I wished that I could see his face, but the starlight was not strong enough for me to read his expression and his tone gave nothing away. "I should have married Tommy and we would be living at Chestnut Knoll, his family plantation." The words evoked no emotion as I pictured my life as it would have been. I had cried myself to sleep for weeks after we left Charleston, but the long year in Nassau had changed me.

"Tell me about your betrothed."

Images of Tommy filled my mind, but I was suddenly loath to share them with Hunter or anyone for they held a part of me I was not sure still existed. Instead of answering, I turned to look at Hunter, wondering what he was thinking. "Why?"

We rode in silence for several moments and I realized that I had once again behaved more like a guest than someone employed by the family. I swallowed a sigh and prepared myself to accept the consequences of my question.

"I guess I am just curious about the sort of man you would choose to spend your life with, Faith," he said at last, his tone thoughtful. "You are very different from most of the young ladies I've met and I wondered if your life in Charleston is the reason."

"Tommy is rather like David, full of fun and daring, always ready for adventure. He was among the first to join the cavalry unit and most eager to show the Northerners that they could not force us to accept their will. Of course, we knew each other all our lives and he . . ." I stopped, suddenly out of words as I realized I had no more to tell him.

The images that filled my mind were of the laughing boy who had shared my girlhood, given me my first kiss behind the summer house when I was fifteen, escorted me to my first grown-up ball and later asked me to share a future that might never happen now. But what was Tommy really like without the teasing Barrington brothers, giggly Sylvie Harris and David and the other half-dozen young people who had spent their time with us? It was frightening to realize that I had no idea.

"Forgive me, Faith. I had not thought how painful this must be for you, not knowing where he is these days." Hunter broke into my thoughts. "I fear I tend to ask questions first and think later—a fault that Sarah points out to me frequently." The kindness in his voice shamed me because I could not correct his interpretation of my silence.

"It just all seems so long ago," I murmured. "As though it happened to someone else and not to me."

"I do understand something of what you say. Mother brought us here to English Wells after my father was killed, but she was never happy on the island. After a few years, when she felt we were settled with Grandfather, she returned to Savannah. She wrote often of life there and I remembered everything she described, but it never meant as much to me as it did to her."

"Is she still there?" I was touched and intrigued by his words; no man had ever spoken to me so openly of his feelings.

"She remarried several years after she left the island and more recently moved north with her new husband and his family. We still receive letters from time to time, but since the war began . . ." His sigh spoke of sadness.

"It must be difficult for her not being sure how you fare here," I ventured. "Does she know that you have been running the blockade?"

"She had no interest in our business, so I doubt that she would be worried. She is likely more concerned with her adopted family." He straightened. "But enough of that. I suggested this ride for your enjoyment, not to make you sad. Tell me, what do you think of our island?"

"English Wells is charming. I wonder that any of you want to leave it."

"Dark Thunder is beautiful, too. And Harlan has built a magnificent home there. Sarah will love it once she accepts the fact that it is to be her home. For everyone's sake, I hope that you can help her do that. If she is unhappy, we shall all be troubled."

"Are you eager to move to Dark Thunder?" I had to ask.

"My home is the sea, so one snug harbor is much like another to me. I shall miss my friends here, but I expect to make new ones on Dark Thunder and, of course, we will continue to unload some of our cargo here until we complete our new facilities. Which will happen more quickly now that the house has been completed and the laborers can be put to work on the docks and warehouses."

"It sounds very challenging and exciting. I think I shall enjoy being a part of it."

"I knew from the beginning that you would feel that way." Hunter caught my hand and squeezed my fingers. "You are just what we all needed."

"I shall do my best," I promised, not sure whether it was his touch or the warm appreciation of his words that set my heart to pounding in my ears; either way, I liked the feeling.

Hunter sighed as the horse turned off the road and headed for Latimer House without direction. "Perhaps we may dine earlier tomorrow night, then we can drive to the west end of the island and watch the sunset. It is a magnificent sight and one I know you would enjoy."

"I am sure I would." I hoped I did not sound too fluttery, but the very thought of watching the sunset with Hunter took my breath away. Besides, he had given me a glimpse of his life tonight and I very much wanted to know more about him. I was only sorry that we had reached the house so quickly.

Hunter escorted me to the front door, bidding me "good night" before he left to take the carriage to the stable. There was no sign of Mrs. Higgins or any of the other servants about, though lamps had been left burning in the parlor and the hallway. Sighing, I climbed the wide stairway and headed for the room I had been given. While I had not thought myself weary, I slept the moment my head touched the pillow.

The next few days were the happiest I had ever known. I had expected to begin my duties at once, but Hunter would hear none of it. Instead he arranged family picnics and excursions for all of us, then while David was busy helping Harlan, he insisted that I try one of the horses from the stable. Once he was assured that I could ride passably well, he took me on a guided tour of the island's trails. I felt as though David and I had become members of the Latimer family and I loved it. Then, too soon, it was the day before the *Sea Pearl* was due to sail.

"Will you ride with me again today, Faith," Hunter asked as we finished our midday meal. "There is a small stream at the far end of the island and I forgot to show you the waterfall there."

"But I was to help Sarah with the selecting of linens to be shipped to Dark Thunder," I began, feeling guilty because I so longed to accept his invitation.

"Surely that does not require two of you?" Hunter's gaze was teasing. "Sarah, you can get along without Faith's help for a while, can you not?"

"Go with him, Faith, or he will make my life a misery. We can do the linens as well tomorrow after he sails." Sarah turned her bright smile toward her brother-in-law. "Just be sure to stop by Gideon Green's cottage, Hunter. I have heard nothing about Miranda and if she has not yet given birth . . ."

"Then Gideon will be unhappy about sailing," Hunter finished for her. "Would you like to see Miranda again, Faith? I know you two became acquainted on our journey here."

"I would love to see her." I had not thought of the quiet woman since landing here, but now I wondered about her. She had confided that this was her third attempt to bear a child and the first that had lasted near to term. She attributed this fact to the care she had received from a woman in Nassau who claimed to have special powers in such matters. "I hope she is all right."

"I am sure we would have heard if anything was amiss," Sarah murmured, frowning. "If the babe has not arrived, Hunter, must Gideon make this trip? She truly needs him now."

Hunter sighed. "I need a first mate, too, Sarah, and Gideon is one of the best, but if you really think . . ." He turned to me. "What would you think of my asking David to act as my first mate, Faith? I am sure that Harlan can easily spare him now since the *Sprite* will only be sailing between English Wells and Dark Thunder with household goods."

"I expect he would be pleased to help you if you need him." Far more pleased than I would be to see him go, that was sure. Knowing that Hunter was sailing into danger was bad enough; I had counted on spending as much time as possible with David during the ordeal of moving everything between the two islands.

"I shall speak with Harlan before our ride then." Hunter was already on his feet. "In an hour, Faith?"

I nodded, not trusting myself to speak since his smile addled my head so completely. Sarah's sigh drew my

65

attention back to her. "I am sorry about David, Faith," she said. "I know that you have had far too little time together, but poor Miranda Green has suffered so much trying to give Gideon a child. It would be too cruel for him to be at sea when she comes to term." She sighed again. "And since you are still an innocent, I should not be discussing such things with you, should I?"

"I understand how important it must be for Mrs. Green to have her husband nearby when she bears this child," I assured her, not adding that I had spent enough time around the fine horses my father bred to know quite a bit about the processes of life. "David and I will have plenty of time once the *Sea Pearl* returns."

Sarah got to her feet and started from the room, then turned back, a tiny frown marring her face. "You and Hunter seem to get on very well, Faith."

Though her words were spoken casually, I sensed a question behind them and it gave me a chill. "He has been most kind showing me about the island."

"It has been some time since Hunter has had someone as pretty as you to escort and I know he has been lonely. I also realize that he is a most attractive man and your Tommy is far away." She stopped, then smiled. "And Hunter will be waiting for you soon, so you had best go and change into your riding clothes."

She was gone before I could speak, which was just as well, since I could think of nothing to say. Her warning had been gentle, but clear and it rather matched the ones I had continued to hear from David. It seemed that everyone was watching me and worrying about my behavior. Righteous indignation blazed through me for a moment, then I remembered how eagerly I had accepted Hunter's invitiation and the chill returned. Could they be right to worry?

I rejected that idea as I hurried up the stairs. Hunter and I had done nothing but talk and laugh together these past days and, most of the time, we had been surrounded by people. Besides, I talked and laughed with Harlan and David, too. I ignored the niggling little doubts that nibbled at my firm resolve to forget Sarah's words. She was just being overprotective, that was all.

Our visit to the Greens' cottage was pleasant and the joy that greeted Hunters' words made me ashamed of my misgivings about David taking Gideon's place. My own eyes burned with tears when Miranda Green wept in gratitude after Hunter told Gideon that he would be free to remain with his wife until the child was safely born. They were still calling their thanks after us as we rode away.

I truly admired the way Hunter treated the men who sailed with him. Many were older than he, but they all appeared to respect him and he tempered his command with what seemed to be genuine friendship. Without giving a thought to how it might sound, I voiced my opinion of his leadership as we stopped the horses at the edge of a tiny hidden pool.

"You can credit Grandfather for that," Hunter explained, his smile telling me that he did not resent my speaking my mind. "He started both Harlan and me as ordinary seamen and made us learn each task that is done on our ships. He said it would teach us to respect the men who sailed with us in the future and he was right." A shadow of pain crossed his clean-cut features as he dismounted, then turned to help me down. "I wish he were here now to see how it has all come out."

"You miss him still, do you not?" I reached out to touch his tanned cheek, caught by the loneliness I could read in his eyes.

His hands tightened on my waist as I freed myself from the sidesaddle. The air seemed to still around us as though the very breeze was holding its breath. Hunter lowered me so slowly it was like floating, yet I felt each of his fingers burning like fire on my waist. I put my hands on his shoulders to steady myself, but when my feet touched the ground, I was powerless to step back.

He was going to kiss me, I read it in his languorous, half-closed eyes, in the softening of his lips. Deep inside I knew that I should pull away, but instead I lifted my head, unable to deny my own desire. I desperately wanted Hunter Latimer to kiss me.

Chapter 5

At first his lips were light, tender, caressing as the wings of a butterfly. I closed my eyes, savoring his touch, waiting for him to deepen the kiss. One hand came up to tangle in my hair, while he slipped his other arm around me, drawing me even closer.

Only then did his tender wooing become a demand. His lips devoured mine in a way that stole the strength from my knees so that only his arms kept me on my feet. Tingles of lightning pulsed through me as I yielded to the pressure of his mouth, parting my lips to taste the sweet wildness of his kiss.

The assault of sensations overpowered my senses so that the world no longer existed for me. Then, abruptly, Hunter dragged his mouth from mine and stepped back. Dizzy from the magic he had unleashed, I staggered and would have fallen had he not caught my arms and steadied me.

"God forgive me, Faith, I never meant . . ." He looked as dazed as I felt. As I watched, he took several deep breaths as though seeking for control of some shattering emotion, then he began to speak again. "I had no right to do that and I apologize for my behavior."

"Hunter, I . . ." My mind refused to produce any words and my lips felt so bruised I was not sure I could have formed them anyway. I had no desire for his apology. To my shame, I wanted only to be back in his arms, to cling to his broad shoulders and feel the heat of his mouth on mine.

"I shall water the horses here," he went on, no longer looking my way. "If you wish to drink, there is a small waterfall just on the other side of that red hibiscus. The water is sweet and fresh."

Dismissal chilled his words. He was ashamed and sorry that he had kissed me! Humiliation flamed in my cheeks as I turned away, blinking hard at the tears I vowed he would never see. He probably thought that I had thrown myself at him, that I let just anyone . . .

The food I had eaten earlier twisted inside me and burned in my throat as I stumbled around the huge hibiscus plant. The waterfall splashed down over the rocky ridge with a merry sound, but I took no notice of the beauty. At the moment, I was interested only in wetting my handkerchief in the cool water and holding it to my face.

How could I have been such a fool? David and Sarah had both warned me and I had laughed at their words, behaving like a silly girl with no more sense than Caroline had. Only I claimed to be an adult, I was betrothed and had accepted employment by the Latimers, which made my indiscretion far worse than the innocent flirting Caroline did.

What was I going to do? I asked myself as the first awful pain settled into a wretched ache inside me. How could I face Hunter even for the duration of the ride back to Latimer House? How could I face anyone ever again? Perhaps while Hunter and David were on their way to their rendezvous, I could take the inter-island ferry back to Nassau and . . .

"Is this not an enchanted place?" Hunter's voice broke into my misery like a cooling breeze on a hot night. "I discovered it the first year I lived on the island, but I rarely have time to come here anymore."

"It is very lovely," I murmured, not turning to look at

70

him as I dipped my handkerchief in the water and patted my face again, trying to cool my cheeks and wash away the heat of my embarrassment.

"Are you all right, Faith? I did not hurt you?" The concern in his voice reached out to me like a friendly hand. "I would never intentionally hurt you. Nor did I mean to frighten you, Faith. It is just that you are so lovely and sweet and I thought to steal a single kiss before I sail away tomorrow."

"I am quite all right, Hunter." I gathered my courage and turned to face him, meeting his worried gaze boldly even though I knew I could not hide my feelings from him. I could not leave a lie between us, no matter how the truth embarrassed me. "If you owe me an apology, then I owe you one for not stopping you. What happened between us was as much my fault as yours. I should have known better than to come to such a secluded place without a chaperon."

"There will be no need for a chaperon in the future, Faith. Now that I know what my feelings are, I would never risk hurting you again. As long as your heart is pledged to another, I will do nothing to dishonor you. Please believe that."

As he spoke, he took my wet hands in his and the warmth of his fingers soothed away the cold hurt. For a moment, I basked in the sweet sensation, then I realized the danger. He might make a promise not to compromise me, but what of my feelings? I still wanted his kisses.

"Faith, you do believe me? You know that I would never hurt you?" His gaze became anxious because I had not answered and his hands tightened.

"Of course I believe you, Hunter. I never doubted your intentions or I would not have come here with you. It is only that I have been lonely for a long time and as you say, this place is enchanted." My explanation for what had happened between us was pretty lame, but it was the best I could manage while his touch was sending quivers of longing through me.

71

"Then you have forgiven me?"

"There is nothing to forgive." This time I met his gaze without flinching, knowing that he would read the longing in my eyes. Perhaps perversely, I was glad to have him know how I felt. Only when I saw the flames of desire in the depths of his eyes, did I turn back to the waterfall. "Perhaps we should return to the house now. You do have to tell David that he is to sail with you."

"Whenever you wish, Faith." His tone was proper, but my heart heard the disappointment behind his words.

After what we had shared, did he really think we could sit here quietly and enjoy the beauty of the silvery waterfall? Or did he expect me to forget the fiery passion he had ignited within me as quickly as he appeared to have set it aside? I feared the answer to that question because of the lack of character it would imply. Right or wrong, I wanted Hunter to remember our kiss.

We made the ride back to Latimer House mostly in a silence that became steadily less painful after we left the intimacy of the tropical forest. It grew easier to smile when our eyes met, but I still trembled inside when he lifted me down at the stable. To my shame, I longed to feel his arms around me again. Tommy, the sweet, laughing boy of my girlhood dreams, had faded even further into the shadows of the life I had left behind.

Fortunately, I was no longer tempted. Sarah had planned a lavish evening meal and David proved disgustingly pleased about going with Hunter. I had no doubt David was anxious to escape the tedious labor of moving the Latimer household to Dark Thunder, but I also sensed that he had a growing appetite for adventure, which frightened me. I hated the thought that he might be sailing into danger, but there was nothing I could do to stop him.

I watched them as they steamed away in the predawn darkness and prayed for the *Pearl*'s safe return, then firmly ordered my fears away. As it turned out, there was plenty to occupy my time, if not my wayward thoughts. Once Hunter was gone, Harlan began to press us to finish our preparations for the move to Dark Thunder.

I watched Sarah closely as we worked together and, though she spoke often of her excitement about going, I sensed that she made the statements more to please Harlan than because she really wanted to go. I found her attitude difficult to understand. If Hunter had built a wonderful new home for me . . .

"Blast!" I whispered to myself. Hard as I tried, I was still having difficulty putting my memories of that kiss to rest. Whenever I allowed my imagination free rein, Hunter dominated my daydreaming.

And something else was happening to me. My memories of Tommy Anderson were fading with each passing day and no amount of trying to recall them seemed to produce any new ones. Seen from this distance in time and geography, our decision to wed appeared to have sprung more from the excitement of his joining the cavalry than from a genuine love. Such realizations shamed me, but I could not deny the truth of them. I could only hope that David would bring me some word from Tommy, because that alone might revive my feelings for him.

The actual move to Dark Thunder took surprisingly little time once everything was carried from the house to the dock and loaded on the *Sprite* and the half-dozen other boats that Harlan had employed to carry everything from clothing, furniture, crystal and china to horses, tack, plants, and livestock. My heart lifted with excitement as we steamed out of the harbor at the head of our flotilla, but I hid my feelings as I comforted Sarah. I could understand her heartbroken sobs, but I could not share them.

"Please stop crying, Mommy," Penny wailed, frightened by her mother's grief. Then she, too, dissolved into tears. "I promise I will be good so we can go back home."

Her words shocked me. In the fuss and flurry of preparing for the move, none of us had taken much time with Penny, and now I understood why she had been so silent the past few days. I knelt before her and took her in my arms, remembering clearly just how punished I had felt when Papa insisted that we all go to Nassau without him.

"Penny, we are going home," I began, trying to choose words that she could understand. "To a wonderful new home that your Papa has built just for you and your Mama and little H.J. It will be a special place and we can all explore it together. You will like that, will you not?"

Her dark blue eyes, which always made me think of Hunter, regarded me dubiously for a few moments, then the flood of tears slowed. "Will you stay there with me?" she asked.

"Of course, and I shall teach you to read and to write so that you can send letters about Dark Thunder to all your friends on English Wells. Would you like that?"

"You will adore it, Penny," Sarah reassured her, wiping her own tears away. "You must never be afraid of new places. I am only crying because I will miss much about English Wells, but you shall grow up on Dark Thunder and it will be your home."

I could hear the doubt in Sarah's tone, but Penny seemed to accept the words without question, much to my relief. It was then that I remembered the warning that David had given me my first night on English Wells. Like Sarah, he had feared the move to Dark Thunder, yet he had been unable to tell me why. I hugged Penny again, trying to put such thoughts out of my mind, but it was difficult when I had to watch the friendly harbor of English Wells fading behind us.

Because of our late start, we did not go ashore on Dark Thunder that night, even though we had reached the harbor. I was still at the rail enjoying the quiet of the night when Harlan ordered the *Sprite*'s anchor dropped. While the nearby island was but a dark smudge between

74

the restless water and the cloudy night sky, I could see a few tiny points of light that I suspected marked the homes of the islanders.

Did they know that we were out here? I wondered. And would they welcome us ashore in the morning? It was a question that had not occurred to me before, but now I was curious as to how the people of Dark Thunder felt about the coming of Latimer Trading. Did they welcome the enterprise or would they resent us? Such thoughts made going to sleep difficult when I retired to my pallet in the tiny cabin I shared with Penny, Dorry, and H.J. The next morning I woke weary and unready to face the endless problems of setting up a new household.

Daylight gave me a clear view of the island, which was strikingly beautiful. As on English Wells, a small village fringed the harbor, but there were far fewer homes here and the warehouse was but a roofed shell, the sides only partially enclosed. The dock, however, matched the one we had left behind and I could see another being built on the far side of the warehouse. Latimer Trading would indeed be able to expand when all was finished here.

Harlan went ashore to arrange for several wagons and a carriage to take us to the new house. Since I knew that Sarah had visited Dark Thunder before, I looked to her for information as we helped the children into the carriage.

"The house is on the other end of the island," she explained with a smile that did not lighten the sadness in her eyes. "The drive here is not as long as the one from the village to Latimer House, since this island is smaller; but the area we pass through has not been cultivated, so it seems less welcoming."

"There are no farms here?" I was surprised.

"Each home has its own garden, but the land has been left unplowed, perhaps because it is not as rich as that of English Wells." Her voice broke and it was several

75

minutes before she continued. "We shall have to see to the cultivation of a garden and the planting of trees near our new home if we want to have fresh fruits and vegetables."

The carriage moved off smartly with Higgins at the reins and Mrs. Higgins and Dorry helping us with Penny and H.J. I looked around with interest as we drove between the cottages of the village. I could see people about through the windows of the houses or working in the gardens that did indeed surround each of them; but no one looked our way. It was as if we were ghosts trailing unseen and unheard along their dusty street. I shivered though the morning was warm and the sun had easily dispelled the clouds from the night before.

"Friendly lot," Sarah murmured as we left the village and bounced along the rutted road that wound between the banyan, palms, and fig trees that shaded it.

"Is there a problem with the people here?" Could this be what had troubled Sarah? It made more sense to me than believing that she would be worried about some curse story.

"Harlan says not." Her tone held no conviction. "He claims they are just a bit clannish and shy with outsiders. I suppose he gets on well enough with them, since they have been working for him these past months."

"Was it like this when you visited the island before?" I tried to keep my tone as calm as hers so as not to alert Penny to my discomfort. So far the child seemed quite happy and I had no desire to set her to crying again.

Sarah nodded. "I hoped it would have changed since that was so long ago. I thought they would welcome us now that we have come to stay."

"Perhaps they will eventually. I mean, they could be shy like Harlan said, couldn't they?" I knew she could hear the doubt in my voice, but I had promised Hunter that I would try to help her adjust to this new place and I had to do my best.

Sarah gave me a slight smile. "I hope that is all that

76

troubles them. Meantime, do you think it would help if I offered employment to some of the women here? We could use day workers to help with the unpacking and, if they worked out well, perhaps a permanent maid or two after we are settled."

"That sounds like a good way to start meeting the inhabitants." I looked out at the wilderness that we were passing through. The flowers and bushes were familiar, but they seemed larger here and more vigorous than when they grew in the formal gardens of Nassau and English Wells. The untamed growth reminded me of the tales an old sailor friend of Papa's had told me— frightening stories of a jungle where wild natives hid with spears and poison darts and all manner of . . .

I forced the thoughts away, reminding myself that I was supposed to be helping Sarah overcome her fears, not cultivating my own. So Dark Thunder was less settled than English Wells; that did not mean that it was dangerous. And as for the people who lived here, it would just take us a little time to get to know them, then we would all be great friends. I wanted to believe that, but my doubts refused to disappear.

The road continued up and down the hills, sometimes shaded by the trees, sometimes crossing meadows of thick grass that seemed to disprove the idea that the land was poor. It was quite beautiful, I realized, yet I felt no desire to stop and pick the flowers or wander through the trees as I had on English Wells. Even warmed by the bright sunlight, I felt no more welcome from the land than there had been from the people.

"It is not much further now, Faith," Sarah said as I caught a distant glimpse of the sea just before the road turned away from it and headed through a dense grove of trees and bushes, past a rocky outcropping or two, then turned again. Sunshine gleamed ahead as Higgins stopped the horses.

"There she be, Miss Sarah," he announced.

I gasped, shaken for a moment by the similarity

between the house that rose before us and the Latimer House. The setting was different, of course, for no carefully tended gardens spread out from the veranda; but for just a heartbeat, dizzy confusion swept through me. I half expected Hunter to pop up from behind the nearest hibiscus bush and shout, "Surprise!"

"Oh, look what Harlan has done!" Sarah's voice rose with joy and excitement. "Is it not wonderful, Faith?"

"It surely is," I agreed. "I had no idea."

"Mommy, it looks just like home." Penny jumped off Mrs. Higgin's lap and landed on my feet, clapping her hands with delight.

"It is our home, silly Penny." Sarah's giggle sounded so normal that I was embarrassed to remember how uneasy I had been on our journey here. She pulled Penny into her arms, then turned to me. "Harlan promised that he would build me a house that I would love as much as I loved Latimer House, but I never dreamed he would do this. Now I understand why he refused to bring me back to the island once the walls were finished. What a marvelous surprise."

"You really had no idea?" I studied Sarah's face, struck by the change in her expression.

"Harlan brought me to the island to see the area, but at that time the house was not much more than a framework, so I had no thought of what the finished building would be like. He said it would be even finer than Latimer House and more spacious, but that was all." Her gaze dropped and a little color burned in her cheeks. "Because of the way I felt about coming, I never asked many questions."

"I am sorry he did not see your face when first you glimpsed it," I murmured.

"Did I appear as surprised as you?" Sarah chuckled. "Did you really think it was a ghost house transported here from English Wells?"

I had to laugh as I felt myself blushing. "For a moment I thought I was dreaming."

Sarah squeezed my fingers as Higgins started the horses forward again. "If you are dreaming, then so am I," she whispered, "and I hope no one wakes us. If we must live here, having an all-new Latimer House will make things much easier."

I sensed there was more she wanted to say, but before she could, Penny claimed her attention with a number of questions and by the time Sarah had answered as many as she could, the carriage had stopped and Mr. Higgins was helping us down. The wagon load of servants creaked to a stop behind us. It was time for all of us to begin exploring our new home.

The next hours flew by as we wandered through the strangely empty rooms of the huge house. The arrangement of the first floor was similar to that of Latimer House except for the addition of several rooms but I soon realized that Harlan had made the upstairs far more suitable for his family.

To begin with, the entire east end of the second floor had been constructed with the children in mind. As governess to Penny, I was to have a suite of rooms consisting of a small sitting room and a fair-sized bedroom with a door that connected to Penny's bedroom. Next to our area there were several small rooms that Harlan identified as playrooms and a schoolroom. Opening on the other side of them was the nursery, which connected to the bedroom Dorry was to occupy. On each side of these rooms were still other very practical arrangements which offered plenty of room for expansion.

As we explored, furniture was already being brought in from what was to be the stable. The pieces, Harlan explained, were a part of the cargo he had brought to the island after his last voyage. At Sarah's insistence, I helped her examine them and together we exclaimed over their well-preserved beauty as she decided where they were to be placed in the rooms.

Even while I listened to Sarah's delight at the prospect

of having such treasures in her home, I could not help wondering about the people who had been forced to sell them. The war being so young, it seemed strange that people would already be reduced to selling their prized possessions. And what of all that we had left behind in Charleston? Would Papa someday be selling Mama's beloved Chinese chest or the wonderfully carved bed that she had loved?

"What is it, Faith?" Sarah broke into my thoughts. "Do you not like the arrangement of these new chairs and tables?"

I looked around the huge front parlor quickly, noting that she had allowed plenty of space for the many sofas, chairs, and tables from English Wells that were no doubt being unloaded even now. "I think you have done most handsomely, Sarah," I assured her, speaking the truth. "I was only speculating about the family that once owned these pieces."

"According to that man Jones, they were glad enough to have a buyer with gold to offer," Harlan snapped, startling me, since I had not seen him enter the parlor.

"I only meant that it is sad to care for something with love and then be forced to part with it." I kept my words soft and my eyes down, sensing his displeasure.

"Oh, Faith, how like you to always think of someone else's pain when I was only enjoying my own pride of possession." Sarah's eyes glazed with sympathetic tears and I cursed myself for even mentioning the former owners. I wanted Sarah to be happy here and if these furnishings could do it, I had no desire to taint her pleasure.

"I think the former owners would be pleased to have their treasures here under your care," I told her. "I know you will love them as they did."

"Better safe here than taken by some thieving Northern blockader." Harlan's smile did not hide the glare he directed my way as he came to put his arm around his wife. "You shall have to go to the stable and

80

look over the rest of what I had stored there, Sarah," he continued. "I thought since we added a number of guest rooms, you might wish to use the lesser pieces in them."

"This house is much bigger than the one we left," Sarah agreed, her brief sadness fading as she concentrated on the challenge ahead. "I had no idea we would need so much more furniture. We could have brought some things from the attic."

"Later, when you have more knowledge of what you will need, we shall make a visit to English Wells, so you can select from what is stored there. Or we can go to Nassau and visit the shops. Would you like that?" Harlan's face softened with love as he looked at Sarah and I felt a momentary twinge of envy, my wayward heart aching with the memory of Hunter's kiss.

Forgetting my feelings for Hunter was proving more difficult than I expected, especially when Harlan was around. Though I had no difficulty telling them apart, a sudden glimpse of Harlan across a room or coming around a corner could set my pulse racing and bring back every wondrous moment of the kiss Hunter and I had shared. What troubled me most was that I so enjoyed remembering.

Fortunately, at that moment I was distracted by the arrival of the first wagon load of our belongings from the *Sprite*. Since it was quickly followed by others from both the *Sprite* and the other ships that had accompanied us, I had no more time for idle dreaming about the past or a future that could never be. Instead I spent the rest of the day helping Sarah and Mrs. Higgins direct the men as they carried everything into the house.

That set the pattern for the next several days. We rose at dawn and all worked together until we fell into our beds, exhausted, each night. Unfortunately, the confusion seemed to make Penny's sleepwalking worse, which meant either Dorry, Rose, or I must be at her bedside when she napped and I worried each night that she might pass by my bed without my hearing her.

On the third morning, I was helping Sarah sort through a box when I came upon a charming little silver bracelet hung with tiny tinkling bells. "What an adorable bracelet," I said, shaking it so the music rang in the quiet room.

"Hunter brought it to me the year before Harlan and I were married." Sarah's smile glowed as she took it from my suddenly cold fingers. "He said it reminded him of my laugh. He was such a romantic in those days, always saying wonderful things to me."

The chill moved to my spine at this proof that Hunter had once loved Sarah, but I forced my jealous thoughts away. "Do you wear it often?" I asked, a plan already forming in my mind.

"Never. The constant chiming of the bells bothered Harlan, so I put it away. I had not thought of it until now. Do you fancy it, Faith? If you would like to have it . . ."

"I was thinking that it might be a perfect gift for Penny," I began, my heart twisting painfully at the thought of wearing the gift that Hunter had given to another. "If she can be persuaded to wear this all the time, I could be sure of hearing her when she slips from her bed at night."

"What a wonderful plan!" Sarah clapped her hands with delight. "And if I know Penny, once she sees the bracelet, she will never want to take it off. She adores pretty things." Sarah turned the bracelet over in her hands. "Before I give it to her, I shall ask Higgins to remove a link or two, just so it will not fall off by accident."

Sarah was indeed correct in her assessment of her daughter's love for the bracelet and, though the charming tinkling of the little bells reminded me of Sarah's words about Hunter, I was grateful. That night for the first time since our arrival on Dark Thunder, I

82

slept easy, sure that Penny would not be roaming the house without my knowledge.

Then, suddenly it seemed, the endless flow of wagons from the harbor came to a stop and there was no more rearranging of the furniture, no more mad searching through barrels, trunks, and crates for misplaced items. There were still a few rooms empty of furniture, but the new Latimer House on Dark Thunder was beginning to look very much like the one we had left behind.

For the first time in what seemed months, I had a few moments for myself, time to rearrange the books on the shelves beside the little desk in my sitting room, time to really examine my clothes and choose what I wanted to wear instead of simply putting on the first shirtwaist and skirt I found. Time to remember and to ache with longing for Hunter's return.

My dreams of Hunter had wakened me well after midnight of our seventh night in the new house, when I heard the faint sound of the bell bracelet. I had hoped that when the confusion of moving had ended so would Penny's sleepwalking. Now swallowing hard, I got up and went through the open door between our bedrooms.

Her bed was empty, but as I looked around, I realized that she was not in her room. Frightened, I opened the door that led to the playroom, sure that she must have gone that way; but the playroom was empty, too. Then I heard the bells behind me and turned to look through her window toward the balcony that formed the roof of the veranda Harlan had ordered built across the front and on both sides of the house. My heart stopped as I watched Penny gliding along the rough wood toward the railing.

I stumbled on shaking legs through my room and out my door to the balcony, then forced myself to step slowly so that I would not frighten Penny as she wandered along the balcony toward the rear staircase. Guilt swept through me. Why had I not realized that a sleepwalker could climb through an open window? Thanking God that I had heard her in time, I took her hand and gently led her back inside without awakening her.

Once she was safe in her bed, I closed the window firmly, then watched her sleep for several minutes before returning to the balcony, still shaking inside. What if I had not heard the bells? She could have climbed up on the railing or slipped down the stairs and gone anywhere. I shivered even though I had taken time to slip a robe around me after I put Penny into her bed.

Seeking release from the horrible "might-have-beens," I gazed out at the distant wooded ridges trying to formulate a plan to protect Penny. It was then that I saw them. Lights moving through the trees, appearing and disappearing as though carried by a line of people moving along the road. But that was not where the road ran, I realized. In fact, according to Harlan, that was the wild area of the island, a section unused by anyone.

I hurried along the rail, trying to see exactly where the lights were going, but even as I watched, they vanished. Curious, I waited for them to reappear; but the night was still and dark. Finally, shivering with the dampness of approaching dawn and a strange sense of foreboding, I retreated to my bed, wishing mightily that I could believe that the lights were a figment of my ever-fertile imagination. Unfortunately, I had a feeling they were all too real and an omen of trouble to come.

Chapter 6

Penny, as usual, rose with the sun and I, as her governess, could not remain in my bed no matter how I longed for more sleep. Since Penny knew nothing of her midnight adventure, I kept my own counsel, but I could not forget the sight of her wandering along the balcony. That must not be allowed to happen again and as soon as I could I left Penny under Dorry's watchful eyes and went to talk to Sarah.

I found her in the morning room with her embroidery. She smiled as I entered. "Faith, thank goodness you have come to talk to me."

"Was there something you wished?" I asked, surprised at her vehemence.

"Only your company for a time." She sighed. "I thought when we were so busy with the unpacking and arranging everything in the house that I should be grateful for some time to myself, but now that I have it . . ."

To my horror, I realized that she was near tears. "What is it?" I asked, sitting down on the sofa beside her. "Has something happened, Sarah?"

"I have suddenly realized how alone we are here, Faith. Do you know that not one woman from the village has come to call? When Harlan sails tomorrow, we shall have only each other and I am not sure that I can bear never leaving the house, never having guests to

85

entertain." She stopped to take a steadying breath. "I had hoped that by now we should have made friends with at least a few of the ladies who live here."

"Perhaps they are just waiting to be invited," I suggested, relieved to know that nothing more terrible was troubling her.

"How can I invite people that I have never met?" Sarah dabbed at her eyes. "I have spoken with Harlan about taking me to meet some of the village ladies, but he seems to feel I should wait until they are ready." She sniffed. "Ready for what, I ask you? Am I not a stranger to be welcomed? I have done nothing to make them dislike me, so why are they pretending that we do not exist?"

I shrugged, wishing that I could offer her some answers, but the truth was that I, too, wondered at the way people shunned us. Except for the wagon drivers, no one from the village had come near the house. Most of the heavy work of moving in had been handled by the crews from the ships and they were from English Wells, not Dark Thunder. Since our arrival, the only women I had spoken to were those who had come with us.

Because I could think of nothing to reassure her, we sat in silence for several minutes, then I sighed and broached the subject that had brought me here. "Penny was sleepwalking again last night," I began, wishing that I could spare her my worry, "and this time she was on the balcony."

"Outside?" Sarah sat forward, her loneliness forgotten. "But how could that be? I thought with the bells . . ."

"She went through the window. Luckily, I was awake and heard the bracelet, but I think we must keep the window closed at night. I thought you would want to warn Dorry and the rest of the staff not to leave it open."

"Dear Lord, perhaps we should have it nailed shut, Faith. If she should wander out there, she could fall and . . ." Sarah shuddered, obviously imagining the

86

same terrible possibilities that had haunted me since last night.

"The new window frames are so stiff, I doubt that nailing will be necessary. I could scarce raise the window myself, so Penny will be safe so long as no one leaves it open as I did last night." I watched her, wondering if I should mention the mysterious lights I had seen after I put Penny back into her bed.

"Oh, Faith, I thank heaven every day that Hunter brought you to us. I do not believe I could bear being here without you." Her hug surprised me, but I welcomed it. In many ways, I had long been as lonely as she was now.

"I love being here with all of you," I assured her. "And I will do my best to keep Penny safe, I promise."

"I trust you. Now, let us talk of something happier. Have you decided when you will begin Penny's lessons? And what shall we do to entertain ourselves until Harlan and Hunter return?"

"I have begun writing a story about Dark Thunder for Penny. I thought it would be more interesting for her if she could read about places she knows and I did promise to help her write to her friends on English Wells." It was easier to plan for Penny's education than to think of ways to keep Sarah content while the men were at sea.

"A story of Dark Thunder, how grim." Sarah's smile disappeared. "Every day the same, nothing new to do, nowhere to visit; I knew everyone on English Wells, Faith. I cared about them. They were like a part of my family and now . . ."

"I think we should begin planning for our garden," I interrupted, sensing that she would soon be in tears. "That would be fun for both Penny and H.J. and I could teach Penny the names of the plants and trees that we will need."

Sarah smiled ruefully. "Ever practical, Faith, how I envy you. I would sit and mourn for what I have left behind, but you are all ready to begin building something new here. By the time Harlan returns, you will . . ." She

87

let it trail off as Hannah Watts appeared in the doorway with a question about the list of supplies that she was making for Harlan to take with him. There were many items that could only be purchased in a port like Nassau and Harlan had promised to do some shopping while he was taking care of business.

Knowing that making the list would keep Sarah distracted for some time, I excused myself to go in search of Harlan. Since I hesitated to tell Sarah about the lights I had seen, it seemed a good plan to let him know—just in case there was something evil afoot on the island. A chilling thought, but one I was unable to ignore.

Unfortunately, Mrs. Higgins informed me that Harlan had already left for the harbor and would not be returning before midday. Still unable to dismiss the image of bobbing lights from my thoughts, I picked up my bonnet and stepped out onto the veranda. Perhaps there was a simple explanation for what I had seen, I decided. Maybe I should just investigate a little before I talked to Harlan.

The morning was bright with sunshine and the thick growth of flowering bushes and trees seemed much less menacing now that I had grown used to it. Trying to behave as I thought David would if he had been confronted by such a vision, I followed the wagon road away from the house, trying to judge just where I had glimpsed the lights. It took only a little while to confirm my suspicions that the lights had been nowhere near the road.

All right, so what did that leave? I asked myself, glaring at the untamed oleander bushes that seemed to crowd the edge of the road shielding the land beyond from my view. Looking back toward the house offered no answers since everything but the steep-pitched roof had vanished behind a thick growth of red and white hibiscus. A shiver traced down my spine in spite of the warm sun and I turned back, feeling a coward, but somehow afraid to push through the bushes that edged the road. There had to be another way.

Once I reached the house, I made my way along the side to a point exactly below where I had stood last night. To my surprise, the view here was much less intimidating. There were still a lot of shadows cast by the banyan and wild fig trees, but the ground was rockier near the cliffs that dropped to the sea, so the bushes that grew there were smaller.

Gathering my courage and determination, I started walking in a straight line from the veranda, trying hard to keep my sense of direction by aiming for a tall palm that I remembered as being near where I had seen the lights. The rough ground quickly slowed my steps and forced me off my planned route; but I kept one eye on the palm, following it like a beacon as I negotiated the small ridges and detoured around the trees and bushes.

My mission had me so engrossed that I scarcely felt the wild thorn bushes that snagged at my skirt as I hurried forward, barely aware of the thunder of the waves that dashed against the cliffs to my right. Rocks cut through the soles of my shoes, bruising my feet, but I refused to give up. As long as I could see the palm I had to keep going.

Panting with the effort of climbing yet another small ridge, I paused to wipe the dampness from my forehead. A breeze tugged at my bonnet as I stumbled down a short, but steep incline, then staggered around a tall clump of cane grass before shuddering to a stop. The sentinel palm rose ahead of me—just across what was obviously a path.

A well-used path, I realized, noting that what little grass grew there was stubby or worn away. But where could it lead? What, besides the house Harlan had built, was on this end of the island? We were supposed to have no neighbors nearer than the village, so why would there be a path through this area? Once I caught my breath, I decided that I would find out.

Following the path was certainly much easier than finding it had been. I enjoyed walking along the tree-shaded trail as it wound downward toward the sea. Soon, however, the vegetation was replaced by rocks and the path narrowed a bit as it curled between outcroppings then curved again before rounding one last cliff face and opening to reveal a little pocket of sandy beach.

"Well, well, well," I murmured, entranced by the lovely scene. The cove, though too small to accommodate a ship as large as the steamers, was charming. The water shaded from pale green to deep blue as it moved outward. Gentle waves lapped the sand, then receded to the wilder water beyond the rocky ridges that sheltered the cove.

I had no trouble picturing this as a perfect picnic spot. Sarah would adore it, I was sure, and here the children would be able to play in the water without fear. In fact, I was quite tempted to pull off my own shoes and stockings to test the temperature myself. It would be a treat to just stretch out on the warm sand and . . .

But what was I thinking? I had come here seeking whoever had carried the lights last night and I was still no closer to learning their identity. Frowning, I turned away from the sea and began the climb back up to the wooded area. Since it was not here, it seemed likely that the answer lay at the other end of this path.

The part of the trail I had not yet explored led toward the bluffs where the house was located and once I passed the sentinel palm, I caught occasional glimpses of the buildings as the vegetation thinned. The powerful waves thundered loudly as I neared the headland, but then the path turned again, angling in the direction of the house until it stopped suddenly at a grassy clearing that spread from the base of a small cliff.

"What in the world?" I looked around, seeking something—a continuation of the path or some sort of structure—that could have been the destination, but there was nothing. Wild vines looped down from the lush growth on top of the cliff and a number of flowering bushes thrived in the high grass of the clearing, well sheltered by the rocky outcropping; but there was no sign of human habitation.

I turned back to the path. Had I missed something? Was there a turnoff that led somewhere else? I retraced my steps a short distance, seeking some sign, but again, I found nothing. The path obviously led from the cove to the clearing, but I could not imagine why—or what anyone would be doing there in the middle of the night.

Thinking of the mysterious lights reminded me again of how alone and vulnerable I was while exploring out here and I gladly cut through the trees, scrambled up the rocky incline and headed for the house. That was more than enough exploring for me; I would be happy to entrust further investigation to Harlan.

As I reached the veranda I heard the sound of approaching hoofbeats and, sure that it would be Harlan returning from his visit to the village, I made my way around the building to await him on the stable side. I waved to Harlan as young Ben, the stable boy, came out to take his mount.

"Was there something you wished to speak to me about, Faith?" he asked as soon as he reached the veranda.

I nodded. "If you could spare me a moment?"

His expression held a touch of impatience, but he leaned against the ornamental railing that edged the veranda. "What has happened?"

It took me a moment to calm his fears after I mentioned Penny's sleepwalking adventure, but finally he was disposed to listen as I described the line of lights I had seen last night from the balcony.

"Are you sure that you did not dream this, Faith?" he asked while I was seeking the words to tell him about my morning's explorations.

"I am not disposed to such wild imagining." Angered by his words, I met his mocking gaze boldly and continued, "Besides there is a path in the area where I saw the lights. I found it this morning. It leads from a small cove to a clearing near the house." That wiped the smile from his face.

"Did you find any sign of damage or locate anyone living in that area?"

"No, I did not." I was forced to admit. "But there was someone out there last night, Harlan, I would swear to it. I just have no idea what they were doing."

"Did you tell Sarah this?" His frown deepened.

"Only about Penny's sleepwalking."

"Good. I must ask you to promise not to mention the lights to her, Faith. I do not want her further upset; she is unhappy enough that I must leave tomorrow."

"But what of the lights, Harlan? If there is someone prowling through the area, should we not take some action? We shall be quite unprotected with you gone."

"I think what you saw is something that the islanders call the "Pirate Parade". I was told about it long ago, when work first began on the house, but I had forgotten. You need have no fear."

"Pirate Parade?" I was definitely not reassured.

"It has to do with an old legend, from the time pirates actually lived on Dark Thunder. The story is that they unloaded their ill-gotten gains into small boats and sent them ashore in that cove. At night the treasure was carried to a pirate's lair somewhere in the area for safekeeping. The ghosts still walk on occasion and their lanterns were what you saw." His smile was back in place, but I sensed no real amusement behind it.

"Ghosts? Harlan, I saw lights last night, not ghosts. I cannot believe that you want me to pretend that I . . ."

"All right, I have no belief in ghost lights either. In fact, I would be inclined to suspect that some of the villagers may have done it, perhaps hoping to unnerve all of us." He sighed, looking suddenly older than before. "Not everyone on Dark Thunder has welcomed us, Faith. Most are pleased with the work and money that Latimer Trading brings to their island, but a few . . ."

"You think they would try to frighten us away?"

He shrugged. "It may have been meant only as a

harmless prank, but either way, I should like to keep it just between us. If the servants should get wind of ghost talk, they would never stay and I doubt that Sarah would wish to staff the house from the village."

"Since we have met no one from the village, I doubt that it would be possible." I could definitely see why he wanted me to keep my bobbing lights a secret, yet I resented having to do so. Besides, I could not help feeling uneasy at the idea that someone might resent our presence here enough to try and frighten us.

"Will you keep it a secret, Faith?" He caught my hand, forcing my attention back to him.

"Unless someone else sees them," I conceded, aware that I really had little choice since I had no desire to frighten Sarah or the servants.

"I shall make sure that the villagers know that we are not frightened, then I doubt they will be so foolish as to trespass again." He released my hand and stepped away from me. "Now, perhaps we should go inside. Cook will have the midday meal waiting and I wish to spend as much time as I can with Sarah before I sail."

"Of course." I left him to go up the backstairs, eager to spend a few moments alone in my room. I needed to change from my snagged skirt and to wash away the stains of my explorations before I ate; but more than that, I needed to consider his words.

His explanation seemed to make sense, yet something bothered me. If they wished to frighten us, why wait until so late? They would have no way of knowing that anyone would be awake to see their little parade. I frowned at my reflection in the mirror as I tried to repair the damage my walk had done to my hair.

And there was the path itself. My hunch was that it would take more than a few "pirate parades" to wear it down so easily. But what else could it be? I had followed the entire path and there was nothing untoward at either end—so what did it mean?

Since I could find no explanation better than the one

Harlan had offered, I went downstairs to join him and Sarah at the table. From now on, I would keep a watch for whatever had been out on the bluffs last night, and if it returned, I would investigate further. No way did I believe in ghostly pirates.

The first days after Harlan sailed passed quietly enough. Sarah spent long hours in her rooms, so I concentrated all my time and energy on Penny. She was a delight to teach, soon mastering the strokes that produced first her name, then mine and more slowly, the names of the other members of our household.

Since Penny also adored stories, I spent many happy hours making up new ones to tell her. To compensate for her lack of playmates, I invented Princess Penelope, a little girl who lived in an enchanted castle on a mysterious island where she had many wonderful adventures.

The third morning after Harlan left, I was in the middle of describing Princess Penelope's adventure with Sparkle, the magical goat with the curly horns when Sarah suddenly came into the playroom. The moment I looked into her troubled gray eyes, I knew this was no casual visit; but I could ask no questions until Sarah sent a reluctant Penny off to help Dorry entertain H.J.

Once we were alone in the toy-cluttered playroom, I waited expectantly for Sarah to speak, but instead she began pacing about picking up the toys that Penny had left scattered around. Unsure what else to do, I helped her, hoping that she would sit down and talk to me once the room was tidy. When we ran out of toys to put away, however, she went to the window and stood there, staring out at the bright afternoon, her back to me.

"What has happened, Sarah?" I asked, too worried now to care about being polite.

"Oh, Faith, I have done something terrible and now I need your help, but I have no right to ask for it." When she turned to face me, I could see that she was near tears.

"But of course you should ask," I told her. "I will do anything to help you, you know that. What is it?"

Her gaze remained troubled, but she sank down on one of the chairs with a sigh. "Did you not once tell me that you helped your father keep his ledgers?"

"Ledgers. Yes, of course. He taught me to keep them and I did so for several years before I left Charleston. Why?" Ledgers were the last things I wanted to discuss, but since she had asked, I had to answer.

"Before he sailed, Harlan asked me to handle the keeping of the ledgers for him. He showed me what to write where in the account book and I told him that I could do it, but now . . ." Her voice broke and tears began to flow down her cheeks. "Oh, Faith, I fear I have made terrible mistakes and I know not how to repair them before he returns."

"Harlan asked you to keep his ledgers?" I had to swallow a wayward giggle at the idea. I had been with the family long enough to know that Sarah could not even keep the household accounts straight—Cook handled them. "Oh, Sarah, why did you not tell me sooner?"

"Because I wanted to please him. He was so impressed at what you told Hunter of your talent with figures and he seemed sure that I could do the work. He said it was most simple, but somehow . . ." She shrugged. "I do feel a fool, Faith, but I cannot let my failure cause my husband trouble."

"There is no reason to worry, I am sure. If you wish, I will do what I can to straighten out the ledger. I suspect the errors are small and easily corrected. With neither *Pearl* nor *Sprite* having brought in any cargo since Harlan left, there should not be much to keep track." I stopped, suddenly realizing something. "But how do you know what is to be posted?" I asked. "You have not left the house."

"Higgins goes into the village each afternoon and returns with a page of figures for me to transfer to the

95

books. Harlan would never ask me to go there since people have behaved so strangely toward us."

So that explained the long hours in her room. I was relieved to know what had occupied her, for I had wondered if she was too morose to spend time with me or her children. "Why not show me the ledger and the sheets and I shall see what I can do." I gave her my most reassuring smile.

"Oh, Faith, I truly wonder if I could have survived this move without you." She shook her head, then stood up to hug me.

"You would have been fine," I assured her. "You simply do not realize your own courage and strength, Sarah. Now, come along and show me what you have done."

The desk in the sitting room of Sarah and Harlan's suite was strewn with papers and when I stared at the pages that bore Sarah's script, I began to reconsider my assurances. Where I had expected a few entries, there seemed to be dozens, perhaps hundreds and nothing she had noted looked right to me.

"It is beyond hope, is it not?" Her bleak words broke through my concentration on the figures. "I shall simply have to confess my failure to Harlan when he returns."

"Oh, I would not say that," I began without my former confidence. "I was only surprised at the number of entries you have made. Do you still have the sheets that Higgins brought each day? Perhaps if I begin with the first entries, I will be able to make sense of this."

"Everything is there." She swept a hand over the top of the desk, sending several sheets of paper cascading to the floor. "I am hopeless!"

"I think you need some time away from this," I suggested, realizing that she was going to be of no help at all. "Why not take Penny and H.J. out for a stroll through the garden? I know they have missed spending time with you while you have been so busy with the accounts."

"What garden? I have had no time to supervise any planting since Harlan left." Sarah sank down on a chair, obviously still too dispirited to leave.

"Then why not start now? You could take Higgins with you and explain your plans to him. I am sure he would be happy to begin work on the grounds now that the house is in order." I pressed the idea, sure that she would feel more herself once she became involved in planning the formal gardens.

"You are sure that you will not have questions? Perhaps I can explain what I have done and then . . ."

I waved her away, sure that her explanation would only add to my confusion. "I shall make note of any questions I have, Sarah; meantime, I will just begin at the beginning and try to learn your company's method of record keeping."

"Well, if you are sure . . ." Her frown quickly changed to a smile as she washed the inkstains from her fingers and located the watercolors she had painted to show how she wanted the gardens to look.

I felt a touch of envy as I watched her leave. While I did enjoy keeping accounts, I was not sure I could ever get these straightened out enough for normal posting. I simply could not believe that so many transactions had taken place at the Dark Thunder dock. Even if the warehouse was now finished, it had not seemed large enough . . . I turned back to the entries made several days before Harlan left.

Two hours later, I straightened up, rubbing my eyes and groaning as my neck and shoulders creaked. I had made my way through the tedious lines of figures, correcting and changing the small errors that Sarah had made; but I still had questions. Not about the figures, since I had the sheets to consult, but about the business itself.

I pushed the neatly stacked papers to one side and closed the ledger then got to my feet. My rumbling stomach announced that it was nearing time for the midday meal and I was most anxious to talk with Sarah. There was no way I could continue to keep the accounts without going into the village to talk with the people who provided the sheets from which I would work.

"Oh, Faith, how are you doing?" Sarah burst through the door, nearly crashing into me. She looked wonderfully happy, her eyes sparkling, a touch of color blooming in her cheeks.

"Well, I think I have corrected most of the mistakes, Sarah, but I still have questions that need answering and I really must talk to the man who keeps the records. Do you think I might ride into town with Higgins this afternoon?"

"Can you not work from the sheets? Harlan said that I could get everything I needed from them." Her smile faded.

"If the figures are correct, that should be true; but I find it hard to believe that business is transacted the way it appears on the sheets. They show undescribed cargoes arriving one day, being stored overnight, then shipped out the next day on a different ship. I fear that there may be a misunderstanding between the person keeping the records and what Harlan told you."

Sarah frowned. "You think that I misunderstood what Harlan told me? Did I, Faith? Have I ruined the ledgers completely?"

Her guilty fear shamed me as I realized that she blamed herself for everything. Yet how could I explain the problem that was tormenting me? I had to try. "As a matter of fact, I found the pages Harlan did were quite similar to yours, Sarah, so I doubt that you misunderstood. I suspect it may be a different method of keeping records and I shall need to understand it, if I am to continue to keep the ledger until Harlan returns."

"You would be willing to do that?" Her relief was almost amusing. "I feared to even ask such a favor."

"I would not mind at all. Keeping the ledger will give me something to do after Penny is safely in her bed."

"Would you do me one more favor?" Sarah's solemnity surprised me.

"What is that?"

"Will you promise not to tell Harlan what has happened? I should be so ashamed to have him know of my failure."

"Of course. It will be our secret, I promise." I made the vow easily enough, but as I hurried to my own room to prepare for the midday meal, I felt the weight of it. I now held two secrets, one from Sarah and one from Harlan, and I was comfortable with neither.

Chapter 7

Higgins held his back rigid with disapproval as he drove me away from the house. Although he had protested only that Harlan would not wish me to go, I sensed his displeasure. A garrulous man most times, he had said nothing since he helped me into the pony cart. It was a situation I could not allow to continue.

Deciding on a straightforward approach, I asked, "Why do you so mislike taking me to the village, Mr. Higgins?"

For a moment, he kept his gaze on the pony's head, then slowly the starch seemed to slip from his spine and he turned to look at me. "We be not wanted there, Miss Faith. The man what gives me the pages, will say naught beyond business words to me, and likely, he be saying less to you. Mr. Harlan instructed me to keep Miss Sarah safe at the house and I be knowing he meant the orders for you also."

"But Sarah has some questions about the figures you have brought to her and cannot continue with her work on the ledger until she has the answers. I am sure Harlan would not like to have the ledger pages unfinished on his return." We had already informed Higgins that, since I was more familiar with the keeping of accounts, Sarah felt I would be better able to get the needed information.

"Mr. Harlan will not approve." Higgins straightened again.

"Then perhaps it would be wise not to mention this trip to him," I suggested. "Besides, what harm can come to me; you will be at my side, will you not?"

"Of course, Miss Faith. I would not be leaving you alone with the likes of these islanders." The dislike in his tone chilled me because I had always found him a friendly man.

I had not been to the village since my arrival, so had no idea what could have made him resent the islanders. Unless he was simply unhappy to be living here since English Wells had always been his home. Sighing, I hoped that was the reason. Still, I could feel his tension seeping into my body as we left the meadows and groves of trees that made up the middle part of the island and neared the houses on the outskirts of the village.

There were few people about in the afternoon heat, but as we rounded a thick growth of hibiscus a woman stepped back abruptly, obviously not having heard our approach. I forced a smile and called a friendly, "Good afternoon."

For a moment her dark eyes met mine, then she turned away without a word or a smile. The only reply to my greeting came from the yapping of a small dog behind the fence that enclosed the garden of the house next to hers. I settled back in the seat, anger and uneasiness twisting inside me.

"As you see, Miss Faith, these folks be different from those on other islands." Higgins seemed unsurprised at the snubbing I had suffered.

"But we are here and they will have to accept us sooner or later," I protested, my cheeks burning.

Higgins said nothing as he turned the pony toward the warehouse, which had indeed been finished since our arrival. To my surprise, there were a half-dozen sailing ships of various sizes tied up at the dock, where men were busily loading or unloading their cargoes. More boats were anchored in the brilliantly hued harbor as though waiting their turn.

At that moment I realized that I might be wrong to question the number of entries on the sheets that Higgins had brought to Sarah. "Is it always this busy, Mr. Higgins?" I asked.

"There be plenty of boats in and out. Mr. Harlan says that he has to accommodate those who been trading at this port for years. Says 'twill be good for business."

I nodded, remembering the fees that had been noted in the ledger. I knew storing cargoes while they awaited transport to other locations was a legitimate form of business for any trading company, but Papa had never kept the cargoes so short a time. And he had always carefully recorded the contents of each cargo he stored so as to be protected from any errors made by those who contracted to ship the goods elsewhere.

"Have you changed your mind about talking to Mr. Decateur, Miss Faith?" He sounded hopeful. "You could spend a bit of time at the shops while I collect the sheets from him."

"Could I not do both?" I asked, my curiosity stronger than my reluctance to chance another snubbing. "I would like to see the shops but I feel I must speak with Decateur since I promised Sarah that I would question him." I swallowed a sigh, hating the necessity for the lies.

"Hannah Watts is never without a list of supplies for me to purchase." Higgins stopped the pony at the end of the dock near the open door of the warehouse and helped me down. "If you will follow me, I shall take you to Mr. Decateur."

A warehouse was familiar ground for me, since I had often accompanied Papa to the warehouse he owned in Charleston and for a moment I grew misty-eyed from missing him. I would so much rather have stayed in Charleston and chanced the dangers of war.

"You be early, Higgins." The man's tone was cold and

unfriendly and when I turned to look at him, his expression matched his voice.

Higgins quickly introduced me, saying that I had come for the mistress of Thunder House with questions regarding the keeping of the ledger. I swallowed hard, forcing back a cowardly desire to retreat from the man's bold gaze, reminding myself that I had stared down worse when I was far younger.

Decateur's glare eased slightly as I began asking questions about the cargoes. His answers were short and not very informative, mostly consisting of his claim that Harlan had told him it was unnecessary to examine the cargoes that were scheduled to remain less than a week in the warehouse.

His attitude began to change slightly when I pointed out an error on one of the sheets and a discrepancy on another. He was no less surly, but at least he was respectful as he adjusted the figures and checked his sheets for today. When he finished, I decided to try a little charm and see if I could change his attitude further.

"You seem to be very busy here," I observed. "Has this port always served so many ships or has the new warehouse attracted them?"

The slight thaw congealed as his expression hardened and his gaze was stony as he handed me the new sheets along with those I had brought with me. "If ye've no more questions 'bout the figures, I've much to attend to, miss." He turned and stalked away, shouting angry orders to several men who had been lounging against a stack of crates. I had a feeling his ire was meant for me, not the hapless men.

"Be you ready to go, Miss Faith?" Higgins asked, bringing my attention back to him.

I nodded, swallowing a sigh and wondering why my idle question had so incensed the man. I had been trying to engage him in a pleasant conversation and had succeeded only in angering him. Perhaps all my months of avoiding male company had left me out of practice when it came to charming men.

Unbidden, images of Hunter filled my mind disproving that ugly suspicion. Hunter had found my conversation diverting enough to spend hours with me. I ached to discuss this with him, to ask his opinion of the ledgers. I had to smile. Hunter at least would be willing to answer my questions about the activity of the small port.

Thanks to my memories of Hunter, I faced the village with renewed courage. I might have failed to make friends with Mr. Decateur, but I had gained his respect and that meant somthing. I was ready to try to melt the reserve of any women I met in the local shops.

The buildings devoted to commerce, which were located on the single street that wound along the edge of the harbor area, were few and none too promising. Several had been closed for the day and the largest, which was the General Store, appeared almost deserted when we entered. A sallow middle-aged man hurried forward, unsmiling, to take Mr. Higgins's list, while a dumpy woman leaning against a wall near the rear door merely turned her head to stare at me.

Not exactly the welcome I had hoped for, but I was never one to give up easily. I smiled at the woman and headed for a small display of fabric, ribbons, laces, and other sewing supplies. I still had several dress lengths to make up, but I could always use another bit of material, if it would ease the strain between the villagers and those of us at the house.

At Thunder House, I reminded myself, remembering what Mr. Higgins had called it. An appropriate name, considering the constant raging of the waves against the bluff on which the house was built. I wondered why Harlan or Sarah had never told me what the place was called. I should have to ask her when I get back. I forced those thoughts from my mind and smiled at the woman, who had finally left her doorway, probably because she wanted to keep a closer eye on me.

By the time I had selected two bits of lace and a length

of ribbon for trim on a dress I had finished in Nassau, I knew that I was fighting a battle I could not win. The woman never met my gaze and her answers were so brief they were almost rude. I could hardly wait to leave the dim store for the heat of the afternoon. Even the burning sun was better than the frigid air of dislike that seemed to have surrounded us the moment we entered the village.

"Be you ready to go back to the house, Miss Faith?" Higgins asked, his expression reflecting an anger that matched mine.

"I have seen more than enough of this village," I admitted, clutching my purchases as he helped me into the cart.

"'Tis a sorry place filled with sorry people." He slapped the reins on the pony's back and we headed along the street. He stared straight ahead, but I watched both sides, trying to see just how many of the villagers were busy ignoring our passage. Of all those I saw only one, a boy of six or seven, actually met my gaze and he turned away when I lifted my hand to wave.

We were halfway home before I thought to ask, "Why did you say I had come from Thunder House, Mr. Higgins? I have never heard Sarah or Harlan call it anything but Latimer House."

"That be what the villagers call the place. 'Twill take no notice of you, be you calling the place anything else. Even Mr. Harlan uses that name when he be speaking to Decateur or the others what work for him."

"But if he prefers the name Latimer House . . ." I began, then let it trail off, realizing that it was a foolish protest. The villagers would call the place what they pleased. I decided not to mention the name change to Sarah, certain she would not understand.

"People on English Wells call a man's house by the name he chooses, but here . . ." Higgins's lip curled and he glared at the few goats that grazed in the meadows near the road. "Here there be no respect."

Since I could not argue, I only nodded and leaned back

wanting to at least enjoy the ride home. Staring sleepily at the lovely landscape, I surrendered happily to the images my imagination presented. My daydreaming carried me forward to what I was sure would be a happier time.

Once Hunter and David returned from their trading foray to the mainland, everything would be different. Harlan had been preoccupied with business since our arrival, but David and Hunter would have time to get to know the villagers. And once Hunter began to charm them . . .

I allowed myself to drift into a daydream where Hunter ordered the building of a second house on the island, which had magically become as friendly a place as English Wells. I could even picture the house, for it would be much like the one I had left behind in Charleston. A perfect home, one where I would be content to spend the rest of my life.

The cart wheel slipped into a rut and jolted me from my reverie. Shock brought me stiffly upright, embarrassed heat burning in my cheeks. I had tried to put such impossible dreams behind me; but it seemed the moment my guard was down, they slipped back to taunt me with what could never be. Once the war was over, my home would be with Tommy at Chestnut Knoll.

To combat my longing for Hunter, I tried to remember Tommy, to recapture the sweetness of our time together; but instead I saw Hunter's lean, hard features and drowned in the deep blue of his eyes. His being away had not helped at all, I realized. I still wanted him as passionately now as I had the moment his lips first claimed mine. My heartbeat quickened as I speculated about what would happen when he returned.

And exactly when would that be? I wondered. Sarah, who kept a small calendar, had marked the week ahead as the one when we could begin to expect the *Pearl* to return; but I knew well how many things could delay them. As we neared the house on the bluffs, a chill touched me though the air was still heavy with the damp heat of early fall. I forced the ugly images from my mind, unwilling to think of the many dangers they faced.

Sarah greeted me on the veranda with a cooling drink and the new paintings she had made of her design for the formal gardens. My worry over Hunter and David ebbed a little as she asked my opinion of the plants and trees she had chosen, then enlisted my help in determining the layout for the paths she wished to have between the massed floral plantings.

Having already volunteered to add account keeping to my efforts as a teacher, I should have know better; but I could not resist the idea of helping to plan the first real garden to be planted on this island. Sarah and I worked happily over the pictures and plans until Mrs. Higgins summoned us to our evening meal and I would have returned to them afterward had not Penny's sad face intruded.

"You promised to tell me what happened to Princess Penelope and Sparkle, Miss Faith," she complained as Dorry brought her in to say "good night" to her mother and me.

"In the morning," I began, my attention still partially on the decision of whether or not night-blooming jasmine should be planted next to the veranda.

"I want to know now." Penny's lower lip protruded. "I waited all day."

I met Sarah's gaze. She smiled. "Perhaps this can wait for one story, Faith. I shall spend the time searching for the list of seeds that I made last spring. I know I packed it, but . . ."

"One story, Penny," I conceded, picking her up and hugging her. "Then you promise to go to sleep?"

"I promise." Her big blue eyes were already closing. "I just want to know if they escape the evil giant under the hill."

"The evil giant," I murmured, thinking that the creation of my imagination now had a real face. Tonight

107

Mr. Ebban Decateur would be suffering defeat at the hands of Princess Penelope and the clever curly-horned goat Sparkle.

Thinking of Decateur reminded me that I had, as yet, done nothing with the sheets of figures he had given me. I swallowed a sigh. When I left Nassau, I had hoped to keep myself occupied, but the many claims on my hours were proving to be more of a challenge than I expected. Still, I preferred my new life to the aimless months I had spent with Caroline.

The days flew by filled with a variety of enjoyable activities. The more time I spent with Sarah, the more I liked her. She seemed interested in almost everything and was widely read thanks to the extensive library of books the Latimers had accumulated through the years. Also, she seemed genuinely interested in my tales of life in Charleston and describing the city and the people there revived my own memories of those happy times. I could ony hope the war would end soon so that I could someday invite Sarah and Harlan to visit me in South Carolina.

And what of Hunter? I wondered as I settled myself to spend the morning working on the accounts. Living in Charleston would mean marriage to Tommy Anderson; could I bear to see Hunter once I belonged to another completely? Hunter had openly admitted to courting Sarah, yet he seemed to live in peace under the same roof with her and Harlan, so perhaps marriage itself made a change in the longing. A sigh of confusion and frustration escaped my lips. I could only hope that it would be thus for me.

"Are the ledgers so difficult, Faith?" Sarah had entered the room unnoticed while I was so deep in thought. I forced my mind back to the present.

"I was just finishing with yesterday's figures." I blotted the numbers I had written down as I pondered the future. "Was there something you wished me to do?"

"I was hoping we could take a stroll through the new area of the garden before it becomes too hot." Sarah looked guilty. "I should not bother you while you are doing my work, but Higgins and young Ben have just finished planting some of the cuttings we brought from English Wells and I would like your opinion."

"And these figures will wait," I agreed. "I can finish them while Penny naps this afternoon." Thanks to my other activities, I no longer spent quiet afternoons reading as I watched over Penny while she slept.

After my report to Sarah about my meeting with the villagers, Sarah had enlisted Higgins's help to send a message to English Wells requesting applicants for the positions she had hoped to fill from the inhabitants of Dark Thunder. We now had two young girls in training and available to watch over Penny, as well as four strong lads to assist with the extra outside work the new garden had produced.

Although I had made no mention of my feelings to Sarah, I was grateful for the newcomers as I still worried about the bobbing lights I had seen. Not that the "pirate parade" had recurred so far as I knew. I made it a practice to watch the area any time I arose during the night, but as Penny was sleepwalking less, there were many nights when I slept straight through. The path, which I had visited only once in the days since that night, appeared exactly as it had the first morning—neither more worn down nor overgrown.

"Well, Faith, what do you think? Will Harlan be pleased?" Sarah forced my attention from the distant sentinel palm to the charming flowerbed that spread before me.

"You have truly wrought a miracle," I told her. "I never thought so much could be accomplished so quickly. Harlan will fear he has come to the wrong island."

"Sometimes I fear that myself," Sarah murmured and

for just a moment I could see the sadness in her eyes, then it was gone as she smiled. "I only hope he will soon be here to see it."

I nodded, but my thoughts were on another steamer—it was the *Sea Pearl* I longed to see in port. "So what have you decided will be the next area of the garden to feel the spade?" I asked, hoping to divert her from any lingering sad thoughts or worries. "Have you . . ." I stopped as I caught the sound of hoofbeats approaching along the road.

"They be coming," a young voice shouted as one of the new lads came riding up the drive toward us. "The *Sea Pearl* be enterin' the harbor."

"Hunter and David are back safe." The words came out like a prayer and with them relief, so strong it threatened to drop me to my knees. For the first time I realized just how worried I had been. "Oh, Sarah, they are back!" It seemed quite natural to hug her and both our cheeks were wet when we stepped apart.

Sarah, more used to the comings and goings of the seafarers, began issuing the necessary orders, then we went inside to inform Mrs. Higgins and Hannah Watts, the cook, so that food and freshly made up beds would be waiting when David and Hunter arrived. Later, I fled to my room, trying to quell my eager heart as I selected a gown of green and brown and repinned my hair, which the breeze had turned into a wild tangle.

I still was not satisfied with my reflection when I heard the sound of carriage wheels approaching. In spite of my bonnet, the sun had touched my cheeks with color and my eyes glowed with anticipation. Like a girl awaiting her favorite suitor? The description came to mind only too easily. I might tell myself I was excited only because David had returned, but I was not sure anyone else would be fooled and that frightened me a little.

My fears faded as I followed my eager charge down the front staircase and watched as Penny hurled herself at Hunter. Though I envied her the hug and kiss she received, it was wonderful to throw myself into David's arms. I had missed my brother desperately even though I knew from the twinkle in his eyes that he would soon be teasing me as unmercifully as ever.

"Now who might you be, miss?" he asked as he held me at arm's length. "You look a bit like my sister Faith, but she has no freckles on her nose and as a proper governess, she would never come racing across the hall like a child."

"And just what would she do when her baby brother came home safely to her?" I could feel the heat in my cheeks as I realized that I had not exactly behaved with the proper decorum I had been trying to teach Penny.

"She would probably cry, then laugh at herself for worrying." David's eyes grew tender and he spoke softly so that I could hardly hear his words above the shouts of greeting from H.J., Dorry, and the rest of the staff. "I have missed you, Faith. And worried about you being on this island."

"We have been fine," I assured him as I glanced at Hunter, just in time to see him take Sarah in his arms and kiss her cheek. "Just lonesome and worried about you."

"We had a terrific voyage." David grinned, then let his hands drop as his expression sobered. "But I still have no word for you from Tommy. 'Twas said he rode north and was in a battle there, but that is the end of the story. The Andersons have been trying to learn his fate, but so far they have had no success."

"He asked everyone we came in contact with, Faith, of that I can assure you." Hunter turned to me and when I looked into his eyes, I nearly melted from the heat of his gaze. The other sounds and people surrounding us seemed to fade like mist under the onslaught of the sun and for several heartbeats there were just the two of us. I ached to be in his arms, yet I held myself rigid, afraid that any movement would betray my longing.

"Then you were able to keep your rendezvous in the Charleston area? You had no need of the alternate

111

dock?" I formed the words with lips that throbbed with the need to touch his.

"We never even saw a Yankee ship," David answered from beside me. "'Twas a fluke that Harlan and I had trouble last trip."

"We took on a full cargo of cotton and delivered it to the broker in Nassau," Hunter continued, his eyes burning into mine. "And we have already taken on another cargo to be delivered to the same place in a few weeks' time."

"So you will be here on Dark Thunder while you wait?" Sarah asked the question that I most wanted answered. "If you have already loaded the cargo . . ."

"We shall happily spend every moment ashore." Hunter's eyes never left mine as he answered her question, so I knew that he meant the words to have special meaning for me.

I felt reality fading again as my heartbeat pounded in my ears and the heat of the afternoon seemed to swirl in clouds around me, making breathing difficult. If he touched me, I knew I would be powerless to resist throwing myself into his arms. It was madness, but I was fully caught up in it.

"I have some even better news for you, Sis," David said. "When we return, Papa will be our contact for this cargo. He sent word with the broker who met us this time. I will actually get to see him and talk to him, so if you want to write him a letter, I can make sure he gets it."

"Then he is well and safe?" The mention of Papa broke the heated bonds between Hunter and me and I managed to turn away from him to look at my brother. "You have talked to someone who has seen him?"

"My contact knows your father quite well," Hunter replied before David could speak. "So I have promised David that he will travel with me next voyage and Gideon will act as Harlan's first mate now that the babe is safely arrived."

"Miranda has her child?" Sarah asked. "I had not

112

heard. How did you know?"

"I stopped by English Wells to leave a part of my crew with their families." Hunter laughed. "I need only a few hands with me for the short trip between there and Dark Thunder." He stepped forward to drape a casual arm about Sarah's shoulders, sniffing the air like a hunting hound. "Now, is it spice cakes I smell, Sarah, or has the salt air totally destroyed my senses?"

"Do you really need to ask, Hunter?" Sarah's giggle and the sight of them together filled me with jealousy. "Cook began stirring them up the moment she heard the *Sea Pearl* was entering the harbor."

"Come on, Sis, I have more news for you," David said, taking my arm and forcing my attention away from the pair who were following Dorry and the children down the hall toward the kitchen.

"Do you not want some spice cakes?" I asked, hating myself for my jealousy, but not wanting to let Hunter out of my sight.

"In a moment; give them a little time to talk. I am sure Sarah has family matters to discuss with Hunter as I have with you." David's tone had changed and when I finally looked into his eyes, I could see the questions there.

Aware that I had no right to feel anything about Hunter, I forced a smile. "I was only remembering that you have a fondness for sweets yourself and I thought you would not want to miss out on Cook's handiwork."

"I suspect Hunter will save some for me; he has been a fine captain to serve. Now is there somewhere we could go to talk?" He looked around and I realized that he had not seen the house since it was furnished.

"This way. We can use the small parlor." I led the way, pointing out several of the rooms as we passed them.

"All very impressive and elegant," he observed as we settled on the loveseat. "But then, I would expect nothing less of the Latimers. Harlan was determined that this house should be even grander than the one his grandfather built on English Wells."

113

"We have been working very hard to make it so."

"But is it a happy house, Faith? Is everything truly all right here on Dark Thunder?" His eyes probed at me, bringing back all the fears I managed to suppress most of the time.

"The island is lovely and the house is wonderful as you see." I had no desire to tell him more right now. "What other news do you bring me? How are our friends? Is Charleston still safe? What of the war? Have there been more battles?"

David leaned back with a sigh. "Remember Sam Taylor? He is working with the broker who brings the cotton to the docks for us. According to Sam, everything is going well enough at present, but he thinks that some of the cooler heads are beginning to worry that England will be forced to honor the blockade and they will lose their market for the cotton."

"But I thought the English would take all the cotton you could bring to Nassau?" I felt sick, understanding only too well what losing the market for their crops would do to our many friends who raised cotton.

"At the moment, that is true enough, but those who understand the politics of this war say that England cannot continue if the other governments press them. They are a nation of sailors and they have often demanded that others respect their blockades." David raked his fingers throught his thick brown hair. "I am not sure how much to believe. Sam could be wrong. He was still in mourning for his brother Jay. Jay was killed at some battle up north, near a place called Bull Run."

"Jay's dead?" For a moment my problems seemed petty and unimportant, especially when I remembered laughing and dancing with Jay at a long-ago ball. I could not bear to think that he was dead on some distant battlefield, so I returned to the safer subject. "What does Hunter say of the prospects for the cotton market?"

"That only time will tell, but that if the war goes on very long the South will suffer more than the North, since we have no factories and need free trade."

"What of our other friends?" I almost hesitated to ask, fearing that the news would be bad.

"Sam knew of only a few." David quickly named them, making me feel a little better as he reported them safe. Still, I could not forget that Tommy had ridden out of Charleston with Jay. If one had fallen on a battlefield . . .

"David, Faith, come along to the morning room," Sarah called from the doorway, interrupting my worry-some thoughts. "Cook has just taken another pan of cakes from the oven and Hunter and the children will eat every one unless you two come and claim your share. You will have plenty of time to discuss all the news later."

"I am not sure I want to hear any more news just now anyway," I admitted, getting to my feet. What I wanted was to be with Hunter, I realized. All the feelings I had been trying to deny since he left had flared to life the moment our eyes met and I no longer cared what anyone thought. I might be betrothed to Tommy, but there was no reason why Hunter and I could not be friends.

My step was light as I followed Sarah across the hall, but deep inside I knew I was still fooling myself. What I felt for Hunter Latimer had nothing whatever to do with friendship. Not that it mattered; the moment our eyes met the rest of the world just seemed to fade away.

Chapter 8

"Do you have time for a stroll through the garden, Faith?" Hunter asked later as we watched a very sleepy Penny follow Dorry and H.J. up the stairs for their much-delayed naps.

"I should sit with Penny," I began, half afraid to be alone with him even in the sunlit garden, yet longing for a few moments away from David's increasingly disapproving glare.

"I am sure Mary will be happy to keep watch over Penny," Sarah said, coming along the hall. "You deserve a few moments to yourself, Faith." She turned to Hunter. "She had been working much too hard helping me with everything."

Though she did not look back at me, I sensed that she was feeling guilty about the still unfinished ledger postings and the fact that Higgins would be bringing me more sheets of figures later this afternoon. Could that duty now be passed to Hunter? I wondered, not sure whether I would miss the work or not. I was still not comfortable with Harlan's casual bookkeeping methods, but I did enjoy the tidy way accounts could be brought into balance. I only wished my emotions could be handled as easily.

"I should like the tour, too," David said. "I could not believe how everything has been changed since I helped

Harlan bring the furniture to the stable for storage."

"I would prefer that you go and supervise the work being done on the *Pearl*, David," Hunter said. "When we were tied up at the dock at English Wells, I could trust them to follow my orders exactly, but here . . . .I know so little about the men Harlan has hired."

David looked for a moment as though he would like to object, but he nodded and, after giving me another stern gaze, turned to thank Sarah for her hospitality. Her gentle laughter echoed in the entrance hall. "Do not be thanking me, David," she teased. "Faith has become like the sister I always wanted and, as her brother, you must also be a member of the family. We shall expect you back in time for the evening meal and, by the way, Higgins has taken the cart into the village, so he can bring your belongings from the ship. We definitely want you to stay here with us."

David looked toward Hunter as though expecting orders, but Hunter only nodded and grinned at him. "You heard her, David. Staying here at the house will give you more time with Faith and there will still be a couple of our lads on board." He took my arm and turned to let his eyes rove caressingly over my face "Now, about that guided tour, Faith."

My breath caught in my throat so that I could not even thank Sarah for her kind words, but Hunter did not seem to notice my silence as he led me out the front door and down the veranda steps to the grass. I was wildly aware of the heat of his arm through the fine linen of his shirtsleeve and had to concentrate to keep my fingers still. I ached to caress the corded muscles that moved beneath my hand.

"So tell me, what have you ladies planned for this area?" His casual question eased my confusion, bringing my mind back to reality. I looked around quickly and realized that we were now standing at the east end of the house, right in front of the flowerbed that Sarah had ordered spaded up this morning.

117

"We have been discussing that. Sarah has a lot of flower seeds she brought with her, but I think it might be nice to fill the bed with night-blooming jasmine plants. This close to the veranda they would soon fill the entire house with their scent."

"Jasmine." He released my arm, then took both my hands in his so that I faced him. "Such a sensuous scent, Faith. Do you not fear it would fill your nights with dreams of love?"

I quivered as he lifted my fingers to his lips and began to lightly kiss them. The heat of the afternoon seemed to pool inside me, then pulse to every fingertip. I wanted to snatch my hands away and at the same time, I prayed that he would never stop the light caresses. "I only thought it a pleasant scent," I murmured, suddenly conscious of the silence that was broken only by the sleepy birds and insects.

"And so it is," Hunter agreed between kisses. "Pleasant, but stirring. When it blows on the night breeze from the sea, it always makes me think of long lazy evenings, of kisses shared and the dreams that two people build together."

He turned my hand over and gently kissed the palm, sending a shiver through me. I wanted to speak, to break the spell that he seemed to be weaving around me, but no words came. I looked into his eyes and felt myself drowning in their midnight-blue depths. I wanted his kiss.

Sanity broke through like a chill wind and I pulled my hands free as I dragged my gaze from his face. What secret power did he hold over me? Resolutely, I turned toward the flowerbeds that were finished and began a hurried and probably confused recitation of all our difficulties.

Hunter followed me along the as-yet-unfinished pathways, listening without comment until I finally ran out of words. He reached out and gently took my hand again, this time weaving his rough fingers through mine.

118

"Forgive me, Faith," he began. "I did not mean to frighten you. It is only that I thought of you every day I was away and missed you more than I believed possible."

"I am not frightened of you." My words sounded angry, mostly because I was embarrassed; yet even as I snapped at him, I realized that I spoke the truth. It was not Hunter I feared, but my own weakness. "It is only that I am promised to another and you know that. We must not . . ." I paused, seeking the right words. "We can only be friends."

Hunter's gentle smile faded as something very like anger burned for a moment in the depths of his eyes, then as quickly as it had come, it was gone and he was smiling again. "You are right, Faith. I should not take advantage of your trust. But I must ask, may a friend give a friend a gift?"

"What?" I was intrigued by the wicked sparkle in his eyes. It made him seem enchantingly boyish instead of slightly predatory, yet still so exciting to be near.

"It's one of the reasons I suggested our stroll, Faith. I brought you a small gift and I wanted us to be alone when I gave it to you." He extracted a box from his vest pocket. "I hope you will accept this token of friendship." His tone slightly underlined the final word.

"Oh, Hunter, I . . . .I do not know what to say." Again, I spoke the truth because I was too benumbed to make any of the casually flirtatious comments that I had been taught before I was introduced into Charleston society. My quiet life in Nassau had left me sadly out of practice at handling a gentleman's romantic attentions.

"Why not open it before you decide?" Hunter suggested, the heat of his gaze once again bringing fire to my cheeks.

"But I should not even consider accepting." Even as I spoke, I fumbled with the top of the box and looked inside, then gasped. An exquisite cameo lay on a bed of black velvet, the snowy silhouette pale as moonlight against the dark background.

"I could not resist her, since she looked so much like you."

"Like me?" I lifted my gaze from the lovely brooch and for the first time caught a glimpse of something like doubt in his face.

"Please say you will wear the cameo, Faith." His eyes met mine solemnly, the sparkle gone now as though vanquished by a stronger emotion.

"It is beautiful, but I cannot accept such a gift, Hunter. It would not be proper."

"Not even for a friend, Faith? I have no plan to compromise your good name, you know that. I am well aware that you are promised to another. This is just a pretty little carving that I saw in a shop in Nassau. She looked so much like you, I knew she had to be yours." He looked away as he spoke and there was a touch of sadness in his tone.

I lifted the cameo from its velvet nest with shaking fingers. I wanted it, not only because it was truly lovely, but because he had selected it just for me. It would be a talisman that I could cherish later when I returned to Charleston and Tommy. "I shall wear it proudly," I whispered, pinning it carefully at the bottom of the modest vee neckline of my gown.

Hunter's grin returned as he studied the effect. "I was right, you know, that cameo could have been carved as a likeness of you."

"I thank you for thinking of me, Hunter. It is a lovely gift and I shall treasure it always."

For just a heartbeat I thought that he would say more, but instead, he took my arm again and led me toward the bluffs where the waves thundered endlessly. "Sarah seems fairly content here," he observed, surprising me with the change of subject.

"We have been kept busy," I temporized, unsure how much I should tell him about our troubled relationship with the villagers. And what of the bobbing lights? I wondered. Did my promise to Harlan mean that I should not confide in his brother?

"And how is Penny? Has her sleepwalking eased?"

"It grew worse after we first arrived; but lately she has slept through a night or two without sleepwalking, so perhaps it was the turmoil of the move that brought it about."

"So you have helped them both."

"We have all helped each other." I met his gaze, controlling my longing firmly. "Sarah welcomed me into her family and I, too, feel as though I have gained a sister as well as a niece." I meant the words as a warning—to myself as well as to Hunter. Changing the desire that flamed between us to friendship would not be easy. I needed his help to keep the fiery passion he had awakened within me from raging out of control.

"So do you like Dark Thunder now that you have had a chance to spend some time on the island?" He paused, his attention seeming to be on the horizon and not on me; yet I felt his tension when my shoulder touched his arm.

"What I have seen of the island is beautiful." I sensed that his was not a casual question, yet I was not sure what it was he wanted me to tell him.

"And the islanders?"

So that was it. I took a deep breath, determined to give him the truth. "I have officially met only one or two of them and they have shown no interest in furthering the acquaintance. They refuse to come to this end of the island to work and when anyone from here goes to the village, they speak only of business matters."

"Blast!" Hunter sighed. "I was afraid of that. Harlan swore that they would come around once they saw how they would profit from having the company here, but this island has a long history of clannishness. They have never really welcomed anyone to their shores."

"Well, they have not changed." I thought again of the bobbing lights, but since I had seen them only that once, I decided to keep quiet about it. If Harlan had settled the matter, reopening it with Hunter might only make things worse with the villagers.

"Has this standoffishness troubled Sarah?" His concern showed in his eyes as he finally turned to face me.

"Of course, it has. She misses the friends she left behind on English Wells and as I suppose you heard, we had to bring several more staff members from there instead of hiring them from the village."

"I did hear that when we stopped at English Wells," he admitted, his expression troubled, "and I wondered."

"I only wish I knew how to change things. If there was just someone I could talk to. If the people here knew how kind and sweet Sarah is, surely they would change their stance and become friendly." I could not keep my frustration from showing. "They give us no chance, Hunter. Even the children turn away when we pass."

"Then you must give them time, Faith."

"And while we wait for this miracle?"

"We shall enjoy what we have. How would you like to see the site I have chosen for the house I shall build here?"

"You are building a house here?" The idea intrigued me, for it was one that had not occurred to me.

"Did you think I would be forever content to live on the *Pearl* or in a room at Harlan's home?" There was a note of sadness mixed with his amusement.

"You did tell me that you were wed to the sea," I reminded him, trying to keep the conversation light.

"For a long time, I believed I was; but now I suspect that will change one day soon. A man needs more than a company and a ship to make his life complete. I want a wife and children to return to after my voyages." He was gazing again at the sea beyond the bluffs, but this time I sensed that he saw none of its beauty.

"And you intend to settle here on Dark Thunder?" I choked back the question I really wanted to ask—whether or not he had chosen that wife.

"This is to be Latimer Trading's headquarters, so

where else shall I build my house?"

"I thought perhaps you might settle in Latimer House on English Wells. I do believe Harlan did mention that you meant to keep your interests in that area." I had to be careful, I reminded myself, because my knowledge came from documents that I had seen in Harlan's desk, not from any conversation.

Hunter's chuckle surprised me. "Your interest in business always intrigues me, Faith."

I sighed, hating the thought that he was laughing at me, yet aware that I had, once again, overstepped the bounds of my place here. "Forgive my curiosity, Hunter, but I was often privy to my papa's business planning and old habits die hard."

"I love your interest, Faith." His gaze was solemn now. "It fascinates me and I would like to discuss my plans with you. Harlan and I have talked of this often and he would like me to remain on English Wells to oversee our interests; but I feel we can trust those we have put in charge there. This is the place we plan to expand, so why should I remain behind?"

"Then you have given up hope of ever returning to Savannah?" I tried to hide my disappointment, well aware that it would reveal the secret fantasies I had indulged in, fantasies that had no place in my future with Tommy Anderson.

"I fear the war has made those plans precarious, Faith. No matter who wins, it will be years before everything is back to the way it was and I no longer want to wait." He sighed and seemed to banish his sober mood. "So tell me, will you ride with me tomorrow? I would like your opinion of the spot I have chosen for my home."

"If Sarah can spare me for a few hours," I began, half frightened by the surge of excitement that swept through me. Friends, I repeated in my mind, he just wants the opinion of a friend. I thought again of the unfinished ledger pages, trying to banish my weakness for this man. "There is much to be done, Hunter, and I should return to my duties now."

"Whatever you wish." He turned his steps back toward the house that so arrogantly rode the ridge above the bluffs, not slowing until we were near the veranda. "There is one thing I have to say before you go inside, Faith." His words stopped me easily because I really had no desire to leave him.

I turned to him, meeting his gaze without hesitation, suddenly not caring if he could read my heart in my eyes. I touched the cameo, feeling the warmth of it, a warmth that just looking into his eyes sent burning through me.

"Please promise me that you will spend time with me, Faith. I will respect your betrothal, but I swear I cannot bear to stay here if you run away from me. If friendship is all you can give me, it will be enough. Just promise me that you will not deny me even that." He caught my hand and held it between both of his and in his face I could read a hunger that matched mine. "Promise?" His fingers tightened until I winced, yet I had no desire to free my hand.

"I will spend all the time I can with you, Hunter." A dozen conditions rose in my mind—we must never be alone, we should refrain from touching, we must fight our feelings. But my mouth was too dry for me to speak the words. Besides, deep down, I knew that I would never adhere to them. Right or wrong, I wanted to spend time alone with Hunter—I needed to explore what I was feeling or I should regret it the rest of my life.

Hunter opened his mouth, but before he could say anything further, we both heard the sound of an approaching cart and when I looked around, I saw that it was Higgins, back from the village already. "I must go in now," I murmured, my mind on the waiting accounts.

"And I had best be about my business, too." He lifted my hand to his lips for just a moment, then turned away, going around the house toward the stable area. I watched him until he disappeared behind a white hibiscus bush, then sighed and went inside.

The house was quiet, but I found Sarah waiting for me at Harlan's desk. She got up at once. "I was going to finish these, Faith, but when I look at them, I get so confused. I knew that I would only make mistakes that you would have to correct."

"There is no need for you to work on them, Sarah. I can do them now while Penny is sleeping. Or will you be asking Hunter to do the accounts for you? He is out at the stable speaking with Higgins, I believe."

"Oh, I could not ask him, Faith. Harlan specifically forbade my asking anyone else to handle these. Besides, Hunter has his own ledger for the *Sea Pearl*, I believe." She moved toward the door. "I shall go down and get the sheets from Higgins."

Swallowing a sigh, I nodded, then tried to focus my concentration on the figures before me. That proved very difficult because I kept seeing Hunter's face instead of the numbers and I could not forget the exquisite torment of his touch. "Friends," I whispered to the cluttered desk, "we must be just friends."

I managed to adhere to that resolve through the evening meal, mainly thanks to David's distracting presence. He and Hunter entertained us with tales of their voyage and their discussion of what they expected to find the next time they reached the redezvous place. Since Papa was to be involved, I had plenty of questions and suggestions to occupy my thoughts. It was only afterwards, when we all moved to the veranda seeking the cooling night breeze, that my longing for Hunter returned.

My spirits soared when Hunter seated himself beside me on the rustic wicker sofa that was part of the arrangement Sarah had ordered placed on the east end of the veranda. He kept his voice low. "Sarah has assured me that you will be free while Penny naps tomorrow, Faith, so I shall have our horses ready then, if you will go riding with me."

"I am looking forward to it," I admitted, only dimly

aware that David was prowling the veranda like a nervous cat. Although he and Hunter had seemed great friends while we ate, the moment Hunter came near me I could almost feel David's disapproval surrounding me.

"When do I get a tour of the grounds here, Sis?" David came to stand right in front of us.

"Perhaps in the moring?" I suggested, caught between amusement and irritation. I loved the fact that he was worried about me; but being two years older than he, I resented his assumption that I could not take care of myself. "I fear it is a little dark to see the flowers tonight."

"You will have plenty of time before we go to the harbor, David," Hunter told him and I was relieved to hear the amusement in his voice. I would not want to cause trouble between David and Hunter, since I knew how much this chance meant to my brother.

"Perhaps you can join the debate that Sarah and I have been having, David," I suggested, hoping to distract him before he noticed that Hunter was holding my hand beneath a fold of my full skirt.

"What debate is that, Faith?" Sarah asked from the chair to my left.

"What to plant just along the veranda," I reminded her. "I think jasmine would be nice, but Sarah has all these seeds . . ."

"Jasmine has my vote." Hunter squeezed my fingers and I knew he was remembering our earlier conversation.

"Their scent is so heavy," David protested, giving up his nervous pacing to settle on a chair he pulled around to face us. "When it is hot, they can fair choke a person."

"And planted so close to the house, there would be no escaping them," Sarah agreed. "I love the scent, but perhaps it would be better planted between the house and the stable; that way we could really appreciate it."

Hunter laughed easily. "A practical suggestion, if ever I heard one; but why not a few plants on this side, too.

126

Maybe mixed with all your flower seeds. They climb well and could be trained to drape over the rail here."

"I am beginning to think we shall have to wait for Harlan's return to make a final decision," Sarah said. "Meantime, do you think you could obtain some fine white rock or crushed shell for the paths, Hunter? I may as well get them done while we are considering what to plant where."

"I was only teasing about the jasmine, Sarah. You must plant what you think will be right in that bed." I was beginning to feel guilty about my insistence on continuing a debate that should have been settled the moment Sarah made her wishes known. "After all, the gardens at Latimer House on English Wells were beautiful."

Sarah sighed. "I can take no credit for them, I'm afraid. I only kept the patterns and plantings that Harlan's grandmother set out. Besides, this is an entirely different location, so I think it should have its own style."

"Your style," I agreed. "You have marvelous taste and an excellent sense of color."

"Harlan is going to be impressed no matter what you plant in that bed," Hunter told her as his fingers traced intriguing patterns in the palm of my hand, sending shivers up my arm. "Now, tell me what else you have planned for this house."

His question set Sarah to chattering and left me free to lose myself in the magical sensations his fingers evoked, sensations that stole my breath and made me want to cling to his hand so that he could never stop. Though no other part of our bodies touched, the quivers started by his caressing fingers reached from my toes to the top of my head.

I would have gladly stayed there forever, had I not caught the sound of bells on the breeze. Janie, one of the new maids, had been asked to sit with Penny, so I had been unworried, but the sound brought me to my feet, everything else forgotten. Sarah must have heard it, too, because she was right behind me as I raced up the stairs.

The jingling led us to the open playroom door where we stood to watch Penny as she moved like a pale ghost through the dimness. I looked around for Janie, but she was nowhere to be seen. After a glance at Sarah, I moved into the cluttered room, doing my best not to stumble over the toys the children had left out.

Penny's fingers were warm as I took her hand and she offered no resistance as I guided her back to her bed. I waited while Sarah tucked her in, then together we stepped through the connecting door to my room. As I had expected, we found Janie sound asleep on my bed.

Sarah's hand was rough as she shook the girl awake and her voice dripped with anger as she told her what had happened. I pitied Janie, but I, too, felt cold fear as I imagined what might have happened had we not heard the bells through the small playroom window someone had forgotten to close. Once the sobbing girl had been ordered to her room, Sarah turned to me, her anger fading into grief.

"I thought Penny was getting over this, Faith," she wailed. "You said it had not happened for several nights and . . ." Her voice broke.

Unable to offer any words of comfort, I held out my arms. Sarah was crying on my shoulder when Hunter stopped in the partially open doorway of my little sitting room. "Is something wrong?"

I explained quickly as Sarah dried her eyes.

"Penny is perfectly safe?" His worry reflected the love I knew he held for Penny and H.J. and for a moment I thought only what a fine father he would make one day.

"She slept through it all. In the morning she will have no recollection of leaving her bed."

"Unless we wake her with our talk," Sarah murmured, having regained her composure. "I apologize for giving way like that, Faith. It is only that I had so hoped . . ."

128

"She will stop sleepwalking, Sarah, do not despair. And until she does, we shall just have to keep her safe."

"From now on, Rose or Olivia will stay up here with her and the new girls will spend more time on hard work." Sarah turned from me to take Hunter's arm. "Now, Hunter, come along with me and I shall show you what I have planned for the guest room at the far end of the hall."

I watched them go with mixed feelings—relief that I had not let Hunter know how deeply his touch on my hand earlier had affected me and an aching longing to be the one showing him the distant room. But that was the prerogative of the mistress of the house, I reminded myself firmly, and I was only the governess here. Such thoughts offered no comfort as I closed my door and retreated to my bedroom where I could hear Penny if she left her bed again.

Now that the evening had ended so abruptly, I knew I should go to bed myself, but restlessness plagued me and I finally slipped out onto the balcony where the fresh breeze could ease the heat from my cheeks. As I leaned on the railing, I heard a sound from the veranda below me and smiled as I recognized David's tuneless whistling. A moment later, I heard the low rumble of Hunter's voice as he and David talked quietly. It seemed I was not the only one too keyed up for sleep.

The distant sentinel palm drew my eyes and I stared at the area of the path, wondering what would happen if the bobbing lights appeared now. I had no doubt that David would help me investigate, but it was not his aid I wanted. If I ventured into the dark undergrowth, I wanted Hunter at my side, not my brother.

"Blast," I whispered to the night breeze. I had to put such foolish thoughts aside or I would be unable to keep my resolve to treat Hunter with no more than friendship. Suddenly weary, I retreated to my room, carefully securing the door that led to the balcony.

Never had I felt so confused. Other young men had paid court to me before I left Charleston. Some had even stolen kisses as we walked in the gardens or rode home after the various balls and parties, but none had stirred my senses as Hunter did with the touch of a finger. I feared to even think what this madness might mean. I was just lonely, that was all. Once I had a letter from Tommy, my feelings for him would revive and everything would be just fine.

Tears burned in my eyes and spilled over my cheeks as I took down my hair and brushed it out before braiding it for the night. No matter how often I told myself that everything was going to be all right, I still could not believe it. But what could I do?

Must I deny myself these few precious days with Hunter? He had promised to honor my commitment to Tommy, so what was the danger? He might hold my hand or even kiss me, but I did trust him not to press his suit beyond that. He would never force his attentions on me.

Force his attentions? I choked on a giggle. Hunter would never have to force his attentions on me, not when I so willingly accepted his touch every chance I got. I was tempting fate, pure and simple. Spending time with Hunter would never banish the feelings he stirred inside me.

But denying them had not helped either. I had tried to forget him after he left English Wells and I had failed miserably. I pulled off my gown, then carefully unpinned the cameo and, after a moment of hesitation, pinned it on my nightdress before I lay down on my bed. I had no doubt that sleep would be a long time coming. I just wished I had someone I could talk to about my feelings.

What would Mama expect me to do? Since her death, that was always my criteria for judging a situation. The answer was obvious. She would expect me to honor my promises. I shifted on the soft mattress. But which promise—the one to Tommy or the one I had made to Hunter in the garden, when I had said I would spend time with him?

I closed my eyes, picturing tomorrow when I would be riding with Hunter. We would have to talk, I decided. We needed to discuss the limits that must be placed on our time together. I would simply tell him . . . I drifted into a dream where I knew no limits as I lost myself in the ecstasy of his kiss.

Chapter 9

David was waiting for me in the dining room when I came down the next morning. "You rise early," I observed after greeting him with a kiss. I could not help remembering how often Mama had sent me to rouse him when we were all living together.

"So do you." His eyes seemed to follow me as I went to help myself from the warming dishes Cook had set out for us.

"I care for a four-year-old who rises with the sun." I felt a chill in the air between us and wondered suddenly if Hunter had said something about me to David when I heard them talking last night. I took a chair opposite him, then began moving the food around on my plate, because I had quite lost my appetite.

"How is Penny this morning?" he asked, finally breaking the long moments of silence that had stretched between us.

"Very eager to help me show you about the garden. She is most anxious for you to know how well she has learned the names of the bushes, trees, and flowers. She may even try to spell them for you."

"You will have to tell her whether or not she is correct." Some of his normal good humor lit his green eyes. "If you remember, I was never very good at spelling."

132

"Penny is still quite creative, but she tries hard and she is very bright. We make up stories and she can hardly wait to be able to write them down herself."

"You always were a natural-born teacher, Sis. I have not forgotten how often I asked your help with my lessons."

"I have missed it. I know I never got a chance to be a full-fledged teacher at the academy, but I did teach some classes my last year and . . ." I let it trail off, not wanting to remember how happy I had been, how sure of what my future would be.

"I know how lonesome you have been, Faith, but I . . ." He stopped, looking uncomfortable. "I worry about you."

"I am perfectly safe and content here, David. You heard Sarah last night. She truly does treat me more like a sister than a governess and as for Harlan and Hunter . . ." I knew the moment I spoke Hunter's name that I had made a mistake.

"It is Hunter that worries me, Faith. I know you see him as an honorable man, but . . ."

"Hunter *is* an honorable man and since you have sailed with him, you should know that yourself. He has been kind to both of us and I am ashamed to hear even a hint of doubt on your lips." Since my stomach had knotted, I gave up any pretense of eating and got to my feet. "If you wish to see the garden, let us go out there now."

David glared at me as he stood up. Red blazed in his tanned cheeks at my words. "Please finish your meal, Faith. I meant no disrespect toward Hunter. It is only that I know how much you miss Tommy since you have had no word in so long. Besides, there are things that you have no knowledge of and I know that Papa would expect me to protect you since he cannot be here."

I sank back into my chair, my brief flare of temper fading at the mention of Papa. "Please do not trouble yourself about my behavior, David. I will do nothing to bring shame to our family. Hunter knows that I am betrothed and has promised to honor my decision."

"You spoke of it?" His surprise was as amusing as it was irritating.

"We are friends, David, nothing more. Now, why do you not tell me more about your meeting with Sam Taylor. Did he tell you anything about the Howells or the Devanes?" I took a mouthful of the eggs and ham on my plate, hoping that the question would distract David. I definitely did not want to discuss my feelings for Hunter with David, because I already knew he would not understand.

Fortunately, Penny joined us before David ran out of stories about our friends in Charleston and with her chattering between us, our stroll through the garden passed pleasantly enough. Once we returned to the veranda, Hunter claimed David's attention and I was free to take Penny upstairs for her lessons.

I tried to concentrate on teaching Penny, but my thoughts strayed all too often to the proposed afternoon ride with Hunter. Should I beg off? There were a number of reasons that I could offer for the change of plans, yet even as I listed them in my mind, I knew that I could not lie to Hunter. Besides, I was curious to know where he planned to build his house.

The hours until midday seemed endless, yet all too soon I found myself joining Hunter and Sarah in the dining room. They had been closeted together in the study since Hunter returned from the harbor and were laughing merrily when I entered. Hunter rose to hold my chair, but continued with his tale about someone they both knew from English Wells.

Sarah laughed until tears spilled down her cheeks and I felt a sharp pang of envy as Hunter offered her his handkerchief. They seemed so close that, had I not known better, I would have thought them husband and wife. In fact, I thought bitterly, I could not remember Harlan making her laugh so joyously.

"Forgive us, Faith," Sarah said when she caught her breath. "It is just that you would have to know Molly to really appreciate the story."

"I understand that you share many friends," I murmured, embarrassed by how easily she had read my mood. "David and I were reminiscing a bit earlier today, too. I was happy to hear you laughing, Sarah."

"It is good to have something to laugh about," she agreed. "Now if only Harlan will return soon." The shadows returned to her eyes. "I am sorry that David must remain at the harbor through the day. Our Hunter is a stern taskmaster."

"Most of the work should be completed in a day or so, then David will be free to spend all the time he wants with Faith." Hunter met my gaze. "Meantime, I shall enjoy her company myself."

"Beware of this one, Faith. He has a fearsome reputation with the ladies." Sarah's giggle told me she was teasing.

"I shall be on my guard," I acknowledged with what I hoped was a stern look. Sarah might be teasing, but I had a feeling I should take her advice seriously.

"A reputation I have done nothing to deserve." Hunter's look of pious innocence was too much for me, I surrendered to a giggle.

My sides still ached from laughing as I went up to change into my riding clothes. Although I could not remember exactly what had been said that was so funny, I had not laughed so often since I left Charleston. Having Hunter here on Dark Thunder had obviously driven away all the evil spirits that flowed our way from the villagers. I only wished that he could stay forever.

Rose greeted me when I peeked into Penny's bedroom. "She be sleeping like an angel, Miss Faith."

"I know she is safe with you here and I am grateful you

135

have the time, Rose. I know you have other duties."

"Miss Sarah say watching Miss Penny be my first duty."

"She will need all of us to care for her until this sleepwalking stops." I stared at the sleeping child and wondered once more if I should suggest that protective lattices be constructed to cover all the windows and special locks be placed on all the doors in the children's area of the house. It was not my place, of course, but I knew that Sarah would order the work done, if I made a firm request.

Not today, I decided, banishing all thoughts of Penny from my mind. Today I would think only of Hunter and the house he planned to build on this island. His words about David soon having more time to spend with me had been a warning of sorts and I meant to heed it. I wanted to enjoy every moment of the little time alone we were to have.

Alone. The word shivered through me as I secured the heavy weight of my hair on the nape of my neck and settled my riding hat in place. For a moment I studied my reflection, wondering what Mama would think if she were here to see me riding off with Hunter while I still wore the betrothal ring Tommy had given me.

"Riding out with a friend to see where he is to build his home," I murmured, turning away from the mirror. Surely she would find nothing wrong with that. I hurried down the back stairs and out through the kitchen, which was empty and silent since Cook was taking her afternoon rest.

The doubts that haunted me when we were apart vanished the moment I saw Hunter leading two horses out of the stable. His welcoming smile lifted my spirits so that my feet scarcely seemed to touch the ground as I hurried to him. When I looked into his eyes I knew that being with him was all that mattered.

Hunter's tour of the island included most of the central area. We crossed and recrossed the single road so often that I had no idea exactly where we were when he finally dismounted on a grassy bluff. Only when I looked down at the sea did I realize we were standing above the small cove I had discovered after I saw the bobbing lights. When I looked across the cove, I could see the same tall palm that I had used as a landmark in my search for the source of the lights.

Hunter lifted me from the saddle and set me gently on the ground, pointing in the direction of Latimer House. "As you can see, the second floor is clearly visible from here now and once my house is built, I expect we shall be able to communicate with lights."

"You are going to build here?" I was too stunned to hide my feelings.

"Do you not like this spot?" Hunter's frown told me clearly that my dismay had been visible in my face. "I thought the view even better than from Harlan's balcony and here I would be close to the little cove you see below. If I can find an easy path down there, I might build a dock and keep a small boat there for fishing."

"It is a lovely place, Hunter," I began, turning away from the sentinel palm and the memories it evoked. The view inland was stunning with many trees and flowering bushes growing in the deep grass. The road was hidden by the thick undergrowth, but I could see goats grazing on the grassy hillside that rose on the other side of the road.

"What is it, Faith?" He rested a hand on my shoulder, turning me back so that I had to meet his gaze. "Is there something about this part of the island that troubles you?"

"I was only surprised," I murmured, wishing to keep my feelings to myself. "You have chosen a charming place to build your home."

"Faith." His tone held a note of command that I could not ignore. "What is wrong?"

Sighing, I told him the same story I had once told Harlan, adding only that I had not seen the mysterious lights since that night. He, at least, did not mock me or question my statements. Instead, he frowned as he stared down at the beautiful water of the cove.

"Has Harlan ever told you of this 'pirate parade'?" I asked.

He shook his head. "I know some of the stories about the men that settled Dark Thunder, but I have not heard that one. It sounds a bit wild to me."

"I can show you the path I discovered, but I have not seen the lights again. It may be that a word from Harlan was all that was needed to convince the villagers that we were not going to be frightened away by their foolishness."

Hunter nodded. "That does seem likely. And is that the only reason you have doubts about my building here?"

His smile washed over my uneasiness like a cooling wave bathing the pale sand below us. "I have no doubt that your house will be grand and that everyone who comes to the island will want to visit you."

"And would you enjoy living on Dark Thunder?" His gaze suddenly became intense as though my reply was very important to him.

"I already enjoy living here," I murmured, both frightened and intrigued by what he seemed to be saying more with his eyes than with his words.

"Then you do not share Sarah's dislike of the place?"

I chose my words carefully, not sure what he was asking me; but aware that he wanted more than the answer to his simple question. "I understand her fears and her longing for the home she just left, but I see the possibilities of this island. If the villagers can be persuaded to accept us, I think it could be as fine a place to live as English Wells."

"You found English Wells a good place to live?" He lifted a hand and began tracing a line around my lips with his fingertip.

A quivering began deep inside me banishing all thoughts from my befuddled mind. I stared deep into his eyes, trying to read his feelings there; but I saw only my reflection, the longing naked in my eyes.

He was going to kiss me. I knew it and did nothing to stop him. His fingers stole, warm and caressing along my jaw and my eyelids were suddenly too heavy to support. As his hand cradled the back of my neck, I lifted my lips to meet his.

Wild heat exploded within me as his mouth covered mine and he pulled me close. His touch was tender, but commanding as he parted my lips and took into his mouth my soft gasp of wonder. I clung to him, measuring the broad strength of his shoulders with my hands, feeling the rippling muscles of his back beneath my fingers as he held me even tighter against him. All my longing blazed into flames that burned away the questions as I answered the magic of his kiss and lost myself in the ecstasy.

It seemed a lifetime and yet too soon he broke off the burning kiss and pressed my face tenderly against his shoulder while he stroked my back. "Oh, Faith, I promised myself that I would not kiss you again, but when I look into your eyes and see that you want me, too . . . Forgive me. I have no right to demand what is promised to another, but as God is my witness, I cannot help myself."

The anguish in his tone stripped away the mists of longing that were swirling through my mind and I felt the awful shame sweeping over me. I could not face him. If he could read my desire in my eyes, that made me no better than some harlot on the waterfront. Feeling sick with my need for him, I pulled away and stumbled toward my horse, wanting only to flee this spot and the temptation that I had not been able to resist.

"No, Faith." He caught my arms firmly, forcing me to face him. "I will not let you run away from me. You must not feel that my kiss shames you and I cannot be sorry either. What we feel for each other is not wrong, only the times are wrong—the war has changed everything and . . ." He stopped and I could see the pain in his eyes.

"If your betrothed was here, I would go to him and ask that he release you from your contract. I would never bring you shame, that I do swear."

My shame fled as quickly as it had come leaving me calm, though no less troubled in spirit. I could not allow him to bear the guilt of what had happened alone, not when I could see how much it hurt him. "I would not run from you, Hunter," I murmured, finding it hard to speak when just looking at him made my mouth dry with longing. "I would run from myself. I think it best that we return to the house now before we say things that are better left unsaid."

For a moment I thought that he might dispute my words, but after a time, he nodded, then a smile touched the corners of his mouth, turning them up seductively. "Shall we return by the cove? That way you can show me this path you found."

"We will have to leave the horses behind," I warned him, trying to distract myself from the shivery teasing of his touch as he helped me mount. "The path is narrow and steep as it goes down between the rocks."

"A little walk will be pleasant." His eyes met mine and I felt a jolt of heat. "The cove appears most appealing from up here."

"It seemed enchanted when I was down there." I regretted the words the moment I said them. Enchantment was the last thing we needed to share. Or was it? As we reined the horses away from the bluff and into the trees on a line that I hoped would lead us to the path, I had to wonder. Perhaps denying the emotions that blazed between us only made them stronger; maybe if I stopped fighting my feelings . . .

By the time we left the horses on the path and started down the rocky cut to the beach, I had made no decision, but I sensed that Hunter had. He chatted easily, talking about the house he planned and speculating on the fish that might await his hook in the sea outside the cove. He made no move to touch me, except to keep a steadying hand beneath my elbow as we climbed back to where the horses waited. But he still wanted me. I read the longing in his eyes when he lifted me to my saddle for the ride back to the house.

There had to be an answer, I decided, as I followed him through the trees and around the house to the stable. Somewhere there must be a solution to the dilemma I found myself in. If only I could go to my room and lie down for a while, perhaps my mind would stop spinning and I should be able to think clearly again.

Unfortunately, I was not to have the opportunity as David came striding from the veranda even before Hunter could lift me down. He was smiling, but I sensed no warmth in his gaze as he greeted Hunter and politely answered his questions about the *Sea Pearl*. Hoping to escape, I started for the house as they spoke.

"Faith, could you spare me a few moments?" David's voice stopped me midstride.

"I would like to change," I began, sensing trouble.

"Surely you can spare a little talk with me." David took my arm, his fingers bruising my skin through my sleeve.

"You are hurting me," I protested as he led me around the house toward the bluff above the sea.

"Not as much as you are hurting yourself." His tone was like a slap and when he stopped and I faced him, I could see the suspicion and anger in his eyes.

"I have done nothing." I jerked my arm free of his grip and concentrated on rubbing away the pain he had inflicted.

"I saw you and Hunter on the bluff, Faith."

"You were spying on us?"

"I was riding along the road as anyone could have been." His cheeks burned red. "You told me that you meant to honor your commitment to Tommy, Faith, so how can you allow Hunter to take such liberties? Must I take you back to Nassau to protect you from him?"

"He took nothing from me, David." Anger banished

141

my embarrassment. Suddenly, I knew what I wanted to do. "I offered my kiss."

"Faith, how can you . . .?"

"I have not heard from Tommy in more than half a year and before that I had only one letter. I scarce remember what he looks like, David, and I know now that I should never have accepted his proposal. I want you to talk to Papa about finding an honorable way to set aside the betrothal. Likely Tommy has changed as much as I; perhaps he has even found someone else and that is why he has not written." I stopped, out of breath.

David opened his mouth, but no words came out as he just stared at me. I fought a need to squirm beneath his scrutiny, aware that it was not friendly. "You have become a stranger to me," he said at last, sounding both sad and very young.

"Is it strange that I have changed, David? Have you not become a man since we left Charleston?"

"What has that to do with your kissing Hunter Latimer?" Now he looked a bit uncomfortable.

"Would you be willing to return to the life we left behind in Charleston?" I lifted a hand to stop his reply. "I do not mean just the house or our friends or being with Papa, David. I mean the days of lessons and being ordered about as a boy. Would you find that acceptable now?"

"Of course not, but . . ."

"I was a girl when I pledged myself to Tommy. I fell in love with the romantic image of a soldier; he seemed so brave and exciting in his uniform, but I did not really know him. If there had been no war threatened; if he had not insisted on joining the cavalry; if Papa had not been determined to send us away . . ."

"If you had not met Hunter Latimer, you would not be saying such things." David's gaze was hard. "The man has turned your head and will make fools of all of us. You must stop this madness, Faith, before you destroy both our lives."

"What I feel for Hunter is not madness." I sensed that my battle was lost, but I could not give up. "You must talk to Papa for me. He would understand, I know. He would never force me to marry someone I do not love."

"You think he would prefer to see you in the hands of a man like Hunter Latimer?" David's eyes were cold as green ice and there was a bitterness about his words that chilled me.

"What do you mean by that? What grudge do you hold against Hunter?"

"There are things that a proper lady . . . I am simply trying to warn you that he has a bad reputation."

"No, David, I will not accept that. If you know something about Hunter, I think I have a right to know what it is. You ask too much, if you wish me to give up my feelings because there has been gossip about him." I faced him, sure that he knew nothing that could change my mind about Hunter.

"It is more than gossip, Faith. I have talked to the men who sail with him on the *Pearl* and they tell of his visits to other islands. They speak of the mistress he once kept in Nassau and of the widow on another island who welcomes him each time the ship docks there. He has twice been sought by angry fathers who wished him to wed their daughters and each time he sailed away."

"I do not believe their stories." Even as I spoke, I knew that I was lying to myself as well as to David.

David did not waver. "Those who know him best say that his wild behavior began when Sarah chose his brother as her husband. They claim that he has never loved anyone else. Perhaps it is because they are twins that they . . ."

I could bear to hear no more. "I must go and see to Penny," I called over my shoulder as I half ran toward the house, fighting the tears that burned my eyes, nearly blinding me. It could not be so! Other men took mistresses or made liaisons with women they did not love, but that did not mean they could never love.

143

I stumbled around the corner of the veranda heading for the front steps, then ducked back as I heard the sound of voices coming from the other side. Frantic not to be seen, I hid in the shadow of the thick red hibiscus bush that Sarah had ordered left at the corner of the house.

"So did you have a good ride, Hunter?" Sarah asked.

"Splendid, really. I am now quite sure that I shall build in the spot I showed you the first time you came to the island. It appeared even more beautiful today."

"Are you sure that you truly want to settle down on Dark Thunder, Hunter?" I could hear the surprise in Sarah's voice. "You have talked so often of building a place of your own, yet somehow no foundations are ever laid."

"Perhaps I am growing old and wise." Hunter sounded amused by her question.

"Are you sure that it is not that you have met someone who makes you think of more than the sea and building the company?" Sarah's tone was serious.

I held my breath, hoping to hear Hunter say the words that would prove David was wrong in what he had said about Hunter loving Sarah too much to care for anyone else.

"A man needs a home, Sarah. I have seen Harlan's happiness when he comes to you. I think it is time that I have a place to call my own, do you not agree?"

"A house becomes a home only when it is shared with someone special, Hunter. Have you thought of that? And what shall Harlan and I do, if you desert us for a house of your own?" Her tone was teasing, but the words chilled me.

"I have thought of many things, darling Sarah, but mostly now I think I need to go up and change." Hunter chuckled. "I should mislike coming to our evening meal still smelling like my horse."

Sarah giggled. "You can evade my questions, Hunter, but I still have eyes and you had best have a care. I would not like to see you hurt, you know."

"Do not worry your pretty little head," Hunter said as they made their way inside, leaving me alone with my dark and troubled thoughts.

Feeling old and far wearier than I had been when David dragged me away from the stable, I made my way slowly around to the kitchen entrance so that I could go up the back stairs. I had no desire to have anyone see me, even though my tears had dried without falling. As I neared my door, I heard Hunter and Sarah's laughter echoing from the family wing of the house and my heart began to ache again.

All my doubts came swirling back and only the fact that I had to keep my feelings hidden from Penny, newly awakened from her nap, saved me from collapsing in tears. A governess had little time for a broken heart I discovered, and was glad. I needed some time away from Hunter if I was to overcome this burning attraction I felt for him.

For a time, I considered pleading weariness to avoid the evening meal, but when I thought of David being there, I knew I could not. At least I had the daily posting that must be done afterward, I reminded myself, so I would have only the meal to get through.

I had not realized how agonizing the pretense of indifference could be. Nor had I calculated the pain I felt when I saw the hurt in Hunter's eyes when I avoided talking directly to him. I welcomed the moment when Faith and I excused ourselves and left David and Hunter to their port.

"Shall we go out on the veranda to await them?" Sarah asked as we left the dining room.

"I think perhaps I should repair to your sitting room and attend to the pages that Higgins brought from the village." I had not had a word alone with her since morning, but I had seen Higgins returning from his daily journey.

"Could the pages not wait until morning? You must be weary from your long ride and you have had so little time with your brother today." She tempted me with a pleading glance.

"If Hunter is right and Harlan will be returning soon, it would be best not to get behind in the posting," I murmured, using the work as an excuse to fight my stubborn desire to spend a few more stolen moments with Hunter. "Please tell David that I have retired early out of weariness, so he will not wonder where I am."

I pressed her arm lightly, then fled up the stairs before I could weaken. I only hoped that denying my feelings would grow easier with practice. Right at the moment, all I wanted to do was cry and I had no illusions about being distracted by the ledgers.

I tried hard to keep my mind on the figures, but I was uncomfortably aware that Sarah had not returned by the time I finished with the accounts. She would be sitting beside Hunter on the veranda, I thought bitterly. David was probably long abed and the two of them . . . The jealousy clawed at me, shaming me. I fled to my room, hurriedly dismissing Rose, then taking her place at Penny's bedside instead of preparing myself for bed.

After a while the warmth of the closed room drove me to my own bedroom where the night breeze flowed in after I opened the door to the balcony. Although I knew it must be only my imagination, I thought I caught the scent of jasmine in the air and the aching inside me deepened.

Unable to bear the walls that seemed about to close around me, I went out onto the balcony. The sentinel palm drew my gaze, but this time I looked beyond it to the bluff where Hunter had taken me in his arms and . . .

"I thought I might find you out here." Hunter came around the corner, then stopped just a step away from me. "I missed you on the veranda tonight, Faith."

"I had other things that required my attention." I pressed my lips together to keep from admitting that I

146

could not bear to be near him now.

"Are you angry with me, Faith?"

"Of course not. I simply have a number of duties and since I took the afternoon to ride with you . . ." I had to let it trail off as memories of being in his arms threatened to destroy all my good intentions.

"Did David say something that hurt you?" He seemed unwilling to accept my words.

"He reminded me of my commitment to Tommy Anderson." I kept my voice flat and unemotional, though I felt my heart breaking within my breast. "I fear I forgot it for a moment this afternoon."

"Perhaps after so long a time . . ."

"Honor has no time limit, Hunter." I swallowed a sob and turned away from him, fearing that I would weaken if I looked too deeply into his eyes. "Now I must say good night."

I went inside and locked the door behind me, but no walls or locks could save me. My heart remained on the balcony, bound to Hunter with the invisible ties of an emotion I feared to even name. I waited in the darkness until I heard his retreating footsteps, then I buried my face in my pillow and cried for my lost love.

... ... better we each leave for our ... ... left for the harbor and ... ... shortly.
... ... turned toward ... ... his
... ...
... ...
... ...

Chapter 10

As I made my way downstairs the next morning, I could not help wondering if Hunter would be waiting in the dining room for me. While I had spent much of the night pondering our brief exchange of words on the balcony, I still had no idea what I would say to him when we came face to face again. Now I wished that I had ordered my breakfast served in the big playroom where Dorry, Penny, and H.J. were having theirs.

David met me at the dining-room door, looking somewhat guilty. "Are you all right, Sis? I never meant to hurt you when we spoke yesterday, only to protect you."

I peered over his shoulder and saw that we were, for the moment anyway, dining alone, then met his gaze firmly, determined not to admit to any pain. "I am perfectly fine, David. Why do you ask?"

He turned away, obviously unable to face me. "You left us so early last night, yet you look tired."

"I had work to do, duties that I had neglected when I went riding." It took all my self-control to keep my voice from breaking as I mentioned my ride with Hunter. "Did you have a pleasant time on the veranda?"

"I stayed only a short while." He sighed. "It was just as well as Hunter has come up with a number of things

148

that must be done before we can leave for our rendezvous. He has already left for the harbor and expects me to join him shortly."

"Have you eaten?" I peered under the covers of the warming dishes, not sure that I would be able to swallow around the lump in my throat.

"I only waited to speak to you. To apologize for hurting you." The sadness in his voice brought me around to look at him. "I did not mean to be cruel. I . . . I like Hunter, too, Faith. I just . . ."

"I have considered your reasons for saying what you did and last night I told Hunter that I must honor my promise to Tommy, so let us not speak about it again."

"As you wish." He slipped his arms around me, hugging me hard before he left the dining room. "See you tonight," he called over his shoulder, sounding much more like his normally light-hearted self. I envied him.

I was still staring into the warming dishes when Sarah came in yawning, what seemed hours later. I braced myself for more comments about the shadows beneath my eyes; but she seemed not to notice and as we discussed the day ahead, my spirits revived. I had taken the action that honor required, but as long as Hunter was on Dark Thunder, there was no reason that I could not be with him when others were around.

Besides, after a long night of thinking about everything, I still had doubts regarding the stories David had told me. I refused to believe that Hunter could kiss me the way he had if he cared deeply for Sarah. Our kiss had made it clear to me that my feelings for Tommy had changed, so why not his for Sarah?

I smiled as I finished my coffee and stared down at my plate. For someone who had come into the room with no appetite, I had done quite well. A new plan formed in my mind. David had offered to deliver my letter to Papa, so in it I would ask Papa to set aside my betrothal. Once that was accomplished, I would be free to discover exactly

149

what Hunter felt for me. My hearbeat quickened at the thought.

The next few days passed quickly. I saw little of Hunter and David because they spent their days at the harbor and Hunter frequently returned there in the evening after we ate. Since Hunter left David at the house with Sarah and me, I suspected that he was trying to avoid me, yet he seemed eager enough to spend time with me when Sarah and David were around. I wished that I dared ask him what he felt, but since he was honoring my request, I had no right.

I was in my room finishing my letter to Papa while Penny napped, when I heard the drumming of approaching hoofbeats. Curious to know who would be in such a hurry, I stepped out onto the balcony and hurried around the corner in time to see David leap from his mount. I called out to him, frightened that something might have happened to Hunter.

"The *Sprite* just came into the harbor," he shouted, his wide smile banishing my fears. "Hunter sent me to fetch Sarah to meet Harlan at the dock."

I dared not leave Penny, but I could feel the change that stirred within the house even before Sarah stopped by to ask me to have Penny ready to greet her father when she returned with him. While I waited, the servants scurried through the halls and intriguing scents rose from the kitchen as Cook set about her work early.

For my part, I was anxious to learn what Harlan thought of the small changes I had made in his ledgers. Once Sarah told him the truth about our little charade, I was sure he would be pleased to turn the keeping of the records over to me and then I hoped to make some major revisions in the way Decateur submitted the figures I worked from.

Penny slept late, then became so excited at the prospect of seeing her father that I had difficulty getting

150

her suitably dressed. She was barely ready in time to go down to meet the carriage when he finally came from the harbor. The thorns of envy clawed at me again as I watched Harlan and Sarah and no amount of stern resolve could keep me from imagining myself in her place, welcoming Hunter back from a trading voyage.

The evening meal was merry as Harlan told tales of his various stops about the islands; but later, as the five of us gathered on the veranda to enjoy the rising of the moon, his mood grew somber. "There is much talk about the blockade," he began.

"We saw no Northern ships," Hunter reminded him.

"You were lucky. There have been three ships reported missing just since I left here." Harlan sighed.

"Missing or taken?" David asked from his perch on the veranda rail.

"Vanished." Harlan got up from the sofa where he and Sarah were sitting and paced the length of the veranda. "That is the devil of it. No one seems to know what happened to them. If they were taken by the blockading ships, no word was sent out regarding the men aboard them."

"Perhaps they were merely driven off course trying to avoid discovery or capture," Hunter suggested.

"Then why have none of them returned? All sailed before you did, Hunter, and you have been in port nearly long enough to be leaving again." Harlan's frown made him look older than his twin. "They have not been seen since they sailed from Nassau with their cargoes."

"Are these people you know?" I asked, unable to hold my tongue even though they were speaking of men's concerns.

"Two of the ships called regularly at English Wells and I know the captain of the third. He sailed with my grandfather before he got a ship of his own." Harlan named the men.

Hunter swore, getting to his feet, too. "I mislike this, Harlan. I, too, have heard talk; but I thought it foolish at

151

the time."

"What sort of talk?" Again I spoke up when I probably should have kept silent.

"Idle chatter in the pubs and inns of Nassau. The men there spoke of ships from the islands that disappeared, but there was also talk of ships that sailed from Southern ports with goods and families coming to our islands, ships that never made it." Hunter's frown deepened to match his brother's.

"Could the blockade have grown so strong already?" David inquired.

Harlan shrugged. "I hope not. If it has, we shall lose a most profitable source of income and our only chance of helping our friends in the South."

"I do not know how Northern ships could be scarce one day and ruling the seas the next." Hunter paused near my chair, resting his hand on the back of it so that his fingers touched my shoulder sending shivers of anticipation through me.

"What else could it be?" Harlan asked.

Hunter shrugged. "Perhaps we shall find out when we sail. Or mayhap some of these missing ships will return to port with the truth."

"Oh, I hope so," Sarah murmured as Harlan returned to his place beside her. "Meantime, could we not speak of happier things?"

"A fine idea," Harlan agreed. "I have been eager to compliment you on the ledgers, Sarah. You have done a fine job. Still, I should like to know how you arrived at the figures for the Harper account and . . ." He continued, but I paid little attention to his questions after Sarah's soft gasp.

Hunter, uninterested in ledgers, had begun talking quietly to David about their upcoming rendezvous, but I could not concentrate on their words either. Instead, I sat frozen, waiting for Sarah to confess her failure to Harlan. I waited in vain. Her stumbling answers to his questions made me wince as did her feeble attempts to change the subject. I sought through my own mind for something that might distract Harlan, but I was trapped by my own part in the deception.

Luckily, Hunter, though unaware of the growing discord, had a question about one of the missing ships and once Harlan had answered it, the ledgers were not mentioned again. Still, as we left the veranda and separated to our various rooms, I sensed the strain between Harlan and Sarah. I swallowed a sigh, hoping that her hesitation came only because she meant to tell him when they were alone in order to spare herself the embarrassment of admitting her failure in front of the rest of us.

What would her telling him mean to me? I wondered as I prepared for bed. She seemed to feel that he would be angry, yet I could see no reason why he should be. I had kept the books properly, even improved on his methods, so why should he resent my taking over the work for which she was so ill suited? Sarah seemed a fine wife and mother in all other respects; surely he would not be angered by such a small flaw in her talents.

I sensed a change in Harlan the moment I reached the dining room the next morning. His expression was grim and his greeting lacked warmth, though he spoke politely. Had she told him? I braced myself for accusations or reprimands, but Harlan ate in silence until Hunter joined us at the table. After that, he simply ignored me, leaving me free to talk to David when he came in. I was happy when I could escape to the children's wing and my teaching duties.

It was near midday before I had an opportunity to speak with Sarah. We talked a few moments about Penny's progress and other household matters and it was only when I realized that she had no intention of mentioning the accounts, that I finally brought up the subject. "Were you able to satisfy Harlan's curiosity

153

about the ledgers?" I asked, trying to sound casual, but unable to hide my worry.

"What curiosity?" Sarah looked out the window and in the bright light of the sun, I could see the shadows beneath her eyes.

My fears deepened. "He seemed to have many questions when we were talking on the veranda last night."

"He did not pursue them, so he must have been satisfied with what I told him." She sighed. "I do wish I had paid more attention when you tried to explain what you were doing, Faith; but so long as Harlan is pleased with the result, no harm was done."

I just stared at her, unable to believe my ears. Could she be so blind to her husband's mood? "What about when he leaves again?" I asked, unwilling to accept her casual dismisssal of what we had done.

"I told him that I might not have the hours to work on the ledgers in the future because they consumed more of my time than I had expected." Her smile turned mischievous. "I think he will make other arrangements before he sails again."

Could I have been wrong about the source of Harlan's displeasure this morning? I wondered as we continued to talk of other things. It was, of course, possible that my own guilt had made me oversensitive, but somehow I did not think so. Still, there was nothing more I could do or say, so I resolved not to worry and enjoy the remaining days that Hunter and David would be on Dark Thunder.

The afternoon passed quietly enough and when the men returned for the evening, Harlan's temper appeared to have improved dramatically. The evening meal was rowdy as the brothers goodnaturedly teased each other and Sarah spent much of her time acting as a giggling buffer between them. A role I sensed she had played for years.

When we finally left the table, David surprised me by suggesting that we take a walk along the bluffs. While I

154

could not help wondering if I had done something to inspire another of his lectures on decorum, his smile seemed genuine as we made our way along the crushed shell path toward the rocky cliff where the waves that had given the island its name thundered unceasingly.

"So how are plans going for your next rendezvous?" I asked, more to fill the silence that fell between us than because I really wanted to know. I did not even want to think of the day when he and Hunter would leave again.

"There is nothing more to be done to the *Pearl*. We are only waiting until the date we have set is nearer. If there are more Northern patrol boats, Hunter feels we would be safer waiting here than trying to hide along the coast."

"Do you really doubt that the blockade has grown stronger?" Now I was curious.

"Hunter knows men who trade with the Northern cities as well as with the Southerners and they all speak of the North's shortage of ships to patrol. The coast of the Confederacy is a long one, Faith, and they would be foolish to concentrate all their forces near one port."

"But if it is not the blockade boats taking a toll of the ships, who . . ."

"I have no idea, but I did not bring you out here to speak about the war." His smile was gone and I braced myself for another lecture.

"I have scarce seen Hunter except at meals, so . . ."

David gave me no chance to finish. "This is about Harlan, not Hunter."

"What?"

"He drew me aside this morning, Faith, and asked me all manner of questions about the time when you helped Papa with the ledgers. He seemed most interested in your talent for figures. Do you have any idea why that should be? Could he be considering offering you a different position?" His confusion seemed quite genuine.

The cold chill started in my stomach and moved slowly over my entire body as the full implications of David's words dawned on me. Harlan's suspicion had not been

155

allayed at all; he had simply made an obvious deduction. But what did it mean? Was he truly considering asking me to do the accounts or was he just confirming his suspicions before confronting both Sarah and me? At this point neither of the alternatives seemed very attractive.

"Faith, what is it? Would you not want to take a new position? I told him of your liking for working with figures, so I hope that you . . ."

Gritting my teeth, I forced the guilt away. "I was but stunned at the idea," I lied. "You were right to tell him the truth, David, and I will happily abide by whatever he wishes." I could only pray that Harlan's wishes would not include sending me from Dark Thunder for my part in Sarah's charade.

"Are you sure that is all that troubles you?" My brother was getting disgustingly adept at reading my moods.

Knowing that I must distract David, I sought wildly through my mind for something I could say that would divert his attention. I looked away to avoid his penetrating gaze and recognized the sentinel palm rising strong in the moonlight. I shivered as that memory brought its own chill.

"Faith?"

"Do you not find this an eerie place?" I asked.

"What?"

I hurried on, hoping for the best. "There's something about this island, David. Remember how you warned me before I came? Well, I have hesitated to tell you, but I think you were right about there being evil forces at work here."

"You said nothing about this before." David's expression told me that he was wondering if I had lost my senses and I could not blame him.

"I promised Harlan not to mention it to anyone else, but now I think maybe I should tell you what happened." I hurriedly began the tale of the bobbing lights, leaving

156

out only the fact that I had already shared it with Hunter.

David listened with flattering attention, not interrupting me once. As I spoke, I could see that I had definitely diverted his mind from the question of the ledgers. I only hoped I had not brought up something that would prove more disturbing to him.

"You have not seen this 'pirate parade' again?" he asked when I finished.

"No, but with Penny sleeping through the night more often now, I have not really watched for it. Of course, if it was just some of the villagers trying to frighten us . . ." I let it trail off, regretting my rash choice of diversions now that it was too late.

"Why would the path be well used if they did it simply to frighten you?" His question echoed my own doubts.

"But what else could it be?"

"Perhaps if we explore the area together tomorrow, we might learn something."

"Will you have the time?"

"I shall be free most of the time until we sail, since Hunter and Harlan will be spending their days together making plans for the trading company." He sighed. "They are very intent on expanding here on Dark Thunder, so if there is something strange happening, it would be best to let them know about it before they invest more in this place." He grinned at me. "Unless my sister is simply being haunted by pirate ghosts."

I stiffened at the amusement in his tone. "I hope you see them yourself, David, then you will not be laughing at me." That said, I forced myself to relax, aware that I preferred his amusement to his believing that the lights were a danger to all of us.

"I would like to see them." David took my arm. "But now I think we had best go back and join the others. They could be forming a 'pirate parade' of their own to come in search of us."

I offered no argument as we made our way back to where the formal garden began, but I was once again very conscious of the darkness beneath the trees that spread between the house and the cove. Every single person from the village could be hiding out there but we would never know it.

"Well, here you are," Hunter greeted us as we approached the veranda. "I was about to call out the servants and start a search."

I felt his gaze on my face and knew that he suspected David of lecturing me again. I forced a smile I was far from feeling. "I am happy to know that we are missed, but I doubt we could get lost with the house like a beacon against the sky."

Our eyes met and heat rushed through my body. Never had I been so instantly aware of another human. Sometimes I felt I might explode if he so much as touched my fingers. Other times, like at this moment, I craved the sanctuary of his arms and the wondrous escape of his kiss.

"'Twas not that I feared you lost," Hunter continued, shifting his gaze to David. "One of the men from the village just rode out to deliver this to you, David. It seems it just arrived on one of the sailing ships that does business with a small trading company not far from Charleston, so I thought it might be important." He extended an oilskin pouch to David.

"Is it from Papa?" I gasped, everything else forgotten.

"Perhaps you should take it inside, Faith, David," Sarah suggested. "There is not enough light out here to read anything."

David nodded and I followed him inside, grateful for the privacy. My heart was pounding with fear as a thousand ghastly possibilities crowded my mind. "Is it from Papa?" I asked again, when I realized that David had the pouch open and was reading the single sheet of paper inside.

"No, from Sam Taylor." His face was grim as he passed the sheet to me.

"Is Papa . . .?" I was too frightened to even read the

158

words on it.

"As far as he knows, Papa is fine, Faith. This letter is about Tommy." He took my elbow and gently lead me to a chair, then lit the lamp on the table beside it. "The news is not good, I am afraid."

"Tommy." For a moment, I felt only relief, than guilt swept through me as I scanned the lines. The message was brief. Sam had managed to reach a friend who had followed our soldiers to the battle area of the north. From him Sam had learned that Tommy had been seriously wounded during the first battle in which he was involved. There had been no chance for Tommy's companions to reach him during the fighting and afterward, they had found no sign of him. Though it was not official, there was little hope that Tommy had survived.

I closed my eyes, sickness twisting inside me, then burning in my throat so that I had to keep swallowing. For the first time in months, clear memories of Tommy flooded my mind. I could see his laughing face, hear his cheerful words, remember how the girl I had been then had loved him.

"Are you all right, Faith?" David sounded worried and I felt his fingers on my shoulder. "Should I summon Sarah?"

I shook my head, not trusting myself to speak just yet. I swallowed again. My eyes burned, but no tears came. My betrayal of Tommy with Hunter held them back. I had no right to mourn Tommy when I had been planning to . . .

"May I help, Faith?" Sarah's voice penetrated the rising mist of guilt. "Was it bad news about your father?"

I opened my mouth, but no words came out, so David explained what the letter had said. I could hear the sadness in his voice and I suddenly remembered something else. Tommy had been like an older brother to David before he had grown up enough to give me my first kiss.

"Why do you not go back out to the veranda, David,"

Sarah suggested softly. "I will see Faith to her room. I expect that she will want to be alone just now. Am I right, Faith?"

I nodded, grateful for her understanding since I seemed incapable of speaking or even feeling. It appeared that numbness had crept into my very bones as she helped me to my feet and it took my full concentration to follow her up the stairs and along the upper hall to the sanctuary of my sitting room.

Once there, she and Rose, who had been sitting with Penny, prepared me for bed, then Sarah stayed with me while Rose went to fetch some soothing concoction from the kitchen. Only when Sarah held the glass beneath my nose, did I revolt against her tender coercion. "I cannot," I protested, fighting nausea. "Please, I would just like to be alone."

"Perhaps it would be best if you take Penny to sleep in your room tonight, Rose," Sarah suggested. "That way Faith will be able to rest without worrying about her."

"No." I shook my head violently. "I thank you for your consideration, Sarah, but I would prefer to go on just as I have been. It was a shock, but I will be fine. Having Penny to watch over will make me feel better."

"Are you sure, Miss Faith?" Rose asked. "'Twould be no trouble to take Penny with me. You be needing sleep after such bad news."

"I will sleep, but first I would like some time to myself. You have both been most kind, but . . ." I felt the sobs rising in my throat as I urged them out the door, closed it, then rested my cheek against the cool wood. Tommy, I thought, oh, Tommy, I am so sorry I could not offer you a love worthy of your sacrifice. My eyes continued to burn, but still no tears came. The guilty memory of Hunter's kisses kept from me the sweet relief of crying.

After a while, I blew out the lamps and lay down on my bed, hoping for the release of sleep; but the night was haunted. When I closed my eyes, I saw Tommy. When I opened them, his face was still before me. As my weariness grew, I picked up the glass and sniffed the contents, tempted to accept the release it promised. But I set it back down untasted, unwilling to risk Penny's safety by drinking it.

Later I heard the sounds of footsteps in the hall as David went to his room, which was not too far from mine. For a moment I considered calling him to come sit with me. I wanted desperately to talk about Tommy, to use words to make him real in my mind; but I stayed where I was, trapped by my guilt. What if David hated me for having turned to Hunter when I was promised to Tommy?

I tried again to sleep, but the room had become stuffy and hot. Or perhaps it was only my emotions that swirled suffocatingly around me. Feeling as though I might smother, I got out of bed and opened the door to the balcony. The night air that blew in was sweet and cool with the tang of the sea. I slipped on a pair of shoes to guard my feet against splinters, then covered my pale nightdress with a dark cloak before I stepped out on the balcony.

The moon had grown distant while I lay awake and the night was still as I crossed to the rail and as always, looked off toward the distant tall palm. My thoughts were far from the story I had told David earlier, so at first I paid no attention to the spark of light; but as it was joined by another, then still more, I realized that the ghostly parade was under way.

Without pausing to think, I raced through my rooms and down the hall to pound on David's door, calling his name softly. He wore only his trousers and a worried expression as he opened the door. "What by all that is holy . . . ?"

"The lights, David. I saw the lights. Come to the balcony and you can see them, too."

He followed me through my rooms to the balcony, carrying his shirt and boots. The lights were still visible. He watched for a moment, then asked, "Can you take me

161

to the path?"

I nodded, my excitement having banished my despair for the moment. "If we hurry, perhaps we can catch them and discover what they are about." I closed the balcony door carefully, then David and I raced along the balcony and down the rear stairway.

I ran confidently through the gardens, but as we neared the wild section of the island, my enthusiasm began to wane a little. What had been shadowy undergrowth in the full light of day was now a jungle of total darkness.

"Perhaps we should have summoned the others," I panted, slowing my headlong pace as I tried to find an opening between the thick bushes and trees.

"If we wait for everyone, we shall have no chance of seeing your ghosts." David plunged into the underbrush then cursed the thorns and branches that snagged at him. "Come on, which way?"

I did my best, stumbling through the darkness, guided only by occasional glimpses of the tall palm. I was shaking with exhaustion by the time I scrambled down an unseen incline to the path. "This is it," I gasped, fighting my need to drop to the worn grass to catch my breath and ease the pain in my side.

"So where are they?" David was breathing hard, too, but his eyes blazed with excitement in the starlight that penetrated this area. "Which way?"

"They must come from the cove, so they would have to leave the same way," I reasoned. "If they are anywhere, it would be there." I pointed the way, then followed David as he plunged ahead.

Since I no longer had to give all my energy to staying on my feet, other fears began to rise in my mind. For the first time, I wondered just what we were going to do if we actually met the "pirate paraders." I was no longer sure whether I was more afraid that they would be ghosts or that they would not be.

The rattle of stones ahead forced my mind back from

dark images of what could happen if David and I confronted a group of the surly villagers. The well-lit shore of the cove lay ahead and below me and it was empty of all but David. I followed him down and collapsed on the sand, caught between relief and anger.

David wandered the length of the sandy beach, then returned to drop beside me. "We were too late."

"What do you mean?"

"I found marks in the sand where two small boats were drawn up and I suspect we could find tracks, too, if the light was better. Not that it matters; whoever was here is long gone."

"But who . . ." My curiosity revived.

"I would be more interested in knowing the why." David got to his feet again. "I think this time Harlan will have to take your observation seriously."

I allowed David to help me to my feet. "He does not wish Sarah to know."

"Since someone is trespassing on his land late at night, I think he has more serious concerns than Sarah's fears."

"But they do nothing to disturb the household, David. I have seen them twice and each time, there are just the lights. The path leads to a clearing near a cliff face; it goes nowhere near the house or the gardens." It was easy for him to dismiss Sarah's fears, but I hated the thought that she might live in dread because of something I had seen.

"Are you saying that you wish to keep this a secret?" He sounded angry at the idea. "What do you think they do here?"

I cast through my mind quickly, seeking inspiration. "Do you think it could be a trysting place for those in the village who fear to meet in public? I should hate to have Sarah frightened because a couple sought privacy here."

We trudged along the path in silence for several minutes, then David sighed. "I suppose it could be something so harmless and everyone at the house will be long asleep. Perhaps we could wait until the morning. After you have shown me the other end of the path, I will

163

decide about telling anyone."

Relief swept through me. "I mislike secrets, too, David, but in this instance . . ." I let the words trail off as we reached a turn in the path that gave us a glimpse of Thunder House. Lights blazed from the windows on the east end—the children's area! "Penny!" I gasped, suddenly realizing that I had left her alone and unprotected.

Chapter 11

David cursed and raced toward the house, blundering through the bushes and trees like a wild creature, while I stumbled after him, so sick with guilt I could scarcely breathe. I had taken no more than a dozen steps when a flash of movement caught my eye. Something stirred in the shadows and I heard a familiar whimper.

"Penny?" I took a tentative step toward a clump of tall cane grass.

"Faith?" Her voice was so faint I thought for a moment that I might be dreaming, then she crawled out from behind the grass, her pale nightdress easy to see against the dark vegetation.

"Penny, how in the world . . ." I caught her in my arms, hugging her so hard she squirmed in protest.

"Did I do it again, Miss Faith?" The despair in her voice banished my own terror, reminding me of how difficult this was for her.

"I guess so, Penny," I murmured, keeping my tone as close to normal as I could as I stroked her hair back from her face and tried for a smile. "Though how you could have come so far . . ." I looked down at her tiny bare feet.

"Penny! Penny!" Several frantic voices filled the night and I hurried toward them, holding her snug against me, blessing whatever miracle had brought Penny this way instead of sending her toward the dangerous bluffs above the sea.

"She is here!" I shouted, stopping to catch my breath after I burst out of the thick underbrush into the open at the edge of the formal gardens. "I have her and she is safe!"

A number of people, David among them, came racing toward me. Harlan reached me first and snatched Penny from my arms, frightening her back into tears. Sarah was right behind him and when he put Penny into her mother's arms, the child's sobs eased. My guilt returned full force as I looked from Penny's tear-stained face to those of her parents.

"This is all your fault," Harlan roared, fury contorting his face. "How could you let the child escape? We trusted you to watch after her and you . . ."

"Stop it, Harlan!" Hunter's voice cut into his twin's tirade before Harlan could go on. "Faith has found the child, be grateful for that."

"You shoud have roused the household so that we could all have been searching for her sooner." Harlan's foice dropped to a less furious level. "When Rose woke us, we had no idea how long Penny had been gone or in which direction."

"Rose?" My head was spinning as I tried to make sense of his words.

"'Twere me who woke them, Miss Faith." Rose joined us, looking nearly as guilty as I felt. "Woke up, I did, and was afeared in your distress you might be overtook by sleep and not hear the little one, so I slipped in for a look." She frowned. "That be when I found Penny's window open to the night and her bed empty."

"The window! But was it not closed when you left the room, Rose? How could it have been opened?" My guilt faded slightly as I was again overtaken by confusion.

"You did not open it, Faith?" Sarah's eyes met mine.

"You know I would never do that." The fact that she would even ask me hurt nearly as much as my realization that I had left Penny vulnerable and alone.

"Then how was it opened?" Harlan's expression had not changed at all; the suspicion fairly burned in his eyes when he looked my way. "And what were you doing out here in the middle of the night?"

"She was doing what the rest of us were doing, looking for Penny. Luckily, she found her." Hunter took my arm, his fingers tightening protectively. "Now, I would suggest that we all go inside so Penny can be put safely back into her bed."

"Did you hear her and follow her, Faith?" Sarah asked.

"I did not hear her," I began, trying to find the words to tell her exactly what had happened. "I thought I saw something and David and I were . . ."

"Mommy, Mommy, my bracelet is gone!" Penny interrupted my explanation.

"Gone?" I gasped, realizing suddenly that I had not heard the reassuring tinkle of the little bells since I found her. "But where?"

"Then there was no way you could have heard her leaving the house." Harlan stared at me. "How did you find her?"

"This is no time for asking questions, Harlan," Sarah interrupted him. "We should just be grateful that Faith found Penny. We can worry about how in the morning."

"Faith has been through enough, Harlan," Hunter agreed. "First the bad new about her betrothed, now this."

His mention of Tommy proved more than I could bear; shivers began to shudder through me. The excitement of chasing the bobbing pirate lights, then the shock and guilt I had felt after finding Penny out here had momentarily banished my grief; but now it all swept over me in a dizzying rush. Luckily, Hunter seemed to sense my weakness, because he held me tight against his side until I could gather my strength again.

"Are you all right, Faith?" he asked gently. "Do you think you can walk to the house or would you like me to carry you?"

"I can walk." The thought of being carried in his strong arms was too tempting. I dared not yield to my longing to be in his embrace. Honor would not allow me to sob out my grief for one man in the arms of another.

"I will escort my sister to her room." David was suddenly beside me offering his strong arm.

For a heartbeat, I thought that Hunter might argue, but he merely nodded and allowed David to lead me away. When I looked back from the veranda, I felt his gaze still upon me, but he was too far away for me to read his expression.

"You did not tell them about the lights." David's accusing tone brought my attention back to him.

"Sarah was far too upset over Penny being lost; I could not add to her burden."

"Will you tell them tomorrow?"

I could only shrug. Nothing seemed to be making sense. Even as distraught as I had been over the news about Tommy, I was sure that the window in Penny's room had been closed when Sarah went in to call Rose to help her undress me. I also knew Penny lacked the strength to open it. Beyond that I could make no sense of what had happened. Aware that David was still staring at me, I murmured, "It seems unimportant when I think of Penny wandering alone into that wild area."

"Are you saying you want me to keep quiet about the lights?" Obviously David was unwillling to give up the subject.

"I wish I knew what to do, David. Harlan refused to believe me when I told him before and I suspect he will treat your story the same way he did mine. I am more concerned about what happened to Penny. She could have been hurt out there and it would have been my fault for leaving her alone to pursue some ghostly lights." Guilt swept through me again.

"I never thought . . ." David looked guilty, too.

"I was hired to think of Penny first, David, and I

168

failed. All I cared about was finding out what the lights mean and . . ." The tears I had not been able to shed earlier welled up and spilled over my cheeks. "If anything had happened to that sweet innocent little . . ."

"Hush now, Faith, nothing did. You found her safe and sound. Besides, you never opened the window and if she has lost her bracelet, you might not have heard her even if you had been there."

I knew he spoke the truth, but that did not help. Every time I closed my eyes I saw horrible pictures of what could have happened to Penny while she was sleepwalking in the night. Once David left me, I hurried into Penny's room, sure there must have been some mistake about the window.

The cool breeze that caressed my hot cheeks told me there was not; the window stood wide open. Unnerved, I went to straighten the covers so that the bed would be ready for Penny when Sarah brought her up, and there I found the bracelet. The clasp, which had been bent to make releasing it difficult, was open. As I stood there staring at the shiny silver bracelet, Sarah and Rose came in through the playroom.

"What is it, Faith?" Sarah asked, hurrying forward, her sleepy daughter cuddled happily against her shoulder.

"The bracelet." I could say no more.

"But how . . .?" Sarah began, then let it trail off as Penny revived to exclaim over her bracelet. Rose closed the window while Sarah and I refastened the stubborn clasp so that the bracelet was again safely around Penny's tiny wrist.

Penny settled into her bed and slept almost immediately. Sarah stayed to watch her for several minutes, then came tiptoeing into my bedroom. "What are we to do, Faith?" she asked. "If you had not found her . . ." She shuddered.

"I swear by all that be holy that I never opened that window, Miss Sarah," Rose began, her face twisting with a mixture of fear and entreaty.

"I know that it was closed when I peeked in after you left," I agreed. "And I certainly never opened it."

"But Penny is so little. How could she . . .?" Sarah's voice broke.

"Perhaps people are stronger when they are sleepwalking. I know they do things they would not attempt when they are awake, so . . ." I let it trail off, not believing my own words.

"How can we protect her?" Sarah looked to me for help.

"Perhaps lattices could be made to fit over all the windows in the children's area. With them in place, the windows could be left open and there would be no danger as long as my door to the balcony is latched and the playroom is secured from the hall." I spoke quickly, my thoughts returning to what had happened earlier tonight and the confession of failure that I owed Sarah.

"What a wonderful idea." Relief banished the lines in Sarah's face and lit her smile. "Oh, Faith, I am so grateful to you. If you had not come to us . . ." Her hug lifted my heart and added to my burden of guilt at the same time, for I knew then that I could not tell her about my betrayal of her trust without hurting her. I had no right to salve my conscience at the cost of her peace of mind.

When I went down for the morning meal, I spoke to David about finding the bracelet and the open window in Penny's room and, reluctantly, he agreed that my mentioning the pirate lights to Sarah would only trouble her deeply. "Since you feel you cannot say anything to Sarah, Faith, I shall explore the area this morning just to be sure they have done no damage. If these prowlers are up to no good, however, I must tell Harlan so he can deal with it."

I nodded, both relieved that we should be protected and apprehensive about the result. I had no illusions about Harlan's reaction if he knew that I had been out pursuing ghostly lights while his daughter was sleepwalking. "I mislike asking you not to speak up, David, but I know not what else to do."

"It was an evil night for all of us, but at least Penny is safe." David's gaze probed at me. "And there is still hope, Faith. Sam's news could be in error. Perhaps Tommy was not so gravely wounded as they thought and is now a prisoner of the Northerners. That would explain why you have heard nothing."

"Of course there is hope. And I shall keep him in my prayers, David, you know that."

"Just be sure that you remember him when you are around Hunter." David's gaze was stern, reminding me of Papa's.

"I assure you . . ." I let the sentence trail off as Harlan and Sarah came in to join us. Sarah's smile was open and warm, but when I met Harlan's gaze, I felt the chill. Though he said nothing toward David or me, I sensed that he was still suspicious either about last night's events or about my secret involvement in keeping the ledger accounts for Sarah.

The next few days seemed endless. I spent as much time as I could with Penny, avoiding both Harlan and Hunter except at meal times and when Sarah insisted that I join the family in the evenings. It was a lonely time since David was kept busy helping Harlan, who was readying the *Sprite* for a trading venture in the islands. And Sarah, naturally, spent every moment she could with Harlan, obviously dreading the day he would sail away.

Once I was able to think of more than my guilt and grief over Tommy, I began to wonder if Harlan's questioning of David about my skill with account keeping had been forgotten. When Harlan made no further comment about the ledgers, I shifted my attention to Sarah. She, however, appeared to have decided to forget our charade with the ledgers.

171

When the two of us did spend quiet time together, Sarah talked only of Penny and H.J. or her plans for the future. Harlan had promised that, as soon as he had some free time, they would visit English Wells and invite some of their friends from there and the other nearby islands to come to Dark Thunder for a stay. Sarah was eager to bring more outsiders to the island in the hope that more friendly faces would help bridge the strain between our end of the island and the people in the village.

After a few days of being treated simply as a friend, I began to wonder. Had Harlan said something to Hunter, perhaps mentioned his suspicions about the keeping of the ledgers or even about my carelessness the night that Penny had disappeared through the window? Hunter had defended me against Harlan's anger when I first brought Penny out of the trees, but what if Harlan had been more convincing later? My stomach knotted as I realized that I was guilty of many of the accusations Harlan might bring against me.

I was relieved when Harlan left the island, for I was sure that once he was gone, Hunter would have more time for me. After he sailed, however, nothing changed. For two long, empty days, I waited, hoping, expecting Hunter to seek me out; but he seemed to have forgotten everything that had happened between us.

Had David been right in his assessment of Hunter's character where women were concerned? I asked myself bitterly. Had kissing me been a game with Hunter, a mere amusement to pass the boring days on Dark Thunder? Had his flattering pursuit come only because he knew I was safely betrothed to someone else?

By the third morning, I began to wonder if I could bear to stay on here, seeing Hunter every day, yet not being truly close to him. But where could I go? There was no way I could return to Nassau. Caroline wrote me regularly and every letter was full of comments about Aunt Minerva's continuing disapproval of my decision to become a governess. To return to her house would mean admitting that I had made a mistake and, in spite of the pain I felt because of my feelings for Hunter, I loved my time with Penny.

"Are you not feeling well this morning, Faith?" Sarah's gentle voice startled me out of my dark thoughts. I had not heard her enter the dining room.

I tried for a smile as I looked up from my plate. "I am perfectly fine, thank you."

"You seem sad. Is it that you were thinking of your Tommy?" Her eyes were full of sympathy, tempting me to accept the excuse she offered, but before I could say anything, she went on. "I think you need a change of scene. Perhaps Dorry could keep watch over Penny this afternoon and give you some free time. Would that make you feel better?"

"I would love a chance to go riding," I admitted, suddenly remembering that Hunter had said something about spending time at the site of his future home. "Do you think I might do that?"

"Of course, you may, Faith, I know that you need some time to yourself these days. I am sorry that I did not think to suggest it sooner. Anytime you would like to ride, all you need do is ask one of the maids to sit with Penny."

"You are very kind."

"I want you to be happy here, Faith, you know that. And I owe you so much for helping me with the ledgers." Sarah looked away guiltily.

"Did you ever tell Harlan what we did?" I asked, glad of the opportunity to inquire.

Sarah shook her head. "I know I should have acknowledged your help when he first began to question me, but he had already told me how pleased he was with the work. After accepting his praise, I simply could not admit that I failed him so completely." She sighed. "Fortunately, he soon found someone in the village to take care of the ledgers, so I will have no further secrets from him."

"He never asked you any more questions?"

Her smile was sunny as she shook her head. "I am sure he never gave the ledgers another thought. He was only curious in the beginning."

"Of course." I rearranged the food on my plate without tasting any of it. Sarah might believe that, but I had grave doubts. Harlan had not been satisfied with her answers that evening at dinner, so his lack of questions probably meant he had drawn his own conclusions from what David had told him about me.

"But let us talk of happier topics," Sarah continuted. "Did you know that Hunter has ordered work begun on his house? He truly seems set on having a home of his own now." She sighed. "Which probably means we shall see even less of him. He left near dawn and Cook said he took his midday meal with him."

My appetite returned. If Hunter had taken food with him, that must mean that he would not be spending the day in the village where he could dine with David and the other members of his crew at the Cock's Crow. Pictures of a romantic picnic on the rocks above the cove filled my mind. Foolish or not, I had to ride over there and talk to Hunter. I desperately needed to know if his feelings for me had changed.

"My goodness, the mere promise of a ride this afternoon has you looking better already," Sarah commented as we left the table to begin the day's activities. "You must plan other excursions, Faith. As a member of the family, I want you to be content here."

Our eyes met and I knew that she meant the words and I wished that I dared confide my feelings to her. But so long as I was still betrothed to Tommy, I had no right to feel as I did, I reminded myself firmly. As David had pointed out, Sam's letter reported only a rumor and I truly did want to believe there was a possibility that Tommy was still alive.

Knowing that thoughts of Tommy and his possible fate would only dim the brightness from the day, I banished them as I hurried upstairs to begin Penny's lessons. Today I was going to dwell only on happy thoughts—like the prospect of spending the afternoon with Hunter. If he wanted me to. Not being sure of his feelings dampened my enthusiasm slightly, but not enough to keep me from donning my riding clothes and going to the stable as soon as Penny was settled for her nap.

Savannah, the gentle bay mare that I had ridden before, was saddled and waiting for me when I reached the stable. "Would you like me to accompany you, miss?" the young groom asked as he helped me to mount.

I hesitated, torn between my longing to be alone with Hunter and my continuing apprehension about what might be going on in the wild area of the island. My plans for an "accidental meeting" with Hunter won and I gave the groom my best smile. "I am sure I will be safe enough and I know you have many duties here."

"I would be pleased to ride with you, Miss Faith." His disapproval was obvious.

"I will be fine." I touched Savannah with my riding whip and trotted away before he could object further. Only after we were out of sight of the stable, did I slow the mare and look around. Though I wanted to talk to Hunter, my pride demanded that our meeting appear to be a casual happening, not a deliberate confrontation.

"Exploring," I murmured, patting the mare's neck. "I think I should take another look at the area of the path. David said so little about what he saw the morning after we followed the lights."

Riding through the wild area was quicker than walking had been, but it was still not an easy passage, for the underbrush made parts of the area difficult for Savannah. Once we reached the path, however, she trotted without hesitation to the clearing near the cliff. As before, there was nothing to see. Whatever the light-bearers did, it left no mark on the area. Somehow I did not find that particularly reassuring.

What if the ghostly lights had no one carrying them?

That was a prospect I had not even discussed with David, yet looking at the clearing, I could not deny it. Humans needed a purpose for their actions and I could think of none that would involve carrying lanters to this place. I reined Savannah back into the shady path, following it until I reached the sentinel palm. From there I rode slowly through the brush toward the distant bluff where I hoped to find Hunter.

The moment I left the path, I sensed the change in Savannah. She shied at a clump of cane grass, then dodged away from a rustling palm frond. I patted her neck, trying to soothe her with words, but she continued to snort and eye each bush as though she expected it to attack her. Was it my fault? Could she sense my uneasiness? I was well aware that animals could sense fear in people, so perhaps the beast was sensitive to my doubts about the meeting I was seeking.

Suddenly I became aware of a rustling noise and the crackling of dry underbrush behind us, sounds that I had not noticed earlier. The shadows seemed to have deepened while I was exploring on the path and now I wished that I had chosen to ride along the road instead of cross-country. I leaned forward, urging the mare to move more quickly, as anxious as she to escape this haunted area.

Savannah leaped forward as though I had struck her, nearly crashing into a tree before she dodged to one side, almost unseating me. Frightened, I jerked back on the reins, hoping to steady her and regain my seat; but instead of slowing her, my action only caused her to plunge sideways. The terrified mare bucked, nearly stumbling into a thicket of spiny plants.

I tried again to rein her in, then realized that I was jerking her sideways, for only one rein was still attached to the bit, the other hung from my hand. In that paralyzing moment, I had no idea what to do, then Savannah reared and leaped forward again and I had no choice. I let go my hold on her single rein and freed myself from the saddle, trying desperately to jump into a

176

cushioning clump of cane grass. Pain exploded through me when my head hit the hard ground, then darkness welcomed me.

Consciousness seeped slowly through the peaceful dark, bringing pain even before I cautiously opened my eyes, afraid to move. Where was I? Everything was so quiet. I could hear the birds and the insects, the rustle of the palms, but I could see little beyond a patch of sky above and the broken blades of grass where I lay.

Memory swept over me. I had been thrown. Savannah had gone mad and the bridle . . . no, the rein had broken and . . . I moved slowly, testing my legs and arms before I even tried to sit up. Everything seemed in working order, though every part of my body ached in protest and my head spun wildly the moment I lifted it off the ground.

"Savannah?" I looked around slowly, since any sudden movement made me both dizzy and ill. There was no sign of the mare. Had she headed back to the stable? I hoped so, since her return without me would bring about a search. I gazed at the sky and the shadows, wondering how long I had been lying here. It was well past midday, but I could tell nothing more.

And how long would it take to find me? The prospects seemed pretty dim, since I had told no one where I planned to ride. Sighing, I tried to get up. The world tilted alarmingly for several moments, but closing my eyes helped a little and when I finally opened them again, I was still standing. Feeling sure that my entire body could shatter like crystal at any moment, I made my way slowly toward the nearest tree. Leaning against it helped.

Since I had no idea exactly where I was, I continued to move from tree to tree until I reached a small rise. From there I could see in several directions. I looked first toward the bluff where I had expected to find Hunter. There were signs that work had begun there, but the area appeared deserted now. Sighing with a disappointment that hurt even more than my bruises, I turned my attention to the road. That seemed my best hope, because if I

177

could just make it down the hill and through the thick floral barrier that protected it, surely someone would come along and take me to the house.

I was barely halfway down the hill when I heard the sound of approaching hoofbeats. Knowing I could not run, I began to shout. Within moments, Hunter broke through the thick bushes and slid from his horse's back. "Faith? Good Lord, what has happened to you?"

Relief struck me with the same force as the ground had earlier and I staggered into his arms before sliding back into the darkness. When I opened my eyes again, I was lying on the ground, my head pillowed on Hunter's jacket as he wiped gently at my face with his handkerchief.

"Hunter." I could barely whisper.

"It is all right, Faith, you are safe now." He set aside the cloth and tenderly smoothed back my hair, then helped me to sit up. "Can you tell me what happened?"

"I was riding and Savannah suddenly went wild. I tried to stop her and the rein broke and . . ." I shuddered, not wanting to remember falling.

"You were riding alone?" Hunter's frown chilled me. "Where were you?"

"Sarah told me that you had begun work on your house and I thought I might ride over and see what has been done."

"This happened on the road?" His expression told me that he sensed I had not told him everything.

"Not exactly. I was riding along that path I showed you when I decided to cut through the brush the way we did the day you took me riding." Why did he not smile at me now or touch me again? His remoteness frightened me. He had seemed so concerned about me at first, but now . . .

"Let me understand, you . . ." He was interrupted by his horse's sudden whinny. And a moment later an answering whicker came from a short distance away.

"Savannah," I gasped as the mare came limping out of the underbrush. The saddle was askew on her back and

178

her dark bay hide was scratched, scraped, and torn as though she had fallen hard. "Oh, Hunter, she is hurt." I dragged myself to my feet as Hunter hurried over to catch the single trailing rein.

He turned back to me, his expression disapproving. "Faith, you should stay still. If you are hurt . . ."

"I may be a bit dizzy and sore, but I have walked away from worse falls," I informed him, then returned to gritting my teeth as I limped forward to rub the mare's velvety muzzle.

"Looks like she went down somewhere along the way," Hunter said as he loosened the cinch and shifted the saddle back into place, tightened it, then led her forward a few steps. "But she seems sound enough."

"Just sore and dizzy, old girl?" I asked, stroking her neck.

The mare nuzzled me as though in apology.

"I have no idea what caused her to act that way, Hunter," I began as he moved around to the other side of the mare. "One minute she was trotting along quiet as you please, the next, she was jumping at shadows and shying from sounds. Then she bucked and . . ." I let it trail off, realizing that his attention was focused on the mare's haunch. "Is there something wrong?"

"I think I see what could have set her to bucking." Hunter's tone was so serious that I scarcely noted the pain as I hobbled around to see what he was looking at.

The wound was small, but different from the scrapes and scratches below it on her side. "What is it?" I asked, looking up to see Hunter's gaze. His frown chilled me.

"It looks like something hit her, maybe a sharp branch or a thorn."

"Could she not have done that when she fell?"

"Not likely, unless she rolled over and with the saddle still intact, I doubt that she did."

"What are you saying?" The implications of his words sent shivers through me.

"I am not sure, Faith. I could be worrying over

179

nothing, but I want you to promise me that you will never go riding alone again." For a long moment our eyes met and I knew that he was warning me, yet I was also intensely conscious of his hand on my arm and of his magnetic closeness. Suddenly he seemed to shake himself and a smile replaced his frown. "But right now I am more interested in getting you home. Do you think you can ride Savannah that far?"

"Better than I can walk," I assured him, then gasped as he lifted me to the saddle.

"Are you all right?" The concern in his face warmed me.

I nodded, biting the inside of my lip to keep from groaning. "But you will have to lead her, since the rein . . ." I looked down, not seeing the expected worn or frayed bit of leather hanging from the bit. There was, in fact, no sign of the rein I had thought broken.

Hunter, who had followed my gaze, looked up to meet my eyes. "I will definietly speak to the groom about sending a horse out with improper tack." he sighed. "And I will have him look at the mark on her haunch. Meantime, I just thank God that you are all right."

I nodded my agreement. For the moment, it was enough that Hunter had come and that he wanted to take care of me. Besides, I had my hands full just staying on the horse as she limped along behind Hunter's mount. I refused to even think about what had happened to me or what it might mean.

Chapter 12

The flurry that greeted our arrival at the house quite took my breath away. Hunter shouted for the groom to take the horses, then insisted on carrying me up to my room while Sarah stayed below issuing orders for a bath to be prepared and sending someone to summon David from the village. At my insistence, Hunter laid me gently on the loveseat in my sitting room.

"Are you sure you are not in pain, Faith?" he asked, taking my hand between both of his.

"Nothing that a few days' rest will not cure." I lost myself in his gaze, even more intensely aware of my feelings for him than I had been when I was in his strong arms. Could this be love? I wondered, dizzy at the prospect. I had spoken of that emotion so easily when I promised myself to Tommy, but I had never experienced anything like this.

"If anything had happened to you . . ." He let the words trail off as Sarah came hustling in, but he continued to hold my hand and the warmth of his touch spread through me easing my stiffening muscles.

"How did this happen, Faith?" Sarah asked, her fingers cool on my cheek as she came to stand beside Hunter. "Surely, young Ben chose a gentle horse for you."

Hunter's fingers tightened on my hand until I winced

and when I looked up at him, I read the warning in his eyes. He did not want Sarah frightened. For a moment I felt a sharp pang of resentment at the way everyone protected Sarah, then I was ashamed of myself. Everyone protected Sarah because she was sweet and gentle and deserved protection. "Ben was not at fault," I replied, not quite meeting her worried gaze. "Something frightened Savannah and when I tried to control her, the rein broke. That's when I jumped off into a clump of cane grass. I would have been all right, except that I hit my head."

"And why was Ben not with you?" Sarah's frown deepened, making it clear that she was not ready to accept my story.

"I was just going to ride in the area near the house, so I told him I had no need for an escort." The words sounded false even to my ears, but how could I confess that I had ridden out hoping to spend time alone with Hunter? "It was foolish of me," I added, by way of apology.

"It certainly was." There was relief as well as admonition in Hunter's face as he reluctantly freed my fingers and moved out of the way as two of the young menservants carried in the bathtub. "Since you no longer need me here, I shall go and speak with Ben about that bridle." His eyes met mine for a moment longer and my breath caught in my throat, for his gaze was like a caress. Though my room was full of people, it seemed empty once he went out the door.

"Faith, are you sure you are all right? I only wish there was a physician on this island or at least nearby." Sarah's worried tone drew my attention back from the sensuous thoughts Hunter inspired. "Are you feeling confused? I have heard that in head injuries that can be a danger."

I managed a smile to reassure her. "I will be fine once I soak some of the soreness from my muscles. I just feel foolish. I used to consider myself quite a good rider; I should have been able to handle Savannah better."

"Even a good rider cannot control a horse with one

182

rein." Sarah turned away to inspect the containers of heated water that the servants brought in.

I lay back against the cushion she had placed behind me and closed my eyes. It felt good to allow someone else to handle the details of my bath. In fact, I almost wished I could go straight to my bed now for the throbbing in my head was worsening. I smiled to myself, well aware that I sought sleep because it would allow me to dream that I was in Hunter's arms again.

I must have drifted off, for I was startled when Rose began to help me out of my battered and filthy riding clothes. Even more surprising was my realization that the two of us were now alone in my sitting room. I had not heard Sarah or the others leave.

"Ah, miss, you be bruised all over," Rose moaned as she stripped away the last of my underclothing. "You be lucky to walk away from such a fall."

Looking down at the already darkening areas on my arms, legs, and side, I had to agree. The thick grass had offered only slight protection from the ground, but my own quick action at freeing myself from the terrified horse had probably saved me from serious injury. Had I still been in the saddle when Savannah fell, I would most likely have been crushed. I shuddered at the thought.

"Be you steady enough to bathe, miss?" Rose's strong hands supported me.

I hesitated a moment, but the lure of the fragrant, steaming water was too great to deny. "If you will help me, I think I can climb into the tub."

I remember little else about the day. Once I left the cooling water, I could barely keep my eyes open long enough for Rose to dry me and slip my nightdress over my head. I woke once in the evening and found David sitting beside my bed and then later one of the maids was dozing there; but I slept again before I could offer a smile to either of them. I was even too tired to dream of Hunter.

It was midmorning before I woke completely and near midday before Sarah would allow me out of my bed. Not that I was much disposed to argue, for even the slightest movement hurt. Still, once I had consumed a sumptuous feast from the tray Cook sent up, my busy mind made me impatient with my battered body.

I wanted to know what Ben had made of the strange wound on Savannah's haunch and the missing rein. How could it have been worn so badly and not be noticed? And where was Hunter? So far as I knew, he had not come by my rooms since he carried me in and I longed to see him. I needed to know if he still suspected that my fall was not an accident.

David came in just as I was hobbling to a chair in my sitting room. "Should you be out of bed, Sis?" His worried frown told me that I looked nearly as feeble as I felt.

"I will only get stiffer lying still," I reminded him, trying to straighten up slightly and finding that I could not walk if I did. "How is Savannah?"

"I saw the groom leading her around and she moves about like you do." David's frown stayed in place. "Are you ready to tell me what really happened yesterday?"

"What do you mean?"

"I have seen Sarah ride that mare and she is quiet as a lamb. What would set her off that way?"

I shrugged and smothered a groan. Was there no part of me that had been spared? "Something frightened her and when I tried to stop her, the rein broke. I jumped free because she was acting wild and I could not control her with one rein."

"What frightened her?"

"I honestly have no idea." That was the truth, anyway.

"Where did this happen?" David was as tenacious as a hungry mosquito.

Knowing that he would never give up until he was sure

184

he had the whole story, I described my movements, leaving out only the fact that I had set out originally hoping to meet Hunter at his home site. As I spoke, memories filled my mind—I heard again the rustling sounds behind me, the crackling of dry twigs.

"What is it, Faith? What are you not telling me?"

"It is possible that I may have upset the horse myself, David. After I left the path and headed through the brush toward the bluff, I thought I heard something or someone in the bushes behind me and I sort of panicked."

"Did you see anything?"

"Only stars when my head hit the ground."

"Then you really cannot say for sure that someone was following you?"

I shook my head. "Something was bothering Savannah, though; she was snorting and shying and she is normally a perfect lady's mount."

"Could she have been reacting to someone hitting her with a rock or maybe poking her with a sharp stick?" David's gaze was intent.

"Have you been talking to Hunter?"

"No, to Ben. He told me what Hunter asked and I have seen the wound on the mare's haunch. What I want to know is if she acted like something had hurt her?"

It took me only a moment to decide. "That could explain why she fought me. Remember the day the bee stung my pony? That was the way he acted."

"That was no bee sting on Savannah."

"But who . . . ? And why, David? I was just riding through the area and . . ."

"And you had just come from that cursed path."

"But I saw no one and nothing amiss there, David." I met his gaze and read in his face the same confusion I was feeling. "It makes no sense."

"The only thing that makes sense to me is your immediate return to Nassau, Faith. You cannot stay where you are in danger."

"You want me to go back to Aunt Minerva because I fell off a horse?" I swallowed my own fears and feigned amusement at the idea, hoping that he would see how ridiculous it was.

"It is more than that and you know it." David's stubborn look made me wish I had kept my own counsel about this. Or waited to discuss it with Hunter. I definitely did not want my brother hovering over me, insisting that I needed protection.

"What is it then? Do you believe in ghosts? Maybe one of the parading pirates stayed around during the day and frightened the mare. But then, what would they do with their lanterns in the daytime?" I sounded hysterical, but I could not seem to control my tongue. I had to convince him that my fall had been an accident. There had to be something . . . Inspiration struck. "Or maybe it was a sharp branch. The mare was shying a lot, she could have spun into one. Besides, I would have seen a person if anyone had been out there." I stated that firmly, wanting desperately to believe it.

"I mislike it, Faith." David was on his feet, pacing the small space of my sitting room like a caged beast. "I must be sailing soon if we are to keep the rendezvous and you will be here alone."

"I have already promised Hunter not to ride without one of the grooms to escort me."

"But what if there really was someone out there?"

"Nothing would have happened if the rein had held. I could have controlled Savannah, calmed her. It was the broken rein that caused the trouble."

"That broken rein bothers me, too. I saw the bridle you were using and Ben swears that there was nothing wrong with the reins. The one still attached looks fairly new."

"We will know what happened when we find the rein that broke." I could only hope that it would be worn or flawed in a way that would reassure David and me that what had happened was just an accident.

186

"Well, I . . ." David stopped as someone tapped on my door.

"Come in," I called, welcoming the interruption. I needed someone to divert David while I thought about what had happened.

"Sarah told me that you were up to receiving visitors." Hunter offered me a fragrant bouquet of flowers. "How are you feeling today?"

"Not bad for someone a hundred and fifty years old." I tried for a joke, hoping to keep the tone of his visit lighter than David's had been.

"We were just discussing her so-called accident." David glared first at me, then at Hunter. So much for a diversion.

I squirmed in my chair while David recounted everything I had told him. While he listened, Hunter's frown matched David's and once David finished, they both turned to look expectantly in my direction. I began to wish that I had stayed in bed, safely away from their curiosity.

"Are you sure you saw no one, Faith?" Hunter finally broke the silence.

"Not a soul." I closed my mouth, refusing to repeat my recollections about the sounds I had heard. At the time I had thought they must be caused by the breeze or birds or maybe small animals, so why should I think now about whatever had carried the ghostly lanterns?

"Could you tell us where you fell?" David asked.

"Not really. I mean, I left the path near the tall palm and headed cross-country toward the bluff where Hunter is building his house, but as to the exact spot . . ." I let it trail off. "Why?"

"I, for one, would like to see that broken rein." David's jaw was set with determination.

"So would I," Hunter agreed. "Can you tell us anything about the spot, Faith?"

I closed my eyes and tried to remember, but the images were a bit blurry. "I was pretty busy with Savannah," I murmured. "And there really was nothing to set the area apart." I gave them another smile. "Just look for a large clump of cane grass with a person-size depression in it."

Hunter came over to touch the scratch on my cheek with gentle fingers. "I admire your spirit, Faith, but I wish you could have been spared this. If I discover that someone was out there stalking you . . ." His eyes narrowed and I shuddered away from the fury that blazed in his face.

"Shall we go see what we can find?" David asked, breaking the spell of the moment. His tone was polite, but I could sense his disapproval. I only hoped that his working relationship with Hunter would keep him from expressing that disapproval to Hunter when they were alone.

"Promise you will rest while we are gone?" Hunter's grin set my pulse to racing and when his gaze rested on my lips, I could almost feel his kiss. The man had the most disturbing effect on me.

"That is one promise I will find easy to make," I assured them both, thinking fondly of my soft bed. Being up was a lot less pleasant than I had imagined. "Maybe I will do some reading."

"Good plan." David hustled Hunter toward the door.

"Please come back and tell me if you find anything," I called after them. If there was someone out there who wished me ill, I needed to know.

The rest of the day inched by. Sarah visited for a while, but mostly I dozed or read, seeking escape in a volume of poetry Sarah had brought up from the library. Unfortunately, lilting phrases about larks and flowers and sunny skies did not quite banish the shadows that creaked and rustled in the corners of my mind. No matter what I had told David, I had a sick feeling that there had been someone or something out there.

Though I needed Rose's sturdy arm to lean on as I went slowly down the stairs, I was glad I had refused Sarah's offer of a tray in my room for the evening meal. I wanted no more of my own company; I needed diversion. Besides, neither David nor Hunter had come by to report on their explorations and I wanted to know what they had found.

Though my high-neck, long-sleeve dress covered the bruises on my arms and body, I was deeply conscious of everyone as I settled myself at the table. David and Hunter both greeted me warmly, but nothing was said of their afternoon activities. For a moment I considered asking if they had found anything, then I realized that they were, as always, protecting Sarah from the unpleasant facts about what had happened to me.

Resentment swelled inside me, then slowly abated as Sarah and Hunter took up a cheerful banter that quickly included both David and me in the teasing. Maybe they were right not to involve her, I could not be sure of anything until I knew what they had found. If the rein had been worn or poorly made . . . I pushed all thoughts of yesterday from my mind and concentrated on Sarah's plans for plantings in the next area of the garden.

By the time the dessert was cleared away, I felt better than I had since my fall. Hunter's high-spirited teasing had made this seem like any other evening and I needed the escape from my fears and doubts. As I struggled to my feet, however, David came quickly to my side. "May I help you to your room, Sis?"

"Are you not going to spend some time on the veranda?" I asked, unwilling to have the evening end even though I sensed that David wanted to talk to me, probably about whatever they had found in their search.

"You are not too tired, Faith?" Hunter came to my side at once.

"I am feeling much better." Not exactly true where my battered body was concerned, but my spirits improved mightily just being around Hunter. "I think I would enjoy watching the moon rise."

"Then I shall be pleased to help you." Hunter swept me into his arms before I realized what he was about. "I

189

will need you to open the door for me, David," he ordered as he carried me out of the dining room.

"I could have walked," I murmured, hoping that he would not feel the excited pounding of my heart when he held me so close.

"But this is so much more fun," he whispered, his warm breath sending shivers along my spine and at the same time creating a pulsing warmth within me. "I want you to conserve your strength, Faith," he continued in a louder voice. "Sarah will be needing your help after we sail and a fall like you took can have a debilitating effect if you try to do too much too soon."

"Listen to Hunter, he probably took more bad falls from horses than all of us put together." Sarah's giggle followed us out into the warm, flower-scented night air. "He always insisted on riding beasts that misliked the saddle."

"We usually managed to come to an understanding." Hunter's chuckle rumbled deliciously beneath my fingers as they rested on his broad chest. "Where would you like to sit, Faith?"

"How about the settee, Faith?" Sarah suggested. "That way you can sit up or even recline, if it is more comfortable."

Since I was given no say in the matter, I was delighted to find myself resting comfortably on the settee with Hunter's arm still around me and my head and shoulders cradled against his chest. At Sarah's suggestion, she and David drew chairs up so that I could see all of them without moving. David glowered, but offered no complaints.

The light-hearted conversation continued and for a time, I did my best to keep up with Sarah and Hunter; but before long, I found my spirits drooping as my aches and pains once again asserted themselves. Though I loved every moment of being so close to Hunter, even the warmth of his body could not erase the stiffness nor soothe the throbbing.

"I think perhaps I should be retiring, Sarah," I began when the conversation slowed a little. It was a painful idea, when I thought of ascending the endless stairway to my rooms. "If you could summon Rose to help me . . ."

"Now why would you need Rose's help?" Hunter chuckled as he eased away from me and got to his feet. "Were you not telling me before how quickly you recovered when your pony threw you over a fence instead of jumping it?"

I winced at the memory. "I was much younger then."

"Well, ancient one, I suppose it is only fitting that I see to your safe trip up to your rooms." Hunter slipped his arms around me and lifted me in his embrace once again.

"I could carry Faith up," David protested.

"Next time," Hunter told him, moving toward the door, which Sarah already held open for him. "Since I chose the horse that caused this accident, I feel an obligation to aid in any way I can."

Something about Hunter's tone made me look into his eyes. A thrill of excitement coursed through me as he winked at me before crossing the hall and starting up the stairs. I surrendered happily to the magic of being close to him, thinking how wonderfully romantic it would have been if my disapproving brother had not followed us, glowering.

The moment Hunter laid me on the loveseat, David said, "I shall be happy to wait here for Rose, so that you can go back to Sarah, Hunter."

"Take good care of her." Hunter's fingers trailed across my cheek for a moment, then he sighed as though loath to leave. "See you in the morning, Faith."

David waited until the door closed behind Hunter, then he sank down on the chair opposite me. I lifted a hand before he could speak. "If you plan to lecture me on my behavior, I am much too weary, David. All I want to know is whether or not you found the broken rein."

For a moment uncharacteristic anger flared in his

eyes, then it faded and he leaned back with a sigh. "We found both the place where you jumped off the horse and the spot where Savannah fell. It was pretty easy to backtrack the horse since Hunter saw her come out of the brush."

"Then you found the rein." I sat forward, forgetting to be careful and nearly screamed. It was several minutes before I could catch my breath enough to ask, "Where was it? Was it broken or had it somehow come unfastened from the bit?"

"We never found it. Are you sure you dropped it where you fell, Faith?"

"Of course. I had it in my hand when I jumped and it was gone when I tried to stand up." That much I did remember, though other details of those moments were less clear. "Are you sure you were looking at the right clump of cane grass?"

"We found this there." David pulled a small scrap of fabric from his pocket and handed it to me. "It was snagged on a thorny branch you must have landed on."

"Then the rein has to have been there."

David shook his head. "We looked everywhere, Faith. I doubt there is a leaf or blossom that we missed. The rein seems to have vanished."

"But that is not possible unless . . ." I stopped, not wanting to go on.

"Unless there really was someone there." David finished for me, his gaze relentless. "Are you sure you want to stay on this island? I could book passage for you on the next inter-island ferry. Aunt Minerva and Uncle Edward would be pleased to have you back, you know that."

"I am staying here." Disturbed and frightened or not, I refused to leave Dark Thunder. "I want to know exactly what happened out there, David, and I cannot find out if I leave."

"Then you do believe something happened?"

"Savannah was frightened by noises in the brush

behind us, but that could have been wild chickens or one of the barn cats stalking them. The rein broke when I tried to stop her from bolting. When I realized I had no control of the mare, I jumped off and hit my head. Perhaps I threw the rein as I fell. Did you look in the trees or farther away from the cane grass?"

"Faith, this is . . ." David stopped as Rose tapped on the door, then entered without waiting for an invitation.

"Miss Sarah bade me come and take care of you now that she be in her room with Miss Penny," Rose explained. "You must be most weary, Miss Faith. Going downstairs be too much for you so soon after such a fall."

David rose immediately, looking frustrated, but accepting Rose's assessment of my condition. "We will talk further tomorrow, Sis," he told me before he bent to kiss my cheek. "Rose is right, you do need your rest now."

I sighed and yawned, then allowed Rose to assist me to my feet. My spirit might be willing to stay up, but my body was ready to surrender. I had no desire to consider the implications of what David had just told me, at least not until tomorrow; right now I wanted to think about the joy of being in Hunter's arms. I wanted dreams of him, not nightmares of bobbing lights and invisible stalkers.

Once Rose left, I settled back against my pillows and closed my eyes, grateful that I had no worries about Penny, who had spent last night with Sarah and would continue sleeping there until I recovered enough to care for her again. It was pleasant to just drift on the edge of sleep, to imagine what it could be like if Hunter continued his tender care and . . . I slipped into dreams where I was free to enjoy Hunter's kisses and caresses without the doubts and fears David fostered in my mind.

Something woke me—a sound or perhaps something disturbing from my dream world. I sat up, heart pounding, listening for the sound of silver bells; then I remembered that Penny was not next door. The connecting door between my bedroom and hers stood open and through it I could see the spill of light from her window. Dawn was very near.

I got up slowly and was relieved to discover that I felt much better. It would be several days before I could move without reminders of my fall, but the worst was obviously over. I limped to my window and parted the curtains to look out. The sentinel palm drew my eyes and my thoughts. What if there was something or someone out there?

Hunter and David would be leaving soon for their rendezvous with Papa and Harlan might not be back before they had to sail. What would happen to us then? Sarah knew nothing of the bobbing lights or the sinister sounds I had heard before Savannah became unruly. Were we wrong to protect her? What if our protection placed her in danger?

I watched as the sun rose and bathed the pleasant vista in early sunlight. I looked beyond the wooded area to where the bluff rose, wondering what kind of house would stand there and who would share it with Hunter. If only it could be me. I was shocked at how deeply I wanted it to be me.

But how did he feel? Last night's actions seemed to say that he still cared for me, but how could I be sure? Hunter Latimer was no doting swain courting me with kisses and proposals the way Tommy had.

Tommy. I swallowed a sigh, thinking of the letter I had proposed to send to Papa. Now it seemed terribly cruel to even think of breaking the betrothal contract when I could not be sure that Tommy still lived; yet what else could I do? I wanted to be free so that Hunter . . .

It was back to that, back to my need to know what Hunter felt for me, what his intentions were. If he wanted only kisses and stolen moments, I needed to know it. If he was holding back declaring his true feelings only because I had asked him to, then I would send the letter to Papa, no matter how cruel it seemed. But how could I find out?

My only hope was to do what I had set out to do yesterday. I had to talk to him alone. The question was when and the answer was simple—as soon as possible. Gritting my teeth against the pain of my stiff muscles, I set about getting dressed for the day. Hunter was an early riser, so perhaps I could meet him in the dining room before David or Sarah came down.

As I pinned up my hair, I heard the sound of Penny's giggle coming from the playroom and felt a pang of guilt. Sarah was unused to dealing with her daughter so early in the day. I could only hope that she had chosen to go back to bed once Dorry took charge of Penny. There was no way I could talk to Hunter if Sarah was about.

I left my rooms without seeing Penny and made my way along the hall toward the front staircase. I paused at the top, suddenly curious to know if Sarah was up. It would take only a moment to listen at her outer door. If Sarah was not singing to herself, it was likely that she had gone back to sleep.

As I neared the door, I heard the soft rumble of a male voice inside. Had Harlan come back? Sarah had said nothing about expecting him to return so soon, but then trading could be an uncertain occupation so . . .

The door knob rattled and I stepped back quickly, ducking into the shadowy alcove opposite the door. I had no desire to encounter Harlan, since I was sure he would have questions about my accident. As the door opened, I heard a muffled giggle, then Sarah stepped out clad only in her nightdress, a shawl thrown about her shoulders, her thick golden hair spilling over it.

"You are wicked, Hunter," she murmured, standing on tiptoe to touch her lips to his beard-stubbled cheek. "You had best get back to your room before the servants are about or we will both be answering hard questions."

Hunter chuckled. "You think about what I said,

Sarah. This time I am serious." Tears filled my eyes as I watched him pad barefoot down the long hall to the guest room that he had taken as his own. The door of the master suite closed, but I could not move for my heart had truly broken and all my dreams lay shattered around me.

Chapter 13

Hunter and Sarah? My heart rebelled at the implications of what I had seen. There had to be another explanation. An emergency that had made her summon him for help and . . . And ended with her giggling and saying he was wicked? Sure, that was a great explanation. The pain within me deepened.

Had he spent the night with her? Held her close, made love to her in the very bed she usually shared with Harlan? The images that filled my mind made my stomach twist and for a moment I feared I would be sick right in the hall. Then I remembered that Penny was to have spent last night with Sarah.

Had Sarah left her innocent daughter sleeping in the great carved bed and met with her lover in the suite's elegant sitting room? More pictures haunted me as anger dried my tears before they could spill down my cheeks. Why had I not listened to everyone who had told me about Hunter's passion for Sarah? Why had I ignored my own good counsel and succumbed to the magic of his kisses?

Furious at myself, at Hunter, and at the woman I had considered my dearest friend, I hesitated at the top of the stairs, not sure what to do. There was no way I could sit at the same table with either of them, at least not now. Nor was I prepared to face David and his too-seeing gaze.

In the distance, I heard the bright sound of Penny's laughter and followed it, seeking escape. I had come to Dark Thunder to care for her; this seemed a good time to get back to work. As long as I kept busy with her, I could avoid thinking about what I had just seen. Sure, I could.

By the time I took my midday meal in the nursery area with Dorry, H.J., and Penny, I had devised a dozen innocent reasons for Hunter's early-morning visit to Sarah's rooms. I only wished that I could fully believe them, because my heart ached worse than any bruise and I knew that when I saw Hunter again, it would feel even worse. How could I have been so foolish as to fall in love with a man who could not return my feelings in any but the most casual fashion?

"Faith, how are you feeling?" Sarah came into the nursery, smiling brightly, her gray eyes sparkling with good spirits. The very picture of a happy, satisfied woman. All my good excuses faded. Hunter had made her happy and in that moment I hated her.

"I am able to care for Penny now," I replied, realizing that her smile had changed to a frown as she awaited my reply. I could not bring myself to meet her gaze even though it was she, not I, who should be ashamed. My knowledge made me feel guilty of their ugly secret.

"You do not look well, Faith." Sarah came over to touch my forehead. "Are you sure you have not contracted a fever? Perhaps you tried to do too much yesterday. Rose and I can watch after Penny if you would be more comfortable in your bed."

I gritted my teeth to keep from flinching from the cool touch of her fingers. I had no need for her kindness, not when she had stolen . . . I forced the thought away, reminding myself coldly that Sarah had known Hunter first and that she probably had no knowledge of his romantic behavior toward me.

198

"I am a bit tired," I murmured, pushing away my nearly untouched plate of food. "Perhaps I shall nap when Penny does. What do you think, Penny?" I focused on the child so that I would not have to look at Sarah.

"Is that why you have had your meals brought up here?" Sarah settled herself on one of the low chairs. "We missed you this morning and now it appears that I shall have to dine alone since neither Hunter nor David will be returning for the midday meal."

"We." The word grated along my nerves. She and Hunter? But would they have even noticed my absence? Only if David joined them, I decided bitterly. "The stairs make it difficult." Now why had I said that when it made me remember the strength of Hunter's arms as he had carried me up to my room last night?

"Hunter would have been delighted to offer you help this morning," Sarah teased, her giggle sounding so innocent I almost believed that I had misunderstood what I had seen—almost, but not quite. "If you are still feeling too stiff to come down when you awake this afternoon, I am sure he will oblige. We cannot spare you from the evening meal."

"David can help me." I tried to smile as I spoke, but from the tiny frown on Sarah's face, I knew that I had not managed to disguise my feelings very well. Still, she remained with us at the table, talking to Dorry and the children as they finished their meal.

Though I had no desire to sleep, I did lie down after I put Penny to bed for her nap. Sarah's visit to the nursery had made it clear that I needed to do some thinking about my feelings toward her and toward Hunter. No matter how much I tried to convince myself otherwise, what I had seen this morning changed everything. The question was, could I continue to live here feeling as I did?

Unfortunately, I soon realized that I had a great many more questions than answers about what had happened this morning; the most important being: What if I was wrong in my suspicions? What if there was an innocent explanation for Hunter being in her room while Sarah was still in her nightclothes? I cursed the fact that I had no right to ask either of them for an explanation. Too late I realized that it would have been simpler if they had seen me, because then I could have read their guilt or innocence in their faces.

So where did that leave me? Confused and unhappy, that much was sure; but how could I change that? One fact was very clear, hiding up here with Penny was not going to help me find the answer. I had to know what Hunter felt for me and for Sarah and the only way to find out was to spend time with them.

That decided, I finally closed my eyes and slept, not waking until the tinkling of bells announced that Penny was moving about. When I sat up, she was standing beside my bed. "I got lonely, Miss Faith. Could you please tell me more about Princess Penelope's 'ventures? Like where did Sparkle go to hide when the evil king tried to tie the golden rope around his curly horns?"

Guilt swept over me as I looked into her big blue eyes. "My goodness, you are right, Penny, we have neglected the Princess's adventures. If you will climb up here beside me, perhaps we can find out what happened next." I spoke easily, but my mind was reeling as I tried to remember where I had left off with my story-telling. My own adventures had commanded far too much of my attention the past few days.

By the time I had extricated the magical goat from the evil king and reunited him with his mistress, Penny was giggling and I felt a little better. Fairy tales had a wonderful way of working out so everyone lived happily ever after; I only wished I could do as well with my life. But fairy tales depended only on the teller's imagination, while my life seemed to be ruled by people and emotions over which I had no control. A very sobering thought.

I felt a chill of apprehension when someone tapped on my door just as I finished dressing for the evening meal. What if it was Hunter? I could not even call out, for my tongue seemed paralyzed. When I opened the door and found David standing on the other side, I was caught between relief and disappointment and so could hardly manage the words to greet him.

"Are you feeling all right, Faith?" His response to my confusion echoed Sarah's earlier concern. "If you are truly not up to taking the meal with us, I am sure Sarah would understand."

For a moment I wanted to accept the excuse to hide here in the safety of my room, but I could not. Hiding from Hunter would tell me nothing and not knowing was intolerable. "I am perfectly all right, David. I was just hurrying to get ready." I brushed invisible lint from the skirt of my dark blue dress and adjusted the large blue and white lace collar I had used to brighten it.

"Then you are feeling better?" He did not sound convinced.

"Much, thank you. And how did you spend your day? Did you go look again for the broken rein?" I welcomed his strong arm as we headed down the hall toward the stairway. Walking was no longer difficult for me, but I had not yet tried the stairs today.

"Hunter and I scoured the area, Faith. It simply is not there."

I nodded, suddenly wishing that I had not asked. If the rein was gone, someone or something had taken it—there was no other explanation. But why? And who? I shivered as I pictured myself lying unconscious in the clump of cane grass while a shadowy form . . .

"Faith?" David's worried tone snapped me back to the present and I realized we were at the top of the stairs. "Are you sure you can walk down? If you are stiffer today than you were yesterday, I can carry you, you know."

201

"Nonsense." I held onto the ornately carved banister with one hand and gripped his arm with the other. The first step was the worst, after that it was much easier than it had been last night when Rose had helped me. I would probably even be able to climb back up them on my own; which was just as well, since I had no intention of allowing Hunter to carry me to my room again. Even if he wanted to.

"Well, it is about time you came down to join us," Hunter greeted me from the door of the parlor, his grin caressing me like a hot August breeze. "I was about to come up and see if you needed a pair of strong arms."

"We were worried about you, Faith," Sarah agreed, coming over to give me a very gentle hug. "Your nap this afternoon seems to have helped, though, you look much more like yourself."

"I am feeling much better," I assured them both, uncomfortable at being the center of attention. This was not going as I had planned; I wanted to be an observer, to see how they looked at each other, how they . . . The hot stab of jealousy made me wince and for once I was grateful for all my bruises; at least I had no need to explain my pain.

It proved to be a very long and quite unproductive evening for me. Though I mentioned Penny's staying with Sarah several times, neither Sarah nor Hunter shied away from the subject. In fact, Sarah said that she worried about Penny's sleepwalking only because she slept so soundly herself and feared she might not hear the bells.

Hunter, too, seemed quite casual as we discussed his niece. Could they be so deeply enmeshed in their sordid affair that they felt no guilt? I found that hard to believe, but I was no longer sure I could trust my traitorous heart since I knew a single smoldering glance from Hunter could turn my mind to jelly.

I could scarcely swallow my food for worrying that

Hunter would find a way to sit next to me on the dark veranda. I knew I could never concentrate on my suspicions if he so much as held my hand. Luckily, an evening thunderstorm kept us inside and David managed to sit beside me on the sofa in the parlor.

Not that being physically separated from Hunter by a few feet truly helped. Whenever our eyes met, I felt the heat flare inside me and my heart ached in a strangely delicious way. Though it made no sense, I longed to be in his arms, to have him hold me tight and tell me that I was the only one he cared for. The most disturbing moments came when I decided that I had had enough of the exquisite pain of being near him.

Hunter got to his feet immediately. "I shall be happy to see you safely to your room," he announced. "Since you bravely walked downstairs to be with us, it is only fair that you ride back up."

"Nonsense, I can walk," I gasped, trying to move quickly to evade his arms. "I . . ." A muscle spasm in my back stopped my words and I might have fallen back on the sofa if Hunter had not caught me once again in his embrace.

"Please allow me this pleasure, Faith," he whispered, his lips touching my ear so that even David could not hear him. Shivers of desire coursed through me.

"Look, Hunter, I can help my sister to her room." David's protest was strong, but too late.

"You can go up the stairs ahead of us and open her door." Hunter's arms tightened just a little. "I want to make sure that Faith does no more harm to herself. We shall have to sail no later than day after tomorrow if we are to be sure to make the rendezvous point at the right time."

"So soon?" I made no effort to hide my sadness at his words. I had been aware that the sailing date would be soon, because I knew from David's conversation that Papa could promise to have a full load of cotton waiting at the hidden dock for only a limited time without risking discovery by the blockaders.

"I am afraid so." He brushed a kiss on my forehead as he carried me out of the parlor. "And I want you able to go up and down these stairs under your own power before we leave."

"How can I practice, if you insist on carrying me?" Somehow my arms seemed to have found their way around his neck and I was wonderfully conscious of the pounding of his heart so close to mine.

"How can I let you struggle when this is so much nicer?" His eyes sparkled wickedly and his lips were so close I had but to lift my head and . . .

As we reached the top of the stairs, I forced myself to look beyond him to the door where I had seen him at dawn. I had to remember that he had been with Sarah, that she had kissed his cheek and called him wicked.

"Faith, are you all right? Are you in pain? Does my holding you this way hurt you, love?" He stopped, a frown furrowing his tanned forehead as the laughter left his eyes.

"Perhaps if you set me down." I had to force the words past the lump in my throat. I had no desire to leave his arms, to ever let him go and yet . . . Even before my feet touched the floor, I realized a terrible truth. No matter what I had seen, no matter how little I trusted him; if I was near Hunter, I would never be able to resist him.

"Are you sure you can walk?" Hunter kept his arm around me and the warmth of it taunted me like an accusation. What kind of person was I to love a man who would betray his own brother?

"I am fine, truly," I assured him, carefully not looking up into his eyes. If I saw concern in them or the desire that had sparkled there earlier, I knew I would surrender to my longing. "It was just a muscle cramp."

"Faith, is something wrong?" David came back down the hall from my room and took my arm, firmly easing me away from Hunter. "Would you like me to see you to your room?"

"Please." I managed to thank Hunter for his efforts, then leaned on David's arm as he led me down the hall. It took all my self-control not to look back to see if Hunter was watching us.

David said nothing until we were both in my sitting room and the door was closed, then he came to stand in front of me, frowning. "I want to know what is going on between you and Hunter, Faith."

"What do you mean?" I could not meet his gaze.

"Whenever you are near Hunter . . . He touches you so easily and you . . . I can see that you like his touch, Sis." The pain in his voice forced me to look into his eyes. His anger had faded, leaving confusion behind and he suddenly looked younger than his eighteen years. "Do you love him, Faith?"

"I am trying not to." Since he cared so much, I felt I owed him honesty.

"And what does he feel for you?"

I shrugged, wishing that I knew the answer to his question. "He knows that I am betrothed to Tommy, so honor dictates that we must be only friends."

"And is he content with that?" David moved restlessly about the room, obviously uncomfortable with the questions he felt he had to ask.

"Not completely."

"Does he . . . does he try to take advantage of your being here in his brother's house, Faith? If he has taken liberties, I will . . ." David clenched his fists, his grim expression telling me that he would do battle to protect my honor.

"Hunter is a gentleman." My heart ached as a little voice inside me added: Except where his brother's wife is concerned. At least I spoke the truth so far as I was involved, for Hunter had taken nothing from me that was not freely offered—that was the problem.

"You are troubled, Faith, what is it?" David put his arm around my shoulders.

The gentleness in his voice was too much for me. The tears I had been denying all day suddenly spilled over. "It is nothing," I wailed against David's strong shoulder. "I am just sore and frightened and confused and . . ." Desperation overwhelmed me. "Oh, David, can I not go with you when you sail? If I could just talk to Papa, I am sure that . . ."

"What?" He let me go so abruptly I would have fallen had I not caught hold of the back of the loveseat. "Are you mad, Faith? Papa would skin me alive if I brought you back to the Charleston area now. He sent you away so you would be safe."

"But just for a visit? We could talk while the ship was being unloaded and the cotton put aboard. You are going to be there and he sent you away, too." Though I knew not where the idea had come from, now that I had made the suggestion, it seemed like the perfect answer to my problem. Once I was with Papa, I was sure I could persuade him to let me return with him to Charleston. He probably even needed my help now.

"I am a grown man, Faith, and this is my war, too. If you do not wish to remain here, you should go back to Nassau. I am sure Sarah would understand if you explained about your feelings for Hunter. Or I could talk to her, if you . . ."

His words drove all other thoughts from my mind. No way could I allow him to speak to Sarah. If she knew of my feelings for Hunter—I could not bear to even think of such a thing. "No, no, I am just being foolish. I will be fine here with Sarah. You will be sailing in a few days and by the time you return, I will have my feelings under control. It is just the weakness from my fall and the shock of Sam Taylor's letter that has made me forget my resolve."

I held my breath, hoping that David was so uncomfortable with our conversation that he would ask me no more questions. I could feel his gaze on my face as I dried my tears with his handkerchief, but I had nothing more to say. Besides, I could be right, could I not? Maybe once Sarah and I were alone here, I would be able to forget my feelings for Hunter, then my suspicions about his relationship with Sarah would no longer matter to me. Of course and maybe I would wake up tomorrow morning and discover I had dreamed the whole thing.

"If you are sure you do not need my help." The relief in David's face would have been amusing if I had not been so desperately unhappy.

"I will manage, but I thank you for caring. I am positive everything will be much brighter in the morning." As it had been this morning? Bitter pain knifed through me again, but I kept my head up and refused to give in to it. All I wanted now was to be alone and I knew that David would not leave me if he sensed my suffering.

David started for the door, then paused and turned back. "There is one thing, Faith. You can rest easier about being here without us."

"What do you mean?"

"Hunter called together the villagers who work at the warehouse and told them that if anyone at Thunder House was harmed, they would all suffer."

"He accused them of scaring Savannah?" I was too shocked to hide my dismay.

"He said only that he expected them to protect all who lived in the house as they would protect their own families. He made it clear that their futures rested on their cooperating with Latimer Trading." David grinned. "If any of them were involved in the bobbing lights or had a part in what happened to you, they have to know that Hunter means business. He is not a man to be crossed casually. He has a reputation for being able to take care of what is his."

"What is his." The words echoed in my mind long after David was gone. Though I knew David had not meant that I belonged to Hunter, a part of me ached for just that eventuality. How could I be such a fool? How could I love a man I could not trust? The pain from my fall paled in contrast to the ache in my heart.

Once again I was glad that Sarah had insisted on keeping Penny with her for a few more nights. If I could find no solace in sleep tonight, I vowed to seek escape by drinking the soothing draught that Cook sent up each night. Luckily, I had no need of it, for I slept deeply and well in spite of all my doubts and fears about the future.

The next morning Sarah came by the nursery where I had again chosen to take my morning meal with Dorry and the children. "Would you like me to help you downstairs, Faith?" she asked, frowning. "The *Pearl* sails at dawn tomorrow, so you should spend as much time with David as you can."

"Tomorrow." The word chilled me in spite of the warm air that flowed through the open window.

"David seems so excited about seeing your father," Sarah continued, her gaze quizzical. "He mentioned that you had not yet given him the letter you were writing."

"I will finish it today." What else had he told her? I wondered, the possibilities chilling me further. If she had talked to him already, why had she not remained in the dining room and sent one of the servants to summon me? "And you are right, I should go down and spend time with David." No matter how I felt about avoiding Hunter, I did need to be with my brother. Also, once I saw David with Sarah I would know whether or not he had spoken to her about my feelings for Hunter.

"Tomorrow we shall be alone on this island again," Sarah observed sadly as she offered her arm for support as we started down the stairs. "At least until

208

Harlan returns."

"I hope that will be soon." I stole a glance at her. The longing in her face when she spoke of her husband seemed genuine. Once again I wondered if I could be wrong about what I had seen. I wanted desperately to believe that Sarah loved only her husband and that Hunter's heart could be mine; yet they were so close, so intimate with each other. Surely that kind of feeling came from much more than simple friendship.

"Hunter tells me that Harlan will be waiting here until the *Pearl* brings your brother back. Harlan wants David with him when he makes his run through the blockade. Your brother has really been a godsend, Faith. His knowledge of the Charleston area and the people there makes it much safer for both Harlan and Hunter."

"David knows the area well. He was forever sailing about with his friends." My lips felt stiff as the impact of her words sank into my mind. Hunter would be here while David was off with Harlan. A shiver stole down my spine as I realized just how vulnerable I would be without my brother's protection.

"Well, well, so you were successful in getting Faith to join us, Sarah." Hunter rose to greet us. "How are you feeling this morning, Faith?"

His welcoming smile banished my shiver with a burst of heat that coursed through me. For a moment I could scarce draw a breath. How was it possible that this one man could so easily make everything and everyone else vanish? "I . . . I am much better today," I managed when I finally realized that David and Sarah were both looking at me as though I had lost my mind. An assessment I feared might not be far wrong.

David was at my side immediately and, once I tore my gaze from Hunter's mesmerizing eyes, I recovered enough of my senses to carry on a decent conversation over our morning meal. Still, I was conscious of every breath that Hunter took. I had barely enough self-control to resist watching his lips as he took a mouthful of food. I kept remembering how it felt to have his mouth on mine, his arms holding me.

I shook my head, wondering if I might have injured my brain when I fell from Savannah. Surely such thoughts were not normal. I had felt none of this madness when I accepted Tommy's proposal and his kisses, while pleasant, had never made me ache for more. I was relieved when Hunter announced that he and David would be at the harbor for most of the day making a final inspection of the ship and its cargo.

Maybe once he was gone, the madness would pass. I wanted to believe that as I tried to keep busy through the morning and into the long, sleepy afternoon; but deep inside, I knew I was only fooling myself. I had discovered the wondrous magic of Hunter's kisses before my fall and nothing that had happened since had dimmed my longing.

What was I to do? I had finished my letter to Papa asking him to free me from my betrothal, but beyond that I had no plans. I could make none until I knew whether or not Hunter was involved in a love affair with Sarah. If he was, I would have to flee this island to protect myself from what I felt for him. If he was not, then I would have to discover if he loved me or only wanted me for the moment.

But how could I learn the truth? I was still no closer to knowing the answer to that question when I changed into my favorite island print gown and dressed my hair in tawny ringlets to frame my face. I smiled as I pinned the cameo to a deep green ribbon that matched the background of my gown, then secured it around my neck. It gleamed against the pale skin exposed by the wide rounded neckline. No matter what, I wanted to look my best tonight—for Hunter.

Sarah, too, had dressed up and at her orders, the table was decorated as for a festive occasion. Though there were but the four of us, we all made an effort to keep the party spirit alive as we laughed and talked and sipped a bit more wine than usual. Near the end of the meal, Hunter and Sarah began to talk about the progress on Hunter's house and Sarah promised to have Higgins check on the rising foundations each time he drove into the village.

To my shame, I felt a stab of jealousy at the idea that Hunter had discussed the house with her and not me. Would it always be so, if I remained here? Would I resent every moment that Sarah and Hunter shared? Or was I right to be suspicious? What if Hunter meant for Sarah to share that house with him? I had been told that he and Harlan had been rivals as boys. Could that rivalry have continued so that now he was building a house that would be more to her taste than this one?

The thought sickened me so that I could no longer swallow and I pushed my dessert away. Luckily, no one seemed to notice my withdrawal from the conversation and the plates were soon whisked away.

"I feel the need of a stroll after such a feast," Sarah announced as we rose from the table. "David, would you lend me your arm and give me some advice about what I should plant on the west end of the garden."

"Have you . . ." I began, but Hunter took my arm before I could frame a question about the garden that would make me a part of what she was doing.

"I should like a few moments of your time, Faith," he said softly. "Perhaps we could stroll toward the bluffs, if you are well enough?"

Warning bells sounded in my mind, but the longing that swept over me at his touch silenced them. We had not been alone since my fall and I wanted some time with him. I desperately needed to know how he felt about me and this would be my last chance to find out before he sailed. "I am quite well, thank you, and I should enjoy a stroll this evening." I met his gaze without shame.

His smile warmed me to my toes and in that moment I

211

could not doubt his feelings for me. My heart thundered
in my ears so that I could scarcely hear Sarah and David
as they led the way out of the house into the sweet-
scented night. My shoes barely touched the shell paths as
we made our way through the gardens and into the
rougher land beyond.

"I have missed being alone with you, Faith," Hunter
said, stopping at last. We stood in the shadow of a
poinciana tree, the moonlit bluff before us, the roaring
thunder of the surf below filling the air.

I turned to look up at him, wanting to speak, but
unable to since my throat was too dry for any words to
come. We needed to talk, but as he drew me close, I lifted
my lips to welcome his kiss. I buried my fingers in the soft
black curls on the nape of his neck and lost myself in the
magic.

Time stood still as the thundering desire in my blood
matched the pounding of the waves and I felt only the
touch of Hunter's hard body against mine as he explored
my mouth with a thoroughness that drove me to the
brink of madness. It was as though he kissed the very
essence of me and made me his. I wanted it to go on
forever. The night seemed colder when he slowly lifted
his lips from mine.

"You love me as much as I love you, Faith." His voice
was hoarse. "You cannot deny it when you answer my
kiss so passionately. We belong together."

"My betrothal . . ."

"You will never belong to another man. I want you,
Faith. We will find a way to be together." He tugged out
the pins in my hair spilling it over my shoulders, then
stroked it as he caught my lips again, stealing my breath
and my will to resist him.

I clung to him, so lost in the wild new sensations that
rippled through my body that it was several minutes
before I felt his fingers stroking my breast through the
bodice of my gown. Startled by the thrill that quivered

within me, I pulled away, frightened by my own desperate hunger for his touch. "We must go back," I gasped.

Hunter groaned, then slowly released his embrace. "You are a fever in my blood, Faith. I meant only to tell you how I felt, but the moment I touch you . . ."

"Hunter? Faith, are you out here?" David's and Sarah's voices broke through the fragile magic of the moment, destroying our private world.

Hunter sighed, then called, "We are over here. We were just enjoying the breeze and watching the moonlight on the water." Within a heartbeat he was talking calmly to them about tomorrow's journey and as we strolled back toward the house, it was as though the madness between us had never happened.

Chapter 14

I did my best to repin my hair as we walked through the darkness to the house, but there was no way I could calmly chat with Sarah and David as if nothing had happened. Had the wild passion that swept through me left Hunter so untouched? Did his whispered words of love mean so little to him that he could act as though they had never been said?

When we reached the house, Hunter suggested that we all sit on the veranda for a while, but I was far too distraught. If I had to sit without touching him, I knew I would never be able to keep back my tears and if he should touch me . . . My skin quivered at the memory of his caresses.

"I think perhaps I shall just go up to bed," I murmured, aware that my voice sounded strange. "The walk was lovely, but I am more tired than I realized."

"I shall see you to your room, Faith," David said, moving quickly between Hunter and me to forestall any repetition of Hunter's carrying me to my room.

"That will not be necessary, David. Let us just say our farewell now. I shall miss you so." I choked back a sob. "I want you to stay and enjoy the evening with the others. I just cannot bear . . ." I hurried through the open door.

"Are you all right, Faith?" Hunter pushed past David and followed me. When I turned and met his gaze, I could see the questions in his eyes.

"I am just tired, Hunter. You stay and enjoy the breeze and the moonlight. It is best that I say good night and Godspeed now, since I know you plan to leave before dawn."

Hunter looked as though he might protest, but in the end he simply reached out a hand to touch my cheek. "Take care of yourself while we are gone, Faith. We shall have much to talk about when I return."

"I am sure you will," Sarah murmured, frowning as she took Hunter's arm. "Rest well, Faith, and if you need anything, I am sure Rose would be pleased to help you."

I muttered a few polite phrases, then fled up the stairs, hardly noticing the twinges of pain. The numbness of my body lasted until my door was closed and locked and I was safe in my room.

Safe? I looked around, seeing Hunter everywhere. But this time the images did not stop with memories. Instead of visualizing Hunter sitting in the chair or moving about the small room, I pictured him taking me in his arms and carrying me through the door to my bedroom. My whole body throbbed as I imagined Hunter making love to me.

Shattered, I sank down on the loveseat. What was I going to do? What was going to happen to me once Hunter returned and David sailed off with Harlan? Tonight's walk had made one thing very clear. If Hunter wanted to make love to me, I was too much in love to resist him.

There was no way I could stay here, not wanting Hunter as I did. If I remained near him, I was in deadly danger of becoming a woman of easy virtue, only too willing to give myself to Hunter without knowing whether his love was true or not. Without knowing if his heart could ever belong to me.

But where could I go? Back to Nassau and Aunt Minerva's disapproval of everything I did or said? In my heart I knew that would not be far enough, for Hunter would come to Nassau with each cargo of cotton and if he

215

was in the city, I would want to be with him.

My own scandalous longing frightened me. Where was the proper young lady my parents had raised? How could I have changed so much? How could I give my heart to a man who might even now be carrying on with his brother's wife? And why, having remembered yesterday morning, did I still want so desperately to be here when Hunter returned from Charleston?

I paced my sitting room, heart pounding. If only David had agreed to allow me to go with them to meet Papa. I needed Papa's wise counsel more now than I ever had. If I could just talk with him and . . . I stopped midstride, wincing as my already tired muscles protested. A desperate plan began to form in my mind.

David had said no, but that was only because he wanted to protect me. If I had been able to tell him what was happening between Hunter and me, I was sure he would realize that I had no choice. Since I dared not tell him because of what he might do to Hunter in a misguided effort to protect me, I would have to make the decision for myself.

I closed my eyes, picturing myself on the *Pearl* with Hunter, the long nights, the shadowy deck . . . I forced those thoughts away. David would be on the ship, too, so I would simply have to stay with him and protect my wayward heart from the temptation. Besides, the voyage would not be long and Hunter would be busy evading the blockading ships.

Once I was back with Papa, I could explain everything to him and he would realize that I needed to stay with him. I did my best to ignore the throb of pain that came when I considered watching Hunter and David sail away, while I remained with Papa. I would worry about that later; right now, I had plans to make.

My first problem was to get aboard the *Pearl* and hide myself. If Hunter or David found me before we were safely on our way, I had no doubt I would be put ashore. I got my small valise and carefully packed the bare

216

essentials that I would need for the journey. Since I would have to walk to the village carrying my belongings, there was no way I could take more. I was only grateful that Penny was still sleeping with Sarah, for I would never again leave her unprotected as I had the night David and I had pursued the bobbing lights.

The valise seemed light enough as I wrapped myself in a dark cloak and slipped from my room to the balcony. The light breeze brought the sound of voices from the veranda below, telling me that David, Hunter, and Sarah were still sitting at the front of the house. I tiptoed carefully toward the rear where the rough stairs led down to the newly cultivated area of vegetable garden.

I held my breath as I went down, expecting to hear a greeting from one of the servants at any moment, but my luck held. I was able to slip into the shadows and make my way carefully around the rear of the house to the west end and the stable area. From there, it was easy to reach the road without being seen.

I shifted the valise to my other hand as I started along the road. It seemed to be growing heavier all the time and I felt my now-familiar aches and pains as I walked. The distance to the village was not great, but with night darkness all around me, I began to think of all the frightening things that had happened on this island.

To battle my fears, I wondered what Sarah would think when she found the note I had left pinned to my pillow. Would she believe my statement that I had been overcome by loneliness for my father or would she suspect I had other reasons for leaving? And what would David say when he discovered what I had done? And Hunter . . . more than anyone, I wondered how Hunter would feel when I revealed my presence on the *Pearl.*

If I made it that far. I shifted my valise again and peered into the darkness. I heard the soft sound of a bell off to my left, which meant one of the villager's goats was grazing in the meadow there. How far from the village was

I? And what was I going to do once I reached it? I dared not march boldly down the street to the dock where the *Pearl* was tied up, yet there was no other way to get on board.

My steps grew slower as I tried to picture the village, the possible approaches to the dock. Was I making this long walk for nothing? And what if I encountered some of the surly villagers? I shivered remembering the rustling sounds I had heard before Savannah bolted. If someone truly wished me harm, I would be easy prey this night.

As if in answer to my thoughts, the wind began to sigh through the bushes that edged the road and when I looked up, I saw that clouds were riding over the stars. I began to move faster, sensing rain in the cooling air. I had no desire to get wet; but if it did rain, I might have a better chance of getting aboard the *Pearl* without being seen.

The night continued to darken around me and I was so intent on keeping my footing in the rutted roadway, I was well into the village before I realized it. Stunned, I stopped and looked around, half expecting to find the inhabitants watching me; but I could see no one. The houses were dark. In fact, there was not a lantern or candle to be seen anywhere I looked.

Swallowing my fear, I moved on, clutching the cloak around me against the growing force of the wind. If anyone was looking out, I doubted that they would be able to recognize me. I would just be another shadow, a part of this stormy night. Clinging to that thought, I headed through the heart of the village and down to the long dock.

The *Pearl* was there, all right. I stopped in the shadow of a wind-whipped tree and studied the sturdy dock. Several other boats bounced and tugged at their moorings as the waves responded to the storm's urging, but there seemed no one about. There were, likewise, no lights aboard the ship, so perhaps the crew was spending the night ashore.

A low rumble of thunder announced that the storm was getting closer. I took a firmer grip on my valise and headed out on the dock. The wind was stronger there, but I hardly noticed it tugging at me; I was too busy bracing myself for the challenge of a watchman or a sleepless sailor. I could scarcely believe my good fortune when I reached the *Pearl's* gangplank without being stopped.

This was it! I raced up the bouncing boards and half fell onto the deck, then scrambled into the deep shadows cast by a mound of deck cargo. I leaned against one of the boxes to catch my breath while I decided where I was going to hide. This was a part of the plan I had not had time to work out.

"Ye hear somethin', Ezra?" The voice seemed to come from right beside me and I could hardly keep back a scream.

"In this storm?" Another voice came from the other side of the cargo. "Likely us be hearin' plenty afore dawn."

The cargo shifted as the ship rolled and an oath sounded from close by. I tried to shrink deeper into the bales and boxes, sure that I would be discovered at any moment. As I did so, the boxes moved again creating an opening just big enough for me to slip through. I dived into the deeper darkness, praying that the whole mound would not come tumbling down on me.

"Ye reckon us better tie some canvas o'er this cargo?" Ezra asked.

"If'n us don't, Captain Hunter be tie'un our hides over it come mornin'," the other man replied. "Best be securin' it, too. Cargo be a shiftin' already and she could git rough if'n this squall be a biggun'."

Totally blind in the darkness, I squirmed through the narrow space until I was out of reach of the wind. Using my fingers, I located boxes and bales on all four sides, then settled myself and my valise in the middle. There was not a lot of room, but I could stretch my legs out if I sat upright, so it would be enough for now. I braced my back against one box and my feet against the other and waited as the cargo continued to move first one way, then another in response to the ship's motion.

Sounds and curses from outside my protective mound told me that the two men were having trouble with the canvas covering. Then I was nearly crushed as someone outside pushed on the boxes, trying to shove them together. Fortunately, I could lock my knees and keep my small space open. They apparently decided that the cargo was packed tight when the boxes refused to yield to their pushing and my sanctuary was secured with me inside. For better or worse, I had found my hiding place.

The storm grew steadily more violent, but the canvas-covered cargo protected me from the driving rain and when the thunder finally stopped, I must have fallen into an exhausted sleep. A familiar voice shouting commands woke me. Hunter was aboard and we were casting off for the voyage to Charleston.

Though very little light penetrated my hiding place, there was enough for me to realize just how precarious it was. I began to regret sleeping after the storm ended, for I should have used the dead of night to find my way to the hold and a more secure place to hide. Still, it could have been worse. By pushing and inching the bales apart, I was able to create a passage to the outer edge of the pile of cargo, which was nearly flush against the rail and out of sight of almost everyone on the ship.

Working to the edge in the other direction, I could see the deck from beneath the sheltering canvas. For a while I watched as Hunter, David, and the rest of the crew moved back and forth through my field of vision, then my weariness and hunger overcame me and I crept back to the center of the mound and curled myself into a ball, sure that I was too miserable to even sleep.

The hours dragged by as I dozed, sometimes dreaming of Hunter's exciting embrace, other times fantasizing about the meals at Thunder House that I had left untasted in my emotional turmoil. How I wished that I had been wise enough to slip into the kitchen for a few supplies before I ran away. How I longed to slip out from under the canvas to face Hunter with my love.

I must have slept at last, for the next time I opened my eyes the world was dark again. Aching in every bone and muscle, I edged out of my sanctuary and looked around. The deck appeared deserted, but I moved slowly, stealing from shadow to shadow as I headed toward the door that led to the cabins and the passage to the hold and the crew quarters. I had no idea how far we had come, but I had no desire to be caught and put ashore before we reached the Charleston area.

The scent of food rose through the passage, drawing me irresistibly toward the ship's galley. As I neared it, I paused, fearing that the rumbling inside me would be audible to anyone around. Holding my breath, I peered around the door frame. The galley was empty! Not taking time to think, I grabbed for the nearest loaf of bread, then picked up a bottle of wine and a wedge of cheese, before I fled back the way I had come.

By some miracle, I made it back to my cargo mound without dropping anything or being seen. I plunged under the protective canvas like a frightened mouse, wiggling between the boxes and bales until I was safely in the middle. I wolfed down the bread and cheese, then used my teeth to pull the cork from the wine bottle. I had been able to drink some rain water trapped in the canvas earlier, but the wine tasted wonderful. I finished the whole bottle before I curled up to sleep again.

Perhaps it was my overindulgence in the wine that eventually brought the dream. I was in the woods, prowling through thorny underbrush that tore at me like reaching fingers. Something was following me, I could hear the panting breath behind me, feel the hot air on my neck as I stumbled on.

The pirate lights were after me! They bobbed and danced first behind me, then in front of me. I was surrounded by them and they shone in my eyes so

221

brightly that I could not see who held them. But I could hear the evil, taunting laughter as the lights drew nearer and nearer and hands reached out of the blackness . . .

Screams echoed around me as I fought the clutching fingers, fought the . . . I opened my eyes and caught my breath, suddenly realizing that the screams were mine. For a moment I had no idea where I was, then memories rushed over me and I clapped a hand over my mouth to keep back a sob.

"What the hell was that?" Hunter's voice came from just beyond my cargo wall.

Answers came from several directions and in various tones, but no other voices that I recognized. Everyone seemed to have heard my cries, but no one knew exactly where they came from. I cowered against the boxes, hoping that they would decide it had been a seabird or even the wind.

"Bless me, but it be soundin' like a woman, Captain," a nearby voice said.

I winced, wishing the speaker into the deepest recesses of the hold. Why could he not have agreed with the man who had suggested that a wounded seagull might be trapped somewhere on board?

"A woman?" Hunter's voice was stern. "Are you telling me that someone brought a woman on board?"

"No, sir. Nobody be that kinda fool, Captain. Us'uns knows the rules."

Silence seemed to settle over the deck. I shifted, longing to crawl to one of my passages to see if they were looking this direction. As I straightened my cramped legs, my foot hit the wine bottle, which I had kept, hoping to be able to fill it with water the next time I slipped out of my hiding place. It rolled less than a foot, but the sound when it bumped into the wooden box was ominously loud in the quiet.

"Someone be in that cargo, sir." The same sailor spoke up again and I knew that there was no point in my hiding any longer.

Feeling doomed and at the same time wishing desperately that I could have time to wash my face and tidy my hair, I edged out through the small passage to the deck. I was shocked to discover that it was sunrise. Thanks to the wine, I had slept through my second night aboard.

"Faith?" The total shock on Hunter's face told me I looked even worse than I felt. "My God, how in the name of all that is holy . . ."

Shame and weakness hit me at the same moment, drying my mouth so that I could not speak and making me wish I had taken more time to think out this plan. He looked so strong and desirable, his midnight hair touched by the first rays of the sun, but there was no glowing love in his eyes as they raked over me. He looked furious and I quailed with the realization that he had every right to be angry.

My shock weakened my knees and I took a step back to lean against one of the bales as the horizon seemed to shift out of rhythm with the sea. "Hunter, I . . ." I closed my eyes, hoping that I would faint and be spared the agony of seeing disgust in his face, but I was not to be that lucky.

"Fetch David Richards," Hunter snarled to one of the crew members, then he caught my arms and jerked me upright so that our faces were only inches apart. "Does he know of this?"

"Of course not." His unwarranted attack on David forced me back to full consciousness. I lifted my head and met his gaze coldly, my weakness banished as I rallied to protect David. "He forbade me to make the voyage, but I must see my father."

"Faith?" The incredulity of David's voice as he crossed the deck to join us echoed Hunter's perfectly. There could be no doubt of his innocence. "What are you doing here?"

"I had to see Papa." Even as I repeated my reason, I had a strong suspicion that neither man was going to believe me. Again I wished for a maidenly swoon to escape their burning glares; unfortunately, the fresh morning breeze was making me feel physically better, not worse.

Hunter's fingers still bit into my arms and I could feel the tension of his body; I just could not be sure whether he wanted to hold me or strangle me. My answer came when he gave me a fierce shake, then released me and turned away. "Take her to your cabin, David. She can rest there while I decide what is to be done."

"Let me get my things," I said, dropping to the deck and ducking back beneath the canvas. At the moment, I craved escape more than having my valise and returning to my sanctuary offered both. I took as long as I dared, hoping to come up with some words that would ease the fury from both Hunter's and David's faces; but I was still uninspired as I crawled back out.

"You have been hiding in there since . . . since when?" Hunter looked even angrier, if that was possible.

"Since the night before you left."

"That was your reason for hurrying off to your room?" Several different expressions flickered across his face as I watched, but I could read none of them. Was he remembering our kisses on the bluffs above the sea or was he just disappointed as well as angry with me? Had he no conception of how he made me feel?

Anger welled up to fill the void despair had left within me. My being here was as much his fault as mine. If he had been a true gentleman . . . Memory of his kisses swept through me and I could no longer meet his gaze. Was it possible to hate a man and still love him or had I truly gone mad?

David's arm slipped around my shoulders as he took my valise and cloak from my nerveless fingers. "Come along, Faith," he murmured. "You look unwell."

I closed my eyes against the pain that seemed to be tearing me apart. I dared not let Hunter know how deeply he wounded me. If I wanted to survive this voyage, I

224

must learn to hide my feelings. "I am just hungry and thirsty. I forgot to bring any supplies with me."

David's arm tightened. "You took the food from the galley last night?"

I nodded, grateful for his support as we stepped into the shadowy passage. My head throbbed and I felt dizzy now that I was away from Hunter's commanding presence. Also, I was terribly thirsty and my stomach was growling again. I wondered how I could bear the scolding that I was sure David would give me the moment we were alone.

"I cannot believe you would do an insane thing like this, Faith." David's tone was less condemning than admiring. "You were always such a perfect lady."

Aware that there was no point in lying to David, I offered him a portion of the truth. "I . . . I just had to talk to Papa about resolving my betrothal to Tommy." It was a relief to be honest, even with a part of the story.

"I would have taken care of that for you." David opened a door and eased me into the tiny cabin where I had first met Miranda Green on my voyage to English Wells. "You stay here, I will get you food and coffee."

"And water to wash?" I had already spotted the tiny mirror fastened to the wall above the shelf that must serve as a wash stand in the cabin.

David nodded, then left me alone. I sank down on the room's single chair, too weary to even look at myself in the mirror. What was going to happen now? Would we turn back? Was Hunter angry enough at me to give up the rendezvous and perhaps put Papa in more danger? The possible consequences of my rash decision began to haunt me.

David brought food and water, then left immediately, promising to come and tell me what Hunter had decided as soon as he could. Though I had thought myself too miserable to eat, I devoured every scrap, washing it down with coffee so thick and bitter I would have normally refused it out of hand.

Once I finished the meal, I ventured to the mirror and nearly screamed. No wonder Hunter had looked so stunned. I was lucky he had realized that the slovenly creature in the mirror was I. Unwilling to undress or change until after I had a chance to talk to David, I washed the grime from my face and hands, then attacked my hair. I had just pinned it back when David returned with Hunter behind him.

I met Hunter's gaze, hoping to find some forgiveness or understanding in his eyes; but his face appeared to have been carved from stone. I could have been a stranger, the casual trollop of one of the crew, for all the warmth he directed my way.

"Are you going to take me back to Dark Thunder?" I asked, bracing myself for the worst.

"I only wish I could." Hunter's impartial tone matched his expression. "We are, however, too far away to return and still be able to make our rendezvous, so you will get your wish to meet with your father."

"Thank you." Relief left me breathless.

"The choice is not mine. It was made by circumstance. If there was a populated area nearby, I would be pleased to leave you there to await our return. Since there is not, I expect you to remain in this cabin unless you are in David's company. I will not have my crew upset any further by your presence on the ship. Is that clear?"

"Yes, sir." My eyes burned with unshed tears, so I kept my gaze on the floor until I heard the door slam. When I looked up, I saw that David had remained behind and he was grinning.

"I have never seen Hunter that angry before," he observed. "I really think he cares for you."

"I think he hates me."

"Maybe he just does not like surprises in his deck cargo." David moved about the cabin, gathering a few of his possessions. "Hunter has said I can bunk in his cabin, so you will have some privacy, but he is right about your staying out of sight. The crew is already blathering over

226

finding a stowaway."

"I did not come aboard to stroll on the deck." His cavalier attitude grated on my already ragged temper. My heart was breaking and he found it amusing.

"Why did you come, Faith?" David stopped in front of me, his eyes probing, his grin gone. "What happened on your walk with Hunter that provoked you into this sort of panic?"

A half-dozen excuses and evasions rose in my mind, but I knew that it was too late for them. "I realized that I love Hunter and I do not wish to remain on Dark Thunder while I am betrothed to Tommy, yet I have no desire to return to Nassau. I mean to stay in Charleston with Papa, David, and I would like your help in convincing him that it is the best place for me."

David just looked at me, his face unreadable. I felt a chill. Had I told him too much? Would he now turn on Hunter and force a battle that could cost him his position with Latimer Trading? I watched as he carefully set his belongings on the single bunk built into the side of the ship, then sat down beside them. I braced myself, not sure what to expect.

"Did he . . . Has he made the kind of advances that you cannot deny, Faith? If he has forced you in any way . . ." I could hear embarrassment along with the violence that was building inside him.

For just a heartbeat, my injured pride urged me to use David to force Hunter into a commitment; then reality intruded and I realized that no one could force Hunter to love me if his heart belonged to Sarah. All that would come from a confrontation between Hunter and David was more pain.

"Stop it, David." I took a stance between him and the door. "Hunter has done nothing to me. This is about what I feel and what I want to happen. My feelings are out of control, not his; that is why I must talk to Papa. He is the only one who can help me."

Much to my relief, the anger began to drain from

David's face. "What do you expect Papa to do?"

"Tell me what to do." It was the only answer I had.

"And that is why you chose to stowaway on the ship? It makes no sense to me, Faith. I just do not understand you." As he spoke, his confusion made David my dearly loved baby brother once again and I welcomed the change from the mature sailor he so often appeared to be. It was far easier to cross the tiny cabin and throw myself in the more familiar David's arms.

"I do not understand myself, either," I whispered. "That is why I need Papa."

David held me for a while, then he sighed. "I just hope that Papa is not as angry about your coming with us as Hunter is."

"So do I," I agreed prayerfully. "Believe me, so do I."

Chapter 15

I had plenty of time to worry during the rest of the voyage. My earlier fantasies of strolling on the moonlit deck with Hunter became a bitter mockery as the hours dragged by. My hope for forgiveness faded painfully as I waited in vain to see him. It became all too clear that Hunter Latimer wanted nothing more to do with me.

David brought me my meals and escorted me to the deck for exercise several times during the day. Times when Hunter was conspicuously absent from the area. Other than that, I was left very much alone to ponder my past sins and lack of future prospects. I began to wish I had never left Dark Thunder. At least there I had duties to attend to and friends to keep me company.

I was just finishing yet another evening meal when there was a tap on my door. "Come in, David," I called, grateful that Hunter could spare him to keep me company.

"It is I, Faith." Hunter stood in the open doorway, looking uncomfortable. "May I come in?"

For a moment time seemed to stand still, I could neither breathe nor speak; all my senses were captive to the wonder of just seeing him again. I had to swallow twice before I could make my tongue produce a sound. "Please do."

Hunter stepped inside, then just stood in the open

doorway. Silence filled the air between us, yet when I met his gaze, I read a longing in his face that matched my own. It took all my self-control to wait to hear what he had to say.

"I . . ." His voice sounded hoarse, unused, even though I had heard him bellowing orders from time to time. "I was wondering if I might escort you for your walk on the deck tonight, Faith."

"I would like that very much." Relief washed through me, followed by a warming tide of joy. I got to my feet, food forgotten.

"I did not mean to rush you away from your meal." His gaze moved from my face down over my wrinkled dress like a caress and every inch of my skin quivered at the memory of being pressed against him.

"I would rather walk with you." I had to be honest with him now, since I was sure that his visit meant that we would reach the rendezvous point tomorrow. I ached at the thought that this might be the last time I would be with him.

Hunter stepped aside, allowing me to lead the way to the deck. I glanced around, expecting to see David somewhere about, but as on other nights, there was no one visible. We could have been alone with the sea, the rising moon and the friendly stars. I trembled inside as he took my arm.

I held my breath as we made a circuit of the deck. Why did he not speak? Why had he brought me out here, if not to give us some time to discuss what had happened between us? I stole a glance at him, but his composed features were unreadable.

An uneasy feeling began to nibble at my joy. What if he was waiting for me to say something? I remembered his anger, his bitter words about putting me ashore on any inhabited island. Was he expecting an apology?

I stiffened for a moment, my pride crying out that he would have a long wait, then I remembered the shock and hurt I had seen in his face when I crawled out of the cargo

230

mound. Perhaps I did owe him at least an explanation; but how could I make him understand what I was doing without admitting to my love for him?

"Are you going to tell me why you suddenly had this violent need to talk to your father?" Hunter broke the silence.

All the excuses I had conjured up filled my mind, but I knew that Hunter would believe none of them. If this was to be our last night together, I owed him at least a part of the truth. "I want to stay with him, Hunter. I am sure that he could use my help in these troubled times and . . ."

"You what!" Hunter stopped and turned, grabbing both my arms, forcing me to face him. "Are you mad, Faith, or is this some kind of ploy?"

"Ploy?" Anger flooded through me. Did he really think I was playing games with him? "Do you find it strange that I should want to be with my father?" His fingers hurt my arms and the anger in his eyes frightened me. I had meant the words as an explanation, nothing more.

"I find it very odd that you should stowaway on my ship to go to him." His voice was low and hard, matching his expression.

"Yours was the only ship going to meet him." I tried to pull away, but I was no match for his strength.

"Why not ask for passage?"

"Would you have taken me?"

"Of course not. Your brother would never have allowed it. Charleston is no place for you, Faith. Your father will tell you that himself. He made the choice to send you away to safety, do you really think he will welcome you back to danger?"

"I have to talk to him." Traitorous tears filled my eyes and formed a lump in my throat that made speaking difficult. I knew if I stayed here with him much longer that I would not be able to keep from crying and I refused to do that. If Hunter could not understand why I had to

231

leave, my pride would not allow me to spell it out for him.

"Faith, if this has anything to do with what happened on the bluffs our last night on Dark Thunder . . ." His tone of exaggerated patience cut through me like a knife.

"You are hurting me, Hunter," I grated, trying again to pull free of his hands. "I would like to return to my cabin now. I do not need any more exercise."

"If you would give me a chance to explain, Faith. I never meant to frighten you. I know that you cannot . . . that you must wait until you can honorably break your betrothal. I assure you that I would never again . . ."

The words struck my heart with the force of blows as I relived those magical moments. I remembered only too well what it felt like to be in his arms, to want him to hold me forever. God help me, I still wanted his kisses! I fought his hold, desperate now to escape before I totally disgraced myself. "Let me go, Hunter, or I shall scream for David."

"Faith, for the love of . . ." Hunter held me one more moment, then abruptly, I was free. "Go then. I would never hold a woman against her will."

Even as I stumbled into the passageway to the cabin, a part of me was aware that his voice had been as full of pain as I felt. But it was too late. There was nothing I could say, nothing that he could tell me that would change anything. As a betrothed woman, I had no right to love Hunter and since I did, I could not trust myself to be near him.

I smiled bitterly as I closed the door behind me. So Hunter thought his passionate kisses had frightened me. How wrong he was. My passion scared me, his only excited me further. Which was why I had to get as far away from him as I could. I leaned against the door, wishing desperately that I had stayed on deck with Hunter.

"Just one more kiss," I whispered to the empty room, then swallowed a sob. With Hunter, I could never stop with one.

A tap on the door forced me to pull myself together. "Who is it?" I asked, sure I could not bear another confrontation with Hunter.

"Are you all right, Faith?" David sounded worried.

"Fine, just tired." I spoke through the door.

"Are you sure? Maybe we could talk for a while?" His tone was so full of caring it brought fresh tears to my eyes.

"Could we do it tomorrow?" I asked. "I really wanted to get some sleep."

"We will be at the rendezvous tomorrow." David could be as stubborn as a plantation mule.

"All the more reason I should get some rest." I swallowed an exasperated sigh. "I really am quite all right, David. I just did not want another argument with Hunter, so I came back to the cabin early."

"Well, if you are sure . . ."

I called what I hoped was a cheerful-sounding "good night," then listened, my ear against the door, until I heard his footsteps retreating. A moment later I heard Hunter's familiar tread approaching. I held my breath as he stopped outside my door, bracing myself for another battle.

The silence tore at me until I was shaking with tension, then I heard what sounded like a deep sigh from the other side of the door and his footsteps went away. Though I told myself that I was relieved that Hunter had given up, the cabin seemed large and empty and I was lonelier than I had ever been. I undressed and crawled into my bunk, but it was a long time before I slept.

David was flushed with excitement when he brought me a plate of food in the morning. "We are near the rendezvous," he said. "We slipped by a Yankee ship about midnight and now Hunter is using the morning mist to cover our approach to the dock."

"Will Papa be there?" My heart began to pound,

233

though I could not be sure whether I felt apprehension or anticipation. In spite of all my time alone on the voyage, I still had no idea how to explain my problem to Papa.

"We should know in about an hour, so be ready to go ashore if he is. We will be at the dock only long enough to unload our cargo and load the cotton. If a Yankee patrol should spot us while we are tied up . . ." He did not need to finish the warning.

"I will be ready." I took the plate, but my knotted stomach told me I would not be able to swallow a bite. While I waited for David to summon me, I packed my few belongings in my valise. I would need to take it ashore with me, since I had no intention of returning to the ship. My fingers shook as I pinned on the cameo that Hunter had given me. No way would I leave it behind. It meant more to me than anything I possessed. I was ready when David returned.

"Papa is on the dock." David took my hand, his expression solemn. "Hunter and I went ashore and I told him that you are on board, Faith. Papa and Hunter are discussing the cargo exchange now. When Hunter comes back on the ship, he says we can talk to Papa while the cargo is being unloaded."

"I have everything ready," I assured him, picking up my cloak and reaching for my valise.

"You had best leave those here, if you wish Papa to listen to you."

"What do you mean?" My doubts expanded into full-blown worry as I realized that David's expression was still grim.

"He is furious, Faith. The moment I mentioned you were with us, he . . . well, he has changed, Faith. He turned on Hunter and would have berated him, had I not explained that we discovered your presence only when the ship was well out to sea. He still had angry words for me for allowing this to happen."

Guilt swept over me as I read the hurt in David's face. Papa's anger had cut him deeply and it was all my fault.

"I will explain everything," I said, wondering if that was possible now. Nothing about this voyage had gone according to my plans.

"He may not be willing to listen, Faith. What has happened in Charleston has made him different." He hesitated, then sighed. "There is something else, something he told me before I mentioned you were with us."

"What is that?"

"Tommy is dead. Evidently his parents received word from some relatives in the North. He was killed during that first battle and is buried not far from the battlefield."

I touched the bodice of my dress, feeling the small mound of Tommy's ring beneath the fabric. I had brought it along so that I could give it to Papa to return to Tommy's family when he asked them to free me from the contract; but now . . . Sorrow swept over me. My feelings for Tommy might have changed, but I could still mourn for all the dreams that would now go unfulfilled.

"Faith, are you all right?" David's light touch on my shoulder reminded me that I was not alone and when I looked into his face, I remembered again how much I loved my brother.

"I just feel so sorry about Tommy. He was a sweet boy and I did care for him. He deserved so much more than a faraway grave. I wish . . ."

"David, Faith, you may go ashore now." Hunter stood in the doorway, his eyes blazing as they met mine. "Your father is waiting."

Was it anger or some other strong emotion that had his color so high and his blue eyes so full of light? I had no time to study his expression, for David hustled me out of the cabin and into the dim light of a very cloudy day. Since the cabin offered no view of the outside world, I looked around curiously as we made our way past the strangers who were helping the crew unload the arms and supplies from the hold.

The dock was not at all what I had expected. A rude structure of logs and planking, it appeared to jut out of thick undergrowth and it was not until I was on the gangplank that I realized the undergrowth was secured to the dock to hide it. It was then I saw the long, low, open-sided building that extended away from the dock, disappearing into the shadows of a number of old trees and more thick brush.

"Faith, is it really you?" Papa's voice forced all other thoughts from my mind and I turned quickly toward the sound, looking past the tall, stooped, white-haired man, seeking my handsome father.

"Papa?" I was swept into the stranger's arms for a hug, then held at arm's length. The stranger vanished as I met Papa's loving green eyes and lost myself in his smile, which seemed rusty with disuse. "Oh, Papa, I have missed you so."

"And I have missed the both of you most cruelly. When Edward sent word of your mother's condition, I tried to secure passage, but . . ." He stopped and the familiar tenderness that had filled his face vanished beneath the stranger's impassive mask. "You should not have come, Faith. It is worrisome enough to know that David is aboard a blockade runner. You must return to the safety of your aunt's home if you have no wish to honor your agreement with the Latimers."

"No wish to honor my agreement?" I stepped back, confused by his words.

"Captain Latimer assured me that his brother's family is delighted with your presence in their home. That Mrs. Latimer considers you more like a sister than a member of the staff." Papa's frown deepened. "Why is it you have come here, Faith?"

I looked to David, unable to face Papa's penetrating gaze. Too late, I realized that I could not explain to him. How could I tell Papa about the torrid moments I had spent in Hunter's arms. What would he think of me? What would honor demand he do to Hunter?

236

Aware that there was nothing left for me to do but stretch the truth, I tried to find the right words. "I was upset when I heard nothing from Tommy, Papa. Then Sam Taylor sent word that he was missing and . . ." My voice broke slightly, but I swallowed hard, then went on, "I just wanted to see you again, Papa. I have been so lonely and I thought perhaps now you would need me to help you at the warehouses or to keep house for you or something." I could see the relief in David's face.

"Did David not tell you the sorry news about Tommy?" The gentleness returned to Papa's face as he repeated what David had already told me.

I listened quietly, feeling the sharp needles of grief once more. When he finished, however, I repeated my offer to stay and help him endure life in Charleston.

"There is no house to keep, Faith, and the warehouses are not a safe place for a young lady of breeding these days. You cannot stay. I have already made that very clear to Captain Latimer. He has agreed to take you either to Nassau or back to his family. There is no other choice for you and I want you to promise that you will never do something like this again. You have been a very foolish girl, Faith, and in these troubled times that can prove dangerous."

I felt the heat rising in my cheeks; yet even as I resented his treating me like a willful child, I knew that I deserved it. It was time I grew up and accepted responsibility for my own emotions. I had left Aunt Minerva's protection because I wished to be on my own, then I came seeking Papa's protection because I was afraid of making my own choices.

"So, Papa, tell us all the news," David said, easing the moment and freeing me to gather up my tattered dignity.

Papa seemed to welcome the chance to lead us away from the busy dock to a quieter area of the building. There we sat with him and the years slipped away. Outwardly Papa had aged ten years since I had last seen him, but as I told him about our life in Nassau and

Mother's last days, he again became the loving father I adored.

The hours seemed to have wings, they passed so quickly. By midday most of the cargo had been unloaded from the *Pearl*, placed in wagons, and taken away, so Hunter was able to join us for a brief meal. I watched, enthralled, as he charmed Papa and made him laugh. My love for Hunter washed over me like the relentless tide and I knew that I would not choose to return to Nassau. Whatever the consequences, I never wanted to be separated from Hunter.

Once the meal was finished, Hunter left and a short while later David followed him because it was time for them to supervise the loading of the cotton bales.

Once we were alone, Papa leaned back with a sigh. "We must talk of your future, Faith. Do you think your aunt could arrange a match for you with someone in the islands? I would rest easier if I knew that you would be protected by a suitable marriage."

I shivered as a chill traced down my spine. Though a light rain had begun to fall and the day had grown cool, that was not the cause of my discomfort. "Aunt Minerva is much too occupied with arranging a match for Caroline," I informed him. "She would have little time for me."

Papa's frown deepened. "Are you sure of that, Faith? You were betrothed when you lived with them before. Tommy's death has changed that."

I shifted uncomfortably, well aware that he was right. "I have no wish to marry anyone that Aunt Minerva might choose for me, Papa."

I braced myself for a reprimand, but instead Papa chuckled. "She is a formidable woman as I recall. Much given to doing the proper thing without enjoying it."

I giggled, unable to resist his description. "Life with her was pretty grim."

"But it was safe, Faith, and if you are unhappy with the situation on Dark Thunder, you must return to Nassau.

238

Whatever else you say about Minerva, she will protect you and see you properly wed."

"I would sooner continue as a governess." The words were out before I could stop them.

"Is it your fondness for the position or for Captain Latimer that would keep you on Dark Thunder?"

The question shocked me and when I looked up, the narrowed scrutiny Papa directed at me brought red to my cheeks. Had David said something to him? Or was it Hunter? The chill spread through me. "What do you mean?" I asked, a bit too late.

"I have eyes, child, and so does the captain. If he has made improper advances . . ."

"Hunter has been a gentleman." I was beginning to get tired of defending Hunter's honor to my family, yet I knew I spoke the truth. So long as I had the good sense to keep my distance, Hunter would be a gentleman. Unfortunately, I could not explain that to either Papa or David unless I wanted to return to Nassau.

"Perhaps I should speak with him once the cargo is loaded. If his intentions are honorable . . ."

My heart leaped at the suggestion. Perhaps my coming here had been the right thing to do after all. If Papa asked Hunter his intentions, Hunter would have to be honest with him and then I would know . . . My spirits rose, then dropped.

Did I really expect Hunter to admit to Papa that he was in love with his sister-in-law? The question haunting me had never been whether or not Hunter had feelings for me—his behavior already proved that he wanted me. What I needed to know was whether or not he also wanted Sarah. That was a question Papa would never ask.

"Faith, do you have feelings for the man?" Papa's probing gaze told me that some of my wayward thoughts must have showed in my face.

"I could have," I admitted. "But I am not sure how he . . ."

A loud report stopped my words and I leaped to my

239

feet, recognizing the sound as a gunshot. I peered toward the end of the dock just in time to see a strange ship emerging from the rainy gloom.

"Dear Lord, the raiders have found this place, too," Papa groaned. "We have to get on the ship, Faith." He started to push me from our sheltered area of the building toward the open dock, but before I could take more than a step, a half-dozen men came swarming out of the brush and onto the dock, guns in hand.

Swearing under his breath, Papa dragged me back and shoved me down behind one of the few remaining cotton bales, then stepped in front of me, his hands in the air. "Keep out of sight, Faith," he warned. "If they see you, it will go badly for you. Let me try to distract them so you can slip away."

I wanted to protest his taking such a risk, wanting him to hide with me since the men had not even looked our direction so far as I could see. Before he could do anything, however, the sound of more gunfire filled the air and I saw one of the raiders fall to the dock, blood spurting from his chest. They were firing from the *Sea Pearl*! Papa stepped back and dropped to his knees beside me. We could do nothing but huddle together and watch in terror as the battle raged before us.

Several of Papa's men, those who had not left with the loaded wagons earlier, were crouched behind timbers or bales; but like us, they had no guns to fire at the raiders. Meanwhile, the men on the *Pearl* scurried madly about the deck, doing I knew not what. The raiders on shore fired furiously at the men on the steamer, taking only occasional shots at the men hiding in the warehouse building. My heart stopped when I heard a shriek of pain from the ship. Had David or Hunter been struck?

A new sound thundered through the thick, wet air, drawing my attention to the intruder vessel. The radiers' sailing ship was smaller than the steamer, but it had two guns mounted along the rail and the roar meant they had fired a shot at the *Pearl*!

I squinted at the worsening storm, trying to see where they had struck the *Pearl*. I could see nothing and drew in a breath of relief just as the second gun blazed and the rail disappeared along with a section of the *Pearl*'s deck. They were going to sink her with Hunter and David on board!

Terror lifted me to my feet. I had to do something to help them. I could not let them die as Tommy had. Papa caught my arm and roughly pulled me back down even as I heard answering fire from the *Pearl*. I gasped with joy as the gun that had fired the first shot disappeared in a massive explosion. It seemed that the crew knew how to use the mounted guns I had noticed on my walks around the deck.

Hope flooded through me, then the crackling of rifle fire grew worse and I realized that just firing the deck guns would not be enough. Though someone had freed the bow rope, the *Pearl* was a sitting duck, for she was still tied to the dock by the stern rope. As long as she was tethered, the smaller ship could maneuver around to fire at will and the men on the dock could pick off the crew of the ship with their rifles. Time was definitely on the side of the raiders.

"We have to help them, Papa," I wailed. "Do you have a gun? Can we not go for help? If they keep shooting at the ship David and Hunter could be hurt."

It was growing dark under the sheltering roof of the open building, but I could see the sad defeat in Papa's face as he looked my way. "My men have orders not to come back under any circumstances, Faith. Those supplies must be delivered to the men who need them. And help is many miles away. The raiders seem to have the devil's own luck at finding our docks. The *Pearl*'s only hope is that someone can cut the ship free. If Captain Latimer could maneuver . . . Oh, dear God . . ."

The look of horror on his face as he peered toward the ship drew my eyes back toward the battle. My stomach clenched as I caught sight of David easing his way along the rail to where the thick stern rope secured the steamer

241

to the dock. He had a huge cane knife in his hand and I had no doubt about his plans to use it. Unfortunately, neither did the raiders on the dock, for they were firing wildly in his direction.

Cursing violently, Papa leaped to his feet and picked up the knife we had used to cut the bread during our noon meal. Without pausing in the motion, he threw the knife with the same accuracy he had so often shown in picnic contests with David and his friends, only this time the target was not a fence post. The knife sank to the hilt in the back of the nearest raider who was firing at David. The man went down shrieking like a madman, effectively drawing the attention of his companions just long enough for David to swing the cane knife severing the rope that held the *Pearl* to dock.

For a heartbeat nothing happened, then slowly the steamer began to drift away from the dock, moving with the tide as David disappeared behind a mound of deck cargo. Above the din of the rain, I could hear Hunter shouting the orders that would bring the engine to life. I shuddered as the single remaining gun on the raiders' ship belched fire, but the shot fell into the water, wide of the drifting *Pearl*.

Hunter and David crouched behind the bales of cotton, firing at the smaller ship even as the rain grew worse and the wind began to blow harder. I heard a scream of pain and scanned the deck of the *Pearl* frantically, unable to spot either Hunter or David through the thick curtain of rain. I could, however, hear the sound of the engine throbbing as the gray-painted *Pearl* plunged to safety, losing itself in the thickening gloom.

Curses and more gunfire brought my attention back to the dock and my joy at Hunter's escape was tempered by the realization that Papa and I were trapped here, along with the half-dozen of Papa's men who had remained to help load the cotton. I was paralyzed with fear, but Papa seemed possessed as he shoved me out from under the

242

sheltering roof of the building into the enveloping fog that seemed to be snared in the thick brush. "Hide, Faith," he ordered, before he turned back toward the nearly empty building.

Terrified, I stumbled into the thorny brush, barely able to see where I was going. I could hear the continuing rattle of gunfire behind me and each rifle shot sent a quiver of fear through me. Why had Papa gone back? If I could hide, why must he remain? A root or vine caught my foot, sending me crashing to the muddy earth. I struggled to my hands and knees, then settled back to the sopping ground. I had nowhere to go. Fearfully, I looked back.

For a moment I could see nothing but a vague outline of the open-sided building, then the rising wind shredded the fog giving me a clear view of what was going on. I bit my lip to keep from screaming as one of the men grabbed Papa, dragging him roughly into the now-empty center of the building. It broke my heart to stay hidden like a cowardly mouse while the man hit Papa and demanded to know where the guns had been taken.

"There is nothing here for you but a few bales of cotton." Papa's voice carried over the rising wind and the pounding of the rain on the roof. "Our supplies have gone to those who will use them against our enemies."

Vile curses filled the air as the hulking man shook Papa as though he weighed no more than I. I stifled a whimper when the monster finally dropped Papa and he lay, unmoving, on the hard ground. As I watched, shivering and crying in the icy rain, the vicious brute had each of my father's men hauled forward for questioning, beating each one when he disliked their answers. If these raiders were the enemies our brave soldiers faced, I wished I could take up a rifle and help to kill them.

While I watched the ugly tableau, the rain began to ease, but the wind continued and the cold seemed to sink into the very marrow of my bones. My jaws ached as I tried to keep my teeth from chattering and a new fear

243

began to command my attention. With the clearing of the rain and fog, my blue gown was becoming more and more visible.

Since I knew I could do nothing for Papa while the raiders were around, I began backing carefully away from the building. There was plenty of undergrowth behind me and if I could just get into the heart of it . . .

"What have we here?" A hard hand clamped on my shoulder and terror sucked the breath from my body as I was forced around to face a leering raider. I had waited too long.

Chapter 16

Terror and fury gave me the will to fight, but I was no match for the muscular raider and he laughed as I kicked and tried to scratch his ugly face. Only when I managed to drive an elbow into the pit of his bulging belly, did he lose his temper and hit me. I welcomed the pain, gladly slipping into the darkness that followed it.

"Faith, my dear child, what has he done to you?" Papa's voice seemed to be coming from a great distance, yet I felt his hands touching my face and I winced as he brushed the bruised side of my head.

Memories of him lying so still on the ground flooded my mind, forcing me back from the refuge of unconsciousness. "Papa? Are you all right, Papa?" I opened my eyes and was relieved to find his dear face bending close to mine.

"I am here, child." Papa's look of relief echoed mine and told me just how worried he had been.

"Have they gone?" I tried to sit up, whimpering as my head throbbed. "Are we safe?"

"Well, well, Richards, I see that your precious daughter is finally awake. Maybe with her help you will feel more like answering my questions."

Though I had heard that voice only from a distance during the storm, I recognized it instantly and my blood turned to ice. I looked up and for the first time saw clearly the face of the leader of the raiders. I had expected him to be some sort of monster, but his features were not brutish like those of the men who followed him. Truthfully, he might even have been considered handsome, had his eyes not been pale as death and filled with malice.

"Spare her, Broderick," Papa said. "She knows nothing and I have no information to give you. The supplies are long gone, delivered to those who fight for our cause."

"So you say, old man." Broderick's smile added to the chill that the nearing of nightfall had brought to the air. "But perhaps your memory will improve as I explore the . . . a . . . possibilities with your daughter." His laughter held no mirth, only venom, and his gaze moved over me leaving an icy trail of shivers.

Since my dress was wet and clinging, I tried to cover myself by wrapping my arms around my swelling bosom. His eyes gleamed with lust and I could almost feel the touch of his grimy hands when he looked at me. Shudders wracked my body and nausea burned in my throat. I began to wish myself safely unconscious.

He grinned at me, his teeth broken and ugly, but vicious as the fangs of a wild dog. "In good time, my pretty." He turned and moved toward the fire that someone had lit in the middle of the warehouse. Several of his men were gathered there tending the wounded, while others stood guard around us, their rifles ready. Their ship was now tied up at the dock and several of the crew seemed to be trying to make repairs in the area where the *Pearl*'s shot had landed.

"What manner of animals are these Northerners?" I groaned, trying to move my arms and legs to warm myself.

"These are not Yankees, Faith," Papa said, his face grim. "That man, Broderick, once traded legitimately with me. Now he has become a true raider, no better than a pirate. Twice have I heard that he offered goods for sale that had been taken from people I know, from folk who were trying to escape this unhappy war."

"He is a Southerner?" I could not believe it.

"I have no idea where he comes from, Faith. His speech is not that of a Yankee, but he could be from anywhere. The devil's own, most likely. If only there was some way to get you away from here." He stirred, then winced and I saw that his left arm hung almost useless at his side.

"Papa, you are injured." I struggled to my knees, my own aches forgotten. "What did he do to you?"

"'Tis but my collarbone. Cracked, not broken, I think. It will heal with time and care. It is you I fear for, Faith. That great beast will . . ." He stopped as Broderick came striding back.

"Feeling better, Miss Richards?" he asked with exaggerated politeness, reaching down to take my hand and bowing over it.

I tried to pull my fingers away, but he lifted my hand to his lips—kissed it, then nipped at the flesh on the back. Furious, I twisted it free and scratched the side of his face. To my horror, he laughed and recaptured my hand so he could yank me to my feet.

"A wildcat, that's what you've bred, Richards. One I shall take great pleasure in taming before I turn her over to my men. They do miss the joys of the flesh while we are at sea. 'Tis a pity you have but one woman for their enjoyment."

Papa started to his feet, his one good arm knotting, but the pain drained the color from his face and he dropped back to the earth looking gray and ill. Terror swept through me as I saw the avid excitement in Broderick's face. He wanted me, but even more, I sensed that he was enjoying my terror and the pain he was inflicting on my father. In that instant I knew that he would have no qualms about doing what he said; he would show me no mercy.

Gritting my teeth, I straightened, banishing the bone-deep fear. Pleading would gain me nothing, but defiance might at least afford me the escape of death. I preferred that to the horror he had planned for me.

"Ah, she is a pretty one, Richards. And proud as the devil, too." He reached out and stroked the side of my face. "Pure, I wager. Saving herself for some fancy cavalry man." His laughter shuddered through me, but I managed to stand still, not cringing from his touch.

"Let her go, you bastard." The anguish in Papa's voice nearly undid me.

Broderick ignored him completely as his hand moved down the side of my throat to caress my shoulder. "What have we here?" He found the cameo pinned to my bodice and began brushing away the thick coating of dried mud that had hidden it from him. Once he got a look at it, his fingers tightened around it and he yanked it free, tearing the fabric of my gown and leaving some of my pale skin exposed. "You'll not be needing this, girl." He pocketed it.

I closed my eyes, thinking of Hunter, of the love in his face when he gave me the cameo. Tears burned behind my lids and sobs clogged my throat as I felt Broderick's hand move lower, touching the mound of my breast, caressing me as Hunter had. I shuddered away from this man's touch, then gasped as he worked his fingers between the buttons on the front of my gown.

His bellow of laughter brought my gaze to his face. "You are a regular treasure trove, lady." He pulled the chain with Tommy's ring from its hiding place beneath my gown, then yanked it hard, cutting my neck with the chain before it parted and the chain and ring joined the cameo in his pocket. "Do you have more hidden treasures for me?" His hands reached for my ripped gown and I knew that he meant to strip me bare here before my father and the avidly watching raiders.

I looked around, seeking some weapon that I might use to end my life before he could dishonor me and add to my father's torment. If only I had a knife or . . .

248

As his fingers grazed the tops of my breasts, the night was suddenly torn apart by an explosion that seemed to rock the very ground beneath my feet. I stumbled back from the massive raider, half expecting a blow; but instead, he bellowed and he and all his men turned to race out of the building toward their ship. Fire lit the night with the glow of another sunset. Their ship was burning!

"This way." Papa grabbed my hand. "Quickly, while they are distracted."

Papa's men, limping, battered and bloody, gathered around us and one huge Negro simply picked Papa up and carried him as we stumbled from the warehouse building into the blackness of the wilderness beyond the light of the fire. Since Papa refused to release my hand even as he groaned with the agony of being carried, I had to run to keep pace with the men.

Another explosion sounded behind us, but when I tried to look back, I could see nothing but the glow of the fire. Already there were too many trees and bushes between us and the dock area. "Stop. Please, I need a moment." Papa's gasp brought the men to a halt.

"What can I do to help you, Papa?" I asked, panting from the exertion.

"Him needin' tied up," the big Negro stated. "You hep me fix 'im, Missy Faith?"

"Plato?" I gasped, vaguely recognizing the voice as I had not recognized the man. "Is that you?"

"Who else be packing yore Papa?" Even in the darkness, I saw the gleam of his teeth as he grinned at me. Though I had not spent much time with the freed Negroes Papa employed at the warehouse, Plato had grown up in our household. His mother Leone, a slave, had been our cook. Plato, too, had been a slave until the day he pulled five-year-old David out of the creek, saving his life. For that Papa had given him his freedom and the opportunity to work at the warehouse.

"What can I do, Plato?" I asked, well aware that Leone had tended most of the slaves when they were injured.

249

"Him need bindin' to keep the arm from moving." Plato sighed. "We gots a hike to where the wagon's hid. I kin pack 'im, but he hurtin'."

"Would strips from my petticoat do for binding?" I felt no embarrassment mentioning my petticoat to Plato. There had been a time during childhood when I had loved him like an older brother and I could still remember standing on the edge of the creek screaming while he pulled David to safety.

"Work fine, Missy."

"There is no time," Papa protested. "They will be coming after us. We have to get Faith away before that . . ."

I lifted my skirt and ripped the limp ruffle from the bottom of my petticoat. "It is soaking wet and cold, Plato," I murmured as I handed it to him, ignoring Papa's protests.

"Better'n nothin'. Massa Richards, you be still now and let old Plato fix ya up."

I shivered as the cold wind raked over my torn and soaked dress, freezing my ankles now that the small protection of my petticoat ruffle was gone. How I wished I had my cloak from the *Pearl*, my valise with dry clothing to change into. A shudder nearly toppled me as I thought of the cabin, of David and Hunter just across the ship's passageway. Would I ever see them again?

"That do ya, Massa," Plato said, just as the distant sound of another smaller explosion broke the relative silence of the night. "Now we gots ta fin' the wagon afore dat scum come ahuntin' us."

"Do you really have a wagon out here somewhere?" I asked, forcing my mind back from the agony of all that I had lost.

"Did you expect me to walk back to Charleston, Faith?" Papa's tone was nearly teasing and I sensed that his strength was returning, which made me feel better.

"Sho' nuff, Missy," Plato answered. "Trick be findin' it."

"I believe that if we . . ." Papa began, then stopped as a strange noise came from the brush to one side of us.

I froze, terror closing my throat. If we had escaped only to be recaptured by the raiders . . . I would run, I told myself. Let them shoot me down, if they chose. I would not calmly surrender to . . .

"Mr. Richards? Faith? Are you here?"

For a moment I thought that I had slipped from reality into a dream, then the rustling noise grew louder and a dim shape emerged from the underbrush. "Hunter?" I gasped, still not believing my eyes or my ears. "Hunter, is that really you?"

"Captain Latimer?" Papa's tone reflected my disbelief. "What are you doing here? Has something happened to your ship? What of David?"

"The ship is safe under your son's command for the moment," Hunter answered calmly. "I left her to come back to help you and Faith escape. I could not leave you to the mercy of that crew."

"You caused the explosions and fire?" Joy surged through me, banishing the cold and burning away the darkness that had filled me as I watched the *Pearl* disappear into the fog.

"Let us say I arranged for the raiders to be very busy for a while." Hunter sounded pleased with himself as he slipped his arm around me, hugging me close to the warmth of his side. "I doubt that they will be able to look for you for several hours, anyway. Now did I hear you correctly, sir, do you have a wagon hidden somewhere around here?"

Papa and Plato answered his questions and asked him the details of what he had done. I listened, but I heard only the warmth in Hunter's voice as I lost myself in the miracle of feeling the beating of his heart beneath my cheek as I rested my head against his chest. He had come back for me! Nothing else really seemed quite as important as that.

"How can I ever thank you, Captain Latimer?" Papa's

251

voice broke through my dreamy vagueness. "If you had not come, that accursed beast would have . . ."

Hunter's arm tightened around me. "I only thank the Lord that I was in time. I had to make sure we were clear before I left the *Pearl* and I feared that I might be too late to stop him." He paused, taking a deep breath. His voice was calmer as he continued, "Now, however, I think you should be on your way. Once they extinguish the fire on their ship, they are going to realize that the other explosions are just harmless diversions and they will come looking for you."

"What of you and Faith?" Papa sounded worried. "Will you be safe?"

"I have a boat hidden nearby. Once we reach the ship, she will be fine and I promise you, she will not be returning to South Carolina until the war is over." Hunter's tone was grim, but I felt no fear, not when he held me so tenderly.

My fear banished, I began to feel the cold even more deeply. There was much I wanted to say, but my teeth were chattering so hard, I could not speak. Hunter rubbed his hands on my arms, swearing. "Why did I not think to bring your cloak from the ship? You will freeze in an open boat on the water and I have but a shirt and it is near as wet as your gown."

"Take my cloak," Papa said. "It is dry and I have only a short walk to the wagon."

"You are injured," I protested, gaining control of my shivers. "I will be fine."

"There be plenty o' sacks an' blankets in the wagon, Missy Faith," Plato said. "I keep yore Papa warm." He stripped off his own heavy shirt and wrapped it around Papa's shoulders once he removed the heavy plaid cloak and handed it to Hunter to put around me.

I hugged Plato, then Papa, doing my best not to jar his bad arm. "I mislike leaving you this way," I whispered. "Could you not come with us?"

"I want you safe with your brother," Papa replied.

252

"And my place is here where I can help my friends. I cannot leave them to fight without the goods I can procure for them. Go with God, the both of you."

"And you." I could not keep back the tears as Hunter gently guided me away from the small group of men. I heard Plato's rumbling voice as he urged Papa in the other direction and deep inside I trembled at the thought that I might never see my father again. Even learning about Tommy's death had not prepared me for the reality of what was happening to the people I loved. Today I had seen men die, nothing would ever be the same for me.

Sobs shook me so that I could scarcely walk. All the fear and anger that had filled me when I regained consciousness to find myself a prisoner of the raiders spilled over. The horror of it, the helplessness, the way Broderick had assumed he had the right to touch me. The memories of it racked me unmercifully.

"It is not much further, Faith," Hunter whispered, stopping to hold me in his warm, sustaining embrace. "I know you need to rest, but we cannot remain here. We need to put some distance between us and the raiders, just to be on the safe side. If their ship survived the fire, they could come looking for the *Pearl*."

The worry in his voice broke through my nightmare memories and helped me to regain control. "I can walk," I assured him. "Please, let us hurry away from here. I never want to see that evil man Broderick again."

"If I ever find out where he hides himself, he will not live to touch another woman." The words were spoken softly, but the menace behind them was chilling. I had no doubt that Hunter would keep his vow and that frightened me. Much as I hated the raider, I did not want Hunter to put himself in danger by attacking him.

"Papa said he was like a pirate, not a Yankee blockader."

"Your father is correct. The man carries no flag. Does your father know anything else about him?"

I sensed that Hunter was more interested in distracting

me as we walked, than in my answers; but I was happy to tell him what little I knew. The wind was steadily shredding the few remaining clouds and as the stars appeared, it was easier to see where we were going. Still, I would never have found the boat that Hunter had hidden along the broken shore of the coast.

"It looks like the fire is out. At least the glow is gone," he observed with a sigh, looking off toward the left as I stepped into the tiny rowboat. "I was afraid that everything was too soaked from the rain to burn well."

"Does that mean they will come after us?" The idea chilled me as I pictured the big sailing ship pursuing us across the open water. They would be able to catch us easily and then . . . I shuddered, not wanting to picture what Broderick would do to Hunter or to me.

"Likely," Hunter replied, "but not tonight. If we can find a safe hiding place by dawn, we should be able to escape them."

"What of the *Pearl*?" Fear knotted my stomach. "Is she not nearby waiting for us?"

"Of course not. David is to anchor in an inlet that I have used before and make what repairs he can. The raiders will be expecting us to head directly out to sea, so with luck, the ship will be safe." He touched my hand for a moment before he reached for the oars. "I could not put the ship and crew at risk, Faith. If we do not rendezvous with them tomorrow night, they are under orders to return to the Bahamas without me."

"Oh." I could think of nothing else to say. The enormity of what Hunter had done stunned me. He had been willing to risk his life, risk being trapped in South Carolina while the *Pearl* sailed back to the islands and all because he wanted to rescue Papa and me from the raiders.

"Just rest, Faith," he whispered. "And try not to worry."

Not worry? I wondered if that was possible. I scanned the shoreline that we were leaving behind. I could see no sign of the dock or the raiders' ship, which was probably just as well, for the moon was peeking out now and we were far from invisible. "Where is the dock?" I asked, more to break the long silence, than because I cared.

"Around that point." He gestured with his head, not breaking his rhythm at the oars. "They will not be able to see us."

"Where are we going?" My thoughts went to Papa and his men. Would they be safe? I hesitated to ask Hunter, not sure I was ready for his reply if it was worrisome.

"There are offshore islands in this direction, lots of them. Most are small and uninhabited, so we can hide through the daylight hours, then go on after sunset tomorrow. Right now, I just want to get as far from here as I can. The closer we are to the inlet, the better our chances of getting back to the *Pearl* in time."

"What about Papa?" I had to know.

"I think he will be safe. Broderick has enough to worry about with a damaged ship. He would have killed all of you before he left the dock, but he lacks the men to pursue anyone into an inhabited area. Your father and that big slave of his will know people they can turn to for help."

"Plato is no slave, Papa freed him long ago. Now he works for Papa." I passed the next hour telling Hunter tales of my life growing up outside Charleston. Talking about Plato and David and all the friends that I had once taken for granted made the horror seem far away. I think for a while after I ran out of stories, I even drifted into a kind of doze, for I remember little of the long journey or the islands we skirted.

"Faith, Faith, are you all right?" Hunter's soft voice brought me back to the cold reality of the hard wooden seat and the damp clamminess that had remained with me in spite of Papa's cloak.

"I am fine," I murmured, stifling a groan as I tried to

straighten my stiff body. "Where are we?" I yawned and looked around, startled to discover that I could see quite well. Dawn was breaking and with the skies swept clear of last night's rain clouds, there would be no morning mist to hide us.

"Somewhere in the offshore islands." Hunter's smile was warm, but I could read the bone-deep weariness in his face. "I thought we should stop now. I hesitate to risk being seen by anyone that might mention our presence to the raiders. Do you see any sign of life on that island just ahead?"

I twisted around to scan the brush and tree-covered scrap of land as well as I could. Calling it an island seemed a compliment, but since the larger islands were quite a distance away, I was in no position to argue. "I see nothing that looks man-made."

"Good." Hunter maneuvered the rowboat into what seemed to be a tiny inlet fully shaded and protected by the thick wild growth of the island. Within moments the boat ground to a stop, its hull dragging on the sandy bottom, the sudden stop nearly toppling me into the water. I grabbed the seat and turned back to Hunter.

To my horror, he was not moving. Instead of getting to his feet to help me secure the boat, he was slumped over the oars, his hands hanging limply, slowly dripping . . . I gasped as I realized that the red I was seeing was blood dripping from Hunter's hands. "Hunter, dear Lord, are you injured?"

He lifted his head so slowly, that I wanted to reach out to him, to clasp him in my arms, and . . . His eyes, always so bright with life and promise, seemed glazed. "Secure the boat. I just need to rest for a moment." His head dropped to his chest again.

Chilled with fear for him, I dropped the cloak and stepped carefully over the side of the boat. The water was surprisingly warm in contrast to the cold morning air. I tugged the rowboat as far under the overhanging trees and bushes as I could, then tied it firmly to a stout limb.

That done, I waded along the side to where Hunter still sat, his hands now hanging over the side of the boat to be washed by the lapping water.

"Can you stand, Hunter?" I asked, my stomach clenching as I saw his blood drying on the oars. "I can help you, but . . ."

Once again his response was terribly slow, but he did rise and, after wavering for a moment, he leaned on my shoulder and stepped carefully from the boat into the water. I slipped an arm around his waist and guided him up the rough bank and into what appeared to me to be a bit of paradise.

Thick grass carpeted the interior of the small island forming a bower completely surrounded by flowering bushes and shaded by palms and other trees. Though the grass was still very wet from last night's storm, Hunter sank down, his eyes closed even before his head touched the grass. A soft snore eased my fear that he might be seriously injured or ill. "I will be right back," I whispered, sure that he was beyond hearing me.

I longed to sit beside Hunter, to perhaps ease his head into my lap and bandage his hands, but instead I eased Papa's cloak from my shoulders. Though it was damp, the cloak would offer Hunter some protection from the morning chill while I took care of another matter.

I had noticed something while I was helping Hunter out of the boat. I hurried back to the craft to investigate the oilskin-wrapped bundle I had spotted beneath his seat. I found the bundle surprisingly bulky and heavy as I carried it back to the clearing. Once there I crouched down beside Hunter to unwrap it. The scents of food made me dizzy as I blessed whoever had wrapped up the two battered loaves of bread, cheese, salt meat, and dried fruit. There were even two containers of fresh water.

Hunter stirred, perhaps roused by the smell of food. I shook him gently, then offered him a piece of the dried fruit as soon as his eyes opened. "Can you eat some of this before you go back to sleep?" I asked, my worry for

257

him overpowering my own hunger.

He struggled to sit up, then moaned as he tried to close one of his hands. "I cannot."

"I can feed you, if you allow me to. Then later, when you feel stronger, I will do what I can for your hands. I can bandage them with cloth from my petticoat and, if we are lucky, maybe this island has the plant that old Leone used to gather to make a poultice for the slaves when they came to her with sores or blisters."

"How do you know of such things?" Hunter accepted another bite of food, this time cheese and bread, then I held the water for him to sip it.

"Leone is Plato's mother. She was our cook, but she also took care of a lot of our people. I used to follow her about and watch. Making pain go away and helping people to be well seemed like a miracle to me and Leone never sent me out of the room the way the doctor did when he was summoned." I ate, too, enjoying the returning of strength and hope that came just from being here with Hunter, as well as the joy of seeing the gleam of life come back into his eyes.

"Always so full of surprises." His grin revived and so did the heat that burned in the depths of his eyes as they moved over my face. "When I thought of you at the mercy of that black-hearted raider . . ." His hands clenched and he winced.

"Forget it," I said, getting to my feet. "If you have had enough to eat, let me see what I can do for your hands, then I suggest that you try and get some sleep. If we are to meet the *Pearl* tonight . . ."

Hunter nodded, his expression grim as he looked down at his hands. "I am not sure how far I will be able to row."

When I looked at the torn and bleeding flesh, I had to swallow to keep from being ill. "How could you have rowed this far?"

"I had to."

"Why did you not wake me? I could have taken over for a time, Hunter, given your poor hands a rest." Anger at my own behavior made my tone sharp.

"You could not row." Hunter straightened, his features hard and set.

"Why not? Do you think I am one of those fragile little ladies who never do anything but sit quietly and embroider?" I pushed back my hair, which having long ago escaped any semblance of order, now hung around my face in wildly curling tendrils.

"Do you know how to row a boat?" His gaze was challenging.

"Of course I do. I . . . we had a pond near our house and I used to take the boat out and row around it." I carefully left out the fact that I had been only seven or eight at the time.

Hunter's eyes narrowed as though he was not quite sure he should believe me, but in the end he simply nodded. "Perhaps, if you could make bandages and if your magic plant works."

"The first thing for you to do is to wash your hands again while I try to find that plant. Without a fire I cannot make a proper poultice, but perhaps if I pound the leaves and mix a little water with the pulp . . ." I left him still shaking his head.

Hunter was back sitting in the clearing by the time I finished preparing my poultice. It smelled slightly different from what Leone had smeared on the injured slaves, but it was all I had, so I put a thick paste of it on his palms before I wrapped them with strips torn from the second ruffle of my petticoat. Helping the injured was proving to be very hard on my underclothing.

"How does that feel?" I asked as I tied the strip just tight enough to keep the poultice in place.

"Cool." He smiled at me, his eyes full of love. "Thank you, Faith. I really do appreciate your trying to help."

"I just wish I could do more." I reached out and gently pushed back the thick black waves that had fallen over his forehead. Just touching him made me feel warm all over.

259

"What we both need is sleep. How about sharing the cloak?"

I looked into his eyes as I lay down beside him. I ached to kiss him, to tell him what I felt; but he still looked so weary, I only smiled as I pulled the cloak over both of us. At the moment, just lying next to him was miracle enough for me.

Chapter 17

At first the tickling was a part of the dream. I was holding a fuzzy kitten and its tail was moving against my neck and then in my ear. When I lifted my hand to capture the errant tail, I was startled by a low, sensuous chuckle. I opened my eyes.

"Hello, sleepyhead." Hunter smiled down at me as he drew a blade of grass slowly across my cheek, then tickled my lips with it. The glow of love in his eyes warmed me even more than the afternoon sun.

For a heartbeat I thought I was still dreaming, then slowly the memories of yesterday's terror and last-minute rescue edged back into my mind, chilling away the sweetness of the moment. Hunter dropped the blade of grass and gently caressed my cheek with his fingertip. "Forget all that happened, Faith," he whispered, seeming to have read my mind. "That was in another place and time; we are here now, just the two of us, safe and together. That is all that matters."

He traced my lips with his finger, sending shivers through me. I kissed the slightly rough skin, then frowned, remembering the blisters. "Your hands," I murmured, finding my voice at last. "How are they?"

"Why not look for yourself, doctor lady?" He turned his palms up. "Your Leone's poultice is a miracle worker."

I stared at his abused hands, barely believing what I saw. The blisters were still evident, but some of the redness had faded and I could see that the healing was already beginning. "How do they feel?"

"A bit stiff and tender, but if you bandage them for me, I should be able to row us the rest of the way to where the *Pearl* is hidden."

"*We* should be able to row there," I corrected him, touching one palm and watching his eyes. He winced slightly, but his grin did not falter. "You will have to navigate, since I have no idea where we are going, but I can certainly row part of the way."

"Such an independent young lady." He began tracing the contours of my lips again and the quivering inside me grew worse.

The air stirred around us, sweet with the scent of rain-washed grass. My eyelids were heavy, threatening to close as my lips parted at his touch. I wanted his kiss, I needed to feel his mouth on mine, his warm body so close . . .

"Oh, Faith, I cannot resist you." There was anguish in his voice as his lips at last claimed mine in a kiss that ignited my blood with the excitement of summer lightning.

I lifted my arms to embrace him, losing myself in the magic of his touch, the teasing thrust of his tongue, the sensual caress of his lips as he awakened the flames of my love. I wanted it to go on forever and when he finally lifted his lips from mine, I could not keep back my moan of longing. Instinctively, I tightened my embrace, lifting my lips to his again.

"I love you so much, Faith," he gasped, still pulling away. "If we do not stop now . . ."

I loosened my hold for a moment, settling back against the soft grass as I caressed the thick waves of hair on the nape of his neck. "Do you wish to stop?"

"Never." His gaze moved over my face, then focused

262

on my lips with a hunger that further enflamed the heat deep within me.

"Then there is no need, Hunter, for I certainly do not ask you to. I love you."

"But . . ."

I stopped his words with my lips. Yesterday's fears and doubts seemed foolish. I had seen death and nearly suffered defilement at the hands of the raiders and even in my terror I had regretted my rejection of Hunter because I knew how much I loved him. Now that his bravery had given us a second chance at happiness, I could not deny him . . . or myself.

His hand moved slowly to cup my breast and I felt the flames of my desire burning away everything but the miracle of being in his arms. When his sore hands fumbled with the fastenings of my gown, I unbuttoned it myself. I wanted his touch, to feel his hands on my quivering skin. I wanted his love and to give him the gift of mine.

"My darling, darling Faith. My love, my brave and wonderful love." His words whispered over my naked skin as he kissed me, caressed me, setting my blood aflame until I scarcely knew where my body ceased and his began. I hardly heard his warnings of pain, nor did I care when the moment came for I believed his promise that he would make me forget the hurting.

His caresses lifted me into a wondrous rainbow-draped cloud of joy as we became one. The brief pain faded like the rain as I learned the magic of love and completion, of giving and taking, of loving. Shattered by wonder, I cried his name and collapsed in his embrace, sobbing with joy.

"Are you all right, love?" His touch was gentle as he traced the path of my tears on my cheek. "Did I hurt you so deeply?"

I forced my eyes open, startled to discover that we were still lying in the grass, the afternoon shadows marching across the bower. Somehow I had expected to find myself in another world. Only when I saw the concern in Hunter's face, did I realize that my tears had disturbed him. "You have made me happier than I have ever been, Hunter," I whispered, rising on one elbow to kiss the corner of his mouth.

"But you are crying." He still frowned. "If I hurt you, Faith . . ."

"You are my beloved, how could you ever hurt me? I am fine. It is just so new and wonderful and perhaps a little overwhelming, that is all." I met his gaze, letting him see the truth of my words before I lay back, too delightfully lazy to even draw the cloak or a piece of my discarded clothing over my still-tingling body.

As Hunter's frown eased, I saw the sparkle of mischief returning to his eyes. "Well, if you are truly all right, how would you like to join me in a swim?" he asked, slowly tracing a finger down my side and starting all the wonderful sensations throbbing inside me again.

"I should love to wash off all the mud," I murmured, not really caring what we did, so long as we did it together.

The afternoon passed too quickly as we explored each other both in the warm water of the inlet and later in the shadowy bower. Hunter taught me the secrets of love and loving and made me sorry that we had to leave this paradise. Though I realized we must go, my heart was heavy when, as the sun set, we finished the last crumb of the food, then climbed into the rowboat. Want to or not, we had to return to the real world.

"Can you row?" I asked, well aware that the strips of my petticoat that I had wound around his hands were small protection against the rough wood of the oars.

"All the way to Dark Thunder if necessary, I will keep you safe." His grin was jaunty, but as we moved out onto the water, I could see the pain in his eyes.

264

I watched him closely as we skimmed along, noticing the moment the tiny furrows of pain creased his forehead, aware of the subtle changes in his posture that told me he was suffering. No matter what he had said about his ability to take care of me, I could bear his agony no longer. I took a deep breath, hoping devoutly that rowing was like riding a horse, a skill not easily forgotten.

"I think it is time you let me row for a while, Hunter," I announced. "I am just getting cold and bored sitting here. Could we not change places for a time?"

"You cannot row this boat, Faith. I thank you for offering, but . . ."

"You do not believe me?" Sensing that he meant to row until his hands fell off, I forced a tone of outrage. "Hunter Latimer, that is unforgivable. I insist that you let me show you my talent."

He continued to argue even as we carefully changed places, but I ignored him. I needed all my concentration to get the proper grip on the oars and to remember how to use them. Far more than my pride was at stake as I managed my first feeble stroke. "If you will just keep us on course, Captain," I murmured, wondering if I would be able to keep us moving in the rough water. This was definitely not like rowing on the old pond.

"Faith, I really think . . ."

Sensing amusement in his tone, I gritted my teeth and dug in. The boat began to move and as I repeated the maneuver, I began to feel better. "So I am a little out of practice," I said. "I told you I knew how to row."

"So you did, Faith, so you did." The warmth and admiration in Hunter's voice spread over me like a soothing salve so I hardly noticed the pull across my shoulders and the stinging in my palms.

He let me row in silence for a while, then he sighed. "You know, Faith, there is something we must discuss before we reach the *Pearl*."

"What is that?" I asked, hoping I did not sound too

much like a winded nag at the end of a long run.

"It might be best if we allow David and the others to believe that we just left your father at sunset tonight."

"But . . ." I began, my mind filled with images of our romantic bower, the delightful hours I had spent in Hunter's arms, then reality intruded. David would not understand our love, the magic, the wonder; in his eyes it would become something else. "I suppose you are right," I admitted, not liking the way seeing our lovemaking from David's viewpoint made me feel.

"It was wonderful being with you, sharing everything as we did; but until we can properly make our feelings known, we must protect your reputation. Your brother has already let me know that he disapproves of our being involved, so . . ." He did not have to finish the thought.

I nodded. "It already seems like a dream." I could not help feeling sad and lost.

"Our dream, my love, and our secret for now. All right?" He leaned forward, reaching out to touch my cheek as I pulled hard on the oars, fighting my sorrow with the pain that came from my efforts.

"All right." I had to agree, but I still misliked the way my promise made me feel. The wonder of what we had shared should not have to be hidden away as though it were evil or wrong. And my love—I wanted to proclaim that to everyone, not hide it away like a guilty secret.

I rowed on in silence until my shoulders ached and my head pounded and I wondered if my hands were dripping blood, too. Then, seeming to sense my misery, Hunter insisted on taking over, saying that he felt we were near the rendezvous point. Though I was not sure I believed him, because I was beginning to wonder if we would ever sight the *Pearl* in the maze of islands, coves, and inlets, I surrendered the oars without argument.

Sunk in a misery that had little to do with my weariness or the cold, damp night, I was half asleep when a strange birdlike whistle broke the silence. Even as I looked around, Hunter sounded the same notes in answer. Immediately a lantern's glow blossomed ahead and off to the right. Before I had time to think, I was on the *Pearl* wrapped in David's crushing embrace.

Relief more potent than any nostrum prescribed by a doctor carried me through the first hours on the ship. Hunter left me to answer David's questions as he set about getting the *Pearl* under way. Though I hated the need to lie, I found it fairly easy to describe everything that had happened before Hunter's miraculous rescue, then simply cover the time after that by saying we all hid until it was safe for Papa and his men to return to Charleston and Hunter and I could come in search of the ship.

Everything explained, I was allowed to share a hot meal with Hunter while David guided the ship toward the open sea. Too soon, however, I had to go to my cabin— miserably alone. That first night set the pattern for the rest of our journey home—too few moments with Hunter and much too much time alone to think, to remember, to ache for his arms and his kisses.

When we neared the islands of the Bahama chain, Hunter and I managed a moment together. As we stood at the rail, my arm tightly pressed against his warm side, he announced that we would stop in Dark Thunder before he took the cargo on to Nassau. "There is something I need to discuss with Harlan," he said, frowning at the churning froth spinning back from the *Pearl*'s prow.

"The same something that has been troubling you ever since we reached the *Pearl*?" I had noticed his change of mood and worried over it. "Is it because of what happened between us?"

."Of course not." His look of shock momentarily pleased me, then I wondered. If he was not concerned about our future, did that mean he had given it no thought at all? "It has to do with the attack, Faith, or rather our escape."

267

"What do you mean?" My romantic doubts vanished at the mention of those terrible moments when the raiders had appeared out of the rainy afternoon. "If you had not come to our rescue as you did . . ."

"I mean the ship's escape. It was too easy, Faith. They had us pinned against the dock. They could have rammed us or fired a shot at the waterline and sunk us, but they did neither."

"And that worries you?" I could not understand his problem.

"The reason does. David thinks they may have hoped to take the *Pearl* for their raids, but I am not so sure. Sinking us in the shallow water near the dock would have given them the ship in a place where they could likely repair and refloat her. Had I been Broderick, I should have chosen that course."

"So he made an error of judgment. I think we should all be grateful," I observed, though his words disturbed me.

"I think he allowed us to escape. That is why I want to stop by Dark Thunder and speak to Harlan before I deliver our cargo. There is something strange about the whole attack and I mean to find out more about Broderick and his crew."

I shivered at the determination I heard in his tone, it frightened me. In the days since we had come back aboard the *Pearl*, I had sensed that Hunter was drifting away from me; but because of our situation, I was unable to seek out the tender lover I had found in our secret bower. If only we could be alone, if we could touch each other and . . . I forced the thoughts away, aware that Hunter was frowning at me.

"I just want to forget everything that happened that day," I murmured. "We all survived, Hunter, can you not allow someone else to hunt down that evil man?"

"How can you even ask that when he . . . If I had not returned when I did, Faith, he would have . . ." Hunter's lips twisted as he held in the ugly words. "I will make

him pay for touching you and for what he planned to do."
For just a moment I could see his love blazing behind
the anger, then it was gone and David was beside me.
There was no more time for private talk. We reached
Dark Thunder the next day.

I closed my valise carefully, suddenly conscious of
what might lie ahead. Before, I had thought only of what
had happened to me since I left Dark Thunder, but now I
began to wonder if I would be welcomed back at all. What
if Sarah refused to allow me to stay? What if all my
belongings were waiting on the dock so that Hunter could
take me to Nassau along with the cargo?

"Are you ready?" David came into the cabin, his
expression impatient. "Everyone is waiting on the dock.
Someone must have sighted us before we reached the
cove."

"Everyone?" I picked up Papa's heavy plaid cloak,
caressing it tenderly, trying to remember the joyous
moments I had spent lying on it, wrapped in Hunter's
strong arms.

"Sarah and Harlan, the children, some of the
servants." David frowned at me. "What is it, Faith?"

"I ran away, David. What if they will not have me
back?"

"Sarah will understand, especially when you tell her
about Tommy. And Penny loves you, you know that."

But Harlan had been cool before I left and if Sarah
truly loved Hunter . . . I swallowed a sigh, not wanting to
remember the morning I had seen them together. Having
tasted the miracle of love, I could not bear to doubt
Hunter and yet . . .

"Come on." David half dragged me out to the deck in
time to see Sarah throw her arms around Hunter,
hugging him with all the familiarity of a lover. My heart
ached and hot jealousy burned through me, yet there was
nothing I could do but step forward to face the woman

who might be my rival for Hunter's love.

"So you have come back." Harlan's tone was cool. "We thought you might choose to stay with your father." Had he hoped that I would not return?

"Are you all right?" Sarah's gray eyes were warmer than Harlan's tone, but I could see the questions in her face.

I nodded, unable to speak around the lump in my throat. At that moment, Penny scrambled away from a pretty young girl and came running to throw herself into my arms. I hugged her, tears spilling over as I realized that she, at least, was glad to have me back. The question now was: would I be allowed to stay?

David and Hunter were busy explaining all that had happened, so I simply followed everyone off the ship and took my place in the pony cart with Higgins, Penny, and the girl, who introduced herself as Nan Prentice, saying that she had moved from the village to Thunder House in order to care for Penny.

"You are from the village?" I tried to hide my dismay at being replaced by focusing on my curiosity. How could they have gotten someone else? Yet what had I expected? Sarah needed someone to watch over Penny night and day and I had left her without a backward glance.

"There are several of us working for the Latimers." Nan sounded proud to be one of them, but her blue eyes were guarded as they met my gaze. She was a pretty blonde of about seventeen or eighteen, I judged, wondering if Harlan had hired more maids or if some of the workers were employed in the stable or working on the garden that Sarah . . .

Sadness swept through me as I thought of all the plans Sarah had shared with me, the closeness between us. I had loved her like a sister until that morning in the hall and now I missed that feeling. Even my jealousy could not change my longing to feel like a part of her family. I looked ahead at the carriage, catching a glimpse of Hunter's dark head and my heartbeat quickened. I wanted to be a part of the family, all right, but as Sarah's sister-in-law, not her sister.

When we reached the house, Sarah directed Rose to show me to my new room, then followed the men into the parlor. Feeling shut out, I trailed Rose up the stairway, caught in the memory of being carried up by Hunter. His presence was everywhere here underlining my longing to be at his side.

"This be where your belongings are, Miss Faith," Rose announced, opening the door of a room near the suite I had occupied. "That Nan be in your room now."

I sensed the disapproval in her tone, but there was little I could say beyond thanking her for packing up my clothes and personal possessions. I had no right to resent being replaced, not after what I had done.

"We be terrible worried about you, Miss Faith," Rose continued. "'Twas Mr. Harlan what said Miss Penny needed a nursemaid and brought in Nan. She be kindly, but Miss Penny missed you something fierce. She be glad to have you back."

"I am glad to be back, Rose," I assured her, wondering as I spoke if I should be allowed to stay. I might consider myself a member of the household, but that could change at any moment.

The hours dragged by, but beyond washing and changing into a more suitable gown and proper under-clothing, I did nothing. Much as I ached to see Hunter again, I could not seek him out now that we were here. If he wanted to talk to me or to hold me, he would have to make the first move. It chilled me to realize that he might not.

As evening drew near, I could no longer deny the rumbling of my stomach. I was about to take the backstairs down to the kitchen, when someone tapped on my door. Praying that it would be Hunter, I hurried to open it. Sarah stood on the other side.

"I wondered if you would like to join me for the evening meal, Faith." Her smile was quite friendly, but I

271

sensed the reservations behind the invitation.

"If you want me, I should love to be with you." I made no attempt to hide my feelings. I did want to be with her, though I could not help hoping that Hunter would be dining here, too.

"There will just be the two of us," Sarah explained as she led the way toward the stairs.

"What? But I . . ." I stopped and took a deep breath, forcing away the pain her casual words brought.

"They all left, Faith. Hunter refused to even anchor for the night, he was so anxious to be rid of his cargo so he could go after the leader of the raiders. Of course, when Harlan heard that, he volunteered himself and Gideon Green to take the *Pearl* to Nassau, so that Hunter and David could take the *Sprite* and start looking immediately." Her tone was bitter.

"He left without telling me?" I could not keep back my wail. I felt betrayed.

"I am sure David had no opportunity, Faith. Hunter and Harlan were like men possessed. I understood little of what they had to say, beyond the terrible things that man Broderick tried to do to you; but Harlan was livid and they both seemed to think it was somehow a personal attack. Do you know what is going on?"

I shook my head, belatedly trying to pull myself together. I had been lucky this time. Sarah had assumed I was upset because David had left without telling me and I must not give her any reason to think otherwise. "I wish I did," I murmured. "All I know is that Hunter seemed to feel the raiders allowed the *Pearl* to escape."

"Did you see anything like that?"

"I was too terrified to notice much," I admitted. We settled ourselves at the table and, as the first course was set before us, Sarah began to ask questions. At her gentle urging, I described much of what had happened to me, beginning with my flight from here, through the raiders' attack on the *Pearl* and beyond to the horror of Broderick's threats and the miracle of Hunter's rescue.

As I spoke, I could see the compassion in her sweet face and when I finished, she reached out and took my hand. "You have been through so much, Faith. To think that you had barely learned of your betrothed's death when the raiders struck. And then to have that awful man threaten you. I cannot think how you had the courage to survive it all."

"When it was happening, there was no time to think of anything but staying alive. And, of course, Hunter managed to save Papa and me from that awful Broderick, so . . ." I let it trail off, afraid that I would cry if I thought about the hours Hunter and I had spent in our island paradise. I suddenly found my dessert impossible to swallow. How could Hunter have left without even seeing me?

"Forgive me for asking you to recall such painful times." Sarah looked uncomfortable. "I fear I have questioned you to spare myself. It is just that I am having difficulty finding the words to explain why Nan Prentice is here in your place."

Relief touched me as I realized that the situation with Nan, not guilt about her feelings for Hunter, was what was troubling Sarah. My smile suddenly felt real again as I met her worried gaze. "You have nothing to explain, Sarah. You hired me to watch over Penny and I left my post." I hesitated, then decided I owed her the full truth about my feelings. "On our return voyage, I was not sure that you would still welcome me back under your roof. I would understand if you wanted me to leave the island entirely."

"Oh, Faith, of course I still want you here." Sarah looked stricken that I should suggest such a thing. "It is only that I am not sure I can put things back as they were. You know how long we have waited for acceptance from the villagers. It was only after you left and we needed help so desperately, that Harlan was finally able to persuade anyone from the village to come. Now we have Nan caring for Penny and Elsie in the kitchen and a new young groom in the stable. If we should change Nan's position . . ."

"She might turn what few villagers have come 'round back to hating you," I finished the thought for her, my mind racing wildly. If there was no position for me here, my pride would not allow me to stay on as a guest. But what could be done? An idea began to form in my mind, but I needed more information. "What exactly is Nan's position? I mean, has she been giving Penny her lessons?"

"Lessons?" Sarah shook her head. "I doubt that Nan can read or write. She is Penny's nurse, as Dorry is H.J.'s." Our eyes met and I could almost see my plan taking form in Sarah's mind. "You could be governess as before, Faith, and with Nan to watch over Penny, you would have plenty of free time to be my companion, too."

"Your companion and Penny's governess?" I was almost afraid to believe my ears, since she was saying exactly what I wanted to hear.

"Oh, Faith, say that you will stay with us. Penny missed you terribly. She was sleepwalking every night for almost a week after you left. She needs you." Sarah hesitated, then added, "And so do I. This house has been far too empty since you have been gone. I find it difficult to stay on this island without your company."

"I have missed you terribly, too." As we hugged each other, some of my pain eased, soothed by the warmth of our friendship. Whatever my doubts and fears about Hunter's leaving without a word, I had Sarah's friendship and that meant a great deal. I had no desire to return to my life of loneliness. More guilt filled me as I realized how much I had hurt Sarah by running away. "I am so sorry I left the way I did, but I knew David would never agree to my going and . . ."

"And Hunter would have ordered you off the ship if he had known." Sarah's eyes gleamed with laughter, surprising me. "I should love to have seen his face when

274

you came crawling out from under that canvas. He is not used to being surprised."

"I seem to surprise him in a number of ways." The words were out before I thought and when I looked into Sarah's face I sensed that she had marked them as carrying a special meaning. "Like my being able to row a boat," I continued, hoping to cover my lapse.

Being in love and trying to hide it was proving more difficult than I had expected. While I was with David on the ship, I had felt no desire to confess, but with Sarah I longed to share my feelings. If only I had not seen her with Hunter that morning. I wanted to trust her fidelity to Harlan, to believe that she would approve of my feelings for Hunter; but how could I? The closeness I had shared with Sarah a moment ago was destroyed by my secret and there was nothing I could do about it.

"Perhaps it is your ability to do the unexpected that he finds so intriguing," Sarah said, her eyes veiled. "My darling Hunter has always had far too easy a time charming the ladies. A challenge will keep him interested."

Her darling Hunter! Though her tone had been amused, the words chilled me. Were they a warning? Had Sarah sensed my feelings and was this her way of telling me to keep away from him? I did not want to believe that, but why else would she say such things to me?

"Faith, are you all right? You seem pale and disturbed." Sarah's concern shone in her eyes as she studied my face. "Were you hurt or . . ."

The genuineness of her caring shamed me, making me hate my own suspicions. Suddenly, I ached to escape the warmth she offered. I needed time to think, to try and understand my own very confused emotions. If I could.

"I am just tired, Sarah. This has been a very confusing and difficult time for me. I still worry about whether Papa reached Charleston safely and now that David and Hunter have gone off seeking Broderick . . . I think, if you will excuse me, perhaps I should just go

275

to my room."

"You have no need to ask. I should have realized that you were not up to entertaining me with all the details of your adventures. Hunter warned me that you might . . . That you were troubled by all that had happened. I thought you might need someone to talk to."

Hunter again. Her easy mention of their closeness stabbed at me because it contrasted so bitterly with my isolation from him. I took a deep breath and tried for a smile that felt too tight on my face. "You have been very kind, Sarah; kinder than I deserve." The words felt heavy on my tongue, weighted down by the lie that was going to be my way of life. "I am sure tomorrow will be a much better day."

I fled up the stairs, not even caring if Sarah thought I was behaving strangely. I could not spend another moment facing her. My new room seemed smaller even than the cabin on the ship. I paced it for several minutes, then stood at the open window staring out at the night.

The view was slightly different from the one in my old suite, but I could still see the sentinel palm and come morning, I would probably be able to see the bluff where Hunter and I . . . Sobs that had been caught in my throat since Sarah told me the men had left now rose to choke me with tears.

"Hunter," I cried. "Why could you not have at least come to say good-bye?"

Chapter 18

I know not how long I lay on my bed, sobbing into my pillow. Perhaps I fell asleep, for when I finally lifted my head, the candle I had left burning on my bedside table was nearly gone. Feeling no better, I struggled to my feet. Time to change to my nightdress and braid my hair or I would face the morning looking even more disheveled than I had after Hunter rescued me.

Since my curtain was still not closed, I went to the window to shut out the night. It was then I saw them—the little bobbing lights moving along the path. Bobbing lights—one of which might be carried by the person who had caused Savannah to bolt, then taken the bridle rein and . . .

Anger sent me climbing out through the open window to run along the balcony to the rear staircase. The lights appeared to be coming from the cove and since I knew where they were going, I meant to be waiting at the little glade to see what they did when they arrived there. I might not be able to convince Harlan that the "paraders" were real, but Hunter and David would be interested in what they did, especially since David had seen the lights himself.

My anger carried me well into the wild area before I stumbled over a rock and fell, twisting my knee. Slowed by my tender knee and a sudden awareness of how alone I was out here, I continued in what I hoped was the direction of the glade. Somehow I had forgotten how dark and frightening the woods could be. I wished mightily that David was with me again. Or Hunter—but no, I must not even think of Hunter now.

An eternity seemed to pass as I wandered through the gloom beneath the trees, emerging only occasionally to try to set my course by the distant palm. I managed to do that surprisingly well, for I almost stumbled into the path. Luckily, sounds from ahead of me saved me from being caught in the open. I staggered to a stop, then inched forward, carefully parting the thick growth of a wild hibiscus.

I had taken too long to reach the area. The lights were approaching not from the sea, but from the direction of the glade. I started to pull back, fearful of being seen; then hesitated. I might not be able to discover what they did at the glade, but this was my chance to find out who carried the lights. Taking a deep breath, I parted the leaves once again.

There was disappointingly little to see. The lanterns cast strange shadows, distorting the features of those who carried them and the men not carrying lanterns were nearly invisible in the well-shadowed path. The second man with a lantern seemed slightly familiar, but he was gone before I could really be sure that I recognized him. The next few were just dark blurs, then another unfamiliar light-carrier.

Weariness settled about my shoulders, reminding me of how far I had come and how little . . . I started nervously as one of the men said something. His voice was too low for me to make out the words, but a chill went down my spine. I recognized that voice! As he came into view, my suspicions were confirmed—Ebban Decateur was carrying the final lantern.

I sank back on the ground as the bobbing lights slowly disappeared around a curve in the path, then winked back at me through small breaks in the vegetation. Why was I so surprised? I asked myself. Had I ever doubted that the villagers were involved? But Ebban Decateur? He worked for the Latimers, so what was he doing out here in the middle of the night?

I shivered, suddenly conscious of the cold night air that easily penetrated my gown. Naturally, I had been in too big a hurry to remember a wrap. I thought sadly of Papa's cloak which Rose had taken down to the kitchen for cleaning. I wished I could surround myself with it and pretend that I was in Hunter's arms. No, I *wished* I could be in Hunter's arms. Or anywhere but here, alone in the dark.

Tears burned my eyes, but I blinked them back, unwilling to surrender to futile sobs. Instead I got to my feet and headed back to the house. There was nothing I could do now, no one I could tell of my discovery. Sarah would be terrified and, of course, she could do nothing about the strange visits to our end of the island.

The moon, which had been hiding behind the clouds, emerged just as I reached the end of the woods and I welcomed its light as I crossed the formal gardens, admiring the way the work had progressed while I was gone. It helped by bathing the stairway in light and making my trip along the balcony easier. My teeth were chattering as I slipped through my window, slamming it closed behind me. I had made it safely back.

I wrapped my own cloak around me and huddled on the single chair, too spent and cold to undress even though my bed beckoned me almost irresistibly. I longed for a warm drink or a fire, but I was too weary to make the effort.

Ebban Decateur. I remembered clearly my meeting with him at the warehouse when I had asked about the ledger entries. I had sensed his resentment and dislike then, but had it been enough for him to follow me in the woods and frighten my horse?

Perhaps what had happened with Savannah had nothing to do with my visit to the warehouse. After all, I had been riding along the path the day Savannah bolted. Could it be that Decateur had seen me and suspected that I had discovered something I should not have? Did he think that I knew what they were doing out there?

Depression washed over me. If he could see me now, he would know how little he needed to fear me. But that was not true. I straightened, my strength returning. I might not know what they did on their "parades," but I knew where they went and now I know who was involved. My returning anger gave me the strength to get up and get ready for bed.

As I slipped between the fresh-scented linens, I smiled, a new plan forming in my mind. I might not be able to take any action to stop the "parades," but I could try to find out more about the island people. All I needed to do was make friends with Nan Prentice. She had been warily friendly when we met, so perhaps with a little effort . . . I drifted into dreams of happier times.

I enjoyed learning more about Nan and I quickly came to like her. Sweet and shy, before long she confessed that she had accepted the post at Thunder House only because her intended, Gordon, had been taken on as a groom and she wanted to be near him.

I learned little that was helpful until late the third afternoon after my return to Dark Thunder. We were together in the little sitting room waiting for Penny to wake from her nap, when Nan let her sewing drop and leaned back with a sigh. "I be not too cozy at Thunder House, miss, for true. 'Tis a place of ill omen and always was." She looked down at the petticoat she was hemming as though embarrassed by what she had said.

"Why do you say that, Nan?" I asked, doing my best to pretend that I was only casually interested, though my fingers trembled so much with excitement that I stuck myself with my embroidery needle.

"Ye be thinkin' I be a fool, if'n I tells ye."

"Not at all, Nan. At home, I often heard tales of places that were cursed by events that had happened in the past." Leone had been full of such tales and David and I had adored being frightened by them. "Is that what happened here?"

"What have ye heard?" Nan's expression changed to one of suspicion.

"About Dark Thunder? Nothing, really. I was just making conversation. I meant nothing by my question." I wanted to scream with frustration. "Is there something amiss here?"

I half expected Nan to either leave the sitting room or change the subject, but she did neither. Instead, she just stared off into space for several minutes, before she sighed and lifted her gaze to meet mine.

"'Tis Thunder House itself, Miss Faith. It be cursed."

For a heartbeat, I just stared at her. That was the last thing I had expected to hear. If she had called the nearby woods haunted, I would have understood, but the house? That made no sense at all. I had to pursue it. "I do not understand, Nan. I thought that Mr. Latimer built this house for his family. How could it be cursed?"

"'Tis built on the very foundation o' the first Thunder House. This part o' the island be cursed by him what owned it. The real Thunder House 'twere burned durin' the time o' trouble, but 'tis said his spirit still be roamin' the bluffs and the woods, cursin' the strangers what be here in his place."

"I suppose he carries a lantern and walks along the path in the woods at night." I was caught between amusement and anger, suspecting that Decateur had used that tale to keep the village people from making friends with us. Only when I looked at Nan did I regret my impulsive statement. She looked as though she had seen a ghost.

"Have ye seen him, miss? If ye be one what has, beware. 'Tis a curse what comes true. Them what tries to seek him, finds death awaitin'."

281

I wanted to protest, but caution kept me from speaking. I had no doubt that Nan believed what she told me and I was far from sure that I could convince her that the ghostly parade was made by real people. Besides, I was not ready to have anyone else know how much I had learned; not until David and Hunter were back on the island to help me get to the bottom of whatever was going on.

"Perhaps we should talk of other things," I murmured, suddenly aware of the silence that was spreading between us. "I had no desire to upset you, Nan. Tell me more about your plans for the future. Will you and Gordon be wed one day soon?"

Since Gordon was her favorite subject, she quickly relaxed, telling me all about their dream of having their own little house in the village. A dream that I suspected was the main reason she had come to live here in spite of her fear of the area. Listening to her brought back my own ache of loneliness. Would I never be allowed to have such sweet, loving dreams of the future? So much depended on why Hunter had left so abruptly . . . and what he chose to do when he came back.

Time passed too slowly from that day on. Though I was busy with teaching Penny and spending time helping Sarah with her various projects, there were still too many hours in the days. Whenever I was alone, my thoughts seemed to turn immediately to Hunter. Where was he? Why had he asked Harlan to take the *Pearl* and her cargo of cotton to Nassau? Where had he gone instead?

The night I had spent pursuing the bobbing lights continued to haunt me. What could they do at the glade? Finally, choosing an afternoon when Sarah was occupied with planning menus and producing a shopping list in anticipation of Harlan's return and Nan was sitting with Penny while she slept, I decided to take a walk.

It was not a pleasant afternoon. Clouds had come

rolling in during the midday meal and the air was already growing damp with the promise of rain. Fearing that I might be caught in the storm, I decided to wear Papa's heavy cloak instead of my own lighter one. Now as I walked, I wrapped it more tightly around me, thinking again of Hunter and longing to have his arms about me.

Cursing my foolish heart, I hurried through the brush and trees, anxious to reach the glade. There had to be something there that I had overlooked before, some clue as to why it was so important for Decateur and his men to go there in the dead of night. I shivered—make that dark of night. I had no desire to think of death in connection with where I was going.

In spite of my determination, I found myself remembering Nan's warning about the curse endangering anyone who saw the mysterious lantern carriers. It might be only a story put about by Ebban Decateur, but if I had not jumped from Savannah before she fell, it might have come true. My sense of foreboding grew with each passing moment and I almost turned back; but I was so close to the glade, my curiosity won over my uneasiness.

It looked disappointingly the same as I had remembered it. The grass still grew thick and lush, the plants appeared healthy, the boulders still protected the rocky base of the small cliff, even the vines that trailed down from the top of the cliff looked the same. I poked around, even marched a few steps down the path, then returned, hoping for inspiration; but there was just nothing to see.

The storm was growing nearer; I could feel the wind rising; I could hear it lashing the tops of the trees, though I was sheltered here by the cliff. I shivered, not cold exactly, but uneasy. The hair on the back of my neck seemed to be rising as though in response to watching eyes. I peered around, trying to see into the shadowed wood. It was not reassuring to realize that a dozen men could be hiding within twenty feet of me and I would be unaware of them.

Time to go back to the house. I looked longingly at the

cliff. Having studied the area from the vantage point of the balcony, I suspected that I was, in fact, much nearer the house here than I had realized. Because of the cliff and the broken land surrounding it, I was forced to take a much longer path back through the wood. If only . . .

A crackling sound that seemed different from the rustling of the wind, brought me around. Naturally, there was nothing to see, but the feeling of being watched intensified until I wanted to scream with it. I plunged into the trees, nearly running, stumbling about in the gloom of the approaching storm. I felt as though a dozen demons were in pursuit, but I saw no one.

I was panting like a wind-broke nag by the time I burst out of the brush and stopped to catch my breath. The wind felt good as it tugged at the heavy, too-large cloak and lifted my tumbled curls off my face. I turned to look back into the trees, knowing that I would see nothing; but still sure that something or someone had been following me.

"I am getting as foolish as the islanders," I muttered to myself as I made my way along the neat shell-paved paths toward the welcoming veranda. Rose opened the front door even before I reached the top step.

"Thank the Lord you be back, Miss Faith," she murmured.

"Has something happened?" A chill traced down my spine.

"'Tis Miss Penny. She had a terrible bad dream and that Nan be of no use calming her." Rose's frown deepened. "Miss Sarah be troubled by an aching head, so she be napping and I . . ."

"I shall see to it," I assured her, running lightly up the stairs. This was one crisis I felt competent to deal with.

I hurried through the playroom, following the sound of sobs into Penny's room. Nan was holding the girl, but her murmuring seemed to have no effect on Penny. Nan's eyes were wet with tears when she looked up at me. "Can ye be helpin' her, miss?"

"I think maybe what Penny needs is a story," I said, allowing Nan to take Papa's cloak from my shoulders as I sank down on the bed beside Penny. "Did I ever tell you what happened the day that Sparkle decided to explore the Golden Grotto, Penny?" I gave her a moment to stop crying. "The grotto that was cursed by the evil troll that lived in the wood."

"What's a troll?" Penny's sobs seemed to have vanished.

"It is a creature that comes from a nightmare. Something dark and scary that wants to frighten. But Sparkle, having curly horns and magical powers, was not frightened. In fact, he never even thought about the troll while he was trotting through the wood. All he wanted to do was bathe his horns in the golden waters of the sacred pool in the grotto."

I held Penny close, feeling her body relaxing against me. As the story unfolded, I asked her a few questions about her bad dream, carefully using some of it in the story. That way Sparkle could banish the dark shapes that terrified her at the same time he used his magic powers to evict the troll from the Golden Grotto so Princess Penelope could swim in the pool with him.

By the time I finished the story, Penny was her bright, smiling self again, quite ready for Nan to dress her so she could go have a special tea with her mother. As I started from the room to go and tidy myself for tea, Nan followed me. "Could I be askin' another favor, miss?"

"Of course, what is it, Nan?"

"Gordon come by at midday and tole me he were in the village earlier and he be hearin' talk that me mum is feelin' poorly and I be wonderin' if ye could see to Miss Penny for a bit. I'd not be stayin' home long, but if'n I could just see her for a wee visit . . ."

"Your mother is ill?" I frowned, realizing that, in spite of all the time we had spent talking, I knew almost nothing of her family.

"Her's been ailin' for sometime, Miss Faith. I be

hopin' to take her to a real doctor one day, but . . . 'Tis likely that her be missin' me and a visit might perk her up. Should I go ask Miss Sarah's permission?"

I could see the desperation in her eyes and, knowing well how I had felt worrying over my own mother, I had to blink back tears. "You go ahead," I told her. "I shall see to Penny's care and explain the situation to Sarah. Rose told me she was feeling poorly earlier. Do not worry, I know Sarah will understand."

"Bless you, Miss Faith, I'd not be askin', 'twere it not so worrisome. I can see to Miss Penny's dressing."

I shook my head, looking out the window at the darkening sky and the rising wind that lashed the trees. "You go now, Nan, and stay the night. I will see to Penny, never fear. Your mother will only fret if you try to return during the storm."

The look of relief on Nan's face lifted my spirits, yet left me feeling a bit guilty, too. If I had known of the situation, I could have offered her other chances to make a visit to the village. I waved aside her murmured thanks as I began helping Penny to dress.

"I be goin' now, Miss Faith." Nan's soft voice interrupted my thoughts and I turned to see her picking up a thin cloak to wrap about her shoulders.

"Wait," I said. "You cannot go without a warm cloak. Take mine. It is big and long, so it will protect you from the storm." I overrode her objections, wrapping Papa's cloak around her and sending her on her way.

The rest of the day passed quietly enough. At tea Sarah seemed to be feeling fine and when I told her what I had done, she was in total agreement with my sending Nan to visit her mother. As we spent time with the children, the storm continued to rage outside the house, making me glad that we were safe inside.

Later, as I looked out at the stormy night, I hoped that Nan had heeded my advice and stayed on with her mother. This was not a time for anyone to be out. Not even the "paraders" I thought grimly as I carried my

286

nightclothes to the room next to Penny's. I would sleep there tonight so that Penny would be protected should she sleepwalk.

It was near dawn when I woke, sensing that someone was in my room. I sat up, clutching the covers to my breast, wondering for a moment where I was, then I remembered. "Nan?" I whispered, the light from the single candle flickered wildly so that I could not make out the face of the woman approaching the bed.

"It be me, miss." It was Rose, not Nan.

"What is it, Rose? Is Sarah ill?"

"No, miss, this be about Nan. Her young man, that Gordon, he come a pounding on the kitchen door. Seems someone come from the village seeking Nan, her Ma be terrible bad." Rose lit the candle on the bedside table as she spoke and I saw the confusion in her face. "I be telling him she went to her ma, but . . ."

"Did she come back after I came up to bed?"

"Not likely, miss, less'n her slipped in. Higgins swears he admitted no one."

"Did you check my room?" I asked, beginning to think more clearly as the cobwebs of sleep were banished by worry. "Perhaps she returned very late and did not wish to wake anyone."

"I'll do that now, miss." Rose left and I got up, shivering in the cold as I pulled on a robe and my shoes. If Nan had, indeed, returned, she would need friends around her. I remembered only too well what it felt like to lose a mother.

Rose was back before I had time to do more than check to be sure that Penny was snug in her bed. Her frown had deepened. "Her be nowhere in the house, Miss Faith. That Gordon, he 'bout roused the dead and Mrs. Higgins, her say there be no sign of Nan."

"Blast." I tugged at my thick single braid, then moved to the window. Though it was still dark, the sky was

287

growing pale to the east and the wind and rain had died out during the night. A light tap on the door announced a second visitor.

Mrs. Higgins came in. Like Rose and me, she was still in her nightclothes, but there was nothing sleepy about her brown eyes. "There's no sign that the girl returned, Miss Faith," she informed me. "You did say that she expected to stay in the village through the night, did you not?"

I nodded. "I thought with the storm . . . What did the man who came from the village have to say?"

Mrs. Higgins shrugged. "I was not the one who spoke with him. The new groom, Gordon, he is the one who came to the house. He is still in the kitchen, if you wish to speak with him. Or should I wake Miss Sarah?"

"I shall talk with him first. Perhaps there is some simple explanation for all this." I turned to Rose. "You will stay here with Penny?"

"Yes, miss."

As I followed Mrs. Higgins down the rear stairs, I felt the chill of premonition. If Nan had not gone to her mother, where was she? Had something happened to her as she walked along the road to the village? I shivered, remembering my own long walk when I had decided to stowaway on the *Pearl*. But Nan had left in the afternoon, not the middle of the night.

I had spoken with Gordon several times, but I scarcely recognized the frantic young man spreading mud across the kitchen floor as he paced. He turned to me, his expression imploring. "Did ye find her, Miss Faith? Be she here?"

"I am sorry, Gordon, but Nan left about midafternoon. She had told me of her worry about her mother and I suggested that she go and perhaps spend the night at home. She has not returned. Are you sure that she was not with her mother?"

"Cal's wife, her been seein' to Nan's ma. Her roused Cal and sent him out to fetch Nan. Where she be, Miss

288

Faith?" His gaze was so full of worry and pain I had to blink back sympathetic tears.

"I guess the only place she can be, Gordon, is somewhere between this house and the village. This man Cal, did he see anything odd on his way out?"

"What ye be meaning, Miss Faith?" Gordon's sun-darkened skin took on a muddy hue.

"Perhaps she fell or maybe she took shelter from the storm and went to sleep or . . . something." I hated saying the words, but nothing else made sense. "I think it would be wise to start a search as soon as the sun comes up, Gordon. I will go dress and I want you to saddle Savannah for me and horses for all the men who work in the stable. Have everyone ready by sunup."

"Yes, Miss Faith." He looked calmer just accepting my orders. I wished I had as much confidence in what I was doing.

"Oh, and have the pony cart readied, too." I winced, his stricken look was like a plea. "If she has injured herself, she will need a ride to the village or back here for care."

"You think something has happened to her, do you not?" Mrs. Higgins asked the moment the door closed behind Gordon.

"She was going to her mother because she was very worried about her, yet she never arrived." I sighed, feeling incredibly weary even though I had gone to bed early and slept well. "I just hope that it is nothing more serious than an injured ankle."

Mrs. Higgins nodded. "I'll have Cook prepare a hot meal for all of you. 'Tis best not to face a search on an empty stomach."

"Thank you. I shall go up and dress."

"What about Miss Sarah?" Mrs. Higgins stopped me with her question.

I hesitated, not sure how the housekeeper felt about my taking charge the way I had. Sometimes I had a tendency to forget that I was not a member of the family.

289

I met her gaze as calmly as I could. "There is little she can do, since she is not fond of riding and does not know the area. Perhaps you should just tell her what is happening when she awakens."

Mrs. Higgins studied my face for several moments before she nodded, a smile warming her features. "I agree there is no reason to upset her further. Leastwise not until we know the lie of the land."

It was a bright and glowing morning full of sunlight by the time I stepped out of the house to join the half-dozen men employed by the household. Horses nickered and stomped their hooves as Gordon helped me to mount Savannah. At my request, Higgins was to drive the pony cart along the road and coordinate our search from there.

We spread out, three riders within sight of each other on each side of the roadway, which was screened from us by the thick bushes. As the least experienced rider, I was placed between Gordon and young Ben. We rode forward slowly, scanning the shadows beneath each bush and tree, pausing every few minutes to call Nan's name, straining our ears for an answer.

Though I had not been on a horse since my fall, I soon found myself enjoying the morning. Thanks to the glowing sunlight and the happy birdsongs that filled the air, it was hard to believe that anything bad could have happened to Nan. Still, as the time passed and we got closer to the village, my joy began to ebb.

Where could she be? This was the only road to the village, Nan would have kept to it, would she not? Or would she? I reined in Savannah, suddenly frowning. I remembered my flight along this way, but that was different. I had been running away from something, Nan had been hurrying to her mother.

"What be it, Miss Faith? Did ye see something?" Gordon was at my side at once.

"Gordon, is there a shortcut to the village? One that

Nan would have known about and used?"

He started to answer, then looked away almost guiltily. "Us be told to stick to the road, miss."

"It was raining and cold and Nan was worried about her mother, Gordon. She was in a hurry to get to her."

"Well, could be her would cut cross-country, but . . ."

"Show me," I ordered. "The rest can keep searching this way, but I doubt they will find her."

"It be this way." He led me across an open field and into the trees that grew between the road and the bluff where the foundation for Hunter's house was now taking form.

A chill touched my shoulders in spite of the warmth of the sun. This was the area I had been riding through when Savannah bolted. It took all my courage not to draw rein and return to the search along the road. Nan would never have come this way, would she?

Suddenly Savannah snorted, pulling at the bit, dancing sideways. I leaned forward to pat her neck, murmuring soothing words even as my own heart began to pound. Suddenly I caught a glimpse of blue in the shadow of a wild fig tree. "Gordon," I shouted. "Gordon, over here."

She was lying curled up, like a person sleeping, my father's cloak nearly hiding her bright blue gown from view. I was shaking so hard, I nearly fell as I slipped from the saddle to the soft earth. Gordon was already kneeling beside her, pulling the cloak away, calling her name, touching her pale cheek. I held my breath, waiting for her eyes to open, hoping that . . .

"Miss Faith, what be wrong with her?" Gordon looked up at me with such pleading, I had to kneel in the mud beside him and take one of Nan's cold hands in mine. I pressed my fingers against her slim wrist as I had seen the doctor do with my mother. My heart leaped as I felt the movement of her pulse beating beneath my fingers.

"Be her dead, miss?" Gordon's voice snapped my attention back to him.

291

"She is alive, Gordon, but she needs help fast. Go and get Higgins with the cart and bring him here. I will stay with her."

For a moment I thought he might argue, might try to lift her on his horse and carry her to safety, then he was gone and I was alone in the haunted area with the unconscious girl. "Nan," I called, shaking her very gently. "Nan, you have to wake up."

There was no response. I touched her cheek, finding it cold and wet. She must be near frozen, I realized, moving closer, trying to lift her head from the cold ground to rest on my lap. It was then I saw the dark matted clot of hair on the side of her head.

Reluctantly, I touched the spot and my wet fingers came away red, telling me what I had not wanted to know. I lifted her head gently, slipping my jacket beneath it to protect her injury from whatever had caused it. A chill shivered down my spine as I saw that there was nothing but rain-soaked soft earth beneath her head, no rock or fallen branch to have caused the injury.

Chapter 19

I had little time to contemplate the meaning of what I had seen as help arrived almost immediately and I could only offer my advice about taking care in moving Nan from the ground to the pony cart. Much of what I told them came from the days I had spent following Leone about the slave quarters as she treated our people's injuries; but I knew it was sound, for most of her patients lived to work again.

Once Nan was successfully settled on Papa's cloak and wrapped with the blankets Higgins had thought to include, he turned to me. "I think we'd best take her to Thunder House, Miss Faith. A rider came from the village to tell us that Nan's mother did not survive the night, so there be no one but her two younger brothers and a sister to care for her at her house."

"Please, Miss Faith, I be wantin' to be near her." Gordon stood beside the pony cart, his young face full of pleading and love for Nan.

"Of course we shall take her back to the house. Is there anyone in the village who is experienced in treating someone who is seriously injured?" I looked to Gordon for an answer, since I knew the rest of the servants had been as rudely treated by the villagers as we had.

He shook his head.

"Cook is a good hand with injuries as is my wife,"

Higgins stated. "And you seem to have the touch for it, Miss Faith."

"Then we had best get her home," I said, getting into the pony cart to hold Nan steady so as not to add further injury to the side of her head.

The next hours were so busy I had little time to think about what had happened to Nan. Sarah was at the door to greet us when we reached the house and, thanks to the fact the other menservants had ridden ahead to let Cook know that we were bringing Nan to the house, everything was in readiness for us.

Before the midday meal Nan had been carefully washed and tucked into one of the two beds moved into a large vacant room across the hall from mine. At my request, Rose took over care of Penny, leaving me free to watch over Nan. Not that there was much to watch. Except for moaning when I bathed the gash and swollen lump on the side of her head, she showed no sign of life.

A tap on the door interrupted my half-dozing vigil shortly after noon. "Miss Sarah says you should go down for your meal, Miss Faith," Mary said. "She be wantin' me to watch over Nan for you, if'n that be all right."

I hesitated, somehow afraid to leave Nan, yet my stomach's rumbling was growing more insistent and I knew that there was little chance that Nan would awaken suddenly. "Thank you, Mary, I would like a little time away. But you must promise to call me if there is any sign of moving or if she begins to cry out or moan in her sleep, is that clear?"

"Yes, miss." Mary's look of anxiety as she crossed the room told me that she would be only too glad to summon me.

My meal with Sarah proved more difficult than I had anticipated because she had a lot of questions that I did not want to answer. Her first came as we were served. "What do you think happened, Faith? Did she fall and strike her head on a rock?"

"There was no rock near where we found her." I was suddenly tired of all the lies that I had told to protect Sarah. "The rain had begun before she left the house, so the earth was already soft."

Sarah paled, her eyes growing wide as she absorbed the implications of my words. "What are you saying?"

"That she did not injure her head falling where we found her." I met her gaze firmly.

"Could she have fallen against a tree or a branch, then staggered there before she fell?"

It was a question I had asked myself as I watched Nan lying so still in the bed. "If she did, she also took off Papa's cloak and pulled it over her after she fell down."

"What?"

"I noticed that she was wrapped in the cloak when we found her, but I gave it no thought then, Sarah. Only later, when I was covering her . . . The cloak was clearly there to protect her from the rain, it was not being worn."

Sarah just stared at me. "Do you think someone hit her, Faith?"

I nodded, relieved to hear someone say the words that had been haunting me since I realized the significance of the cloak.

"But who would hurt Nan?"

"I have no idea." That was the truth, but not all of it. Once I realized that Nan had been carefully covered by the cloak, another horrible truth had intruded. I had been wearing that cloak just a short time before Nan left the house in it—and I had been exploring the area of the bobbing lights.

"You are frightening me, Faith." Sarah's voice snapped my mind back to the present.

"I thought you should be warned. It might be wise to make sure that no one strays from the house until Hunter or Harlan gets back to look into this." I felt again the isolation of living on Dark Thunder; but now that I had told Sarah, I was more angry than frightened by it. If someone had hurt Nan because they thought it was I they were striking, I wanted revenge.

"I will warn the household to avoid that area of the island, but I think it would be wise for us to keep your suspicions between us until the men return." Sarah surprised me by her acceptance of what I had told her. Perhaps Harlan and Hunter were wrong in their insistence that she must be protected like a child.

I nodded, then happily changed the subject to other matters. Though I had told her that I wanted to wait until Hunter and Harlan were back to take any action, my anger still simmered and the flames grew hotter every time I pictured someone following Nan through the storm, sneaking up behind her and . . . And striking a blow that was meant to kill me.

A long night and part of another day passed before Nan showed any sign of reviving. I had plenty of time to brood about what had happened and to consider the possibilities. My guilt grew hourly and with it my anger. If I had not pressed Nan to take Papa's distinctive plaid cloak, she would never have been injured. Someone was going to pay for that.

When Nan suddenly whimpered, I raced to her side. Her eyes opened and I held my breath, fearful that she would not know me or not be able to see or speak or . . .

"Faith, what happened?" Her voice was rough and strange, but once the confusion eased a little, I could see the girl I had come to care about was back with me. I sent one of the maids to fetch Gordon because I knew she would soon have need of his strong young arms.

Slowly, as gently as I could, I explained that she had hurt her head on her way to the village, then gave her the sad news about her mother when she asked. As I held her in my arms and listened to her sobbing, I vowed that someone would pay for her pain and for keeping her from

296

spending those last few precious hours with her mother.

Gordon came shyly to the door and I could almost feel the warmth of his caring as he held Nan's hands and told her of her mother's burial and assured her that her brothers and sister were well and safe. Seeing their love made me ache inside to share such feelings with Hunter and I had to turn away or cry for my own loneliness.

By evening, it was clear that Nan no longer needed anyone to watch over her, for her recovery seemed startling in contrast to the fears I had entertained while she lay unconscious. Still, I visited her after the evening meal and stayed by her side until she slept. As I stared down at her sleeping face, I felt as close to her as I would to a younger sister.

It was past midnight as I crossed the hall to my room suddenly anxious to sleep in my own bed for a change. There would be many plans to make tomorrow, for Nan's future, for my own return to being a governess instead of a nurse to Nan; but now I just wanted to forget everything but sleep and maybe a few dreams of Hunter.

The flash of light caught my eye as I started to close the curtain. A chill filled me as I realized that I was, once more, seeing the bobbing lights. Fury swept through me as I picked up Papa's cloak and opened the window to the balcony. This time I was going to see what they did!

Having had plenty of time to think and plan while I sat with Nan, I chose a new route to the glade this time, one that got me to the cliff much more quickly. I paused at the edge of the open area, my side aching with each panting breath I took. Suddenly a light appeared, seemingly out of the cliff itself. I forgot to breathe as I watched the men emerging from what seemed to be a hole in the cliff face.

A cave! Why had I not thought of it? But where? I had searched the cliff area on my last visit and, except for the large boulders . . . I clasped my hand over my mouth so that the men would not hear my gasp. As the final man emerged, I saw that one of the boulders had been rolled away from its normal spot against the rocks. I waited, expecting them to roll the huge boulder back into place, but they simply marched away, leaving the area both quiet and dark.

Was their leaving a sham? Had they seen me? Were they out there waiting for me to emerge so that they could attack me? I peered at the darkness and caught a distant spark of light. They actually seemed to be marching along the path just as they had been the night I saw Decateur with them.

Fearfully, I edged out of the undergrowth and made my way slowly along the cliff face to the opening. It was larger than I had expected and, once I peered inside, I could see a distant glow, as though a lantern had been left behind. Ducking down, I stepped inside and, after a few steps, was able to straighten as the tunnel ceiling was high enough to easily accommodate a man.

After a slight turn, the tunnel opened into a large cavern where the lantern had been left. I stopped, too shocked to do more than stare. The whole room seemed to be filled with crates, boxes, barrels, and other containers, most open and spilling their goods out. It looked like the interior of a small warehouse.

Confused, I moved slowly around the huge room, noting that more tunnels or caves opened off it and that each one seemed to be filled with containers. There were chests full of jewelry and trunks loaded with elegant silver serving pieces, now tarnished, but obviously once someone's treasured possessions.

I touched one of the handsome plates, feeling the cool sleekness of the design beneath the tarnish. How had all this come to be here? What did it mean? And how was Ebban Decateur involved? A shiver traced along my spine as I stepped away from the trunk. Whose goods were these?

Back in the main cavern, I looked more closely at some of the unopened crates and boxes trying to decipher the markings on them. Suddenly I thought of the pages of ledger entries I had made for Sarah while Harlan was away. Cargoes into the warehouse and cargoes out so quickly . . .

Could there be a connection? The very question made me a little ill. What if the cargoes were left at the Latimer warehouse so they could be transferred to smaller boats and brought around to the cove and . . . A sound from outside the cavern snapped me back to the present. They were coming back!

Terrified of being caught, I dived into the nearest of the side tunnels, seeking the deepest shadows behind a stack of barrels. Laughter rode the dusty air and I heard curses as something heavy was dropped. There were raucous comments in unfamiliar voices as the men stowed whatever they had carried in with them.

"That be everythin' for this load," a familiar voice stated from so nearby I almost cried out. "Best us be gettin' back to the village afore someone misses us." Ebban Decateur's chuckle sent shivers down my spine. "There be too much talk a'ready."

"Mayhap, us'uns should do naught for a time." The voice sounded old and weary.

"Ye be losin' yer nerve, old man? Or yer taste for gold." Decateur mocked him.

"For hurtin' our own."

"The girl be fine. I heered it from her sister. Good as new." Decateur confirmed my worst suspicion. "Next time mebbe her be wearin' her own cloak and stayin' on the road, like her been told."

There was more, but I scarcely heard the words, for my mind was spinning. Decateur had struck Nan down and these men knew it. What manner of evil was this that they would hesitate to expose him even after he injured one of their own? I closed my eyes, crawling even further back behind the containers, suddenly terrified for myself. I had no doubt that they would kill me if I were discovered.

Time dragged by, or so it seemed. Then, suddenly,

everything became still and I dared to open my eyes. Nothing, total blackness surrounded me. The lantern! They had blown out the lantern and left me in the suffocating darkness. Terror rippled over me like an icy wind, I could not keep back a whimper. Even as a child I had hated the darkness.

I closed my eyes again, hugging my knees, wanting to pretend that it was all a bad dream; but each time I opened an eye, the blackness was waiting. Finally, the truth penetrated my terror and made it worse; they had gone all right and I was trapped in the cavern!

Screams welled up in my throat and tears spilled over my face as I realized that there would be no light, not ever, not unless they came back. Panic made me want to run, but I could not take a step without stumbling, so I sank back against the rocky wall of what might well become my tomb. I was going to die here alone in the dark.

That thought did it. My panic congealed as a flame of anger flickered inside me. If I died, Decateur won. I rested a hand on the rocky wall and took a couple of slow, deep breaths, then wiped the tears away with the corner of Papa's cloak. I was not going to lie here and die like a mouse. There had to be a way out and I was going to find it.

Calmer now, I moved cautiously along the wall, trying to remember what I had seen. I had a dim memory of a candle and some old matches. I had glimpsed them as I stepped into this particular cave, but where . . . Using my hands I explored every inch of the rock until I found the waxy stub and the long matches. Whispering a prayer, I struck a match.

The flame seemed blinding, but I managed to light the candle before it flickered and went out. Holding the candle stub carefully, I looked around. It took me what seemed a lifetime to find a small cache of candles. I lit one and put the rest, along with the matches, into my cloak pocket. Now to get out of here.

It took only a short time for me to locate the tunnel that led out, but my elation at finding it died quickly. The boulder had been rolled back into place. I took a deep breath and set the candle carefully in a small pool of cooling wax, then used both hands to push the boulder. Nothing happened.

The terror began to return as I turned my back and tried bracing one foot against the tunnel wall to give me added impetus. It still refused to budge. I pushed and shoved and sobbed, but the boulder might as well have been a solid wall. Finally, exhausted and nursing scratches on my hands, I sank down on the stony ground. I had found the way out, but I was still trapped here.

I could feel the icy panic creeping back to surround me as I stared at the immovable boulder. To fight it, I picked up my candle and left the tunnel. If I could not go out that way, I would simply have to find another way out. I started across the cavern, then stopped as my candlelight fell on the contents of an open chest, one that had not been there when I entered.

"My cameo." I rubbed my dry, sore eyes, sure that it was a trick of my mind; but the cameo was still there, lying atop what looked like a collection of beautifully embroidered linens. I picked it up, holding it close to the dancing candle flame, still sure that I must be wrong; but there was no mistaking the carving in the cameo, I had spent too many hours looking at it to be wrong.

Swallowing the bitter bile that rose in my throat, I moved the linens aside and found my betrothal ring beneath them, along with a collection of jewelry I had not seen before. I shivered as I remembered Broderick's hands moving over me, tearing the cameo from my gown, breaking the chain that held my ring. But how could they be here?

I refused to think about it as I added the ring and the cameo to the candles and matches in the cloak's big pocket. I needed all my strength to find a way out, I told myself firmly, trying not to notice the shadows that danced and reached out to me as I moved carefully across the big room toward the far end. Since I had explored most of the small side caves earlier, that area was my only hope.

At first the back wall of the cavern seemed pretty solid, then a deeper shadow, half hidden by yet another stack of unopened crates, drew my attention and I headed for it. A tunnel! My heart began to pound as I stepped into the narrow space, my feeble light showing me that nothing had been stored in this rocky area.

Another exit? But to where? I had completely lost my sense of direction since being inside here, but I could think of no place in the area where an opening could exist unnoticed. Still, it had to go somewhere, I kept telling myself as I followed the tunnel and tried to ignore the way it closed in on me. Darkness behind, darkness ahead and nothing but rocky walls that grew closer and closer together until . . .

Perspiration trickled down my back in spite of the damp cold and I had trouble catching my breath as I rounded one last twist in the tunnel. My hand was shaking so hard the candle threatened to go out and for a moment I thought I was seeing things. There was a wooden panel ahead of me. The tunnel ended in a wall! A sob caught in my throat as I lifted my candle to examine the barrier.

Light glinted on a metal lever. A handle? Hope pushed the panic back as I reached out and touched the cold metal. It was real, not a figment of my imagination. I caressed it, afraid to push or pull or lift or press down on it. I knew that, if it did nothing, I would be unable to keep the screams inside any longer.

I know not how long I stood there, but finally my courage returned and I pushed down on the lever. For a heartbeat nothing happened, then a creaking filled the narrow tunnel and after a grating complaint, the wall moved away revealing darkness on the other side. Swallowing hard, I stepped through, wondering where

302

I was.

The wall or panel began to swing closed, but I caught it, not sure that I was ready to trade one prison for another. It was then I discovered that the wall was the back of a cupboard and I could see a second, much smaller lever on this side, carefully concealed by the ornately carved design of the cupboard. I released the panel as I realized that I recognized the cupboard. I had seen it on my last trip to the cellar of Thunder House!

Still not sure I believed my own eyes, I crossed the dirt floor of the old cellar, seeing my own trunk in one corner and recognizing many of the other items stored down here. As I climbed the stairs that led to the storage area off the kitchen, I prayed that the door would be unlatched so I would truly escape from this nightmare.

It opened and the dark kitchen welcomed me with the scents of food and life. No one challenged me as I climbed the backstairs and made my way to my own room. I closed the window and the curtain, then lit a lamp, glorying in the light, in being here, in being alive.

The small clock on the mantel told me that I had been imprisoned less than four hours, yet I felt a lifetime had passed. Weary beyond comprehension, I simply wrapped Papa's cloak more tightly around me and lay down on my bed. I slept instantly and without dreams or nightmares.

I woke slowly, feeling groggy, my head aching even before I opened my eyes. The room felt stuffy and when I tried to push back the covers, I discovered that I was wrapped in them. Though the curtain was closed, enough light penetrated to show me that I was in my room at Thunder House.

My hands stung as I untangled myself from the cloak and sat up. What had happened? Had I lain down for a nap or . . . The memories came flooding back like a nightmare left over from the darkness. I shivered in spite of the warmth of the room. It could not be true. It was just a bad dream brought on by all that had happened.

I looked down at myself, at my stained and torn gown and the scratches on my hands. I could almost feel the unyielding boulder gouging my palms and bruising my back as I tried to escape. The cavern was real and so were the goods it contained. Fingers shaking, I sought through the folds of the cloak to find the pocket.

My cameo still had bits of dried mud on it and the ring clearly bore Tommy's family crest. I gasped, suddenly fully aware of the meaning of what I had found. If my cameo and ring had been stored in the cavern, that meant that Decateur and Broderick were connected. The man who had meant to despoil me and kill my father could even live on Dark Thunder!

I wanted to go shrieking to Sarah, to demand that we take some action, but when I tried to stand, dizziness stopped me. I sank back down on the bed as someone tapped on the door. Rose entered at my invitation.

"Be you all right, Miss Faith?" Her worried frown told me that I probably looked as bad as I felt.

"Not really," I replied. "I . . ." Words refused to come. I could not tell her what had happened to me and I was too confused to come up with a plausible reason for my disheveled condition.

"It be all the caring you've done for Nan. Worked yourself into a state, you have. So you collapsed after she woke up safe, I've seen it afore. You be needing a bit of bed rest yourself." Rose came over to pick up my cloak. "Let me help you out of your clothes and into a nightdress, then I'll be fetching you somewhat to eat."

I tried to protest, but after a moment of thought, I realized the wisdom of accepting her diagnosis. I was exhausted and pleading illness would allow me to avoid all sorts of questions that I had no wish to answer. "How is Nan this morning?" I asked, hoping that Rose would not notice the condition of my clothing.

"Right as rain. She be sad about her ma, but her be on the mend. Likely, her be in to see you in a bit. Miss Sarah,

304

too. She's been asking after you."

"I guess I overslept."

"'Bout time, I be thinking. 'Tis too much you been doing since you been back. You need time to grieve for your betrothed."

There was nothing I could say to that, so I simply allowed Rose to tuck me into my bed and closed my eyes. I had no desire to think about what I had discovered, the implications were too frightening. I needed to talk to David. He would know what to do, whom to contact. And where David was, so also would be my darling Hunter.

As Rose left the room, I conjured up my magical memories of our island sanctuary and Hunter's tender loving. Just remembering the wonder of his touch soothed and healed my heart and mind, making me feel whole again. I clung to my belief that last night's terror could not reach me while I was within the circle of Hunter's love.

By late afternoon the hours of sleep and Rose's tender care had restored my strength, if not my peace of mind. No amount of daydreaming about Hunter had been able to clear the implications of the cavern's contents from my mind. I could not escape the fact that the cameo and ring tied Broderick to this island and since Decateur had brought them to the cavern that meant those two were connected.

And Decateur ran the warehouse for Harlan. The words echoed in my mind even though I did not want to acknowledge them. The same Harlan who had told me that the "pirate parade" was just a harmless trick of the islanders. The same Harlan who had warned Sarah to tell no one about the accounts she was keeping for him. The same Harlan who had wanted me off this island.

The chill of my suspicions made me shiver. For the first time, I began to wonder if David and Hunter were right about the raiders allowing the *Pearl* to escape. Had they attacked not realizing that it was a Latimer ship? Or perhaps they had come to steal the cargo of arms that had been put ashore. If they were truly modern-day pirates, such a cargo would be of great value and they might have expected the *Pearl* to be gone. My unexpected visit with Papa had probably slowed the unloading and loading of the two cargoes.

I shook my head, not wanting to believe my own conclusions. It was too horrible. Hunter would have no part of such activity, of that I was sure; but would Harlan? I hated to think so, but the evidence seemed damning from where I stood. Yet how could he allow his own home to be a part of such a ghastly business? And why would he do it?

I paced my room pondering that question. For the gold that would be paid for the goods stored in the cavern? I could not believe that. I had seen enough of the Latimer account books to know that the company was doing well and would, undoubtedly, do better as the war continued. Besides, I reminded myself, the Latimers had ties to the South, to Savannah, so why would they victimize their own friends?

My head began to ache with the strain of my thoughts, but I ignored the pain, focusing on Broderick. Papa had known him before the war and he gave the appearance of a man raised as a gentleman. The manners were there and the refinement of taste in his dress, only his conscience seemed to be lacking. Perhaps somewhere he, too, had a lovely house and an innocent family that thought him good and kind and fair.

"No, it cannot be." I sat down in the chair, weary from my doubts and fears. Hunter and Harlan were too close; if one was involved, the other would have to at least suspect that something was amiss. Hunter had rushed right to Harlan for help the moment we got back, so he could not mistrust his brother.

So where were they now? The long days since the two ships had left the harbor suddenly took on an ominous appearance for me. For the last few days I had been so wrapped up in all that had happened to Nan and to me

306

that I had not even considered that Hunter and David might be in deadly danger.

What if Harlan felt threatened by Hunter's determination to seek revenge against Broderick? How far would he go to protect his secret? I shook my head, unable to accept such a horrible prospect. Harlan would never harm Hunter . . . unless he, too, had noticed the closeness between Hunter and Sarah. What if I was not the only one who had seen them together as they had been that terrible morning?

Shudders shook me as the memories of that moment swept through my mind. This was madness. Speculation proved nothing. If I sat here any longer, I should truly go mad. But what could I do? I could try to find some answers.

I smiled bitterly remembering how often Papa had said, "Knowledge is power, Faith. You can never lose by learning, remember that." I wondered if he would feel the same if he knew that I was trying to find out if the man I loved was involved with the man who had nearly killed us both.

But how to begin? There were not a lot of sources of information available to me, not if I wanted to keep my discovery a secret. Still, there was no reason I couldn't try to learn more about Decateur's involvement with Latimer Trading Company.

Feeling better for having chosen a direction for myself, I got up and tidied my hair before going in search of Sarah. It was time I asked her a few questions about the account books I had helped her keep what now seemed a lifetime ago. I found her sitting on the veranda with a book.

"Faith, are you feeling better now?" Her obvious delight at seeing me gave me a pang of guilt. How could I suspect her husband of such dastardly deeds?

"Much, thank you. In fact, I was just wondering if there might be some accounts to be entered or ledgers to be worked on. I seem to have a great deal of spare time these days."

"Accounts and ledgers? Not that again, please." Sarah laughed. "I told you, Harlan gave all that over to the man who runs the warehouse."

"Did you tell me?" I feigned confusion. "What man would that be?"

"The one you talked to. A . . . Mr. Decateur, I believe." Sarah shook her head. "Harlan said the man was happy to take over the chore."

"I am sure he was." I walked to the rail to stare out at the distant sentinel palm so that she would not see the sadness I could not hide. What kind of man was Harlan Latimer and why had he chosen to build his house on the foundation of a pirates' home?

Chapter 20

I managed to hide my feelings through the rest of that day and the next, but it grew harder with every passing hour. I had no doubt that Sarah was totally innocent of knowledge of what was happening here on Dark Thunder; but no matter how hard I tried, I could not believe the same of Harlan.

For that reason, I found it difficult to summon up any real excitement when Sarah came to the playroom to announce that the *Pearl* was entering the harbor. "We must go and meet the ship," she said, her eyes bright with excitement. "Harlan will bring news of David and Hunter, I am sure. Without doubt, they have rendezvoused somewhere in the islands since Harlan disposed of the cargo."

Penny's excited, "Papa! Papa! Papa!" and H.J.'s enthusiastic shouts covered my silence. I longed for news of Hunter and David, but how could I trust anything Harlan might tell me? And what if he saw through my façade of welcome to the fear behind it? Would he guess that I knew too much?

"Faith, are you not eager to near what Hunter and David discovered about the evil raiders?" Sarah's frown told me that I was doing a poor job of hiding my feelings.

"Of course I am, Sarah. I was just thinking of Papa and wondering how he fares." The lie almost stuck in my throat. How I hated the necessity of hiding my feelings from Sarah, of having no one I could truly and completely confide in. I had known loneliness in Nassau, but none so bitter as the feeling that came from keeping a part of myself hidden from someone I really cared about. "Let me tidy my hair and I shall be ready to go meet the ship."

"I can hardly wait." Sarah blushed like a maiden. "I have missed Harlan so bitterly these past weeks. I only hope that he brings word that this terrible blockade-running is to cease. If anything should happen to him now . . ."

The glow in her face when she spoke of him made me ashamed of all the dark thoughts I had entertained about a liaison between her and Hunter. I could not believe that anyone as open and loving as Sarah could express such love for one man and still be carrying on with another.

My heart was lighter as I hurried to my room, but my relief at this proof that Hunter's love could be mine was quickly tempered by my realization that Sarah could lose her beloved if what I suspected was true. If Harlan was, indeed, involved with Decateur and Broderick . . . I pushed my suspicions from my mind, well aware that I could not hide my feelings from Harlan, if I continued to think such thoughts.

We reached the harbor just as the *Pearl* edged up to the dock. I shuddered as the splintered area of deck and rail came into view. Would I never forget the sight of the shot hitting the ship? Or the fear for Hunter and David that had nearly paralyzed me? My footsteps dragged a little as I followed Sarah out along the dock. So much had happened to me because of my last voyage on the *Pearl* and . . .

"Faith! Sarah!"

I nearly tripped over my own feet as I saw not Harlan, but Hunter standing at the rail as the gangplank was maneuvered into place. "Hunter!" My whole heart went into the word, yet I could not be sure whether I shouted

310

his name or merely whispered it.

Sarah, who was ahead of me, threw herself into Hunter's arms, hugging him, then giving him a light kiss before she stepped back. "What are you doing here?" she asked, her tone light, but worry already showing in her eyes. "I thought that Harlan was to sail the *Pearl* to Nassau for you?"

Hunter looked past her to meet my gaze and for just a moment all the heat that had flowed between us blazed to life. I waited for him to step away from Sarah and come to me, to take me in his arms and proclaim his feelings; but then Penny and H.J. reached him and claimed his attention. When he looked up again, his gaze was veiled and his delayed greeting was merely friendly.

"Harlan did take the *Pearl* to Nassau and we met there not long after the cargo was sold. He had contracted for another cargo and already set up a rendezvous with Daniel Jones, so we traded ships. The *Pearl* needs a bit of repair before we go blockade-running again."

"Harlan has taken a cargo without coming home?" Sarah's voice held real anguish. "But he promised me."

"Now, Sarah, he knew you would just be worrying, and since the rendezvous was set, he thought it best to let me break the news when I got back here. He will be fine, you know that." His gentleness with her ate at me, fanning the flames of my jealousy until it burned white hot and I had to turn away.

"Where is David?" I had a hard time forcing the words past the thickening lump in my throat. I needed David's strong arms around me now that all my foolish dreams of love seemed to be crashing down again.

"He went with Harlan on the *Sprite*. I was just island hopping and asking questions, so I had no need for him. He does know the coastal waters as well or better than either Harlan or I do."

David was with Harlan! Though that had been the original arrangement, I had not even considered it after Hunter and David left Dark Thunder to seek news of

311

Broderick. Now hearing it staggered me so that I had to clutch the rail to stay on my feet.

"Faith, what is it? Are you all right?" Suddenly Hunter's arms were around me, sheltering and gentle.

My dreams revived. I lifted my head, everything forgotten but the wonder of being held. The concern in Hunter's face shattered the illusion—concern, not love, not the blazing passion that had united us before. I closed my eyes to hide my pain. From a great distance, I heard Sarah explaining about Nan's terrible accident and my collapse after she regained her senses.

"I think perhaps we should take Faith right back to the house," Sarah finished. "All this has been too much for her."

"Why not let her rest for a time in my cabin?" Hunter suggested, his arm tightening around me. "I can see her to the house when I have finished here. The rest will revive her."

"But surely . . ." Sarah's tone held a questioning note. "Faith, do you think that would be best?"

Pride ordered me to straighten up and march off the ship without a backward glance, but a stronger emotion made me want to wrap my arms around Hunter and never let him go. "I think a bit of rest would help. And the children will be restless if they are kept from their naptime." The voice did not sound like mine, but no one else seemed to notice.

Sarah quickly gathered our greeting party and led them off the ship, promising to send the carriage back for us. Hunter held me close against his side as we waved to them when they left the dock, then he led me across the deck, shouting orders to his crew until we reached his cabin.

"At last." He closed the door and pulled me into his embrace, his lips taking mine with a hunger that seared me, banishing thought, doubt, and fear. I answered his kiss with an abandon that would have embarrassed me had I not been so lost in my love for him.

312

"I have missed you so desperately," he whispered as he trailed kisses across my cheek and nibbled on my ear before tasting my neck. "I dreamed of this moment, Faith. If you had not come to the dock . . ."

His impassioned words were music to my ears until my memory jolted me with pictures of him holding Sarah in his arms. Though every inch of my body ached with longing, I pulled away from him. "We have to talk, Hunter."

"We can talk later." He reached for me again, the heat of his fingers on my shoulders loosing the fire in my blood and increasing the pulsing need within me.

"No!" It was almost a wail, but by turning my back, I managed to keep from weakening. "You left me without a word, I have to know what is going on, Hunter."

For a moment the only sounds in the cabin came from our labored breathing, then I heard his sigh and the creak of the floor as he moved away from me. "I had no choice, Faith. How could I explain a need to see you again without everyone guessing that our feelings for each other had changed? We agreed that your reputation had to be protected. Did you think I wanted to leave without holding you again, without kissing you?"

"I did not know what to think." The weariness in his voice tore at me. Had I misjudged him again or was he using the blinding passion he had ignited within me for his own ends?

"Did what happened between us mean so little to you?" The anger in his voice forced me to look at him.

"How can you even ask that?" My own anger flared to match his. I would not be treated as though my doubts had no basis. "You sail off without a word and then wonder why I doubt your feelings."

"I went to find the man who would have defiled you. I wanted to extract revenge for what he threatened. I wanted to make sure that your father would be safe." Hunter managed to look wounded and self-righteous at the same time. "Is that not what you wanted me to do?"

"I just wanted you near me." The words were out before I could stop them. In one stride, he had me back in his arms.

"I wanted that, too, Faith, but how could I bear being near you and not holding you this way? Even now, I want you closer, I want all of you. I want us to be the way we were on the island and that cannot be, not until I can meet with your father to declare my intentions and make an honorable offer for your hand."

I just looked up at him, not trusting myself to speak, almost afraid to feel the pulsing excitement that his words sent through me. I wanted to believe him. I wanted it to be perfect and wonderful and magical like it was in my dreams, but even as I met his gaze, I remembered the cavern. The joy drained away.

"Faith, what is it? Is something wrong?" The warming love in his eyes changed to concern as he seated me in one of the chairs his cabin boasted. "Has something happened?"

Knowing that our love might be doomed by what I had to tell him, I still had to give him the truth as I knew it. Yet where to begin? "Did you find Broderick?"

Hunter's frown deepened as he seated himself in the other chair. "Not a trace. No, that is not quite true. I think I have found a lot of traces, but no clue to where the man hides himself between attacks. He seems like the fog, coming up out of the sea, then disappearing when the sun grows too hot."

"What sort of traces?" I sensed that he was confused by my questions, but I wanted to be sure of my ground before I told him of my discovery.

"Wrecks mostly. Bits and pieces washed up on populated islands or stripped hulls on wild islands. Not a clue to prove that Broderick caused the wrecks, of course, but someone has been sinking ships and I doubt there is another raider on the prowl."

"You might be surprised." The bitter words slipped out because I felt so cold and empty sitting here with

314

Hunter. I was finally close to him, yet emotionally I was so far from his arms.

"What are you talking about?" His piercing blue eyes probed at me as though he knew I was holding back something important.

"I made a discovery . . . a lot of discoveries after you sailed away, Hunter." I stopped, not wanting to tell him now. How I longed for one more kiss, one more precious moment in his arms. But his steady gaze told me I had come too far to stop. "It has to do with those bobbing lights and what happened to Nan."

Slowly, carefully, I described my first late-night visit to the glade area and my glimpse of Decateur leaving with his men. Then I told him of my second visit and what had happened to Nan a short time later when she left the house wearing Papa's cape. I watched the waves of worry, doubt, anger, and love as they crossed his face while I detailed my final visit to the glade and my discovery of the cavern and its contents.

"You went inside, Faith? You could have been killed. Of all the foolhardy . . ." He was almost sputtering, he was so upset with me.

"I was trapped inside, Hunter." This was the hard part, but I kept talking, describing what I had overheard, then glossing over the terror of discovering that I could not escape once Decateur and his men were gone.

"How did you get out?"

"The cavern has a rear tunnel to another exit." I paused to take a deep breath. "It opens into the cellar of Thunder House through a secret panel."

Doubt replaced concern in his face, doubt and something else that almost frightened me. He shook his head. "No, I cannot believe that, Faith. Are you sure that this is not all some wild nightmare? Harlan would never build something like that into his house."

I could not bear to witness his pain, yet neither could I deny what I had seen, so I offered him the only explanation that had occurred to me. "Did you know that

315

Harlan built his house on the foundation of a house that was burned? Very probably during the time when the original pirates were driven from the sea."

"You think all this dates from when Dark Thunder was a pirate's lair?" Disbelief and relief were both obvious in his face. "But everyone told us that ugly business was over long ago."

"Maybe so, but it has begun again and the pirates are now led by Broderick."

"That cannot be." He was on his feet, pacing. "The islanders are clannish and unfriendly, but I would know if something so evil was going on here."

"It is happening, Hunter." I rose, too, and reached into the pocket I had sewed into my skirt. "I found these in the cavern; they were a part of the load that Decateur and his men were carrying in that night." I offered the cameo and Tommy's ring to him.

Hunter looked as though I had struck him and for a moment I thought he might even deny the evidence before him. "Broderick on this island? I just cannot believe it. Where is he hiding? How can he be here?"

"I honestly have no idea whether he stays on the island," I admitted, wishing that I could stop now. "It may be that he merely unloads his booty and Decateur decides what is to be stored in the cavern and what is shipped elsewhere."

"What are you saying?" Hunter came back to stand close to me, but he made no move to touch me. There was no warmth in his expression, no love for me; his face was tight with anger and suspicion. "There is no place on this island for cargo to be unloaded except . . ."

I met his gaze, aware that I might well lose his love if I continued, but unable to stop what I had begun. I finished his sentence for him. "At the warehouse you and Harlan built and that Decateur runs and for which he keeps the accounts."

"Accounts? What accounts are you talking about, Faith? And how do you know so much about all of this?"

316

I watched his face as I told him of Harlan asking Sarah to keep secret accounts and of her turning them over to me, even my visit to the warehouse to question Decateur. Each word seemed to age him as he drew the same implications that I had. At that moment I would have done almost anything to spare him the pain he was feeling, but I could not. I had nothing to offer him but the truth.

"This cannot be true." His tone was harsh, angry. "You must have made some sort of mistake, Faith. Harlan would never allow contraband to be stored in our warehouse. How can you even think such a thing?"

I sank back into the chair. "I only know what I saw. The ledgers were full of entries showing cargoes unloaded one day and shipped elsewhere the next day. There was no detailed listing of the contents of each cargo, just the number of bales or crates or barrels. It seemed strange to me, so I . . ."

"So you started snooping around, looking for something. My God, Faith, Harlan is my brother. How could you even question his honesty? Or did you think that I had my hands in it, too? Maybe you believe we are both working with Broderick and his crew of raiders, is that it?"

The words were like blows, each one shattering another part of our dream, driving my hope for our love further away. The pain ripped through me, unleashing my tears as I buried my face in my hands. I wished I had never seen the accursed bobbing lights.

"Faith, Faith, I am sorry. Please stop crying. I never meant that. I know you would never . . ." His hands were cold as they touched my cheeks, but so gentle. "I just know it all has to be some terrible mistake."

I offered no resistance as he drew me into his arms. It felt wonderful to bury my face against his warm, strong chest, to feel his heart beating against my cheek as I pressed ever closer. I never wanted the moment to end. Maybe if we just held each other the world would

317

disappear and we could forget everything that had happened.

The magic lasted until a discreet knock on the door broke the spell. "We be secure, Captain, and the carriage is waiting," the first mate announced.

"Thank you, Gideon." Hunter slowly released me, his face still touched with sadness as he looked down at me.

"What are we going to do, Hunter?" I asked, suddenly afraid of the world that was waiting beyond the door.

He met my gaze without flinching and I could read his love for me in his eyes even though he said nothing for a moment, only smoothed back my hair and traced the path of my tears down my cheeks. His sigh seemed to come from his boots. "Lord help me, I wish I knew, Faith."

"We have to stop them. They could have killed you or David or all of us."

"I know that." His hands dropped and he turned away. "There is fresh water on the stand. I will go make a final check of the ship, then we shall have to go to the house. Sarah will be expecting us." He started to the door, then stopped and turned to face me. "Who knows of this, Faith? Did you tell Sarah?"

"I have told no one." I felt the sharp thorn of jealousy as I recognized the deep concern behind his question. As always, he was protecting his precious Sarah.

"Please promise me that you will continue to keep this a secret, at least until I have time to investigate Decateur and discover . . ." He let it trail off, suddenly unable to meet my gaze.

"If what I say is true?" I finished his sentence, holding myself stiff so that he would not guess how deeply his doubt had wounded me.

"Exactly what is going on here," he corrected me, but without looking up. "I do believe you, Faith; but there is much that we do not know. And there is Broderick to be considered. If he is, indeed, hiding somewhere on the island, you could be in deadly danger."

318

I swallowed my own sigh, knowing that he was right, but still sensing his doubt. "There is no one else to tell, Hunter. When David returns . . ."

"We shall talk later. Now I have a ship to see to." He left the cabin abruptly, closing the door behind him.

Heart aching, I bathed my red eyes and secured my wayward curls; but I could not wash away the despair I felt. No matter what words Hunter offered, I already felt the chasm opening between us and I had no idea how to reach across it and touch the man I loved. The man I hoped still loved me.

With Gordon driving the carriage, there was little we could say on the drive to Thunder House and so the distance between us grew ever wider. Since I could not even hold his hand, I watched him, willing him to forget the terrible things I had told him and see that nothing had changed between us. If only he would look into my eyes as he had earlier, then I would know that he still cared for me, that the ugliness had not killed his feelings.

But he seemed not to even know that I was in the carriage with him. Though he stared at the panorama of meadow and trees, I suspected that he saw nothing but the turmoil in his mind. Turmoil I had created with my curiosity and my discoveries.

Too soon we reached the house and I had to submit to Rose's fussing over me while Hunter vanished into the parlor with Sarah. Always with Sarah. I had thought that Hunter's return would end my torment, but now I suspected that my suffering had just begun. Seeing him was not enough, I wanted his arms around me, his lips on mine. I wanted to . . . I groaned.

"Are you ill, Miss Faith?" Rose asked, her concern shaming me.

"No, just impatient, Rose. I was so hoping that David would be with Hunter. I need to talk to my brother." That, at least, was the truth. I desperately needed to know that David was safe.

"We'll all be happy when Mr. Harlan be back safe. Miss Sarah 'twere beside herself knowing he be in danger now."

"Perhaps you should go to her, Rose," I suggested. "I am fine, truly. I shall just rest until time for the evening meal."

"She be with Mr. Hunter, so she be fine." Rose ignored my hint and continued fussing about my room.

I searched my mind for a comment that would not reveal my jealousy, but none came to me, so I changed the subject by asking about Nan's condition, then closed my eyes. I hated the thought of Hunter and Sarah together, of Hunter and Sarah sharing so many hours. Was he telling her of my suspicions? Somehow I doubted it. With Sarah he would keep the conversation light and loving, full of laughter and . . .

I could not bear it. "Is Penny awake yet?" I asked, getting to my feet.

"Yes, miss, but you'd best not . . ." Rose let the warning trail off. "Miss Sarah said you were to rest."

"Miss Sarah worries too much." I brushed past Rose and headed for the playroom where I could hear Penny's giggle. She might not need a story, but I definitely did. Sparkle and Princess Penelope's adventures just might see me through until someone thought to invite me to join the adults. Someone like Hunter.

I was ready when the summons came. Though I was officially in mourning for Tommy, I pinned the cameo on my gown and pinched a bit of color into my cheeks. No way would I let Hunter or Sarah see how miserable I was.

The sumptuous meal seemed endless as I pushed my food around my plate and tried to make conversation without mentioning any of the subjects on my mind. Sarah was animated at first, flirting with Hunter and teasing me, but as the evening inched by, she, too, appeared to wilt from the effort. Though I longed for a

320

moment of closeness with Hunter, I was grateful when he declined Sarah's suggestion that we sit out on the veranda for a bit.

"I think we have all had a long day," he began, giving us both a smile that did nothing to ease the bleakness in his eyes. "I for one will have an early night."

"I think I should retire early, too," I agreed.

Sarah smiled at me. "Of course you must, Faith, I should never have planned such a lengthy meal. After that odd turn you had on the ship, you must take better care of yourself. You have suffered too much the past few weeks." She came to give me a hug. "Let me walk you to your room while Hunter makes sure everything is secure down here."

I wanted to protest, but, of course, I could not. I glanced over my shoulder at Hunter as we started up the stairs, but he was already checking the door and closing the windows. It was as though our moments of intimacy had never happened and I felt so empty . . . and afraid.

I had been in my room less than ten minutes when there was a tap on my window. Frightened, I stared at the curtain, which stirred in the breeze that entered through the scant inch I had left it open. "Faith, let me in."

"Hunter!" I rushed to lift the window so he could slip inside. "What in the world . . . ?" He stopped my question with a kiss, then stepped back, holding a finger to his lips.

"We have to talk, but we must be very careful. No one can see us alone together. We cannot afford even a hint of gossip until your stowing away on the *Pearl* is forgotten."

"But how . . ." Again he stopped my words with a kiss and this time I answered him with all my longing and hunger. I gloried in the way his body heated against mine, the strength of his embrace and the soft groan he could not keep back when he finally released my lips.

"I should never have come here." He turned away, fussing with the curtain, checking the door to see if it was

321

securely latched.

"Why did you come?" I felt abandoned as I watched him. Did he not want me as much as I wanted him? When I was in his arms, it seemed that he loved me; but each time he pulled away as though he hated himself for wanting me. The thought chilled my desire. Could that be it?

"I need you to show me the cellar entrance to the cavern. I thought we could do it tonight after all the servants are safely up in their rooms." He continued to prowl my small room, not really looking at me.

"When do you want to go down there?" I sank into one of the chairs, his swift movements making my head ache—or was it my heart?

"Could you meet me in the kitchen in about an hour? Everyone should be settled in by then."

"Meet you?" That brought my head up. Did he intend to leave again? "But I thought you wanted to talk."

"I . . . a . . . have a couple of other things I need to take care of, so I think it would be best for me to meet you." He was already at the window, opening it. He turned back before he slipped out. "You will be there, Faith?"

"Of course, Hunter." I met his gaze as calmly as I could, but I was glad when he disappeared through the window, for I feared he would read too much in my face.

The next hour was a torment. Now I paced my room, my mind filled with images of each time I had been with Hunter. Each kiss, each touch, every moment was etched in my heart and no amount of seeking through them gave me any answers. He seemed to care, to love me as he claimed; yet so often he turned away from me, left me when I would have had him stay. Only on our island had he seemed to glory in my nearness, never leaving my side, loving me to distraction. Did he truly love me or only want me when he was far from Sarah?

I still had not found the answer to my question by the time I made my way through the dark and silent halls and

322

down the backstairs to the equally dark kitchen. I shivered, remembering how I had felt when I emerged from the cellar after my escape from the cavern.

"Over here." Light greeted me as Hunter opened the heavy cellar door for me, then led the way down the stairs. He stood aside for me to take the lead, but the lantern's light showed no expression on his face. We could have been two strangers and that chilled me far more than the dank cellar or the memories of the last time I had been here.

"We could talk here," I murmured, more to break the terrible silence than because I really expected him to agree. "There is no one to see or hear us."

"It is late and you are exhausted." He did not meet my gaze as I paused before the cupboard. "I think perhaps I should go ahead and explore a bit tonight. If you will just show me how this works and leave the door at the top of the stairs unlatched for me . . ." His tone, as well as his words, spoke of dismissal.

I smiled bitterly. "I always wondered why there was such a sturdy latch on the door to the cellar. Now I guess we know."

"Harlan had it installed before they moved in because of the children. He feared that they might be injured on the stairs." Hunter tried the hidden lever, then stepped back as the cupboard creaked open. "Thank you, Faith, for showing me this and we will talk soon, I promise." He brushed a quick kiss across my lips, then stepped through the panel, allowing it to close behind him.

I stood alone for several minutes, adjusting to the much dimmer light from my candle and to the chill of emptiness that surrounded me. Talk? Of what? How his feelings for me had changed once he learned the truth about his brother? Or could it be his feelings about Sarah had changed, grown more intense now that he knew she could be free of Harlan?

That thought was so awful I fled from it, running up the cellar stairs as though something pursued me. He could not be that cruel, could he? I cursed the fact that I knew so little of the ways of love between a man and a woman. If only Mama were still alive to advise me. I left the door slightly ajar for Hunter, then returned to my room too miserable to even cry.

I had hoped to escape into sleep, but everything about the day haunted me, so that I could hardly remain beneath the covers. I heard every time the house creaked, every rustle of the trees outside, every . . .

The sound of a footfall brought me upright in my bed. Someone was moving along the hall. I threw back the covers and stood up, pulling my robe around me as I headed for the door. I opened it just a crack. The dark hall was lit by a flickering candle as Hunter tiptoed toward the head of the stairs.

Relief swept through me. At least he was safe out of the cavern, then my curiosity flared. But where was he going? Why was he in this part of the house? Had he come by my room, hoping to see a light and . . . I slipped through the door and followed after him, afraid to call out for fear that I might rouse someone else.

He disappeared from my view as he turned at the head of the stairs, but when I reached that area I saw that he had not gone on along the hall to his own rooms. My whole body turned to stone as I watched him vanish into Sarah's sitting room.

Chapter 21

A century passed as I stared at the door Hunter had closed behind him. Every excuse I had made for him, every legitimate reason I had thought of for his being with Sarah that long-ago dawn now faded from my mind. I had been right to doubt him, to suspect his words of love.

The great tearing pain of that realization cracked the stone around me and for a moment I thought I might collapse there on the floor, then a healing anger rescued me. I turned with great dignity, my head high as I made my way through the dark to my room. I even managed to get back into my bed and close my eyes, but I hurt too much to sleep.

By dawn I felt a hundred years old, but I was calm as I bathed my shadowed eyes and dressed for the day. Now that I knew the truth, I would trouble Hunter no longer. Once David returned with the *Sprite*, I would tell him everything and then we would leave this accursed island. Someone else could hunt down Broderick and all who conspired with him; I only wanted to forget what had happened to me.

Finally satisfied with my appearance, I opened my door, ready to go to the playroom to take my morning meal with those I could trust. In my hurry, I nearly crashed into Rose, who, it appeared, had been about to tap on my door.

"Miss Faith, you are ready."

"Ready for what?"

"Miss Sarah asked me to fetch you for her." Rose looked as flustered as I felt. "Are you well this morning?"

Sarah wanted to see me. The implications threatened to unravel the fabric of my hard-won façade. I nodded, not trusting my voice since my throat felt ominously dry. What if Hunter was there, too? What if he had told her of my feelings for him and they had decided to confront me together?

"You do feel all right, miss?" Rose's worried frown told me that I had not hidden my feelings very well.

"Is there something wrong with Sarah, Rose?" I asked, hoping to change the subject.

"I'd not be knowing, miss. Mayhap, she be lonely since Mr. Hunter rode off at first light."

"Of course." I forced a smile and evaded her curious gaze. "I thought perhaps there was trouble with Penny or . . ." I let it trail off. "Thank you for giving me the message, Rose. I shall see what I may do for Sarah."

I felt her gaze following me along the hall, but refused to look back. I needed every moment of my walk to compose myself for my meeting with Sarah. Even if she knew nothing of my love for Hunter, I could not allow her to sense how disturbed I was. My pride was all I had left.

Sarah opened the door the moment I tapped on it and her expression was grave as she welcomed me in. Something was definitely wrong. I searched her face, seeking some telltale sign of guilt, but I could read nothing but compassion in her eyes as she waved me into a chair and poured tea for us both.

As we sipped in silence, my curiosity grew to match my dread. Why was she torturing me? What did she have to say that was so difficult? Finally, I could bear the silence no longer. "Is something wrong, Sarah? Are you angry with me?"

"Angry?" Her look of shock seemed genuine. "Oh, no, Faith, I am only troubled to see you looking so wan and weary. I see that Hunter is right and I am being selfish keeping you here."

"What?" I reacted to Hunter's name like a horse to the spur.

"We talked this morning about your loss and what it must mean to you and he made me realize that I have been taking advantage of your kindness. You should be with your family in Nassau at this time of grieving for your betrothed. They can offer you the consolation that you deserve and help you heal after that terrible attack. They may even have had word from your father. I know that would ease your mind.

"Papa?" I was confused.

"Hunter was sure you needed to get away, so he has ridden into the village to make arrangements with one of the fishermen to take you to Nassau for a visit."

Shock paralyzed me. Her words spun through my mind, but I could make no sense of them. She could not mean to send me away. I forgot entirely that I had planned to leave as soon as David returned. I opened my mouth to protest, but could force no words past the lump of pain in my throat as I realized exactly what her words meant. Hunter was sending me away so he could be alone here with Sarah.

"Are you all right, Faith? Oh, my dear, I should have seen that you are not yourself. How could you be after all you have suffered from the raiders and caring for Nan? I have been so wrapped up in my own feelings and my need to have you nearby, that I . . ." She took my cup from my nerveless fingers and wrapped her arms around me. She whispered gentle words like a loving sister, seeming as unaware of Hunter's duplicity as I had been. Because a part of me still loved her in spite of what I had seen last night, I sobbed on her shoulder.

When my tears were dried and we had finished our

morning meal, Sarah summoned Rose and supervised as she packed a valise for me. I was given no chance to refuse or object to being sent away. Instead, Sarah talked cheerfully of the many activities we would share when I returned.

As my numbness eased, I watched her, wondering if she could be pretending to save my feelings. But there was no sign of guilt or duplicity in her clear gray eyes and when she escorted me out to the waiting pony cart, her tears mingled with mine as we said our farewells.

Gordon frowned at me as he slapped the reins on the pony's back. "Us'll be missing ye, Miss Faith. Nan be cryin' to see yer go. Mayhap, Mr. David be bringin' ye back afore long?"

"I just hope the *Sprite* gets back soon." Thinking of David and the danger he might be in cleared a few of the cobwebs from my mind. Sarah had suggested that I might see him and Harlan before she did, since they frequently delivered their cargo to Nassau before returning to Dark Thunder, but now I was not so sure.

What if Harlan was working with Broderick? He might bring a part of his cargo to the warehouse for transfer to the cavern and if he did, David would surely know it. A chill slipped down my spine. David had already been suspicious about the *Pearl*'s easy escape from the raiders, if he should question Harlan's actions . . .

"Have you seen Hunter today, Gordon?" I asked.

He nodded. "Him be at the warehouse earlier, miss, after him talk with the fishermen. Him be right concerned for ye."

I tried to smile, but my face felt too tight. Hunter was concerned all right, but not for me. More likely he feared that I would tell Sarah of his behavior, his promises to me. Bitterness twisted inside me, setting my anger off again. How could he just send me away without a word.

"Here we be, miss." Gordon's voice forced my thoughts back to the present and I realized that we were stopping at the dock. "Ye be sailing on that boat." He indicated a rather battered-looking fishing craft. "Mr. Hunter, him say it be right as old Cap'n Edgar be takin' his wife to Nassau this trip."

Leave it to Hunter to make proper arrangements, I thought, only slightly relieved to know that I would not be the only woman on some creaking fishing boat. Even as I followed Gordon out to the boat, I realized that I did not want to go—not without seeing Hunter one last time.

"Gordon, do you think Hunter is still in the warehouse?" I asked, suddenly determined that I would not leave without demanding an explanation.

Gordon peered toward the building, then shook his head. "Horse be gone. Mayhap him be at his house. He be most curious about the buildin'."

Blast! Why had I not noticed him there as we drove by the bluff? Because I had been too angry to even look that way, of course. Feeling defeated, I allowed Gordon to help me aboard the small vessel and introduce me to the owner and his glum-appearing wife. They were polite enough, but in the manner of most of the islanders, they kept their distance. I was shown to a tiny cubbyhole of a cabin and informed that they would not be sailing until evening.

I tried to accept my situation, but after half an hour of being confined to the smelly, rocking ship, I knew that I could not leave without trying to talk to Hunter. I went up on deck and peered at the sky. It was still early afternoon and the bluff where Hunter was building his house was not too far away.

Since the captain and his wife were nowhere to be seen, I simply left the ship and headed back along the dock. If I cut through the village and went cross-country, perhaps I could find the shortcut that Nan had been seeking the day she had been struck down. Thinking of Nan gave me a shiver, but I pushed my fears away. The sun was shining and I was leaving the island, so surely I would be safe enough.

My determination carried me forward for a while, but

329

as the wild growth grew thicker and I had trouble finding my way, my enthusiasm for facing Hunter ebbed. What was I going to say? Did I really want to confront him with what I had seen last night? Accuse him of loving Sarah more than he loved me? I cringed from the images my mind created.

I might be hurting now, but would I feel any less pain if I forced Hunter to admit his feelings for Sarah? The answer was obvious and once I acknowledged that, I began to accept the fact that Hunter had offered me an easy way out. At least by leaving now I would have my pride and dignity intact; if I faced him with my accusations, I would have neither.

"So much for a nice last walk on Dark Thunder," I murmured bitterly, turning away from a glimpse of the still distant bluff. Tears burned in my eyes, half blinding me as I cut through a thick grove of trees.

I had taken no more than a dozen steps when I sensed that I was not alone. Rustling sounds came from my right and from my left. I was being followed! Fear surged through me and I tried to run, but I had no chance. Strong arms grabbed me from behind, locking around me, holding my arms against my sides. Before I could even scream a thick cloth bag dropped over my head, suffocating me as I struggled.

Curses filled the air as one of my kicks found its mark, then something thudded against the side of my head. For just a moment the interior of the bag was bright with pain stars, then the blackness claimed me and I struggled no more.

The cat was against my face, heavy and smothering. I tried to lift a hand to push him off, but I could not move. My hands were trapped behind me and my arms felt numb. My head . . . Suddenly, memories washed over me in a fearful rush. Sheer terror held me still.

It was the cloth bag, not the cat, that covered my face

330

and, as I wiggled my fingers, I felt the ropes holding my wrists. Whoever had been following me had rendered me unconscious, then bound me and . . . And what? Where was I? And who had struck me down?

"What us be doin' with that 'un, Ebban?" The old man's voice was familiar; I had heard it in the cavern.

"What do ye care, Seth?" Ebban Decateur's voice came from so nearby it took all my self-control not to jerk away from the sound.

"Jes curious, Ebban."

"I reckon to use her same's I done when I stole the little girl from her bed and left her in the grass. Since that night, her papa be askin' no questions 'bout the cargo what passes through here. Only I don' be sendin' this 'un back lessen Broderick say so. Us'll jes keep her and Mr. bloody Hunter Latimer be stoppin' abadgerin' me 'bout them ledgers."

Listening to Decateur's words sent a shiver down my spine as I remembered the night I had found Penny in the woods and blamed myself for her disappearance. At the time I had wondered how she could walk so far, but I had never guessed that someone could be evil enough to . . .

"How ye be akeepin' Mr. Hunter away?" Seth's question interrupted my thoughts.

"I lets 'um know, if'n he takes the ledgers, her dies."

My fear deepened at Decateur's calm statement. I had no doubt that he would kill me. In fact, I had a strong premonition that Hunter's compliance with his demands would not be enough to keep me alive for long. The man sounded as though he would enjoy killing me. Icy terror spread through me as I remembered that he had tried before.

"Ben't ye done enough ta the wench?" Seth had moved away from wherever I was lying. "Shavin' her rein and spookin' her horse, followin' her, and strikin' down poor Nan . . ."

"'Tain't my fault this 'un be forever snoopin' round the cavern." Decateur sighed. "Her be trouble, Seth.

331

Likely Broderick be givin' her sommat to remember afore him gets rid o' her."

Broderick. I swallowed hard remembering his touch, the cruel pleasure he had taken in telling me exactly what he planned to do to me.

"Broderick." Seth seemed to spit the word out.

"Ye'll be lickin' up to him right enough, if'n Jones held to the plan and the *Sprite* be bringin' cargo for Big Wood Cay. There be a river of gold awaitin' for a steamer what has the right captain."

Steamer? My fears for myself paled as I realized that he must mean the *Sprite*. What was he talking about? Did he mean that Harlan was the right captain?

"Broderick's gold. Us be gettin' naught but a trickle." Seth's whine grated on me and I wanted to scream at them to let me go.

"Be mor'n us had since the trouble. Mor'n Latimer's warehouse and dock be bringin' in. Put Dark Thunder back on the map, Broderick will and us'll be runnin' it."

"If'n us ben't swingin' from a yardarm. I know'd folks what be hit by raiders, Ebban. Hidin' cargo be bad, but 'tain't same as know'n 'bout a ship bein' sunk or stole."

Sick fear gripped me. David was aboard the *Sprite* and these men were talking as though . . . David was in deadly danger and so was Harlan, if I had heard correctly. Hunter had to be told. Maybe there was something he could do, some way that they could be warned before it was too late.

"Ye be knowin' the rule, Seth. If ye ben't with us, ye be agin' us and ye be knowin' too much." There was no denying the menace in Decateur's voice. He was the perfect confederate for a man like Broderick.

The two men continued talking for a few more moments, then Decateur ordered Seth out and came over to check my bonds. His hands were rough as he rolled me over. "When ye be wakin', wench?" he snarled. "I gots questions be needin' answers afore I be facin' Latimer."

Though I was tempted to confront him and demand

332

some answers of my own, I kept myself limp and still, reasoning that I would learn more with silence. Perhaps if he thought he had injured me, he might untie my hands or remove the cursed cover over my head so I could see where I was. Curious to find out what would happen, I allowed myself a groan.

His response was immediate and painful. He shook me so hard my teeth chattered, but I clung firmly to my pretense of unconsciousness, biting my lip to keep from crying out as he dropped me back on my bound arms.

"So sleep on, wench. Mayhap ye be ready to talk when I gits back." He stabbed a finger in my ribs, nearly destroying my act, then I heard the sound of his boots as he stamped away.

I lay still for what seemed hours, listening, fearful that he was trying to trick me. When I could bear the pain no longer, I rolled over and began trying to work my hands free. At first it seemed hopeless, but as I continued to pull and twist and work my wrists together, I felt the ropes grow damp and begin to slip. The pain was excruciating, but I focused on David and the trap that had been set for the *Sprite* and fought the rope even harder.

Suddenly, the rope gave and one hand was free, then the other. I could not keep back a groan as I tried to bring them forward, to massage the blood back into my aching arms. It was an eternity before I could bend my arms enough to untie the bag and pull it off my head.

A glance at my hands made my stomach twist, for they were red with the blood that still seeped from the places where my bonds had cut through my skin. I had no time to think of my pain, I had to reach Hunter and warn him about the trap that Harlan was sailing into. But first I had to get away from Decateur.

The room was dim, the only light filtering in through chinks in the wooden walls since there were no windows. I looked around, trying to guess where I might be. There was no furniture, I had been lying on what appeared to be a stack of torn and battered sails. A storage area? I limped to the door, discovering that my legs were nearly as stiff as my arms. How long had I been unconscious?

It took only a moment to discover that the door was locked. I glared at it, controlling an urge to kick it and scream for help. I knew it was unlikely that I would get any aid from the villagers. Before I did anything, I needed to know where I was. I located the largest space between the boards and pressed my eye to it.

My heart lifted as I saw the dock, the fishing boat I had been aboard, even the *Pearl* beyond it. Did that mean that it was just late afternoon? The shadows were long, so perhaps it was already early evening and the boat would soon be sailing without me. Would they even notice that I was not aboard?

I forced such thoughts away. I had no time for self-pity now, I needed my freedom. I tried to see more, to judge my exact position. Could I be in the warehouse? I moved to the other side and peered out. I could see the unfinished second dock and beyond it houses and gardens, even a few of the villagers moving about as though it were just a normal day. I sighed. If what Decateur said was true, perhaps it was just an ordinary day for them.

I moved back to the larger opening and stared at the dock with longing, realizing at last exactly where I must be. I had paid little attention to the construction of the huge Latimer warehouse, but I did remember that some sort of shed had been built on the end. That had to be my prison.

So close and yet so far. The ground between me and the dock was clear of brush and the distance was great enough that I doubted I would be able to outrun Decateur. Of course if I could reach the *Pearl* . . . Hunter had mentioned that most of his crew had returned from their visit to English Wells, so surely those aboard would help me. But how could I get out of here to try?

As if in answer, I heard the sound of someone approaching the door. Frantic, I looked around and spotted a pile of cracked and worn belaying pins in the corner. Not sure what I was going to do, I snatched one up and positioned myself behind the door.

Decateur came through the door, then stopped as he realized that the pallet of sails was empty. He was taller than I remembered, much too tall for me to hit him over the head. Yet I had to do something before he saw me. I took a deep breath and swung the belaying pin against his belly with all my strength. I caught him mid-bellow and he went down, whimpering as he rolled into a ball. I leaped over him and plunged into the shadowy confusion of the warehouse.

Two answering shouts echoed in the room, but I paid no attention as I dived between stacks of bales and boxes. I could only hope that the men would go first to find out what had happened to Decateur. If they were not aware of my being held here, I had a fighting chance of slipping out one of the doors that opened toward the dock and once I was free . . .

I swallowed hard, not wanting to think of all the islanders that stood between me and the safety of Thunder House. I would head for the *Pearl*. Once on board, I could ask one of the men to get word to Hunter. I clung to the hope that I would be safe on the *Pearl*, reminding myself that her men would be as anxious as I to save the *Sprite*, for they, too, had family among her crew.

"Seth! Jeb! Close the doors, bar them!" Decateur's voice carried like a fog horn. "Let no one out."

My heart sank as I heard the banging sounds of the men complying with his order. I was still trapped. Feeling sick with fear, I looked around the darkening room. If I could not escape, I had to hide, but where?

The huge space was filled with cargo, everything from tidy piles of crates to lumpy stacks of what appeared to be personal belongings. I headed for the nearest conglomeration of furniture, trunks, boxes, and barrels. Bounty from one of the wrecks Hunter had spoken of? I shuddered even as I moved aside the lid of a barrel and peered into it.

Clothing. There was no time for thought as I clambered into the barrel and shifted the lid back into place, then burrowed beneath the musty-smelling clothes. If I could hide here long enough perhaps Decateur would think I had escaped and then when it was safe . . .

"Decateur. Damn you, I know you are in there. Open the door!" Hunter's voice was muffled, but the pounding was loud enough to wake the dead. "Open it now or you'll be working elsewhere."

I heard curses from frighteningly nearby, then the sounds of a low-voiced conference. Though I caught only a few words, one of them was my name. I held my breath, afraid that Decateur meant to stay hidden until Hunter left. Yet how could he? Hunter sounded angry enough to break the door in.

It seemed Decateur shared my estimate of Hunter's temper, for I heard a door being opened. "Mr. Latimer, forgive my being so long, but I was occupied in the office." Decateur's polite and proper words surprised me. He sounded like a gentleman, yet when he spoke with Seth or the other men, he sounded like an untutored islander.

"I have come for the ledgers." Hunter's voice was quieter now, but no less determined.

"And I have explained that they are not mine to give you. If Mr. Harlan Latimer wishes you to have them, he will give them to you." Decateur's tone was polite, but firm.

"I will have them now or you will be replaced." Hunter was just as stubborn.

"Before you do that, you'd best think about that honey-haired woman of yours." Decateur's voice lost its polish.

"Faith? What has she to do with this?"

"You be wanting to see her again, you will leave this place and stop asking about the ledgers. Is that clear?"

336

The viciousness in Decateur's voice sent a shiver down my spine.

Hunter's curses filled the air and I could almost picture him striking Decateur, then abruptly his invective ceased. "Where did you get that, Decateur?"

"From Miss Richards, of course." Decateur sounded pleased with himself. I cautiously touched my shoulder where I had pinned the cameo what seemed a lifetime ago. I was not surprised to find it gone. "If you wish to see her again, I would advise you to leave this place . . . now!"

"Where is she?"

"Somewhere safe." Decateur's voice was louder now. "But she'll not be safe long if you press me, Latimer. I can have her killed or . . . well, there be plenty who would be willing to pay gold for one so fair and pure." His evil laugh was too much for me.

"I am here, Hunter," I shouted, pushing the lid from the barrel and climbing out. "He had me locked up, but I got away and . . ." I heard the sound of footfalls off to my left and grabbed the barrel lid. One of Decateur's henchmen was heading my way. I threw the lid at him, catching him in the knees, sending him to the floor with a shriek of pain.

"Faith, where are you?" Hunter's voice sounded above the others, then I heard a crash and the sounds of battle. I ran toward the noise, sure that Hunter must be in danger. Strong arms caught me as I rounded a stack of boxes.

"Let me go!" I cried, squirming and trying to free myself.

"Be still, Miss Faith." Gordon's voice hissed in my ear. "Give the captain a chance."

"Gordon?" I gasped, giving up my struggle. "What . . . ?" Then I saw them. Hunter and Decateur were locked in battle and I could see the knife in Decateur's hand. He was trying to stab Hunter, but Hunter had a hold on his wrist. "We have to help him," I wailed.

337

"Decateur has a knife."

"Ye goes out there an' Ebban be killin' him sure." Gordon's grip did not loosen. "She be safe, Captain," he shouted.

Decateur roared a curse at Gordon, then shifted his weight, throwing Hunter off-balance. I held my breath as they staggered back and forth, sometimes crashing into piles of cargo, sometimes disappearing for a moment. Then suddenly a terrible scream tore the air.

"Hunter!" I jerked free of Gordon's grip and plunged forward ready to attack Decateur if he had harmed my beloved.

Hunter turned toward me and I gasped, for his clothes were spattered with blood. Then I saw the knife in his hand and heard the groans from behind the bales. "Are you all right, Faith?" he asked.

"I am fine, but you are injured." I could see the blood welling from a gash on his upper arm and more from the side of his hand.

"What the hell are you doing here?" His eyes held only anger as he glared at me. "You were to be on that fishing boat. How in the name of . . ." He stopped, staggering a little as Gordon moved past him to go to Decateur.

"I wanted to talk to you, so I was going to your bluff and Decateur must have seen me and followed me and . . ." I stopped, remembering what I had overheard. "But that is no matter now, Hunter. We must go after Harlan. He and David are in deadly danger."

"What are you babbling about?" Hunter stopped daubing at his wounds and looked at me.

"While they held me prisoner I overheard Decateur say something about Jones sending a steamer to Big Wood Cay. Broderick is waiting there and he means to have the ship."

For a moment Hunter just looked at me as though he could not understand my words, then he shook his head. "Decateur knew about Jones?"

338

I nodded. "Decateur said Broderick could make more raids if he had a steamer, then the rest about Jones and Big Wood Cay. Is it the *Sprite* he means, Hunter?"

"He be a goner, Captain." Gordon stepped out from behind the bales. "Ye gutted him clean."

Hunter sighed. "All for some damned ledgers."

"Ledgers that will prove that he was handling stolen cargoes for Broderick." Unable to look at Hunter any longer, I turned to Gordon. "Decateur is the one who nearly killed Nan thinking he was striking me."

"Do you know what the ledgers look like, Faith?" Hunter forced my attention back to him.

I nodded. "Let me clean your wounds, then I will look for them. You are still bleeding, Hunter and . . ."

"There is no time. If what you say is true, I have to leave now for Big Wood Cay. It may already be too late, but if there is a chance . . ."

"Then I am going with you."

"No, I want you to take the ledgers and some other papers that I will turn over to Captain Edgar and go to Nassau. If none of us come back, give the papers to your uncle and tell him everything you know about Broderick and Dark Thunder."

"Hunter, I cannot just . . ."

He turned his gaze to Gordon. "Can I trust you to see her safely onto the fishing boat, Gordon?"

"Yessir." Gordon straightened, his expression so full of hero worship it would have been amusing if the circumstances had been different. He was one islander who had given his heart to the Latimers.

"Once Faith is on her way, I want you to go back to the house and have the men arm themselves to protect Sarah and the children. Whatever happens, they are to be kept safe and, when Captain Edgar returns, he is to take them to English Wells. Is that clear?"

"You can count on me, Captain."

"Hunter, please, we . . ." He did not even seem to hear me, for he was already turning away, heading for the

339

door. My heart ached as Gordon led me to the small warehouse office and helped me search for the ledgers. By the time we carried them aboard the fishing boat, the *Pearl* was already on her way.

Captain Edgar cast off as soon as I was on board. I was on my way back to Nassau whether I wanted to go or not. And I did not want to go. My heart still belonged to Hunter, even though he seemed to care little for me. It was over, his insistence on sending me away made his choice clear. Somehow, I would have to learn to live with a broken heart.

Chapter 22

I was awake and dressed when Captain Edgar tapped on my cabin door in the morning. Thanks to my worry over David and my despair over Hunter's rejection, I had slept little and looked it. "What may I do for you, Captain?" I asked without interest.

"Captain Latimer be wantin' ye to have these." The captain produced a thick packet of papers. "There be food in the galley. Us'll make Nassau afore evening."

"Thank you, Captain." I accepted the papers, placing them with the ledgers, not even bothering to see what they were. Though I would have preferred to remain in my musty bunk for the entire voyage to Nassau, my stomach's rumbling made it clear that I would have to brave the rigors of the tiny galley.

After a quick meal of bread, cold meat, and fruit, I returned to my cabin; but no peace of mind awaited me there. Why could I not turn off the images that flooded my mind? I was tortured by pictures of Broderick and Hunter locked in mortal combat while David's life hung in the balance. Or, even worse, images of a sea battle between the *Pearl* and the *Sprite*, now captained by Broderick.

How could I get through the next few hours, let alone several days, of not knowing what had happened to Hunter and David? How could I bear the next few minutes? I paced the tiny cabin until my eyes fell on the papers. Hunter had entrusted them to me, so perhaps I could lose myself in trying to understand what they meant. At least I would be doing something instead of just wallowing in my misery.

I picked up the packet of papers, then gasped as I noted the dark splotches on the top sheet. Blood had been dripped on the paper. I touched it with a quivering finger, well aware of whose blood it had to be. It was then that I saw the folded sheet beneath it—a piece of paper with my name on it.

Shaking so hard that I was forced to set the other papers aside, I unfolded the sheet. It, too, was spotted with Hunter's blood telling me that it must have been written while Gordon and I were searching Decateur's office for the ledgers.

My love,

I found these when I searched Harlan's desk after I returned from the cavern last night. I have not had time to go through them, but suspect they will tell us how deeply Harlan is involved in all this.

Should I not return from Big Wood Cay, I ask only that you protect Sarah and the children, if you can. Her heart would break if she knew that Harlan had betrayed the love they share. Should Harlan and I both be Broderick's victims, the children must not suffer.

Protect yourself, Faith, and guard these papers well. Know that I will do my best to bring your brother back to you.

His signature was scrawled amid the blood spots and I traced over it with trembling fingers, my mind whirling as I tried to make sense of what I had read. Had I been wrong about his feelings for Sarah? Or were his words about her love for Harlan only another lie to ensure that I would carry out his orders if he could not return to protect her himself?

But what if he had been slipping into her sitting room only to search Harlan's desk that night? I recognized Harlan's handwriting on the papers and, in a way, Hunter's words did make sense. If he wanted to hide his suspicions from Sarah, he would have to search the desk when there was no danger of her asking him what he was looking for. And Sarah had often told me that she slept like the dead.

But what of the morning when I had seen them together? I closed my eyes, unable to face the terrible jealousy that still refused to go away. And if he did not love her, why had he insisted on sending me away even after Decateur was dead? Why had he been so angry with me after he saved me from Decateur?

None of it made sense. Nothing in my life made sense. I folded the sheet and put it back with the papers, then put the entire bundle between the ledgers. I could not deal with my life, so why should I think I could understand what other people had done? I curled up in my bunk and closed my eyes seeking escape from everything, but most of all from myself.

By the time I finally woke from my troubled dreams, it was late afternoon and thanks to favorable winds, we were nearing the entrance to Nassau Harbor. I placed the ledgers inside my valise, then went up on deck.

"Be ye well, Miss Richards?" Captain Edgar asked as he came to stand beside me at the rail.

"I am fine, thank you." I tried for a polite smile. His friendly inquiry was the last thing I had expected.

"The captain told me 'bout Decateur. 'Twas good riddance. There be many on Dark Thunder who be singin' today."

I studied his face, not sure whether I should believe his words. He was an islander. How much had he known? And if he was aware of Broderick's activities, why had he not warned Harlan or Hunter long before? It made me feel cold to realize that I no longer trusted people as I

343

once had.

"Captain asked me to see ye safe home. Ye're not to be worryin' no more." His gaze was steady, but unrevealing. I wondered if he was curious about my relationship with Hunter.

"Captain Latimer is most considerate," I murmured. "I will be ready when you are, Captain, and I thank you for bringing me home." I almost choked on the final word. Nassau was not my home and, sadly, now neither was Charleston. I ached inside to realize that, when I thought of home, I pictured the bluff on Dark Thunder or Hunter's arms.

I made my way back to my cabin, shaking my head. I must be mad to continue to love a man I could not trust. A man who had taken my innocence without even the promise of marriage. A man who might even now be planning his life with his brother's wife. A man who . . . who had risked his life to save mine both yesterday and on a hidden dock somewhere along the South Carolina coast. A man who could make me forget everything with one kiss. A man who . . .

A most unladylike curse formed on my lips. A man I must stop thinking about if I was to survive. I fastened my valise and got Papa's cloak from the peg where I had hung it what seemed a lifetime ago. Since my life had been spared, I was going to have to live it—somehow.

The next two days were the longest of my life. Caroline, Aunt Minerva, and Uncle Edward all welcomed me kindly. They asked few questions, yet I could see that they suspected there was a great deal more to my sudden arrival than a need for comfort after learning of Tommy's death. But what could I tell them?

Not about my visit with Papa, for they would be scandalized that I had stowed away on the ship. Nor could I mention any of the bizarre goings-on I had found on Dark Thunder, because that would only bring more

344

questions I could not answer. I could not even share my deepest fears with them, for until I had some word from Hunter or David, I had no proof that they were in danger.

Still, I could not keep Hunter out of my thoughts, and during my solitary hours in the window while I watched for either the steamers or Captain Edgar and his fishing boat, some realizations came to me. I did believe that Hunter had loved me. Seen from a distance with a mind less tormented by jealousy and doubt, I could recognize the love that had brought him back to rescue me from Broderick. I could accept the fact that he honestly wanted to protect my reputation by keeping a distance between us. A distance I had quite often tried to cross because of my need to feel his arms around me.

With all that in mind, I examined my own behavior. My jealousy shamed me. For the first time, I saw clearly just how my continuing suspicions had swelled like dark clouds spoiling the fragile magic between us. If only I had allowed myself to trust Hunter . . . But I had not and that lack of trust had made him so angry that, in the end, he had chosen to send me away without a word of explanation.

Why had I listened to the ugly stories David told me? Why had I spied on Hunter and suspected his motives whenever he was near Sarah? Did I really believe that Sarah was the kind of person who would dishonor her huband with his own brother? I had called her friend and still suspected her of such wrongdoing. What kind of person did that make me? A fool was the kindest answer that came to mind.

As my second full day in Nassau began to dim toward evening, my fear swelled. It was too long. I had located Big Wood Cay on a map and it was not too far from Dark Thunder. Hunter should have reached it before dawn the morning after his fight with Decateur. Had I been wrong to keep silent about the danger he was in? But his note had made it clear that he wanted me to wait to tell anyone about the ledgers. But how long?

345

What if he would never come? What if I never had a chance to see the flames of desire blazing in the depths of his eyes again? What if he had been too late to save David and Harlan and Broderick used the *Sprite* to attack the still unrepaired *Pearl*? What if . . . As I scanned the harbor, I could scarce see it through my tears.

For a moment I thought it was a trick of the light or of my own fevered imagination. I rubbed my eyes, trying to banish the tears, then looked again. A gray steamer was in the harbor heading for the docks. Even though I knew I should wait, should watch and be sure that it was not one of the other steamers that made regular visits to the dock area, I could not.

I grabbed Papa's cloak and raced down the backstairs and out the rear door. No way was I going to be stopped by Caroline or Aunt Minerva's questions. The streets were busy, but I scarcely noted the people I brushed past as I hurried along. By the time I reached the docks, I had a pain in my side and my heart was pounding so hard I thought it might explode.

Now that it was closer, I recognized the *Sprite*. I could see the intact rail, but now dark charred marks on the side and other signs of battle marred the cargo-crowded deck. Fearfully, I scanned the ship, praying that I would find David's familiar form among the men working there. Then I saw him! He was waving wildly, calling my name as the ship was secured. He leaped to the dock even before the gangplank was in place.

"David! You are safe!" It was all I could say as he wrapped me in a hug so tight I feared for my ribs.

"Hunter saved us, Faith. He sailed the *Pearl* out of a fog bank just as we were about to be boarded by that pirate Broderick. He only had one gun, but he laid a perfect shot into the raider ship and set it afire. That's how the *Sprite* got burned. Broderick tried to ram us."

"Dear Lord." I shuddered. "Is Hunter all right? Please tell me he was not hurt. And what of Harlan?"

"I think you had best come along and see." David's

tone was solemn, but his eyes sparkled with green fire as he half dragged me toward the gangplank.

"Where is the *Pearl?*" I asked. "Was she badly damaged?"

"By now she should be anchored safe in the harbor at Dark Thunder awaiting repair."

"And Broderick?"

"Dead. He was trapped in the fire on his ship." David's smile was grim. "Screamed a good bit before the flames got him. I call it a proper preparation for where his soul is bound."

"David." I tried to sound shocked, but I suspect my tone reflected my relief. I could not help myself. Just knowing that Decateur and Broderick were dead made the world seem a safer place. "Then it is truly over?"

"Depends on how you look at it." David's grin broadened as he opened the door of the captain's cabin. "Could be things are just beginning. Anyway, I have some errands to run for the captain, so I want you to wait for me in here." He pushed me inside and closed the door before I could say a word.

"David . . ." I protested, angry at his cavalier behavior.

"He will be back, Faith, and we do need to talk."

"Hunter!" I whirled to see him lying on his bunk. For a moment my joy and relief were so great that I could not even breathe, then I realized that he had not risen. "You are hurt!"

I rushed to him, then stopped, suddenly awkward, not sure I had the right to touch him. So many questions lay between us and yet . . . All my love welled up and spilled over my cheeks in a flood of tears.

"I injured my leg pulling Gideon back to safety when one of the raiders managed to put a ball through his side. My leg will heal itself in a few days, but I could not wait that long to see you." He sat up and when his eyes met mine, all the barriers between us seemed to melt away.

"You are all right?" I asked as I sank down on the edge

347

of his bunk.

"Look and see for yourself." The flames of desire in his eyes ignited an answering fire within me. "Though perhaps you had best not examine me too fully at the moment, since David has gone to fetch your uncle." His chuckle was like a caress.

"Uncle Edward?"

"Since I cannot reach your father to ask for your hand in marriage, David suggested that your uncle's permission would be sufficient."

"You want to marry me?" I felt as though I had stepped aboard a ship being tossed by a stormy sea. His words seemed to echo all the dreams I had treasured through the endless hours we had been apart.

"Did you really doubt my love, Faith? Why?" His look of pain stabbed at me as he took my hand.

Shame made me want to turn away, to deny my lack of trust, but this time I could not. If we were ever to be proper lovers, I had to tell him the truth and demand the same in return. "I thought that you loved Sarah."

"She is my sister-in-law and an old friend; of course I love her." He met my gaze without flinching. "Why would you think it could affect the way I feel about you?"

"When Harlan was away I saw you come out of her room at dawn and she kissed you and called you wicked." I could not bear meeting his gaze, so I looked down at his bandaged hand. "And then I saw you slip into her rooms the night before you asked her to send me away."

"I wanted you off the island only so I could be sure you would be safe, Faith, yet I could not insist on it myself, so I convinced Sarah to do it. As for that night, I was on my way to search the desk. That's how I found the papers I had the captain give you."

"Oh." I could say little more for I was caught between relief and my still haunting doubts.

"Now, as for the morning you speak of, I remember nothing of the . . . Oh." For a moment he was silent, then

348

he lifted his good hand to take my chin in his fingers and forced my gaze back to his face.

"I do remember. Penny had a nightmare. I was up walking down the hall and I heard her screaming, so I went in to help Sarah calm her. Once she quieted, Sarah asked me if I was falling in love with you and I told her that I was. Then I told her that I meant to continue courting you until you asked your father to break the betrothal contract."

"You told Sarah?"

"That is why I was so worried about her guessing what had passed between us. Knowing how I felt about you, she would be extra sensitive to our behavior." He sighed, his fingers moving caressingly along my jawbone. "Lord knows, I was having enough trouble keeping my hands off you before, Faith. After the island, I was afraid to trust myself alone in a room with you."

Happiness burned through me and I could not keep back a giggle. "I had the same problem."

"Which is why I sent David to bring your uncle here. It may not be exactly proper for us to wed so soon, but I am not leaving Nassau until you are my bride and can go back to Dark Thunder with me."

"I will marry you with or without his permission." I lifted his injured hand to my lips kissing his battered fingers tenderly. For a time just holding his hand and drinking in the miracle of being with him was enough, then the questions came. "What of Harlan? Is he safe?"

"Scrapes and burns from the battle and a good bit of anger when he learned exactly what Decateur was doing. According to Harlan, those papers I found should prove that he was already suspicious of Decateur's insistence on keeping the ledgers. The questions actually started when Harlan began to suspect that the furniture Decateur arranged for him to buy might not have been from a legitimate cargo."

"The furniture was part of a stolen cargo?" The idea

349

sickened me, but when I remembered all I had seen in the cavern, I realized that it made sense. "What about Harlan building his house where he did, Hunter? Did he know of the cavern?"

Hunter shook his head. "He just loved the area and used the foundation. He was furious when I told him that those 'pirate parades' were genuine."

"Then he really had no idea what Decateur was up to." I felt weak with relief for Sarah's sake as well as for Hunter's.

"Harlan was just suspicious of the man, that is why he started to question Decateur. Evidently, Decateur resented it because he warned Harlan that there might be trouble on the island if he did not give him more authority in the running of the warehouse. He even hinted to Harlan that the children might be in danger. Can you believe that?"

I nodded, telling him what I had overheard Decateur say about stealing Penny from her bed. "He was an evil man, Hunter, and I think he kept the islanders from being friendly."

"So Captain Edgar told me. It will take time for me to sort it all out with the authorities here, but that will give me something to do while you and your aunt plan the wedding."

"I can think of other things that we might do." I leaned over and kissed the tip of his nose.

Hunter's arms closed around me powerfully and his lips found mine in a kiss that brought back every wondrous moment we had shared on our tiny island. By the time our lips parted, I was weak with love for him.

"You are a wicked woman, Faith Richards," he groaned. "No wonder I love you so."

"We deserve each other." I started to lower my lips to his again, then I caught the sound of approaching footsteps and heard David's voice, loudly saying something to Uncle Edward. Giggling, I stumbled away from

Hunter's bunk and dropped into the closest chair, doing my best to pull myself together. It was a losing battle as I looked into Hunter's eyes. The rush of love I felt for him took my breath away.

The sun glinted like fire on the harbor at Dark Thunder as we entered. I stood at the rail of the *Sprite* drinking in the moment, enjoying it. I was coming home and even though some of my memories of this place were frightening, I loved the island.

"Looks like everyone is here to greet us," Hunter said, coming to put his arm around me. "To welcome my wife home."

"Your wife." I savored the words, then sighed. "I do wish that Sarah had been well enough so that she and Harlan could have come to Nassau for the ceremony."

"We shall just have a second ceremony at Thunder House. I know the reverend from English Wells would be pleased to conduct it and Sarah will be happy to help you plan it."

"Do you think she has recovered now?" I scanned the people lining the dock anxiously until I spotted her. "There she is!" I lifted a hand in answer to her enthusiastic waves.

"She is usually fine after the third month. Or she was with H.J. I was not around much before Penny was born." Hunter grinned at me.

"She is with child?" I gasped, then frowned. "Why did you not tell me, Hunter?"

"I just found out from Gideon when we stopped at English Wells. His wife Miranda spent some time with Sarah while Gideon was being cared for on Dark Thunder. I told him I would not tell anyone, so you must promise to act surprised."

I laughed up at him, knowing well that I would promise him anything. "I shall not be acting, I *am* surprised."

"I should have suspected something when she was so upset that Harlan took that last run to South Carolina without going home first. She must have realized her condition after he sailed and been eager to tell him. At least I am sure he knew nothing of the baby when we talked on Big Wood Cay."

"He must be so happy." I met Hunter's gaze.

"Almost as happy as I am." He bent to kiss me, oblivious to the shouts and laughter coming from the people on the dock. I held him tight, for in his arms I was truly home at last.